BEHIND THE LINES

BEHIND THE LINES

by
W. F. Morris

CASEMATE
uk
Oxford & Philadelphia

Published in Great Britain and
the United States of America in 2016 by
CASEMATE PUBLISHERS
10 Hythe Bridge Street, Oxford OX1 2EW, UK
and

1950 Lawrence Road, Havertown, PA 19083, USA

Paperback Edition: ISBN 978-1-61200-413-6
Digital Edition: ISBN 978-1-61200-414-3 (epub)

A CIP record for this book is available from the British Library

Printed in the Czech Republic by FINIDR

For a complete list of Casemate titles, please contact:

CASEMATE PUBLISHERS (UK)
Telephone (01865) 241249
Fax (01865) 794449
Email: casemate-uk@casematepublishers.co.uk
www.casematepublishers.co.uk

CASEMATE PUBLISHERS (US)
Telephone (610) 853-9131
Fax (610) 853-9146
Email: casemate@casematepublishing.com
www.casematepublishing.com

DEDICATED TO
AUDREY AND PETER
AND THEIR FAMILIES

W. F. Morris (second from the left) with his fellow junior officers circa 1916.

PREFACE

MAJOR Walter Frederick Morris was born in Norwich in 1892. He met his wife Lewine Corney in Bonn, was married in 1919 and had two children, Audrey and Peter, shortly thereafter. They in turn provided him with eleven grandchildren, all of whom knew Major Morris as "Grand Pa Peter". Even to the rest of his family and friends he was always "Peter"; it appears, for reasons we have never been able to clarify, Walter was known by his son's rather than his own given name.

Walter "Peter" Morris was educated at Norwich Grammar School and later at St Catharine's College, Cambridge. On graduating in 1914 with a degree in History, he was appointed by the colonial office to a post in British East Africa, but the outbreak of war intervened and, despite the offer of another appointment after the war, it seems he never set foot on that continent. Instead he joined the ranks of Britain's volunteer army, left for France and later that year was given a temporary commission. It was as an officer he fought on the Somme – no doubt this experience helped him capture so tangibly in his two war novels *Bretherton* and *Behind the Lines* (published in 1929 and 1930 respectively) the everyday horror, squalor and camaraderie of trench warfare.

Awarded the Military Cross and mentioned in despatches for acts of unknown bravery, our Grand Pa Peter, a quiet gentle man, never spoke of the war. However, he continued his close association with the army long after 1918, being appointed a Major in command of a Cycle Battalion in the Rhineland. Even after his retirement in 1920, he was active in the reserve and training corps. He also retained a particular affection for France: his honeymoon was in Clermont-Ferrand and one of his later novels – *The Hold Up* – was set in the Auvergne. As a teenager I read my grandfather's short stories with pleasure and pride at his being a bestselling author but it wasn't until 2015 when, well into middle age and the same year Casemate Publishing rediscovered his work, I actually began to read his wartime novels. Now having done so I am confident future readers will quickly understand as I did, how well my youthful pride was justified.

David Morris
June 2016

BEHIND THE LINES

BY W·F· Morris

PART I

CHAPTER I

I

I WAS asked the other day by my charming young niece what was the quaintest thing I had come across during the war. I assured her that the whole war was "quaint," every bit of it—from the two pals I lost drowned in the mud at Passchendale to the spontaneous combustion which a court of inquiry I once served on decided was the cause of the loss of two Army bicycles. Had she asked what was the most extraordinary thing I had come across, I could have answered her; for I still believe that my eyes did not play me false that morning in March '18 and that it was Peter Rawley I saw in that chalk pit near Bapaume.

Rawley and I were at school together, and later when I went up to Cambridge and he went into an insurance office, we corresponded and met at intervals. We were spending a holiday together on the Broads in August 1914, and when one morning, as we lay at Horning Ferry, a newspaper with glaring headlines "War" was thrown on board, we held a pow-wow over our bacon and tea in the well, the result of which was that we started up the auxiliary and went chugging back to Wroxham.

Two days later we were both full-fledged privates in a Territorial battalion, and after a short period of training we joined our Company on coast defence work. We arrested dozens of spies. But after a couple of months of vainly scanning the night sky for Zeppelins and of watching the sun come up above the North Sea without disclosing an invading flotilla we grew restless. Eventually I was commissioned to a Yeomanry regiment training on the Plain, and Rawley got a commission in the R.F.A.

I got out to France several months before he did, and it was more than a year since I had seen him when one morning as I was sitting down to a meal in the Quatre Fils at Doullens he walked in.

We had lunch together and swopped experiences. He had been out about two months then, up near Arras firing barrages and getting plastered in return. He was the same old Rawley, as interested in things and as enthusiastic as ever, and dead keen on his job. But there was an added assurance and quiet self-reliance about him which I knew meant that he had made good under fire. His brigade was back in Army reserve, and his battery was having a quiet time in a village a few kilometres from Doullens. But I saw no more of him, for I had to get back to the Squadron after lunch, and the next day we trekked north to the Salient.

It must have been about two months later, as we were passing down to the Cambrai show, that I ran across Rawley's division. We billeted a night in the area, and I decided to look him up. I had only a few hours to spare, but I thought I could just do it, and so I obtained from Divisional Headquarters the position of the battery and set out.

I got a lift part of the way on a limber along the usual appalling, pot-holed road bordered at intervals by riven, leafless trees and on either hand by the desolate downland country covered with rank jungle grass. I left the limber by a fork road where a derelict Nissen hut, rusty and full of holes, slanted drunkenly like a dog wounded in the hind quarters. I watched the limber amble over the crest of the slope out of sight and, leaving the branch road with its bordering fruit trees, which brother Bosche had cut down before his retreat last winter, lying like matches across it, I set off across country.

There was not a living soul in sight. An occasional shell waddled across the empty sky and burst distantly or moderately close, though what there could be worth destroying in that deserted and depressing desert I could not imagine. An old trench system ran roughly parallel with my path, and the ground was broken by low banks and hummocks of dirty chalk and half-filled ditches. Bleached and rotting sandbags gaped here and there, and tangles of rusty wire lay half hidden in the rank grass. Bent screw pickets, with a few curled rusty strands at the top like hairs on a wart, showed where the wire had been.

I scrambled across a couple of half-filled communicating trenches and began to descend the slope to the little valley in which the battery lay. The bottom of the valley was flat and rather marshy, and the stream which meandered through it was enclosed by banks about five feet in height. Dug in to the near bank in a broad loop of the stream, which I could see as I walked down hill, I had been told I should find the battery.

As I came nearer I could see the gun-pits, six of them, covered with the usual camouflage netting sprinkled with leaves.

The battery was not firing at the moment, and there seemed to be nobody about. I picked my way carefully, knowing that gunners are usually rather touchy about people wandering near their guns; and I suppose they are right, for two or three people following in one another's steps will leave a trail that is clearly visible in aeroplane photographs. So stepping like a Mohawk Indian on the war-path, I reached one of the pits. The gun was there with its workmanlike polished breech-block glinting in the subdued light under the camouflage netting, a neat pile of eighteen-pounder shells stacked at one side, and a little mound of used brass cases at the back, but no men. I moved along to the next pit, and there, under the netting, crouched another silent gun that seemed to blink at me watchfully with its stolid breech-block. I passed from pit to pit, and in each a gun blinked at me from the gloom like a watch-dog in its kennel; but its masters were not there. I put my head in a little shelter, dug in the river bank. There were blankets lying about it, an open mess tin and other trench furniture, but no occupants. Farther on I found a well-constructed shelter with tree trunks and sandbags for a roof. In here was a rickety table with a map spread on it, a clip of field message forms and the switch-box and headphones of a field telephone. But still not a soul.

I had been wishing I could take a gun or something of the sort, and hide it so that afterwards I could rag Rawley about the carelessness of his battery; but, as I stood in that deserted dug-out and heard the ticking of the watch on my wrist, I began to feel creepy. It was uncanny with all those evidences of suspended activity around one. Not a movement, not a sound. I felt as though I had been asleep for a hundred years and had woken up to find that the human race had ceased to exist.

I went up into the open air and looked about. There were the six silent pits with their six silent guns. Behind them the ground sloped up to a low, near skyline broken by the low earth mounds of derelict trenches, forlorn screw pickets, and short wisps of rusty wire. The long rank grass moved silently in the gusty breeze. Not a sound; not a soul.

I stood gaping like a fool, half scared, till a long-range shell sighed through the sky overhead and broke the spell. Then I turned and walked back up the slope. There was nobody there and I could not wait; I had to get back to my unit.

We moved south the next day, and I wrote to Rawley as soon as we had settled in. A reply came back from the adjutant of his brigade. It said simply that Rawley had been killed, buried in a dug-out by a direct hit on the very day that I had visited that silent battery.

II

The Passchendale show had ended in stalemate, the Cambrai affair, brilliantly begun, had failed through lack of reserves, and things quietened down for the winter. The next move lay with the Bosche. We for the moment had shot our bolt, but he with his vast reserves rolling in from the Russian Front was sure to take the offensive in the spring. Our intelligence merchants prophesied the father and mother of all the pushes that ever were. And in due course it came.

My regiment had been back in the neighbourhood of Doullens since a little after Christmas, and on the first day of the attack we got our marching orders. We saddled up and moved south.

Our route lay across the old Somme battlefields of 1916, a dreary desert of some hundred square miles in extent in which trees were just leafless riven stumps and villages mere heaps of rubble and splintered wood; and it was not long before we had evidences of what was in store for us. The rumble of a really fruity barrage sounded unpleasantly close ahead, and from time to time we met unshaven, hollow-eyed wretches, trudging back in the last stages of exhaustion.

That night we went into action on a bare hillside, with both flanks in the air. Before dawn they pulled us out and sent us hell for leather to stop a gap elsewhere. And so it went on. We strung ourselves out across a gap, and as soon as a few men could be scraped together to relieve us, out we came and were rushed off to do the same elsewhere.

The mornings were misty, and it was jumpy work pushing forward at top speed across unknown country with visibility limited to about thirty yards, and very hazy information of the enemy's whereabouts. Of course the inevitable happened. The game of ten little nigger boys had reduced my troop to something under fifteen men, and I was leading this little push to reinforce some of our men who, I had been told, though hard pressed were holding out in a sunken road, when suddenly a crowd of Bosches loomed up in the mist not twenty yards away. There was only one thing to be done, and we did it. We drew sabres and dug in our spurs.

They must have outnumbered us four or five to one, but we were on them before they could move. It was the only time during the war that my regiment used *l'arme blanche* and then we were only a remnant of a troop, but it was glorious while it lasted; we went through them like a whirlwind, cutting and pointing, and they went over like ninepins. Then we were alone again in the mist, cantering up a slope.

We left our horses in a hollow, scraped rifle pits in the chalk, and settled down to the shooting gallery business. But the machine-gun fire was heavy and our rifle pits shallow. One by one the men were hit, nearly all in the head. The Bosche was creeping up close, and it was evident that we should be overwhelmed by a determined attack.

I brought the half-dozen survivors back to the hollow where we had left our horses, but neither horses nor holders were there. We went off to look for them, and had gone about twenty yards when three or four rifles went off quite close, and we saw a row of those damned goblin helmets right ahead. We scattered for the shelter of a bank that lay a few yards to our right, and I had just reached it when up popped a lanky weed of a Bosche officer with a supercilious grin on his face. I would have removed that pretty quick if he hadn't had a long-barrelled automatic pistol pointed at the pit of my stomach. I could only curse and put up my hands.

What happened to my other fellows I don't know, for only two of them were marched off with me under the escort of a German infanteer and an N.C.O. We went round a hill and up a sunken road where the mist was still pretty thick. Several Bosche wounded were sitting on the roadside, and an officer was strolling about. Farther up on the right was a chalk quarry with three or four men drawn up to form what was evidently a firing party: for about ten yards away with their backs to the chalk cliff were a couple of civilians. They were dirty, bedraggled, miserable looking wretches, and I remember wondering what pretext the Bosche had found for shooting them.

We had drawn level with them before something familiar about the taller of the two attracted my attention. The man's face was unshaven and covered with grime, but it was something characteristic in the attitude that seemed familiar. He was not looking at me, and I was past him before I could put a name to him or call out. Then a big shell, one of our own I think, landed on the road behind us, and the N.C.O. hurried us on. Other shells followed the first, and we needed no hurrying. The tableau in the chalk pit was swallowed up in the mist.

I never saw the man again, alive or dead. One will say that I saw him only for a moment, that it was misty at the time, and that even then I did not recognize the features, covered as they were with grime and stubble. I admit all that. The circumstantial evidence is not worth a straw. Yet I am sure that the taller of the two ragged civilians I saw in the chalk quarry that misty March morning of 1918 was that Lieutenant Peter Rawley, R.F.A., who the official records stated was killed near Arras the previous autumn.

PART II

CHAPTER II

I

PETER RAWLEY surveyed the road behind him. He sat sideways in the saddle, one open palm resting on the crupper, one knee flexed and turned out, the other straight and pressed in against his mare's flank. The road was very straight, but was not monotonous like those farther north in Flanders that are both straight and level. There they stretched like white tapes across a patchwork coverlet, and the traveller toils along them in despair of arriving anywhere. Here in Picardy they are only straight. They lie across the swelling curves of the country like ribbons on a woman's breasts. Like an eager terrier they dip suddenly into hidden hollows and reappear on the slopes beyond, smaller but white and straight and beckoning.

Rawley glanced upwards. The sky was withdrawn from the sunny landscape, a translucent vault infinitely remote, across whose vastness strayed forlorn a few fleecy clouds like sheep lost on a prairie. The sun-hazed country undulated to the purple distance, throwing up broad patterns of growing corn, dark green rectangles of woods, and gaudy patches of mustard—the wide hedgeless fields of northern France.

The road was white and dusty and slashed by the blue shadows of the bordering trees, but where it slid down the opposite slope towards him and disappeared into the hollow to prepare for its sudden swoop out of the dip, something long, narrow and dark like a worm was crawling. No movement was perceptible, though little pin-points of light scintillated from it from time to time; but moving it was, for its worm-like length lessened till it was swallowed up in the hollow and the road was white and bare again.

Somewhere beneath the remote pale vault an invisible aeroplane droned lazily. Distantly, where the gauzy towers and chimneys of a small town sprouted in the eastern haze, rumbling explosions broke the summer stillness. But they were remote beneath the withdrawn vault. The warm, wide-spreading landscape soothed them and took them to itself.

A faint but increasing rumble became audible, and presently the jingling music of metal striking upon metal and the klipity-klop of horses' hoofs emerged from the rolling undercurrent of sounds. A man in khaki rose above the white horizon of the road with an unfamiliar bobbing motion that was absurd till one saw that he was riding a glossy chestnut charger. Behind him came other horses in pairs, a rider to each pair, their necks stretched out and their shoulders lunging rhythmically to the strain. Six of them in pairs, and behind rumbled a field gun painted service green. More horses and more guns followed. The distant worm had disclosed itself. It was a battery of field guns, B Battery, on the march.

The moving column was stippled with sunlight that striped the road between the trees, and as man and beast and gun passed through these yellow bars, button, bit, and polished breech-block glittered like a heliograph. The turnout would have passed the eye of an inspecting general. Even head and drag ropes were as white as snow. But this was no foppish, Bond Street battery. The men wore cloth service caps, but grey painted steel helmets hung behind the saddles, and a jagged twisted gun shield and twinkling points on gun and limber, where the naked steel showed through the bruised paint, were scars that spit and polish could not hide.

But the battery looked well, especially to the eye of a gunner—to the eye of Rawley. And the two leading guns were those of his own section, the spear point of his particular little force.

He glanced back at the cobwebby towers and chimneys in the distant haze, and then again at the battery. It was good to feel the moving flanks of a horse between one's knees on this summer afternoon, good to be in France amid the "real thing," good to be a subaltern of B Battery.

The Major rode up from the rear of the column, his black mare cantering gracefully over the turf bordering the road. He dropped into a walk beside Rawley.

"About another five kilometres," he said with a nod towards an iron sign-post, white embossed letters on a blue ground.

Major Cane was a young man, he could not have been more than a year older than Rawley. He was a regular, and B Battery was his first command. He wore the tricolour

Mons ribbon and the white and purple of the Military Cross that he had won on the Somme.

"It is only a few kilometres from Doullens, isn't it?" asked Rawley.

"About ten," answered Cane.

"Much of a place?" inquired Rawley.

"Which? Doullens? Not bad. Smallish—nothing like Amiens, ye'know; but one can get a passable meal there." He leaned forward and patted the black glossy neck of his mare. "Want to go joy ridin', Rawley?"

"Well I haven't seen much of France yet," answered Rawley; "and there are one or two things I want from Ordnance."

"You can go in tomorrow," said Cane. "I'm going to give the men a day off. You might bring me a couple of collars, and I expect the mess will want one or two things."

He turned sharply and gave a curt order as a large car with a little red and black flag fluttering above the radiator bore down upon them. The men straightened caps and sat more stiffly in the saddle. Heads and eyes turned sharply to the left, and drivers' arms and short-handled whips slanted rigidly across the riderless horses as the car slowed to pass the column. Only the black kitten on top of the high-piled G.S. wagon in the rear forgot her manners and yawned.

"Army!" exclaimed Rawley when Cane's hand had dropped from the salute. "Who was it?"

"Horne, I fancy," answered Cane. "And he's a gunner and knows what's what." And he glanced back again with a critical eye at his battery.

Rawley hummed a little tune. He was enjoying the sunlight and the wide-spreading landscape. The green fields were very pleasant after the bare, tortured earth and rubble heaps from which he had come. This was France as he had imagined it; for although he had been nearly a month in the country, with the exception of a glimpse of the streets of Havre in the grey light of a rainy dawn and what can be seen from the window of a railway carriage at night, his knowledge of French landscapes was limited to that straight, pot-holed road, bordered by riven tree stumps, that led to the saucer-shaped depression covered with rank jungle grass, which was the battery position.

But he had enjoyed it all—the night journey through unknown country to the unknown of the battle line, the ride up to the battery at dusk, across that desert country, where heaps of rubble with a riven, up-jutting gable marked the site of a village and ragged poles, black against the evening sky, were woods that once had been green.

It had interested him. It was experience—life. It was all so different from the quiet East Anglian town in which he had been born and bred, and from which till now he had never been more than a hundred miles. Life was just an accumulation of experiences, he had decided in his youthful philosophy, and the wider and more varied the experiences, the fuller the life.

In that quiet provincial town he had welcomed the war as a new phenomenon—he had been too young to theorise about the Boer War—and the call for men and his answering that call was the gateway to an experience, a great and wonderful man-making or man-breaking experience such as had never before crossed his horizon.

And so he was interested in France and avid of experience. He could still recall the thrill of that ride at dusk across the devastated area when suddenly the pearly sky above seemed to have been ripped like calico and the tiles of a derelict farmhouse nearby had lifted in the air before his eyes and bellied out into a red balloon-shaped cloud, whilst his ears had been smitten with a furious crack of sound. His first shell. And his first casualty too he could remember with an equal though different thrill.

It had been at night—one of those curiously quiet nights when the forward area seemed remote from the civilized world, like some distant uninhabited and unexplored country. He was walking from No. 2 gun-pit to the mess. The ragged wall of the ruined *estaminet* ahead showed fitfully against pale flickerings on the northern horizon—soundless flashes from distant guns. He was sucking contentedly at his pipe and contemplating the seven stars of the Great Bear, when suddenly out of the night came that whistle of a giant whip lash-crack and the flower-like bloom of orange light in the darkness near him. Then silence. And then again that vicious lash-crack. And then silence, broken by a long drawn "Oh-e-e-e-e" that made his scalp tingle.

He picked himself up from where he had flung himself prone and groped towards the sound. A dark form that moved once convulsively lay on the edge of the corduroy road. He overcame a strong feeling of shrinking and went down on one knee beside it. He pressed the button of his torch. Immediately a pair of glassy eyes set in a dough-like face surmounted by tousled black hair seemed to leap at him in the sudden brilliance. One muddy khaki leg stuck out over the edge of the track; the other leg—was not there. All below the thigh was just a tangle of sopping rags. The torch flickered in his shaking hand and went out. He was violently sick.

And the first time he had fired a gun in anger, that too, he remembered. It was his third day with the battery. They were engaged in harassing fire. The familiar, "Ready! . . . Set" had been called, when he had been seized with a sudden desire to fire the gun himself. He squinted through the sight and changed places with the layer on the seat. The smooth polished firing lever was in his hand. 'Fire!' He had pulled the lever and had immediately been blinded by the flash, and his ears had been stung by the report. The gun slid smoothly back and up again, and he heard his shell sizzling away on its flight towards the enemy.

That too had been an experience. He had fired his first round, one among millions it is true, but individually he had performed an act that may have caused death to some of the enemy. He had taken his place in the world war.

It was all intensely interesting. He felt that he was really living. It was all so different from the quiet humdrum life of a provincial insurance office, broken each year by a fortnight's holiday at Lowestoft where one wore carefully chosen *négligé* and had mild flirtations with rather silly girls one picked up round the bandstand.

This was France. Everything proclaimed the fact. That farm wain with its high hurdle arrangement fore and aft and its two long-maned, long-tailed greys was quite different from the creaking tumbrils one met on the roads of Norfolk. And the plodding peasant with his long whip—his deep-throated "Heu!" was quite unlike the sing-song "Arld ye!" of East Anglia. And the *estaminet* they were passing and on which the men cast longing glances; it stood flush with the dusty white road; Café du Commerce was painted in large faded black letters across its flat yellow-washed front, and white blistered shutters were closed against the glare. A few self-important chickens patrolled the doorstep. It was all different, all so different from the "White Harts" and "Red Lions" of rural England.

"There we are," cried Cane suddenly. "C Battery is over there." He pointed towards the grey point of a low spire which rose above a clump of trees a kilometre on his left. "And this is our turning." He swung his riding whip round towards a narrow winding road to the right which left the straight main road a hundred yards ahead.

A low brick building with an ornamental ironwork door stood on the corner where the road forked. Two army lorries were parked on the grass of the roadside, and a third lorry with the front part jacked up and the wheels off stood in a yard bounded by the outbuildings. A man in shirt sleeves carrying a bleached canvas bucket "eyes righted" as Cane and Rawley rode by.

"Some workshop, got a nice cushy billet!" commented Cane. And then he added, "Lead on," and turned his mare to watch the battery turn off the main road.

The narrow road curved round the slope of a hill, thick dark woods above, lush grass and a tiny stream below. Round another curve Rawley rode, and then the village appeared. Yellow or whitewashed cottages bordered the road which now widened and divided to encircle the church, a short grey tower surmounted by a shorter peaked spire. Here they met a procession of first communicants, little girls in white frocks and long white veils, two by two, followed by little boys in black suits and large white bows, whose hands were clasped devotionally but whose eyes strayed to the dun column of horsemen and guns. Behind the church the broad and re-united road formed a little square shaded by two short rows of trees.

"Beneath the spreading chestnut tree B bloody battery stands!" murmured Lieutenant Piddock to Rawley as the battery wheeled and came to a halt beneath the branches.

II

Some hours later Rawley, who was orderly officer, walked back down the village street. The sun had set, but the long evening of the northern summer had not yet turned to night.

The battery had already made themselves at home. Three village girls, arm in arm, were talking to two gunners who straightened their caps and saluted as Rawley passed.

On the other side of the road a driver was helping a farm girl to carry a wooden pail up the railed steps to a cottage door. Beneath the trees behind the church the guns stood parked, and a sentry with fixed bayonet paced to and fro. Up a little lane on the left the reflection of the cook-house fire gleamed ruddily on a white cottage wall, and a slow north country voice was singing some sentimental song.

By the church he met Sergeant Jameson, a tall, well built man with a weather-beaten face and a pair of keen grey eyes shaded by the long peak of his cap. He transferred his riding switch from his right hand to his left armpit and saluted in the correct drill-book manner. Rawley said "Goodnight, sergeant," and "Goodnight, sir," came the sergeant's deep reply.

Rawley liked the way the man saluted him, looking him straight in the eyes. It was the masonic look which one competent and self-confident man gives another whom he considers competent also—the masonry of mutual respect which is independent of position and rank. A good man, Sergeant Jameson. He marched along with his shoulders square, his chest out, head up and chin in. It was not a swagger but the confident walk of justifiable self-confidence. Rawley admired the type. And there were several men of that type in the battery. A good battery; undoubtedly the best in the Brigade. And the Brigade of course was one of the best in France.

He passed up a narrow lane between two cottages, turned to the left under an archway, and passed by the bricked walk round the midden to the door of the mess.

It was a long, low white-washed house with a second floor lit by dormer windows in the high, tiled roof. The mess-room was long and low, brick-floored, and with two windows facing each other. The oil lamp hanging from the uncovered joists was lighted, though the evening sky was still bright behind the open windows. A mess servant was putting crockery on a table, and Piddock on hands and knees was unpacking the gramophone. The various odds and ends of mess property that had been packed with the gramophone lay in a semi-circle around him. He wound up the motor and put on a record. He nodded to Rawley and then, with hands thrust deep in the front pockets of his riding breeches, began a clog dance on the brick floor.

Whedbee, the battery second-in-command, sat in a canvas chair beneath the lamp reading a newspaper. He was a tall, lean, middle-aged man with thin hair. He bent his head and looked over his glasses short-sightedly with contracted brows as Rawley came in, and then went on reading. He wore the green and yellow territorial ribbon. In civil life he had been a mathematical master in a private school, and his habit, when talking, of emphasizing a point by removing his glasses and stabbing the air with them was more suggestive of the class-room than the wagon lines which he commanded.

Suddenly the glass-topped door that led to a room occupied by the family was opened, and a French girl appeared holding in her hand a fry pan. She called in a loud whisper to the mess servant, who was laying the table, and then quickly disappeared. Piddock stopped in his dance to gaze at the now closed door, and then he turned to Rawley with raised eyebrows.

"And very nice, too!" he said, with emphasis.

Whedbee looked up short-sightedly from his paper. "Eh?"

"We were admiring the local fauna, sweetheart," Piddock told him.

"Fauna!" murmured Whedbee absently. "What fauna?"

"Cows and sheep, my old war horse," cried Piddock. "But especially birds." He clapped Whedbee on the back. "Dear little dicky birds, my jolly old Napoleon. A charming little French one popped her pretty head in and popped out—bless her. What a sight for scarred veterans!" And he tripped across the room holding out the corner of his tunic like a skirt.

"Is that all?" murmured Whedbee, and went on reading.

Piddock turned with hands outstretched. "All!" he cried. He walked solemnly towards Whedbee and halted before him. "All! you cold-blooded pedagogue! Has Cupid's dart never penetrated your academic gown? Has luscious love never nestled among the recurring decimals in your heart?"

"Never," answered Whedbee with mock sadness.

Piddock flung an arm across his eyes and gulped. "Teacher, you unman me. My heart is in the coffin there with Gertie, and I must pause till it come back to me."

Whedbee took off his glasses and polished them on a corner of his handkerchief. "I say, old man," he remarked amiably, "do you mind pausing somewhere else; you're right in my light."

CHAPTER III

I

BREAKFAST on the following morning in the clean brick-floored mess-room, accompanied by the clucking of hens on the midden, and the pleasant whirring sound of a separator, was prolonged far beyond the time that meal had taken in the cramped earthy dug-out they had recently left. French-made coffee instead of chlorinated tea, and fresh butter and milk in place of the usual tinned substitutes, were luxuries too rare and precious to be spoiled by hasty consumption.

At last Major Cane pushed back his chair and carried his unfinished cup of coffee to the open window where the sunlight slanted through the apple trees. He placed it on the sill and unrolled his oilskin tobacco pouch.

"Must get some exercise," he grunted between the puffs as he lighted his pipe. He threw away the match and leaned out of the window. "There is a good level bit of turf there. Where's that cricket ball? And Sergeant Johnson has a bat." He paused with his coffee cup half way to his lips. "Rawley you're a bowler, aren't you? How about a knock!"

Rawley went to the window and inspected the pitch. "Pretty good," he agreed. "But you said I could go into Doullens this morning, sir."

"Oh yes, so I did. Here, Whedbee; what about a knock! You are a dark horse I believe."

Whedbee, who was filling a large and very old curved pipe, looked over his glasses and walked solemnly to the window. "I'll bowl you first over," he announced with the same solemn air.

"Good for you!" cried Cane. "Piddock, what about it?"

"Righto, sir. I'm game," answered Piddock who, with a cigarette in the corner of his mouth, was winding up the gramophone.

Rawley strapped on his Sam Browne and put on his cap. "Well, I'll leave you to it," he said.

In the narrow lane outside the house his groom was walking his mare, Lucy, up and down. She looked beautiful with the sunlight glistening on her glossy chestnut flanks, and woman-like she seemed to know it, for she arched her sleek neck coquettishly and lifted her white-stockinged forefeet daintily, every now and then breaking into a little springy trot. Rawley swung himself into the saddle, and with his crop resting on his thigh like a marshal's baton, rode at a walk down the steep track into the village street.

Once clear of the village he got on to the grass bordering the road and broke into a trot. At the fork roads he acknowledged the "eyes right" of an A.S.C. private carrying two green tins of petrol and crossed the main road to the pasture beyond. He had seen on the map that he could save a mile by cutting across country, and he was anxious for a gallop.

He topped a rise and saw below him a little combe with a spinney at the bottom. Down the slope he cantered, trotted round the margin of the spinney and saw before him a long gentle rise. He clapped his knees to his mare's flanks and loosened the reins. She was fresh and needed no encouragement; she stretched her shapely neck and threw out her legs. Black clods spurted behind the flying hoofs. A hare got up and sped away like an arrow ahead. "Oh-e!" yelled Rawley light-heartedly, and, bent low like a jockey, went madly after. Near the crest it doubled almost under the horse's feet. Rawley thundered on up the slope and at the top straightened and pulled into a canter.

The ground fell away to a narrow sunken lane between twelve-foot banks, with the main road at the bottom. He slowed to a walk, but the mare was still fresh and pulled his arms almost out of the sockets.

"Steady, old girl," he cried. "Steady, damn you! We can't barge on to a main road like that. Blast you!" This last as the mare curveted sideways up the bank.

Progressing sideways he reached the end of the steep track where the high enclosing banks fell away abruptly to the main road, and at the same moment an ambulance flashed past with a loud warning screech and sudden swerve to avoid the emerging horseman. This was too much for the mare; Rawley's hands were jerked forward as her head went up, and away she went down the road after the car. He sat back and pulled her in, first to a canter and then to a straining trot.

The mare was still tossing her head and capering as he drew level with the green-hooded car, that had pulled up on the roadside. He saw that the driver was a girl. With one gauntleted hand resting on the steering-wheel she looked up at him. "I'm sorry I startled your horse," she said. "But you did come out rather suddenly."

"My fault—or rather Lucy's!" he admitted readily, and raised his hand in salute. And then he dropped it hurriedly as the mare capered round and presented her hind quarters to the car. He pulled her round again. "She has no manners this morning," he declared. "I apologize for her."

The girl smiled. She was not exactly pretty, Rawley decided, but she had candid eyes and an engaging smile; her voice was pleasant and cultivated, and above all she was attractively healthy and English.

"See! She is apologizing herself," she said, rubbing the silky muzzle the mare pushed against her shoulder.

Rawley rubbed the glossy neck with his crop. "She is fresh this morning. It's the first gallop we have had together for goodness knows how long. And she has taken me the wrong way. That is the way to Doullens, isn't it?" he asked, pointing with his crop.

She nodded. "Yes. It is about five kilometres."

"We are going in to see the sights," he explained. He found the novelty of an English girl's society attractive, and was in no hurry to go.

"The sights of Doullens!" she echoed with a laugh.

"Don't tell me there aren't any!" he exclaimed in pained tones. "After you've brought us out so far, and made us trot so quick!" he quoted with a grin.

"Sorry! It is not a bad little place. One wouldn't rave about it in peace time—and in England; but . . . well if you have just come from the Line you will find it attractive, I expect."

"I breathe again," he answered, laughing.

She dropped her hand to the gears. "Well, I must get on with the war. Goodbye."

The clutch went in, and the car slid away. Rawley turned his mare and trotted on into Doullens.

It was a commonplace little provincial town, but, as the lady of the ambulance had prophesied, it was very attractive to him, fresh from the desolation of the forward area. There were shops with homely unwarlike goods in the windows; things one had forgotten anyone had a use for—white stiff collars, and civilian suits, children's toys and photograph frames, fancy notepaper and ladies' hats. Where the street widened to form a small square was a market. Fat market women sat complacently beneath their large umbrellas before trays piled with stockings, hats, pots and pans, vegetables, fruit, crockery or ironmongery.

Rawley rode slowly through the main street and enjoyed it all. Two army nursing sisters in red and grey uniforms stood before a window hung with silk and linen lingeries, and Rawley smiled to think how remote such fragile garments were from the rough masculine world of gun-pits and dug-outs from which he had come.

For luncheon he turned into the Quatre Fils. It was market day, and there were but few vacant chairs at either of the long tables that ran the length of the dining-room. The atmosphere was redolent of cooked food, and hazy with the steam of hot dishes; and there was a swelling buzz of sound, for the *vin ordinaire*, a bottle of which stood before each plate and was included in the *table d'hôte,* seemed to have loosened the tongues of the taciturn Picardy farmers and to have increased the natural volubility of their wives. A sprinkling of British officers served to remind one of the war.

Rawley was looking for a vacant chair when he heard his name called and, turning, discovered Charles Tankard seated at a small table by the wall. Tankard was an old school friend and together they had enlisted in a Territorial battalion in 1914. They had both been commissioned about the same time and separated, Rawley to the Artillery, and Tankard to a Yeomanry regiment.

Tankard gripped Rawley's hand and grinned. "Hullo, Peter, old cock! Take a pew. I thought we'd run across each other before long." He signalled to a waitress. "Let's have some drinkable juice to celebrate in. Can't swallow the local red ink." He pushed the bottle of *vin ordinaire* aside. "And where are your old pop-guns now?"

"Ervillers—back resting for a bit. We pulled in from La Basse last night."

"That's bad luck," exclaimed Tankard. "Here have we been hanging round here for the last month, and now we go north tomorrow, and I have to get back to the squadron *toute suite* after this, so I shall not see you again. Rotten luck!"

"Rotten luck," agreed Rawley.

"Well, what have you been doing up at La Basse, old son? Pitching shorts on the poor ruddy infanteers as usual?"

Rawley grinned. "You old horse-wallah, you! No—winning the war, that's what we've been doing—you know, the usual harassing fire relieved by occasional S.O.S. calls."

"No fruity barrages yet?"

"Not yet; that's to come."

Tankard nodded. "Sure. You will get all you want before you are through. Well, how does this little war agree with you, Peter?"

Rawley put down his glass and answered thoughtfully. "Well, to tell the truth, I really rather like it. It's deuced interesting."

"Interesting! My God!" exclaimed Tankard. "Look here, young fellow, if you go on like that you will be a general before you know where you are, so be warned in time."

"You old cynic," retorted Rawley. "But after all, that's what we joined up for, isn't it."

"I suppose so," admitted Tankard. "But we were very young in those days."

"Three years younger to be precise," put in Rawley dryly.

Tankard shrugged his shoulders. "One can learn a lot in three years. Oh, ay, I don't want to die," he sang softly.

"Neither do I," retorted Rawley. "But what is wrong with you, Charles, is that you're fed up with hanging about. I suppose you have been spending your evenings loaded up with sandbags and junk, wandering round in the dark among crumps, looking for a map reference and a sapper lance-corporal who isn't there."

"That's about the size of it," agreed Tankard.

"But you know damn well that, if the infanteers made a break and pushed you through, you would be as keen as mustard the moment you got your old quadrupeds on the other side barging among the Bosche."

"Well, that would be a reasonable kind of war," protested Tankard. "Not this damned ditch-digging game."

"They will push you through the gap one of these days," Rawley asserted confidently.

"My God! Have they been telling you, too, about that gap!" exclaimed Tankard in disgust. "When I first came out it was to be a break through—vanguard to Berlin. Now it's this cursed gap. For weeks we have been practising finding that gap. Why, my troop horses wake up in the night and imagine they've found it, poor brutes. The only gap I've ever found—or am ever likely to find—is in the brains of the Brass Hats."

Rawley smiled. "It's not a bad old war," he said.

"It might be worse, I suppose," admitted Tankard. "But not much. Yours a decent push?"

"Quite a good crowd. We are only four in the mess at the moment; we lost a subaltern up at La Basse. The Major is all right—young and keen; a bit regimental, but he doesn't muck the battery about or try experiments. Old Whedbee, the second-in-command, is a rum old bird—dry old stick. Was a schoolmaster in civil life— got the pedagogic manner. Reminds me of old Piecrust at Ventchester. But he's a jolly good sort when you know him. And then there's young Piddock; he's quite a good kid. We are a cheery crush."

"That's half the battle," said Tankard. "What are you doing in Doullens?"

"Having a look round."

"Not much to see, I'm afraid."

"It's new to me and a change from the battery position."

Tankard nodded. "Civilization again. The devastated area is ghastly."

"Yes. And yet it has its own peculiar charm."

Tankard raised his eyebrows and smiled. "Same old Peter," he commented.

"Well, it has," asserted Rawley. "In a way it reminds me of the Broads—Hickling and Horsey."

"Oh, I say!" protested Tankard.

"It has the same loneliness—and timelessness," went on Rawley. "There one might be living in the twelfth century or the ninth; there is nothing to show that it is the twentieth."

"Except crumps," put in Tankard.

"Those great stretches of devastated, uncultivated, deserted downland are rather fine—especially at night, when there is only a faint flickering of Verey lights to the east and the grumble of a distant strafe. The universe seems grander and nearer then—and anything might happen."

Tankard shook his head. "You will be a poet one of these days, Peter, my lad. But I know what you mean."

"And those stark trees, all points and shivered branches without leaves, and the great mine craters in the chalk all white in the moonlight. Did you ever see anything more like a dead world—like another planet, like a Lunar landscape must be?"

Tankard smiled reminiscently. "You haven't changed much since the old days at Piecrust's," he said. "Do you remember that day after the Ely match when you nearly missed the train and we found you up the cathedral tower in the dark trying to light a beacon!"

Rawley grinned. "I had been reading *Hereward the Wake*," he said.

Tankard looked at his wrist-watch. "I must walk march." He beckoned a waitress.

Rawley's hand went to his breast pocket, but Tankard held his arm. "No; this is with me—positively." At the door he gripped Rawley's hand. "Don't go fooling round looking for trouble, Peter," he said. "Cheerio!"

II

Rawley made his purchases with leisurely enjoyment, wandering to and fro in the streets and lingering before every shop window. Some time between three and four o'clock he entered a shop which sold English periodicals and newspapers. It was an old-fashioned shop. A bell jangled when one pushed back the door, and two steps led down to the dark, low-ceilinged interior of the shop. On the shelves and stands round the wall other articles besides papers were displayed for sale. There were fancy notepaper and bottles of ink, gaudily-framed reproductions of the basilica of Albert, gilt teaspoons with the arms of Doullens embossed on the handle, aluminium rings and medallions stamped with a miniature seventy-five millimetre gun, and made from old shell fuses, picture postcards—some indecent to English eyes—and greeting cards of ribbon and lace and celluloid, bearing sententious mottoes.

There were a number of people in the shop when Rawley entered, and at first he was unable to get near the counter on which the periodicals lay. He stood pressed back against the shelf behind him to allow those on their way out to reach the door, and as his eyes became accustomed to the gloom he saw that in addition to the civilians there were three or four English Tommies in the shop, and at the far end a girl in uniform whom, though he could see only half her face, he recognized as the driver of the ambulance that had bolted his mare that morning.

He studied her with interest, and was pleased with what he saw. He disliked uniforms for women. One of a woman's greatest attractions, he thought, was her individuality, and this quality she always exemplified in her dress. And this was just the quality that a uniform was intended to destroy. There was something nauseating and degrading in a row of women all alike.

But this girl had triumphed over the disability. She did not belong to her clothes; her clothes belonged to her. Her skirt hung cleanly and neatly from her hips, and suggested lithe, clean limbs beneath. The ugly uniform jacket hung gracefully from her shoulders. It did not bulge and sag in creases about her figure as did so many women's uniforms he had seen; nor did it hang too loosely, like a shapeless sack. It stressed her girlish figure neither too much nor too little. On her the jacket succeeded in being entirely a woman's garment, and not a ludicrous travesty of a man's. And with the unpromising cap, too, she had achieved distinction, though in what it differed from others of its pattern he could not discover.

Suddenly she turned and made towards the door, passing close to him without noticing him; and just as she reached the door it was opened from the outside. She stepped back to avoid it, and a small parcel she was carrying fell from her hand. Rawley bent swiftly to pick it up, but the girl had already stooped and their heads bumped.

Rawley straightened with the package in his hands. "Sorry!" he said, with real distress. "I'm most awfully sorry."

She straightened her cap and smiled as she recognized him. It was a friendly and expressive smile. It said all sorts of things: that bumping heads was a comedy and not a tragedy, that she was sorry for his evident distress and hoped he would not think any more about it, that she knew it was an accident and was not in the least annoyed.

"We are quits now, aren't we?" she said.

They had reached the pavement outside and he was holding the package in his hands. He did not want her to go. He badly wanted to talk to her in a friendly, sisterly way. War made one like that, made one friendly towards one's kind. After all, it was one show, they were all in it, men and women, for good or ill.

She held out her hand for the package.

"May I carry it for you?" he asked.

Her eyebrows went up slightly, and she looked at him with candid eyes. "Are we going the same way?" she asked, with a droll smile that he found very attractive.

He rubbed his chin in a characteristic manner, and smiled a little ruefully at the rebuff.

"The fact is," he answered frankly, "I thought perhaps we might foregather in some tea-shop if there is such a thing in this metropolis. After all, it's war time, we are fellow dumplings in a foreign land and all that."

"I suppose that does make some difference," she answered with a smile.

"All the difference in the world," he asserted.

"But how did you know. . . . Oh, you saw the address on that package!" she said severely.

He nodded and grinned. "Yes, it was a lucky guess," he acknowledged cheerfully.

"And how am I to know that you, too . . ."

"I dunno, Barney bor, these bunks do cut sumfen haard!" he drawled in broad Norfolk.

"That's proof positive!" she laughed.

"And my name is Peter Rawley," he added.

"I am Berney Travers," said she.

"And now that we are properly introduced, how about that tea shop!"

III

"I rather like this French game of 'Come choose you east, come choose you west, come choose the one that you love best,' " said he, as they stood plate in hand before the tempting piles of confectionery on the *pâtisserie* counter. "Much simpler than our English system of six standard articles on a plate—you know: bun, cream, one; meringue, one; éclair, chocolate, one; conserve, one; cake, fruit, slice of, one; ditto, seed, slice of, one—and the waitress counts up on her fingers what's left and does mental arithmetic with furrowed brow."

The girl laughed and speared to her plate a puffy confection, oozing cream. Rawley knit his brows and eyed it with mock aversion. "I'm afraid you have depraved tastes," he said with a sigh.

"There are plenty more, if you want one," she retorted.

"That's the beauty of the system," he answered, as he calmly transfixed one of the same fearsome confections. "In England you all sit like kids at a party with one eye on the cakes, gobbling up your bread and butter as fast as you can lest someone should finish first and bag the one you've had your eye on."

They sat down at their table. "I'm afraid you were a greedy child," she said reprovingly.

"I was," he avowed unashamedly. "All healthy kids are. And I bet you were, too."

She handed him his cup. "Bulls'-eyes were my vice," she confessed.

He nodded. He liked her clear, low-pitched voice. "I was catholic in my tastes," he admitted. "I don't think I ever ran to a *grande passion*, though I did have an affair with doughnuts."

Her fork was poised half way to her mouth. "Stoge!" she said, with crinkled nose.

It was a graceful hand that held the fork, small and white, but neither incapable nor delicate. And the finger nails suited it. They were not blunt and black, like those of the pretty farm girl at the mess, nor long and pointed, like those of the little girl in black who had laid her hand on his sleeve in the corridor of the Quatre Fils; they had little cream half moons on them, and were nice and honest looking.

"It's good to be drinking out of a cup again," he remarked. "But I miss the eternal chloride of lime."

"It's very good for one," she mocked.

"Which? Cups or lime?"

"Both—one for the tummy and the other for the soul!"

She had a slow, charming smile, that was free from malice, and gave promise of a great sense of harmless fun. He noticed how her lashes curved upwards when her head was bent. She had steady, candid eyes, and talked in a natural, friendly way.

Her hand came across the table for his cup. "More tea?"

"And no sugar, please," he said.

"Sorry! Did I give you some? Patient man. Why didn't you shout?"

"Icklingham is near Thetford, isn't it?" he asked, glancing down at the parcel beside him.

She nodded and put down her cup. "Um—on the outskirts of the heath."

"I've been across it on my motor-bike—rabbits by the thousand and heather and pines."

She nodded her head vigorously. "I love it."

That was rather refreshing. Most people dismissed the country as dull, or thought their own town slow.

"Tell me about it," he said.

He learned that she lived alone with her mother, that she was attached to a stationary hospital at a place called Hocqmaison, between Doullens and Arras, that she had a Scotch terrier at home named Tim, that she brought the Mess President into Doullens once a week to buy stores, that she loved tennis and hated bridge, that she had a brother at Oundle, that she had seen *Chu Chin Chow* twice, and loved George Robey, though he was rather low, and that she was going to see a divisional concert party that was giving a show in Hocqmaison on Friday.

Suddenly she glanced at her wrist-watch and sprang up. "I must simply fly," she cried. "Captain Grant said that he would be ready to go back by a quarter-past five."

They left the *pâtisserie* and walked down the street thronged with civilian carts, army cars, limbers and motor lorries. Her ambulance was in the square, parked with half a dozen other British vehicles, staff cars, box bodies, and a R.A.F. tender. Beside it stood a middle-aged R.A.M.C. captain. Berney began to apologize for being a minute or two late, but he cut in with, "Not a bit, Miss Travers. I have only just arrived, and there is no hurry, anyway." And there was a twinkle in the eye that met Rawley's as he added, "Can I give you a lift anywhere, Gunner?"

"Thanks very much, but I have a four-footed one of my own waiting for me," answered Rawley.

Berney climbed into the driving-seat, and with a wave of her hand to Rawley, drove out of the square towards the Arras road.

Rawley jogged homeward on Lucy through the amber light of the sinking sun which gilded the leafy woods that crowned every hill. The drone of a homing aeroplane served only to emphasize the calm that attends the dying of a summer day. In the A.S.C. billet at the fork roads outside the village an unseen man was singing in the soothing contented manner that betokens pleasant fatigue, a day's work behind and leisure ahead—the way men sing when polishing their boots before walking out for the evening. Round the last bend in the narrow road the first yellow-washed cottages of the village lay bathed in golden glory. Two men of the battery passed him with clinking spurs, whitened lanyards, and soldierly salutes. He rode slowly up the streets and mounted the short, steep lane to the mess.

His canvas bath stood ready filled on the red-brick floor of his billet, and he had a cold sponge down before changing into slacks for mess. Altogether a successful day he mused as he stood clean and clothed, brushing his damp hair before his steel travelling mirror.

IV

The Major, Whedbee, and Piddock were in the mess talking to a stranger who was introduced as Rumbald, a reinforcement from Havre, posted to the battery. The Major asked about the collars he had commissioned Rawley to get him from ordnance, and Piddock asked facetiously whether he had been to the opera or attended a *thé dansant* at the Ritz. Rawley told them of his meeting Tankard at the Quatre Fils, but said nothing of Berney Travers. That would have been to invite facetious remarks, and he felt that it had been too nice an occurrence to become the subject of Piddock's chaff.

The conversation drifted back to London which Rumbald had left only a fortnight previously; and Rawley drew up a chair and covertly appraised this new-comer, who was to share that close intimacy that war had imposed upon them.

He was a big man, probably in the early thirties, though the girth of his waist, which compelled him to buckle his Sam Browne in the last hole, made him appear almost middle-aged. He had the comfortable, well-fed air of a man who finds much in life that is agreeable, and does not spoil his enjoyment of it by vain yearnings for the unattainable. His pink and slightly fleshy face suggested much soap and warm water, and the dark hairs imparted to the well-shaven cheeks a faint, luminous blue gleam. There were little wrinkles at the corners of his eyes, and Rawley pictured him in civil life wearing a tight blue suit and a bowler hat on the back of his head. He lounged in the old horsehair armchair, his head sunk in his massive shoulders, a glass of whisky resting on his crossed knees, and his great buttocks pressing the springs flat; and Rawley, remembering his own shyness as a newcomer to the mess, envied this man for his easy assurance.

He had a humorous blunt way of talking about men and things, and he had, it appeared, a great number of acquaintances in London and scattered up and down England, to whom he referred bewilderingly as old George Kemp, young Tom Conolly, Sam Tatam's missus, or that little armful Patsy Green. Evidently he was very popular in this wide circle of acquaintances, though it did not appear to which particular strata of society they belonged.

He had managed to enjoy life, even in Havre where, it appeared, reinforcement officers were hampered by endless ridiculous regulations. But he had not allowed these to cramp his optimism or opportunism. Evidently he was a very good hand at driving a coach and four through an Act of Parliament, or any other troublesome regulation. He had a breezy, persuasive, "Come-old-fellow,-but-of-course-these-ridiculous-regulations-don't-apply-*to-me*" manner that had procured him sugar in a land of saccharine, meat without a ration card, and drinks in public-houses after hours. A useful fellow to send to brigade or division when they and the battery did not see eye to eye.

CHAPTER IV

THE battery was enjoying its rest in the village after its long and arduous spell in the Line. In the manner of British troops the world over it had made itself at home within ten minutes of the guns being parked beneath the trees of the square. Within an hour it was known throughout the battery which farm sold the cheapest eggs and at which *estaminet* the beer was least insipid, and more than one gunner had taken his place in a French kitchen, with the family, to drink a cup of the coffee that seemed to be ready at any hour.

Two guns had gone to ordnance for repairs, and apart from the routine exercise, stables, and feeds that are inseparable from a horse unit, duties were light. And the weather, as if in expiation of its recent vagaries, was excellent. The dusty white surface of the village street was scolloped with the clear-cut shadows of gables and chimneys. The wood that climbed the slope behind the village street looked cool and inviting, and beyond the houses the heat shimmered above the swelling slopes of ripening corn that undulated to the hazy distance, unbroken by hedge or tree except for an occasional wood upon a hill-top, and in the low ground the winding green ribbon of trees that marked the road.

A football match had been arranged between the battery and the motor transport workshop that was quartered at the cross-roads, and Rawley played in his old school position at right half and fed Piddock, who made a very fast outside right. Rumbald, on the touch-line, proved to be an enthusiastic supporter of his new unit, and his periodic mighty bellow of "Come on, B Battery," sent the birds eddying above the poplars.

He showed a liking for Rawley's company, and Rawley was a little flattered by this tribute from a man older and more worldly wise than himself. They went riding together in the afternoon, following, perhaps not entirely by accident, the route Rawley had taken two days previously when he had met Berney Travers on the road to Doullens. Rumbald was in a confidential mood and spoke of his wife.

"Writes to me every other day, Pete," he said. "Sends me lashings of cigarettes, marching chocolate, and any damn thing the shop people can kid her we want out here. That's the sort of wife to have, Pete, my lad, one that looks after the bed *and* the board. That's a wife's job—a wife that is a wife."

He took a photograph from his breast pocket and handed it to Rawley. "Not a high stepper, mind you, but a nice little armful all the same."

Rawley made some suitable comment and handed back the photograph. Rumbald gazed at it sentimentally for a moment before returning it to his pocket.

"That's the sort we shall have to find for you one of these days," he continued. "How would you like a nice little girl of your own?" and he made a stab at Rawley's ribs with his crop. "Half the trouble in this life is caused by fellows who want a woman and don't know it, or by females who get a kink on religion or uplift or some damn nonsense, when all they really want is a few babies. God never intended a man or a woman to live alone, and He ought to know."

Swaying gently to the motion of his mare, Rawley silently agreed. He tilted his cap over his eyes to look at an aeroplane droning overhead, but his mind's eyes was occupied with the picture Rumbald's words had conjured up—the picture of a little woman of one's own, someone so much a part of oneself that one was never alone, even when separated from her. Someone with whom one could share all the extraordinary thoughts and ideas and emotions that made up life—particularly life in this baffling time of war. Someone who would welcome one even though one came muddy and sweaty and unshaven straight from a gun-pit. And he recalled the daintily dressed girl he had seen at Victoria station, who when the leave train came in had flung her arms round the neck of her muddy husband and had been lifted off her feet and hugged before the world.

His mare half-stumbled in a rabbit hole and curveted affectedly. He soothed her with a little clucking noise while his thoughts ran on.

Of course it was not often that a cultured English girl showed her feelings like that; but it did give one a glimpse into hidden heavens so to speak. Her eyes shining like stars and seeing only one muddy man among all the khaki crowd. There was no mistaking that look—or forgetting it. Lucky devil that infanteer, whoever he was.

Clean, healthy English girls seemed very pally and unemotional, but after that revelation at Victoria one knew that behind their calm eyes that radiant look lay waiting for some man.

He glanced covertly at Rumbald riding beside him and eyed his plump profile with new interest. *He* had not merely surprised such a look as a slightly envious onlooker; he must know what it felt like to be that muddy infanteer. When he went on leave a girl would be waiting for him with that look in her eyes.

He turned his eyes away and patted his mare's neck. How little one really knew about the lives of others; less than the half. Here was this fellow Rumbald, ordinary looking chap, nothing heroic or—or Hamlet-like about him to give a clue, and yet he had been through all that. And that infanteer no doubt seemed just as ordinary to his fellow officers who had not seen his wife meet him at Victoria.

On the way back Rumbald asked, "Ever been to Amiens?"

"No," answered Rawley. "Have you?"

Rumbald shook his head. "Good spot, I'm told—like Havre, only better." He tapped Rawley's knee with his crop and asked mysteriously, "Like to come in with me tomorrow?"

Rawley thought it would be worth doing if it could be managed.

Rumbald shut one eye and nodded mysteriously. "So you shall then," he said. "I've fixed it all up. A nice little dinner and the sights of the town. Like me to tackle the Major for you?"

"Oh no, I'll ask him," said Rawley. "He won't object. He's awfully decent about that sort of thing when we're in rest. But how are we to get there? It must be over thirty kilometres."

Rumbald winked again mysteriously. "Trust your Uncle Sammy," he said. "Know Penhurst?"

"That's the M.T. fellow at the cross-roads, isn't it?"

Rumbald nodded. "Yes. Well, he's going to take us in his car tomorrow afternoon."

CHAPTER V

I

PENHURST of the A.S.C. arrived on the following afternoon to take Rawley and Rumbald into Amiens. Rawley was in a sight-seeing mood and was anxious to be off. Rumbald, however, insisted upon a preliminary drink, and they retired to the mess and shouted for the mess corporal. Rawley disliked drinking whisky on a hot afternoon, but his objections were overruled by Rumbald, whose persuasive, hail-fellow-well-met manner was always difficult to resist.

"Come on, Pete," he said. "You must have just one little spot. You can't see Amiens properly unless you've had at least one drink first. Isn't that so, Penhurst?"

Penhurst nodded agreement.

"Well, so long as I don't see two cathedrals," murmured Rawley doubtfully.

"That's right," boomed Rumbald. "A good stiff whisky for Mr. Rawley, corporal. Puts you in the right mood to appreciate architecture or any other sort of beauty." This with a wink at Penhurst. And so they all settled down into chairs, and it was two drinks later in the case of Rumbald and Penhurst or twenty minutes before they went out into the sunlight and started up the grey Vauxhall car.

They drove along the now familiar shady road into Doullens and turned south past the old grass-covered citadel up the straight, steep Amiens road that climbed over the bare downs. Penhurst drove, and he drove fast, so that Rawley had little opportunity of seeing the country as he would have wished to do, and he absorbed only a vague impression of a straight white road switch-backing over corn-covered downs, hedgeless and treeless, except for a wood-shrouded village here and there on a hill top, and punctuated by villages with hideous new red-brick churches which changed later to picturesque though poverty-stricken wattle-and-daub cottages girdled with fruit trees.

Then the car shot over the low crest of a hill, and he saw the city below him straddling the green Somme valley, a wide sweep of jumbled roofs and chimneys and trees glimmering silver-grey in the sunlight, and the great cathedral, with its long, grey roof and pinnacles towering cliff-like from the tree-shaded quays and bridges where the glassy Somme was shivered into a number of gleaming canals. The view was lost a moment later as they swept into a suburb down a long, straight *pavé* road bordered by trees and broad sidewalks on which dirty urchins played and bedraggled women filled cracked ewers at the stand-pipes spaced before dreary flat-fronted houses. The road narrowed suddenly, and canals, stone quays, and markets opened to right and left. The western towers of the cathedral soared above the houses terraced on the slope ahead. The car bumped over two or three narrow bridges and climbed a steep, winding cobbled street.

They left the car in the courtyard of the Hôtel de la Paix and walked back across the Place Gambetta.

"What's the programme?" asked Rumbald.

"Well, I think that Charley's Bar is indicated."

"Oh Lord!" groaned Rawley. "We are not going to spend the whole day on a pub crawl, surely."

"Well, what did you think of doing, Pete?" asked Rumbald good-humouredly.

"Oh, I don't know. Look round the place—register on the cathedral and all that."

"Righto, Pete. You get the cathedral off your chest while Penhurst and I register on Charley's Bar. Where do we go afterwards, Penhurst?"

"Oh, we'll get tea at Odette's; Rawley can meet us there."

"Oh, and I want to get a bath," put in Rawley. "Where does one bath?"

"Come on, I'll show you," said Penhurst. "This is the three-pebbles street, the local Bond Street, where one can buy anything from a camisole to a smutty post card. That's Odette's." He pointed across the road to a *pâtisserie*. "Where we meet for tea. And these are the baths."

He turned in under a low archway where second-hand books were displayed on shelves. "That's the gentleman's lavatory as we call it euphemistically in English," he said, and murmured "*bonjour, madame*" to an old dame seated on a stool. "These are the baths." He pushed open a glass door on the right.

"Want us to come in and hold the soap or tickle your back?" asked Rumbald. "No? Then cheerio. We'll meet at Odette's anon."

Rawley was led up a broad staircase and ushered into a small room containing a short deep metal tub covered with a sheet, into which steaming water was gushing. He took off his belt and tunic and hung them on the door hook and turned with arms akimbo to examine the unfamiliar type of bath. It seemed a sanitary idea if the sheet were clean, which it was, and anyway, the hot, deep water was an improvement upon the few tepid inches in his folding canvas bath.

II

Feeling comfortably clean and civilized he wandered out past the old woman still seated on her stool, into the crowded Rue des Trois Cailloux. Staff cars, mess-carts, and military motor-cycles moved in a continuous stream along the road, and on the pavements the number of British officers was hardly less than that of the native civilians. The civilized shop windows were enticing, and he lingered at one or two of them before turning down a side street towards the grey pinnacles of the cathedral. The street was narrow, winding, and cobbled, and at each turn he caught a new glimpse of the great grey rampart of stone and glass rising higher and higher above the roofs. He found himself at length in the open space before the west front. The great carved buttresses and recessed door arches were neatly sandbagged to a height of eighty feet or more to protect them from bomb splinters, but above the rampart of bleached sandbags the two great chiselled towers rose in naked splendour.

Rawley gazed upwards till his neck ached, and then he mounted the steps and passed into the lofty tunnel of the nave. The silence and dimness and spaciousness were restful he decided. Rumbald was a good fellow, but his persistent joviality rather swamped one's efforts at intelligent thought.

He found Odette's filled to overflowing with British officers of every age and rank, and among them Rumbald and Penhurst in a corner clapping tea-spoons on plates to attract his attention. He was anxious to see the famous Odette, and when she herself arrived to take their order he was surprised to find not the spoiled and painted beauty he had expected, but a quiet, pleasant-faced girl who had a smile and a friendly word for everyone, and repelled the advances of her too ardent admirers with disarming tact and competence. The ogling glances which several officers of high rank and grey hairs directed at her he found highly ludicrous and a little beastly; but she moved about the room as though unconscious of them and showed favour to none. A very competent little person he decided. Fame had exaggerated her beauty, but did bare justice to her character.

Penhurst greeted her jovially as an old friend, and so did Rumbald, though he had never seen her before. The familiarity annoyed Rawley. How she must hate them all, he thought, though she betrayed no sign of it. She said, "*Bonjour, messieurs*" with disarming naturalness, and a smile that included him though he had not spoken; and he could have sworn that she had divined his annoyance and that her eyes, which for a moment met his, were the kinder on that account.

"Nice bit of goods that," asserted Rumbald, gazing appreciatively at her retreating high heels. "Keep nice and warm at night with that wrapped round you."

Penhurst grunted agreement. "She doesn't wrap too easily, though," he grumbled.

Rumbald guffawed. "So she has given you the frozen optic, Pen, has she?"

"Not only me," growled Penhurst hastily, in self-defence. "I declare I believe the damned woman is a virgin."

Rumbald laughed incredulously. "Particular, is she! That's half the attraction. She's got a head on her shoulders. All the same, if I was a betting man—" He finished by throwing out his chest and giving his tunic a little tug downwards, an affectation which in a man of Rumbald's figure Rawley thought ridiculous.

After tea Penhurst led the way to the Galleries to do some shopping. Rumbald insisted on doing all the talking, and boisterously fanned the amusement which his rusty fourth-form French created among the shop girls. When at a loss for a word in French his method was to say the English equivalent in a louder tone and with what he considered was a French accent. Thus a walking-stick was asked for as "*un steek promanader*," accompanied by dumb show, purporting to mimic a man-about-town twirling his cane in the park. His expression and antics were so absurd that Penhurst and Rawley were reduced to speechless laughter, and assistants flocked from the other departments to watch the fun and join in the game of guessing what it was he was trying to say.

Out again into the Rue des Trois Cailloux they came at last, and led by Rumbald turned automatically, it seemed, into a café. He settled down with a long complaining of springs on the red plush seat and called loudly in his execrable French, "*Garcong*! Garcong!" And there they stayed till Penhurst announced that it was time for dinner.

He led them up a mean and narrow street branching from the Rue des Trois Cailloux and stopped before a small, white-painted shop-front where a few fly-blown pastries were displayed against a background of black-and-white check wall-paper.

"Bloody looking hole outside," he explained; "but they give you a good meal, and it's quiet."

They found dinner laid in a long, boarded room, painted white, with frosted-glass windows high up along one wall and palms and a piano in one corner. A tall, dark girl, dressed in a black-and-white striped frock, whose pallor was emphasized by heavy powdering, took their caps and sticks.

Rumbald moved straight to the piano, called for a drink, and began to play a spirited syncopated tune; and Rawley found himself seized by Penhurst and fox-trotted down the narrow lane between the table and the wall. As he turned at the top by the piano he saw with surprise that there were now a number of women standing at the other end of the room watching him. One of them clapped her hands and cried, "Bravo! Vair-e good, M'sieu," and Rumbald, hearing this exclamation of surprise, looked up and exclaimed, "Oh, the fairies have arrived." He sang, to the piano accompaniment, the first few bars of "If you were the only girl in the world;" then took a long gulp from his glass, stood up, straightened his Sam Browne with a tug and shouted, "Party—'shun! The C.O. will now inspect the parade."

The girls giggled, and arranged themselves in exaggerated attitudes of attention, while Rumbald stumped down the room in the manner of the stage colonel, twirling an imaginary moustache.

Rawley thought them the most depressing and pitiable collection of women he had ever seen. There were six of them. None had any pretensions to good looks, and only two of them were at all young. Deep lines seamed their heavily painted and powdered faces, and their black-pencilled eyes glittered metallically through their thickened lashes like those of a starved cat. And their frocks were the cheapest of tawdry finery.

Rumbald stamped down the line in his facetious mockery of a military inspection, here making a coarse joke about chest measurement, there lifting a skirt ostensibly to check the position of the feet; while the girls tittered and uttered coquettish squeals of dismay. But there was an anxious competitive look in their eyes, which showed that the mock inspection was more than mere foolery to them.

Like a cattle market, thought Rawley in disgust.

Rumbald reached the end of the line and bawled, "Stand at ease! Stand easy!" He turned to Rawley. "Come on, Pete, take your pick."

"But—well," demurred Rawley, to whom this development was a complete surprise.

Rumbald misunderstood his diffidence. "Oh, that's all right. You're the guest. First pick," he cried magnanimously.

The ladies had exchanged their absurd military postures for attitudes of languorous ease. Their mask-like faces smiled beguilingly at him, and they signalled invitingly with their bold eyes.

"It's not that," he protested. "You see, I didn't know these girls would be—"

"I quite agree," broke in Rumbald heartily; and he did not bother to lower his voice. "They're a pretty moth-eaten crowd of hags. Where did you get this bunch of tarts from, Pen?"

Penhurst said that they were the best he could get at short notice, and added something coarse to the effect that faces were not everything.

"Oh, well, if Pete can't make up his mind I'll start," said Rumbald. He took a thin, fair-haired woman by the ear. "I'll have you, skinny Lizzie."

Penhurst announced that he would have the fairy with the chippendale legs.

"Come on, Pete," urged Rumbald, "pick your stable companion and let's get on with the grub."

Unless he played the part of a spoil-sport there was nothing for it but to do as they suggested; but it was a cad's trick to force his hand like that. He chose one of the two younger women, a girl in a shoddy black frock with a wan, pinched face. She looked as though she needed a good meal, and he saw by the momentary flash of fierce joy in her hard eyes that he had guessed aright.

The unchosen three immediately ceased their beguiling smiles and glances, and began putting on their hats in a business-like manner. The market was closed for that day. Penhurst moved among them, distributing a few consolatory notes, and shepherded them to the door.

Rumbald called for drinks all round. They sat down at the table, and the girl in the black-and-white striped frock brought in soup. Rumbald was in excellent spirits, and although most of his remarks must have been unintelligible to the ladies whose knowledge of English was limited, they squealed appreciatively at each of his sallies, though without interrupting the important business of eating the meal.

Rawley, who had recovered from his first feeling of nausea, felt only sorrow for his partner, and was anxious to amuse her, but he could think of nothing to say. As the champagne circulated, however, his awkwardness slipped from him, and presently he found himself talking and even making jokes in his indifferent French. Glasses were filled and refilled. The room grew hot and noisy. This sort of thing was really quite amusing when one was warmed up to it. The girl in the black-and-white striped frock was placing a dish on the table, and he saw Rumbald's great red hand creep out and tickle the back of her knee. She slapped it away with a whispered "*Méchant!*"

Penhurst's companion was laughing heartily, and her chair was tilted back. Suddenly, assisted possibly by an unseen boot, it tilted too far, and she disappeared over backwards, and lay with kicking legs on the floor. The other girls screamed with laughter. Rumbald rose to the rescue, with his face modestly hidden in a table napkin, though one large eye peered unblushingly from behind it; and after some horseplay the girl was re-seated right way up on her chair to Rumbald's spirited chanting of the ribald verses, "She was poor but honest."

Glasses were refilled. Rawley had already, during the past few hours, drunk more alcohol than he had drunk before in any three days. It gave one a comfortable, contented feeling. Rumbald was right. Eat, drink, and be merry, for tomorrow we die. If that were true of anywhere, it was certainly true of Amiens in war time. Though Rumbald, the old satyr, had not yet seen a round fired in anger. But he damn soon would. Wise fellow, then, to make the most of things.

He glanced approvingly at Rumbald, who was doing some fooling on the floor with a wine-glass and his partner's beaded hand-bag, and drained his glass. He refilled it, and refilled his partner's glass, and he experienced an unfamiliar trembling when her hand, with its long, pointed nails, came out and rested upon his knee.

Rumbald moved to the piano and they danced, stopping only to replenish glasses and when overcome by laughter. They all talked loudly and laughed uproariously at anything or nothing, but particularly at Rumbald's absurd antics as he sat thumping out syncopated airs at the piano while his partner held a glass to his lips.

Rawley found the lights and heat and noise bewildering; he was conscious only of circling round and round in a bright, warm haze with the sickly scent of cosmetics in his nostrils; till suddenly he became aware of Rumbald with his cap on the back of his head counting out notes to the girl in the black-and-white striped frock. He stumbled across the room, dragging his note-case from his breast pocket with fumbling fingers. "Let me pay my whack," he cried, pulling out a fifty-franc note.

Rumbald waved it aside. "My show, Pete. Absolutely my show—mine and Pen's. From now on we carry on independently. Meet in a couple of hours at the car—Hôtel de la Paix."

Rawley thrust the note into his breeches pocket, clapped Rumbald on the back, and went in search of his partner. He helped her into her cloak, and she held up her pitiably wan and painted little face for him to tuck the wisps of hair under her hat. Then they went out into the street.

It was very dark, and he had no notion of his whereabouts, but she tucked her arm into his and led him along. He was annoyed with his legs; they seemed to have suddenly grown longer. His feet would keep hitting the ground when he thought they were still three or four inches from it, and it made him stumble as though he were drunk. The cool night breeze that was blowing cleared his head a little, and he recognized an open space they crossed as the Place Gambetta. She led him to a dark, narrow street and stopped suddenly before a door. She ran up the three steps and opened it with a key. "*Entrez, cheri?*" she said.

He leaned against the wall without replying, and she repeated in English. "Cum-en, Darlin'."

He shook his head, and blurted half sullenly, "Not tonight, Josephine—*Pas ce soir.*"

She came quickly down the steps and laid a hand on his sleeve; but he shook her off.

"Oh, you won't lose by it," he assured her, and thrust his hand into his pocket. His fingers closed over the note that Rumbald had refused, and he thrust it into her hand.

She looked at it quickly and cried, "*Merci bien, M'sieu. Vous êtes très gentil.*" But he was already several yards from her. She shrugged her narrow shoulders and went back up the steps; and he heard the latch click, and the door close behind her.

He took off his cap and allowed the cool breeze to play about his forehead. Absolutely chucking money about, he thought—fifty francs, nearly two pounds. No doubt she needed it—poor half-starved little slut.

He leaned against the wall and closed his eyes. He saw again the lights and white paint and littered dinner table of the little restaurant. It moved round and round as it had done when he danced. Faster and faster it moved, till nothing but whirling streams of lights were visible. His stomach rose suddenly, and he was violently sick.

A few minutes later he wiped the sweat from his brow and went on. His brain was excessively active. "My God, what a night," he thought. "Sick in the street—like a Saturday night drunk! Swilling oneself with poison! Paying through the nose to horseplay with filthy little sluts. That was Rumbald's idea of a good evening. My God!"

III

He trudged on through the silent streets that radiated from the cathedral. Little firefly lights came and went in the darkness. One flashed suddenly and blindingly in his face, and a husky female voice said, "Naughtee boy! What would mother say!" The flash-lamp swung round and illuminated the little white powdered face and dark, inviting eyes of her who held it, as though to say, "Don't buy a pig in a poke. See what you are paying for."

He shook his head at her and passed on. Other flash-lamps threw their beams upon his uniform, and other husky voices murmured facetious greetings from the darkness at his elbow. Couldn't one get away from these women anywhere in Amiens? What a reputation British officers must enjoy with the civil population! And no wonder, when even married men like Rumbald couldn't keep straight.

Distantly from above sounded the pulsating drone that distinguished the German night bomber, and the pale fingers of three or four searchlight beams went questing silently across the calm night sky above the dark housetops, pausing now and then uncertainly and then moving on again.

He trudged on through the darkness aimlessly. It would be useless to return to the car so soon. Rumbald had said two hours. He wandered down a winding black canyon and emerged on the deserted quays, where the stars lay reflected in the black water of the canals at his feet. The pulsating drone of engines still sounded fitfully from the north-east.

He sank wearily on to a bench beneath a tree and sat with hunched shoulders listening to the night breeze rustling the leaves above his head. Suddenly the ground and the seat shook as though kicked by a giant foot, and the tapering *flèche* of the cathedral leapt into view for a moment, black against a dull red glow, and was gone again. The familiar muffled crash of the explosion followed and the distant pattering of falling masonry and glass.

He followed the gropings of a searchlight beam with lazy interest. He wondered if the bomb had dropped anywhere near Rumbald. It would be funny if it had landed on the very house and taken off the front as had happened to many houses he had seen near the Line. The surprised Don Juan scrambling out of bed in a room with only three walls and hurriedly pulling on his breeches in full view of the street would be a comic sight.

He laughed softly at the absurd picture his mind had drawn, and glanced upwards as the liquid lucka-lucka-lucka-lucka of aerial machine-gunning came from overhead. But there was nothing to be seen except the halo of a searchlight beam on the edge of a cloud.

The night breeze was cold. He turned up the collar of his trench coat and continued his wandering. The cafés were closed. The streets were deserted and dark, except for the little flash-lamps which still winked hopefully here and there. At this hour it seemed that Amiens provided only one amusement for the stranger within her gates.

He found his way back to the now darkened yard of the hotel and sat in the silent car and smoked pipe after pipe. When at last the other two men did appear, he was warned of their approach by the hearty voice of Rumbald singing the Robbers' chorus from *Chu Chin Chow*. Penhurst was as mournful as his companion was cheerful. He started up the engine sullenly and switched on the headlights. Rumbald fooled round the car and began working the Klaxon horn violently like a mischievous urchin.

Penhurst turned on him in cold fury. "Stop that bloody row for Christ's sake!"

Rumbald desisted after one more provocative wail. "Must get your lousy old 'bus going, Pen," he said cheerfully. And he began to move violently every lever and switch within reach. The engine coughed and was silent.

Penhurst, who had one foot on the running-board, seized Rumbald savagely by the cross strap of his Sam Browne. "I'll twist your flaming neck if you don't keep your blasted hands off things," he hissed.

Rawley dragged them apart. "You come in the back with me, Rumbald," he said. Rumbald did not want to go in the back seat; he wanted to drive. "Not if I know it," cried Rawley.

There ensued a lot of drunken foolery on the part of Rumbald, and a stream of blood-curdling invective from Penhurst, till Rawley lost all patience. He hauled and pushed Rumbald into the back seat. "My God!" he cried in exasperation. "Tight as you are, I swear I'll slog you both if you don't shut up."

He was very doubtful of Penhurst's ability to drive, and he was relieved and a little surprised when they reached the outskirts of the city without disaster. But Penhurst, though not sober, was competent; and once on the open road he drove with a cool, suppressed fury at a pace that would have been suicidal had he been either less sober or less drunk. Occasionally the lime-washed cottages of a village leapt up white in the headlights, walling the road narrowly for a few seconds, to fall away as suddenly as they had arisen, leaving windy darkness on either hand, and the racing pool of light ahead chequered with the shadowed inequalities of the road.

Rumbald made one sudden effort to gratify his wish to drive, and was repulsed by an icy douce of vituperation from the fell Penhurst, and was urgently dragged back into his seat by an exasperated Rawley. He complained almost tearfully of their unkindness, but fell asleep in the middle of his jeremiad.

The familiar buildings at the cross-roads leapt up in the headlights and were gone, and a second later it seemed Penhurst brought the car to a standstill in the village. The now maudlin Rumbald was bundled out and Rawley followed. Penhurst called "Goodnight," turned the car dexterously, the headlights in their swinging arc revealing for a second the white walls and shining windows of sleeping cottages, guns and limbers standing beneath cardboard scenic trees, and a silent sentry with white face and glistening eyes and bayonet, and then the darkness rushed in again and he shot like a rocket back the way he had come.

Rumbald began to sing mournfully, but the words ended in a gasp as an elbow drove into his body. "Shut up, you fool," whispered Rawley hoarsely. "We don't want the sentry to know you are bloody drunk. Shut up!" He put his arm round the huge, sagging body and piloted it towards his billet.

By the meagre light of a candle stuck in the brass cottage candlestick on the marble-topped chest of drawers Rawley pulled off Rumbald's boots as he lay like a stranded whale on the square French bed. They were field-boots and required much tugging before they came off and lolled drunkenly together by the low wooden valance of the bed. And all the time Rumbald talked sentimentally, though to Rawley, kneeling on the clean, red-brick floor, his head was out of sight below the horizon of his prostrate body.

"Damn good of you, Pete—to look after me—like this. Damn good of you," he murmured. "Do same for you— one day."

Rawley set to work to take off the other garments.

"I like you, Pete, lad," the voice went on. "I—like you. Good pals we'll be . . . good pals. Bloody good . . . pals." With great earnestness: "War's hell, Pete . . . flaming hell . . . but not when you've got pals." Tears of emotion stood in his blurred eyes. "We're pals, Pete . . . b-bloody good pals."

Rawley made no contribution to the conversation. He went on steadily with his task, no easy one, of separating the tunic, breeches, and other garments from their close filling of flesh. But at last it was done, and Rumbald was in green pyjamas and lay in bed with a brown army blanket tucked under his chin and his flushed face on the coarse white pillow like a fried egg.

Rawley went towards the candle, but was recalled to remove the watch from Rumbald's wrist. Again he approached to blow out the candle and was again recalled to replace the Sam Browne on the chair. A third time he reached the candle and the voice came again from the bed. "Pete, will you—"

"Oh, God! What do you want now?"

"You're . . . not angry, Pete, are you?" plaintively.

"What *is* it?"

"You're not angry?" This almost tearfully.

"Oh, no—only fed up; damned fed up."

"One little favour, old man. Will you?"

"Oh, I suppose so. What is it?"

"My wallet . . . in my tunic."

Rawley took the wallet from the pocket of the tunic on the chair and brought it to the bed. Rumbald opened it and fumbled in the pockets. He took out the photograph of his wife and gazed at it with a silly smile.

"My old missus!" he faltered. "My half-section. Can't go . . . to sleep without her . . . Pete, lad."

Rawley blew out the candle with such force that the curtains stirred and left him mumbling in the darkness.

CHAPTER VI

I

RAWLEY was awake early. The coarse green curtain had been drawn too brusquely the night before, and between one side of it and the window-frame a narrow shaft of early sunlight penetrated and lay like a shining sword across the red-brick floor. He turned over in his sleeping-bag to avoid the glare and arranged his head more comfortably on the little rubber air-pillow. The village cocks were inquiring after one another's welfare and the engine hum of a high-flying machine returning from dawn patrol passed over and died away. The cool breeze that stirred the curtain carried a tang of wood smoke from the fire kindling at the cook-house.

Rawley dozed; and the shining sword of light upon the floor moved slowly and was twisted on the edge of his valise lying in a brown rumpled heap by the bed.

Shuffling of feet on the road outside announced that the mess orderlies were parading. He turned over drowsily without opening his eyes. That was no concern of his; Rumbald was orderly officer. Rumbald! He sat up quickly as a thought struck him and looked at his watch. Then he disentangled his feet from the flea-bag and slid off the bare box-mattress on which it lay to the floor. He glanced out of the window and saw the orderlies waiting in the road, and then he began pulling on his clothes.

So that was the sort of fellow Rumbald was, he mused. Drink and women were a man's own affair. Debauchery was one thing; but letting the battery down was another. If a bombardier neglected his duty he was broken, and yet an officer. . . .

He pulled on his boots. It was not to save Rumbald he was doing it. The fellow fully deserved the strafing he would get if the Major knew; but the men must not know that an officer was slack. He put on his cap and went out.

He had taken less than five minutes to dress, but even so he was late; and he had never yet been late on parade. Sergeant Jameson called the men to attention and saluted. He looked strong and capable, standing there rigid in the sunlight. His sunburnt face was expressionless, but his blue grey eyes were very intelligent. "Damn the fellow," thought Rawley, "he knows I'm not orderly officer."

Rumbald did not appear at breakfast, and it was after stables, as he was passing the mess, that Rawley heard the hearty voice calling him insistently by name. He looked in at the open window of the mess-room and saw Rumbald standing alone in the room, a glass of whisky in one hand and a cigarette in the other. His cap and crop lay on the table. "Morning, Pete," he cried cheerfully. "You're in a hell of a hurry this morning. Whither away?"

"The section. Some people try to do their job—even in war time," retorted Rawley cuttingly.

Rumbald seemed to be unaware of the thrust. He smiled a comfortable, at-peace-with-all-the-world smile and held his glass to the light. "Let them get on with it then," he answered cheerfully. "Nobody's stopping them. Come and have a drink."

Rawley shook his head. "Had enough of that last night—and more."

Rumbald sauntered towards the window. "So did I," he admitted disarmingly. "But hair of the dog that bit you, you know." He leaned his elbows on the sill. "You won't? Wise man, Pete," he murmured paternally. "Drink has been the ruin of many better men than you and me."

"Why not chuck it then?"

Rumbald drained his glass and dragged a cigarette case from his pocket. "Why not!" he exclaimed as he selected a cigarette with leisurely care. "Alcoholic remorse is all very well if it isn't carried too far. Make good resolutions by all means, Pete, lad: they purify the soul. But, Lord! what a dull world it would be if we kept to 'em! Take it from me, it's a mistake to take life too seriously; you'll find that out for yourself when you are my age."

"Perhaps," retorted Rawley sceptically and turned away.

"The worst of you fellows is that you don't enjoy life," went on Rumbald imperturbably. "You get comfortably tight, but afterwards little conscience comes along and spoils it all. Why in hell be ashamed of a glorious binge?"

"It's not that," retorted Rawley hotly. He found Rumbald's diagnosis of his feelings irritating.

Rumbald blew a smoke ring. "And it's the same with a woman. I bet you got sentimental and overpaid that tart last night—probably wanted to pi-jaw her afterwards. Why the hell can't you take what comes to you without being ruddy virtuous about it?"

"All the same," he continued as Rawley turned angrily away. "Thanks very much for taking breakfast for me this morning—and bedding me down last night."

"Oh, that's all right," called back Rawley, somewhat mollified at this recognition of his services.

"Only, Pete!" bellowed Rumbald after him, "for the Lord's sake don't be virtuous about it."

Rawley went off to the section in an ill temper. Rumbald had a knack of making one feel young and putting one in the wrong; and the irritating part of it was there was a grain of truth in what he had said.

II

Whedbee and the Major rode off for Doullens soon after lunch. Penhurst turned up shortly afterwards and suggested poker. Rawley declined, and Piddock said he did not know the game; but Penhurst and Rumbald offered to teach him, and Rawley left them hard at it round the mess table.

He strolled out through the village and came to the fork roads by the A.S.C. billet. A long convoy of lorries was passing along the main road, and in order to get away from the choking exhaust fumes and the clouds of white dust which rolled like smoke around the clattering shadowy shapes, he crossed it and followed the short cut he had taken on his ride to Doullens. He tramped across fields along the margin of copses and came at last down the sunken track to the main Doullens road where his mare had been startled by the ambulance.

He looked up and down the road, half hoping to see the ambulance with Berney at the wheel, but there was only a Maltese cart jogging along and a despatch rider phutting by on a motor-cycle. He climbed a bank overlooking the road and sat down on the grass at the top beneath some trees. He took out his pipe and lighted it. She might be going into Doullens that afternoon, and if she were she would pass along the road below him. Anyway, it was very pleasant lying there in the shade.

He smoked several pipes and allowed his thoughts to drift idly as he watched the traffic that passed intermittently below him—a G.S. wagon with driver perched high above the horses' tails, a swiftly moving green staff car with a little red flag fluttering above the nickel radiator, a heavy French farm wagon with two long-maned horses harnessed tandem-wise, motor lorries singly and in convoys, a mule-drawn limber wagon, two French *gendarmes* in glittering horse-tailed helmets, a noisy caterpillar tractor dragging the massive mounting of a nine-point-two, and a light ambulance. This last caused him to sit up, and when he saw that the driver was a man he experienced a sharp pang of disappointment.

He sat a long time, longer than he had intended, giving himself another five minutes, and then another, in the hope that she might be on her way back from Doullens; but no ambulance sped along the road below him. Finally he bound himself to go when seven more vehicles of any kind had passed, and when they passed one by one, and the seventh had disappeared round a bend, he threw one last hopeful look up and down the road and rose reluctantly.

III

The Major and Whedbee had returned when he got back, and Rumbald was entertaining them and Piddock with an account of his adventures in Amiens on the previous evening. Rumbald was a good talker and artist enough not to adhere too strictly to the truth if the story could be improved upon by the exercise of some imagination. His breezy narrative style, accompanied by pantomimic gestures in the comic parts, kept the Major highly amused; Piddock was giggling in his irrepressible way, and even Whedbee's eyes twinkled behind his glasses and his lean face broke periodically into an amused smile.

Rawley dropped into a chair and listened with mixed admiration and disgust; for, as told by Rumbald, the sordid events of the previous evening assumed the lustre of comedy and romance. Amiens became a comic opera city in which the most ludicrous incidents were to be encountered at every street corner, and the little back-street restaurant became the scene of such gaiety, beauty, wit, and romance, as is to be found only in the imagination of young novelists. And in this brilliant scene, Penhurst and Rumbald played their parts gallantly and worthily; and Rawley was astonished to learn how witty and amusing he himself had been.

Rumbald's powers of imagination and description appeared to be inexhaustible. Each laugh that he drew spurred him to further efforts. He addressed himself principally to the Major, with an occasional glance at the others, and he dominated the room. General conversation was impossible. The Major and Piddock were his willing listeners, and Whedbee sat silently drawing at his pipe with that non-committal expression on his face that made it so difficult to guess what he was thinking.

Rawley found the persistent voice and the loud vulgar laugh maddeningly irritating. The man was shamelessly showing off, sucking up to the Major. He dominated the place; nobody else could say a word. They all sat and listened like sheep to his blatterings, and laughed obediently when he looked at them. They had been a contented peaceful mess till this fellow had butted in. Why should one man be allowed to annoy the rest? Surely the Major must see that the fellow was just sucking up to him. He couldn't really be amused at that rot.

Rawley sat in a corner and scowled. He at least would not encourage the fellow; and every time Rumbald's eye went round the faces asking silently for a laugh, Rawley's face alone was set like wood and did not respond.

At last he could stand it no longer. He went to the gramophone and put on a record. And so for a few minutes the hearty voice and the syncopated tune contended for mastery; and then the Major, with an exclamation of annoyance, lifted the needle from the record and shut off the motor.

Rawley picked up his cap and went for a walk in the moonlight.

On his way back up the little village street to his billet he met Piddock.

"*Bon soir*, my old war horse!" cried Piddock cheerfully, and fell into step beside him. "Comrade Rumbald was in good form tonight."

Rawley grunted.

"Dashed amusing bloke," went on Piddock. "Livened the place up no end. I must hie me to Armeens. I'd no idea you'd had such a topping time there. Why didn't you tell us about it, you lugubrious old warrior?"

Rawley stopped at his billet. "Rumbald's idea of a good time and mine don't agree," he said.

"You're too hard to please, Rawley. It seemed a dashed good time to me."

"Oh yes, he made it sound all right," retorted Rawley.

"Well, wasn't it?"

"Oh yes, if you think it amusing to muck about with foul women and get disgustingly tight," retorted Rawley savagely, and opened the door of his billet.

IV

The following afternoon found Rawley seated again on the bank overlooking the Doullens road. He no longer hid from himself his reason for being there. He wanted to see Berney again, and if she did not pass that day he would come tomorrow—and the next day, till she did. He sat and smoked his pipe and watched the traffic pass. He had decided what he would do if she came, and he was content to wait.

An hour and a half went by, broken by two false alarms caused by two ambulances coming from the direction of Doullens. He saw Rumbald and Piddock emerge from the sunken track on his left, cross the road, and canter along the edge of the pasture beyond. He himself on top of the bank among the trees was invisible from below. And then an ambulance sped swiftly along the road in the direction of Doullens, an ambulance in which he recognized the figure of Berney Travers. When it had passed he scrambled quickly down to the road, and waited with what patience he could muster till a lorry came along in the right direction.

He left the lorry in the main street of Doullens and began his search. He went first to the little square and was overjoyed to find that the ambulance was parked there. "My luck is in," he murmured, and set off down the main street. He looked in at the paper shop where he had met her, and at the tea shop, without finding her. He visited the canteen by the station without success. Half an hour had passed, and he returned anxiously to the little square to assure himself that the car was still there. Then he made short excursions into the streets, returning periodically to the square to make sure that she had not left.

Time was passing and he was becoming desperate. She would be leaving soon and he would have but a few minutes with her at the most. He began to regret not having shouted to her from the bank. He walked the street rapidly, scanning both pavements for the neat uniformed figure. For the tenth time he looked into the paper shop and the tea shop. He dared not try the station again: that was too far from the square.

Then back again he came to the square, striding fast and answering salutes impatiently, to find the ambulance gone. And he had not said one word to her.

Regardless of military dignity he raced towards the Arras road, but dropped precipitately into a walk as he saw the ambulance emerge from a side street a few yards from him.

He raised his hand to the salute as it turned slowly into the main road. She saw him and smiled. He put a hand on the wing of the car gliding slowly past him.

"Are you going along the Arras road?" he asked breathlessly, with scarlet face. She nodded. "Be an angel and give me a lift," he panted desperately.

For answer she brought the car to rest, and he climbed in beside her. She let in the clutch and they glided down the street and out along the tree-shaded road without speaking.

"Get back all right last time?" he inquired at last, inanely.

She nodded. "Did you?"

"Yes, rather."

He was supremely happy sitting there beside her, but for the life of him he could think of nothing to say. And he wanted to talk. He had wasted so much time already hunting for her in Doullens. Soon they would reach the sunken track which was his way back to the village. Suddenly he remembered the concert party she had said she was going to see.

"I say, did you enjoy that concert party?" he asked, knowing well that she had not yet been.

"I haven't seen it yet," she answered. "It is coming on Friday."

"I am going to try to borrow a motor-bike or else lorry-jump in to see it," he announced.

They had reached the sunken track and passed it. She had given it a glance, but had made no comment.

"Do you think we could go together?" he asked quickly. "I would like to awfully, if you wouldn't mind very much— would you?"

"I should love it," she said.

"That's splendid. It will be great fun."

He found he could talk more easily now, and he was elated at the prospect of spending over two hours in her society. She had pointed out that they had nearly reached the village in which was her C.C.S., but he had replied, "Yes—if you go the nearest way, but is there any hurry?" And she had taken the next turning and driven off into a maze of side roads.

She fell silent at length, and presently she stopped the car and turned to him. Her little face was troubled.

"This isn't fair," she said. "You know you ought to go. We passed your turning hours ago. I ought to be back, and I've taken you all over the place. It isn't fair to make me go on."

He jumped out quickly on to the road and stood with his hands on the wheel looking appealingly at her. He was terribly afraid that he had angered her by his selfishness.

"I say, I'm awfully sorry," he said. "You are absolutely right. Jolly caddish of me. You're not frightfully angry with me, are you? Serve me right if you were. But you are not, are you?" he pleaded.

She shook her head with a wistful smile at his earnestness.

"Beastly selfish of me, but I enjoyed it so much," he said.

She looked down at the ignition lever and rasped it forward and then back. "So did I," she confessed; "but I thought you would never go."

"I'm forgiven then?"

She nodded.

"Till Friday evening, then. Goodbye—Berney."

She let in the clutch and the car began to move.

"Goodbye—Peter."

He watched the car out of sight and then strode gaily along, slapping his field-boot every other step with his crop.

V

A period of rest in a peaceful back area village within reasonable distance of Doullens was an event which any of the hard-worked batteries in France would have hailed with joy, and B Battery were enjoying their stay at

Ervillers. The Major never fussed his command, and apart from the necessary parades of stables and exercise that are inseparable from a mounted unit, he left the battery in peace. The men played football among themselves and matches with the other batteries of the brigade; and several villagers gathered in the dusk outside the billets to listen to the harmonized sentimental songs of the contented men within.

Rawley alone was uneasy. He asked himself irritably why he could not enjoy this spell out of the Line without bothering about Rumbald. But everything the fellow did irritated him, and justifiably surely. They had been playing *vingt-et-un* one evening, Rawley, Whedbee, Piddock, and Rumbald, in the little farmhouse mess-room. Rumbald sat with his back to the old-fashioned mantelpiece on which stood a mirror overmantel. He had been losing, and Whedbee who sat opposite him had been winning. Suddenly, with an exclamation, Rumbald had jumped up from his chair and covered the mirror behind him with a newspaper. Whedbee had merely lowered his head and peered over his glasses at Rumbald's fat hands tucking the edges of the newspaper behind the mirror, and Piddock had contented himself with asking Rumbald sarcastically whether he was expecting the sweep, but Rawley refrained only with difficulty from an outburst at this gratuitous insult.

And there had been the incident of Sergeant Cooper's billet. Sergeant Cooper was a little inclined to be familiar with the men, and in consequence the discipline of his section was a shade below the high standard maintained by the other sections. His billet was a small wood shed, opening off the archway that gave entrance to the farm courtyard on the other side of which the section were billeted. The shed, separated only by a rough wooden partition from the cart-shed beside it, was not more than eight feet long by six feet broad, but a bed composed of a rough wooden frame covered with wire netting had been fitted along one wall and made it a comfortable billet for one man.

As orderly officer Rawley had turned in one night under the archway with Sergeant Jameson to see that lights were out in the men's billets. A streak of light and the sound of a voice came from Sergeant Cooper's door which was ajar, and as they passed it Rawley distinguished the concluding words of a story Penhurst had told that evening in Amiens.

He hesitated at the sound of the laugh which followed the words, and Sergeant Jameson halted regimentally beside him. He hesitated a moment longer and then stepped to the door and flung it open. The little shed was lighted by two candles stuck in cigarette tins nailed to the wooden partition, and on the low, brown-blanket covered bunk sat Rumbald and Sergeant Cooper. Rumbald's cap was on the back of his head, and he was dressed in the khaki slacks and shoes that were worn in the mess back in billets. A half-burnt cigar was in his mouth, and he held an enamel mug in his hand. The collar and top buttons of Sergeant Cooper's tunic were undone, exposing the greyback army shirt and the brown and green identity disc hanging by a greasy cord round his neck. A chipped enamel mug rested on his knee. At the sight of Rawley with Sergeant Jameson standing rigid and sphinx-like beside him, he rose quickly to attention and fumbled to do up the buttons of his tunic. There was a half-guilty; embarrassed look in his eyes.

Rumbald, lounging on the wire-netting bunk, cried heartily, "Hullo, Pete!"

Rawley nodded. His eyes encountered those of Sergeant Jameson fixed enigmatically on his. He hesitated a moment, and then stepped back and closed the door. Followed by Sergeant Jameson he walked in moody silence round the midden to the men's billet. "So that was it," he mused. "Drinking and telling dirty stories with an N.C.O. in his bunk! A little of that sort of thing would play old Harry with the discipline of the battery."

CHAPTER VII

I

A t exercise one morning as the long column of horses filed back along the road to the village, Piddock clattered up beside Rawley. "I say, Rawley," he began, "can't we commandeer a car from somewhere and get into Armeens tonight. This simple life stunt is all right in small doses, but personally, I can't work up much enthusiasm over watching the local ploughman homeward plod on his beery way. I think a drink at Charley's Bar, and a dinner at the Godbert, is the right prescription. Are you game?"

"Sorry, but I've a previous engagement," Rawley told him.

"What, here in the wilds of Picardy!" Piddock exclaimed. He shook his head sanctimoniously. "Peterkins! Peterkins! You're leading a double life, I fear—but couldn't you lead me astray, too?"

Rawley laughed. "As a matter of fact I'm going into Hocqmaison to see a divisional concert party—but it's a secret. Come along, too, if you can keep it."

"Who provides transport?"

"I'm borrowing one of the battery cycles."

"Holy Hindenburg! What, push-biking all the way!"

Rawley nodded.

Piddock spoke soothingly. "My dear old battle-scarred war horse, I hate to shatter your illusions, but the luscious damsels in divisional concert parties are really only anaemic bombardiers dressed up in camisoles and what-you-may-call-ems."

Rawley grinned. "You silly ass, I'm not that type of fool. But there will be some real damsels there."

Piddock nodded uninterestingly. "Oh, I daresay—horny-handed Hebes from the local midden, with black woollen stockings on their fat legs and black-heads on their red faces."

"You're coarse," Rawley told him. "But I don't mean Picardy farm wives; I mean English girls."

"What! Oh, shut up, Rawley. You're delirious."

"I mean it," said Rawley.

"What, little darlings with silk fetlocks and powdered noses?"

Rawley nodded emphatically. "Yes—Army nursing sisters and lady ambulance drivers. There's a C.C.S. in the next village. It's one of those twin arrangements—one on each side of the stream."

"You make me go all over alike. But there's a catch in this somewhere. First of all, how do you know (*a*) that any of these she-angels of Mons will be at the divisional follies tonight, and (*b*) supposing they are there, that we shall click?"

"That's the secret," said Rawley. "Swear to keep it?"

"Wild whiz-bangs wouldn't get it out of me, my old Hannibal."

"Well, the answer to (*a*) is that I know they are going to be there, because I heard one of them say so, and the answer to (*b*) is that I've already clicked."

Piddock smote his booted leg with his crop. "Stout feller. Outsize in stout fellers! Go on, my martial Romeo," he cried lyrically. "Go on, walk march, tell me how you met Whiz-bang Winnie, the battlefield belle."

"Shut up," growled Rawley. "She's too nice for that kind of rot. I met a little ambulance driver when I was in Doullens."

"And you arranged to go with her to this show tonight?"

Rawley nodded.

"Stout feller! 'A guardee or sapper may dazzle a flapper, but for women a gunner, what! What!' " carolled Piddock gaily. "And will there be any more little drivers there?"

"Probably—but you will have to take your chance of that. Anyway, you keep off mine."

"Sure thing, my dear old warrior. You registered first. I'll be as discreet as a blind monk at a grandmother's meeting."

II

They left Rumbald in the mess making up to the adjutant from brigade headquarters, and rode off on two scarred green army bicycles. Piddock had not ridden a bicycle for some years, and his awkwardness was increased by the long field-boots and tight riding-breeches he was wearing. He wobbled erratically all over the road, but it was only when he locked handlebars with Rawley almost under the radiator of a passing staff car that he consented to ride in single file. A long dusty convoy of motor lorries, that drove them to the gutter of the steeply-cambered road, where wobbling meant disaster, completed his discomfiture, but his cheery optimism carried him through, and they reached Hocqmaison in safety.

"The first thing," said Rawley, "is to find somewhere to park our tin chargers."

"And the next," put in Piddock, "is to find some mess where we can get a drink; and then we shall be all ripe and fruity for the sob stuff."

They walked their bicycles slowly up the village street.

"Look!" cried Piddock suddenly. "What a sight for scarred veterans!"

An army nursing sister in grey and red cape and large white coif was coming up the street towards them.

"On the command 'Glad eyes right!' " said Piddock, "we salute smartly with the Mark V smile."

"We do nothing of the sort," protested Rawley.

"Army sisters rank as officers," persisted Piddock. "And I think this one is our senior; therefore we salute."

"It isn't done," said Rawley.

"It is," affirmed Piddock cheerfully. "But the only thing is, how does one salute when wheeling ironmongery? Does one extend the arm at an angle of forty-five degrees across the saddle, turning the head and eyes to the right, or does one cant the cycle smartly upwards with the right hand, revolve the pedals with the left, bringing the bell in line with the right ear and left toe?" He saluted cheerfully as the sister went by, and she gave him a little smile and murmured, "Good evening."

"There you are!" he cried enthusiastically, when she had passed. "She recognized in us two strong silent men from the wide open spaces, men who have never lost a trench, men who have faced the hairy Hun without flinching, men who have played laughing hazard with their young manhood to save her from worse than death! What wonder, then, that her little heart fluttered, that a delicate blush suffused her creamy cheek, that she faltered shyly—the magic words—"

"Good evening!" put in Rawley dryly.

Piddock gazed at him reproachfully. "A lie never passed her cherry lips," he went on imperturbably. "She spoke the truth. It is a good evening, a damn good evening."

"I suggest we ride into the twin village and reconnoitre the concert hut," said Rawley. "We have nearly a couple of hours before zero, and we don't want to be seen hanging about here."

They mounted and rode down a shady, tree-bordered road out of the village, crossed an old stone bridge, and found themselves in the twin village on the other side of the stream. It was a narrow, winding cobbled street up which Rawley went with Piddock pedalling dangerously in the rear. A high stone wall ran along one side, and where it curved inwards to a pair of tall iron gates a flagpole was planted. A small red flag with a white St. George's Cross hung limply from the halliards.

"Some bloomin' corps headquarters," growled Piddock.

Beyond the open iron gates was a grey, flat-fronted château with the usual rows of windows and blistered white shutters. A sentry with fixed bayonet stood properly at ease at the foot of the steps leading to the door, and the broad, dusty space between him and the iron gates was occupied on one side by a couple of green-painted staff cars, a lorry, and a field-pigeon loft, and on the other by one Nissen hut labelled "Camp Commandant," and another nearer the gate with the blue and white board of the signals D.R.L.S.

"We are on the right track," said Rawley, pointing to a notice painted on the wall above him. It ran: To the Corps Concert Party: To-night at 8. A little farther on another notice ran: To the Officers' Club.

"We are in luck," exclaimed Piddock. "A club means a drink—and, by gad, yes, a decent meal."

Presently a large, home-made poster depicting a flashy young lady having her shoe lace tied by an immaculate and tight-waisted Tommy, announced that the 'Iron Rations' would be 'issued' that night at 8 pip emma.

"Well, we've found the concert hut," said Piddock. "And there's the club," he added, pointing to a curious collection of huts in a field, bordering the road.

The nucleus of the club proved to be a sixty foot hut that was used as a dining-room, and radiating from it were four Nissen huts, two on each side. These respectively did duty as a bar, a writing-room, a smoking lounge, and a lavatory. This last was a triumph of field plumbing. Two lengths of timber some two feet apart supported the half-dozen wash-basins which consisted of petrol tins cut in half lengthways and neatly hinged to one of the supporting timbers, so that each tin could be tipped up and the water emptied into the zinc-lined trough below. A water pipe with a tap above each tin completed the equipment. Another hut placed across the end of the large main hut served as the entrance and foyer of the club. This was furnished with a carpet and armchairs. A brick fireplace and ingle nook had been built at one end.

Piddock dropped into a comfortable armchair, and looked about him appreciatively. "It makes my heart bleed," he said, as he sipped his gin and bitters, "to think of all these staff merchants nobly carrying on amid these horrors of war. Think of having to stretch out one of your arms every time you want a drink. Thank God we have such men in England today!"

Rawley, who was wandering round, came to rest at a writing-table. "There is actually notepaper and envelopes here," he exclaimed.

"Good egg!" murmured Piddock, from the depths of his chair. "There is a real ash-tray here too. Positively, I must use it. Give me a cigarette, Rawley." Rawley threw across his case. "You know," went on Piddock dreamily, "it's astonishing how much fun one can get out of simple things that one just took for granted in peace time. After that dirty work on the Somme I went on Paris leave, and I had a gorgeous room at the Edward VII—silk-hung bed, tiled bathroom and lavatory all to myself. I was just like a kid, switching on lights and things—I spent half the first night pulling the plug. It seemed so bally civilized, if you know what I mean. I must have wasted half the water supply of Paris."

Rawley grunted. "Who are you writing to?" asked Piddock. "Haig? Dear Douglas, I hope I shall not spoil your war, but I shall be unable to fight this afternoon. I am going to the pictures with a lady friend. Perhaps at some future battle you will let me bring my cannon, and we will have a jolly time firing them together. Yours affectionately, Peter Rawley."

"I'm trying to fix you up with a companion for this evening," answered Rawley. He had written: "Dear Berney, I am writing this at the Officers' Club in the next village. What swell neighbours you have! There is another fellow from the battery with me—an awfully good chap—and I am rather hoping that you may have a friend who would be kind to a lonely gunner. Anyway, I shall be outside the church punctually.—Yours, Peter."

"I am going to give some fellow five francs and lend him my bicycle to take it down to the C.C.S."

"That's a very sound scheme, my old Napoleon," agreed Piddock. "You ought to be on the gaudy staff."

Rawley sent off the note, and then they had dinner; and a very good dinner it seemed to them, with tablecloths and crockery and wine, and liqueurs and cigars to follow.

"All we want now is a taxi," said Piddock as they left the club. "And of course we ought to call in at the florists on the way."

"Well, we might lorry-hop," answered Rawley practically. "And there are some poppies in that field over there."

III

"Do I hover daintily in the middle distance?" asked Piddock, as they walked towards the church which was the rendezvous.

"When she appears," answered Rawley, "you fall back a dozen paces and become interested in that Maltese cart, or any damn thing till I say walk march."

Punctually to the hour Berney emerged from one of those lanes that in every French village squeeze between the cottages bordering the main street. Piddock, in one rapid glance, took in the neat figure in khaki coat and skirt and broad-brimmed hat. "If only she has a twin sister I am going to enjoy myself," he murmured, as he fell back.

Rawley went forward to meet her. "You are a sportsman to come," he said, feasting his eyes upon her. Little wavy wisps of hair showed beneath her hat, and she wore a broad-ended tie loosely knotted at her low collar; it was khaki, but very different from the narrow, knitted ties that encircled the brick-red necks in the mess. She seemed unbelievably feminine from the brim of the hat that nestled on the little curls at the back of her neck to the well-polished and serviceable-looking brogue shoes.

"They brought me your note," she said.

"Well?" he asked.

"And I have a friend," she answered, with a smile.

Piddock was called up and introduced. "I'm afraid I'm the skeleton at the feast," he grinned. "But just say the word and I will sit in that lorry and read King's Regulations till it's time to take Rawley home."

"It's a shame to keep you from your work," answered Berney, with a twinkle, "but Mary Hamilton promised to come to make a foursome. But I am sure she is frightfully ignorant of King's Regulations."

"Splendid! Then I will read them to her in a low voice during the show," grinned Piddock. "They are awfully entertaining—'when on active service dropping an H: maximum penalty—death.'"

They halted outside a cottage, and Berney called, "Mary! Are you ready?" A feminine voice inside answered, "Coming," and a moment later a pretty girl with a freckled face, dressed in the same manner as Berney, joined them.

The long recreation hut with a stage at one end was nearly full when they entered. A Tommy with freshly scrubbed face and plastered hair conducted them to their seats among the first three rows of chairs. The body of the hut was fitted with benches that were closely packed with men in khaki, though here and there a man was escorting the madame or mademoiselle from his billet.

Just below the stage a lance-corporal, seated at a piano, was playing selections to pass the time till the curtain should rise, while the audience lustily joined in the choruses of the more popular airs. At the moment they were expressing with the full power of some three hundred pairs of lungs their desire to leave France:

> Take me back to dear old Blighty,
>> Put me on the train for London Town.
> Dump me over there; any bloomin' where,
>> Liverpool or Halifax, oh I don't care.
> I should like to see my best girl;
>> Cuddling up again we soon should be.
> I-tidly-ity take me back to Blighty.
>> BLIGHTY IS THE PLACE FOR ME.

The chairs were placed very close together, and Rawley was glad of it. He leaned slightly to one side so that Berney's arm and shoulder were perforce pressed closely against his. The intimacy of it was intoxicating, and the throng and noise around isolated them as though they were alone together.

A loud stamping of feet greeted the turning-up of the footlights. The lights in the hall went out, leaving them in pleasant semi-darkness, and the curtain went up.

The performance was not of a very high order, but the audience was not critical. Every item was loudly applauded, and particularly the provoking and coquettish damsel, whose auburn curls hid the red hair of a sapper lance-corporal. Her beautiful frocks, rich falsetto voice, and twinkling silken-clad legs, stirred the other ranks to enthusiasm. The hut rang alternately to loud laughter and hearty rendering of choruses or was bathed in audible silent sadness as the concert party rang the changes on topical jokes—not always in the best taste—popular songs and sentimental airs.

Berney joined softly in the choruses, and Rawley, with his head slightly sideways so that unobserved he could see her profile in the radiance from the stage, listened greedily to the unfamiliar music of a woman's voice.

"Why are you watching me?" she asked suddenly, in a low voice without removing her eyes from the stage.

He laughed guiltily at being caught. "Because—you are too good to be true," he said at last.

She turned her head slightly, and he saw her eyes for a moment bright in the shadow of her hat. Then she looked back at the stage without replying; but he could have sworn that the arm that rested against his had pressed a fraction of a millimetre closer.

The success of the evening was undoubtedly "Roses in Picardy." It was sung by a man with a really good voice, and the leading lady sang the second verse and chorus off stage. The plaintive, haunting air stirred the starved feelings of that audience of exiles, and after the last verse and chorus which were sung by both characters on the stage, the girl's falsetto blending harmoniously with the rich baritone, the applause was deafening.

The concert ended with the singing of the national anthem; the doors were thrown open, and the crowd of men pushed slowly through into the darkness and cool air outside.

The road back across the stream was stippled with bars of light from the moon that played hide and seek among the bordering trees. The pulsating drone of German 'planes came faintly from a distance, and a pale pencil of light, distinguishable only by its movement, was searching the luminous haze above the dark silhouettes of the trees.

"Jerry up!" cried Piddock cheerfully. He paused in a patch of moonlight, and with upturned face began to chant: "Moon, moon, serenely shining, don't go in too soon. . . ."

The two girls joined in softly, and they moved along the deserted road four abreast singing. Rawley tucked Berney's arm into his, and she did not withdraw it. Piddock began 'Roses in Picardy,' and they sang it through very earnestly and feelingly, the two girls singing the second verses and chorus as had been done by the concert party. At the end of it there was an embarrassed silence which lasted till, all too soon, they reached the other village.

Piddock and Mary Hamilton were left to say goodbye to each other outside her cottage billet, and Rawley and Berney went on alone. They walked in silence with steps that became slower and slower as they approached her billet. Rawley was acutely conscious that the few minutes left to him with her were running out second by second in the silence of the moonlit village street.

"Good fellow, Piddock," he said at last.

Berney nodded agreement. "Mary is an awfully good sort, too," she said.

Rawley agreed. "A good pair," he added, with an embarrassed laugh.

They had turned up the dark, narrow lane that led to her billet. She stopped in the shadow of a small house and patted the plaster wall. "Home—somewhere in France," she said.

He was silent. Time was up, and in deep shadow her face was but a vague blur. Behind him the apex of a cottage gable end, projecting into the moonlight, gleamed like a Chinese lantern above the dark trench of the lane.

Her voice seemed to break the silence reluctantly. "Goodbye, and thanks awfully."

He did not reply, and she moved slowly towards the door.

"Berney!" His tone arrested her slow movement. She waited for him to speak, and when he remained silent she asked, "What is it?"

He prodded the ground with his short stick. "I've had a topping time, and—dash it, I wish you had not to go."

She was leaning against the wall with her palms flat against the plaster behind her. "But I must. It's getting so late."

"Yes, I suppose you must," he answered miserably, prodding fiercely at the ground.

She nodded in the darkness. "I'm afraid so." Her dark form was moving away again.

"Berney!" She stopped again. "Berney!"

She turned and faced him, and he saw her eyes dimly fixed appealingly on his. "I must go, Peter dear—really," she answered gently. "I don't want to, but I must."

He came close to her. "I know, but—but can't we say goodnight properly?"

She fiddled with a button on her coat. "Haven't we said goodnight?" she asked, in a low voice.

"Yes, but not properly," he persisted desperately. "Can't we, Berney?" he added pleadingly.

He slid his arm round her shoulders. Her face was turned from him. He bent his face towards her cheek, but paused with his forehead touching the brim of her hat. "Berney," he whispered, "Berney, you are not angry with me—for this?"

Her head came round slowly, and he saw her eyes quite close, dark and shining in the shadow of her hat.

"You don't hate me?" he whispered earnestly.

The slow shake of her head was almost imperceptible.

"Then this is really goodnight." He bent swiftly and kissed her.

Piddock was waiting for him in the main street of the village. They fetched their cycles from the club and began the ride back. Piddock was lyrical. "She's wonderful," he cried. "Wonderful; they are both wonderful." He apostrophized the moon with raised hand till Rawley's growling warning only just averted a collision. Then he pedalled cheerfully along crooning 'Roses in Picardy' to himself, while Rawley rode in silent happy sadness beside him.

IV

It was after midnight when they rode up the quiet street of the village, but a light still showed through the curtains of the mess-room. They pushed open the half-glazed door and went in. Whedbee in pyjamas and British warm and with a long pipe between his teeth was sitting at the table writing in a squared field note-book. Piddock smote him boisterously on the back.

"Hullo, teacher!" he cried cheerfully. "Want me to help you with your prep! Twice three are six."

He went over to the little sideboard and poured out a drink. Rawley looked at the half-packed gramophone box on the floor, and unbuckled his Sam Browne in silence.

Piddock turned, glass in hand. "I don't care how long this old war lasts," he declared, "or how long we stay in smelly old Bluebottlevillers." He flung out an arm dramatically and carolled nasally: "Though it's only a tumbledown ne-e-st, it's a corner of heaven itself, f-o-r with l-o-ve blooming there why no place can comp-a-are with the little round hole in my v-e-e-st."

Rawley tapped the half-filled gramophone box with his toe. "What's all this about?" he asked.

Whedbee took off his glasses and sat back in his chair. "We are moving up again tomorrow," he said. "Taking over gun positions the same night. Reveille is at 4.30. Cane is up at brigade now. The orders came about an hour ago."

Piddock put down his glass and collapsed into a chair like a pricked balloon. "Oh, my God!" he cried. "And I was just beginning to enjoy life."

"Where are we going?" asked Rawley.

Whedbee shook his head. "In the orders it only says, 'the head of the column will pass 11.b.57 at 6.30.' But Cane will know all about it when he comes back."

Rawley sat down on the edge of the table thoughtfully. "Want any help?" he asked, nodding towards the note-book lying in front of Whedbee.

"No thanks, I've just finished. I would turn in and get some sleep if I were you. Reveille is at 4.30; breakfasts at 5.0, and officers' kits have to be stacked ready outside the orderly room by five-thirty."

"Why the hell do they always wait till the middle of the night to tell us these things!" growled Piddock. He rose wearily from his seat. "Come on, Rawley—to our virgin couches." And he went out singing dolefully: 'Signals have a jolly good t-i-ime, parley vous, signals have a jolly good t-i-ime, parley vous, signals have a jolly good time while poor ruddy gunners go up to the L-i-i-ne, inky, inky, parley-vous."

CHAPTER VIII

I

THE hard-working peasants of Ervillers had gone to bed that night as they had done for the previous week with some two hundred horses and two hundred men comfortably ensconced in their barns and orchards, but when next morning they plodded out to their fields, their barns and orchards were empty and the tiny square behind the church was bare of guns and wagons. B Battery had gone; and the smoking heaps of rubbish on the incinerators and the freshly turned earth on the filled-in latrines were the only marks of their passing.

In the early morning sunlight the long column of guns and wagons uncoiled itself from the village and wound like a dark snake on to the long, straight, tree-bordered *route nationale* that switchbacked out of sight over the rolling down country. In that back area traffic was scarce, and the road unrolled itself ahead white and empty, except for a dusty rumbling motor lorry, and an occasional green car of a divisional supply officer speeding back to Amiens to buy forage. Women worked in the fields. Here the war was remote, though at the entrance of a long, cool avenue hung the black and red flag of an Army Headquarters, and one caught glimpses between the trees of a large flat-fronted château with rows of blistered white shutters closed against the glare.

There was a long halt at midday, when horses were watered and the men ate their haversack rations sitting in groups on the roadside, or lay on their backs in the shade. Then, on again, the column moved on the right of the long, straight road with the tall trees set like palings on either side, while the white chalk dust drifted into eyes and nostrils and set like a mask on the sticky faces of those in the rear.

It was soon after the resumption of the march that Rumbald trotted up beside Rawley and Piddock. "There's a Zepp prowling about over there," he said. "I suppose I ought to tell the Major."

"Zepp!" cried Piddock in astonishment. "Holy smoke! Where?" He tilted his cap over his eyes and looked up.

"It's behind that tree now," said Rumbald. "You'll see it in a minute. There! There it is—just passing to the right of that spire on the hill." He pointed with his switch.

Rawley looked and recognized the familiar bean-shaped bag of an observation balloon hanging motionless a few miles away.

"By gosh, yes!" cried Piddock with a grin. "Damned smart of you to spot it, Rumbald."

"I suppose the Major ought to know," said Rumbald.

"Rather," cried Piddock, with a wink at Rawley. "If you hadn't spotted it it might have bombed us to Hades before we knew where we were."

Rawley was about to say something, but was silenced by a grimace. "That will amuse old Cane no end," cried Piddock, as Rumbald trotted off importantly towards the head of the column.

The appearance of the country changed rapidly as they drew nearer to the Line. The road became congested with traffic. Long dusty convoys of lorries passed ceaselessly. G.S. wagons loaded with hay, pit props or rations passed singly or in pairs. Infantry limbers jogged by on various errands. Despatch riders with the blue and white signal armlet phutted by on dusty motor-cycles. Field kitchens smoked in the orchards around the villages and parties of men in fatigue dress with towels over their shoulders passed on their way to the divisional baths. Notices in English became more frequent on the whitewashed walls—arrows denoting lorry routes, hands pointing to the concert party barn and to the E.F.C. canteen. Lorries, limbers, and G.S. wagons stood drawn up on the cobbled roadside, and barns had their billeting capacity painted on their outside walls. And the open fields on either hand had been worn bare and brown with horse lines, ration dumps, or practice trenches. Tents and Nissen huts were dotted here and there, and in the lee of a copse an observation balloon nestled on the ground. "Rumbald's ruddy Zeppelin in bed," remarked Piddock, with a grin.

They reached the wagon lines soon after sunset, a shallow depression between two rolling hill slopes. The earth was bare of grass, hard and cracked and scored with wheel ruts and hoof marks. Bell tents, Nissen huts, tarpaulins, and shacks built of ammunition-boxes and sheets of corrugated iron occupied every inch of the ground that was not already given up to trusses of hay, wagons, water-troughs, and brick horse-standings. The smoke of a wood fire on the outskirts of the camp rose in lazy loops, black against the pearly after sunset sky. Men in grey shirt sleeves moved between the huts and whistled or sang lazy tunes. A homing aeroplane droned its way westwards.

In the fast-gathering gloom the now reduced column began the last part of the journey, that to the battery position. The road ran gently upwards between two low flat hills that were silhouetted now and then against the greenish glow of a Verey light that was itself out of sight below the crest. Other traffic was on the road; the nightly ebb and flow of the line. Infantry limbers bringing up rations, G.S. wagons loaded with reels of barbed wire, screw pickets, pit props, sandbags and other necessities of trench warfare, gun wagons bringing up ammunition, and parties of men in steel helmets, clean fatigue and gas helmets tramping up for some night fatigue. Occasionally to right or left a flash lit the gloom and some unseen gun banged resonantly; otherwise the evening was very still and undisturbed by the jingle and clink of harness and the steady rumble of wheels on the road.

Suddenly a far distant poop was heard, followed a few seconds later by a distant scream that grew rapidly on a rising note as it approached, and ended abruptly in an earth-shaking bump, and rumbling crash some distance ahead.

"It was a dark and stormy night upon the Caucasus," began Piddock. "The brigand chief and all his men were—"

Again the distant poop was heard. "Here we come again," said Rawley. There followed that hurtling screech and rumbling crash. The infantry limber ahead stopped abruptly, and Rawley pulled up his mare with her head over the back board.

"What are we stopping for?" asked Piddock. "Somebody picking wild-flowers?"

He and Rawley were riding at the head of B Battery. The Major had ridden on to the gun position. "I will see if we can pull out of this jam and get on across country," said Rawley. "No hope there," he announced a few moments later, after surveying the broad ditch and steep bank beyond.

Shells continued to land somewhere ahead at regular intervals of about a minute. The long mixed column of vehicles moved forward a few yards and stopped, moved forward again and stopped again. A corporal wearing a traffic control brassard appeared out of the darkness. Rawley bent down to him. "What's wrong, corporal? Can't we get on?"

"They are shelling the road ahead, sir," answered the man. "All vehicles to move at fifty yards interval."

Gradually, by short advances and frequent halts, like a theatre queue, the battery drew near to the scene of those rumbling crashes that sounded so like a gigantic sack of coals being tipped down a chute. The limber in front had stopped again. The traffic control corporal appeared at Rawley's horse's head. "As soon as this limber is clear, get your leading vehicle through, sir," he said.

Another rumbling crash close ahead, and the limber was on the move, leaving the head of B Battery next to run the gauntlet. At a trot, at a gallop the limber receded into the gloom with a man hanging by his elbows from the back. There came another frenzied screech and hurtling crash, but the bright brief glow showed the road clear. The limber was through.

In response to Rawley's signal the leading gun team moved up beside him and stopped. He heard the distant poop, and touched his horse's flanks. He moved slowly forward, and the gun followed. The high-pitched whistle of the shell rent the night sky, and Rawley turned in the saddle and beat the air with his fist. The gun team behind obeyed the order and had broken into a trot when the shell burst with a bright glow on the roadside thirty yards ahead. They passed the danger zone at an easy canter, and heard the next shell scream overhead and detonate harmlessly behind them.

One by one the other wagons and guns crossed the danger area to safety; and lastly Rumbald, bent low in the saddle, came up the road at a furious gallop, his tin hat askew and his horse in a lather.

"What the hell do you think you're doing?" growled Piddock, into whom he had cannoned in the darkness. "Bringing the good news to Aix or what?"

"Some barrage that!" panted Rumbald, as he struggled with his field glasses, map case, and haversack that had collected in a bunch round his stomach.

"Barrage! That!—one shell today and another next Thursday week!" cried Piddock scornfully. "You wait till you get mixed up in one. You'll skip about like Pavlova and wish you had a tin hat down to your boots."

Cane was waiting for them by a clump of ragged trees that hedged a crucifix outside a village. He led them up the dark, echoing tunnel of the village street, round a corner where the church tower loomed black above them, and made a hard, notched line against the starry sky, to an orchard on the farther side. One by one the guns drove in through the narrow gateway, unlimbered, and were manhandled into the pits on the eastern margin. By ten o'clock the horses were on their way back to the wagon lines.

II

The position was a comfortable one. The orchard wall nearest the enemy was well sandbagged up, and shallow pits had been dug for the guns. Overhead cover from view was provided by greenery covered netting spread between the apple trees. The mess was in a cottage on the far side of the orchard. There was one hole in the roof and one of the corner walls facing east had a ragged bite a few feet below the eaves. The interior, however, was luxurious. There was a mahogany table and a green plush armchair in the mess-room, and an old-fashioned country clock with hands that pointed persistently to five minutes past two. And there was actually a picture on the walls—a coloured print of five bearded sportsmen in a rutted wood ride blazing away with astonishing success at the cloud of birds that was passing over their heads. In the tangled garden outside, four tree trunks propped wigwam fashion against the wall covered the shattered window and protected it from shell splinters.

"This is all very *bon!*" exclaimed Piddock appreciatively, as he came in from seeing the men into their quarters. He dropped his tin hat with a clatter on the table and stood with arms akimbo looking round. "Well-equipped country cottage on the outskirts of old-world village, within easy reach of main lorry routes and station—casualty clearing—telephone, Verey lighting, and gas, modern ventilation by Jerry, Bosche and Co.; owners leaving for reasons of health. And there's old Rumble Tummy well dug in already—damn him," he added.

Rumbald looked up from the depths of the one armchair and winked solemnly. "Plenty of room on the floor, Piddy boy."

"I'm going on duty in half an hour," said Piddock coaxingly. "I'll toss you for it till then. You will have to give it up when Cane comes in, anyway."

Rumbald shook his head. "Nothing doing. But I'll tell you what I'll do. When I die I'll leave it to you in my will."

Piddock shied a map case at him and went out into the kitchen where he whispered with the mess corporal. A few minutes later the corporal approached Rumbald and said, "Sergeant Warner wants to speak to you, sir."

Rumbald growled angrily, but at last reluctantly heaved himself up from the chair and went out; and when he returned a few moments later with flushed angry face,

Piddock was lying back in the plush armchair, singing lustily: "Old Rumbles never die-e, never die-e, never die-e, old Rumbles never die-e, they simply fade away-e."

III

Cane took Rawley up to the forward observation post the next morning to register the battery. The communicating trench began on the left of the road a short distance from the orchard. It was a well-dug trench, and for the first fifty yards or so was neatly floored with bricks from the village. The telephone cable was carried along the wall of the trench by wire staples.

Rawley enjoyed forward observation work. It was far more satisfying than the blind mechanical task at the guns. Places where enemy movement was noticed from time to time were cautiously registered and tabulated so that the tap could be turned on at a moment's notice. And then one morning perhaps when the mist rose suddenly a party of the enemy would be seen approaching one of these points. A few brief directions into the telephone while one watched with galloping pulse the party drawing nearer and nearer to the trap. Then the words 'battery fire' were followed by the pom, pom, pom, pom, pom of the guns behind one and the scream of the shells overhead. The target disappeared in clouds of smoke and spouting earth, and sometimes one had the satisfaction of seeing a body whirling slowly, windmill fashion, in the smoke.

In pre-war days Rawley had vaguely imagined a battlefield as a stirring pageant of cheering men, bursting shells, and charging squadrons. Under such conditions no modern war could last more than a few months: both sides would be annihilated. Men must take cover. It was obvious: but he had never grown quite accustomed to the desertedness of the firing line. One peeped over the parapet, and all one saw was the undulating, shell-scarred country; a shattered wall or two, a few ragged trees, some rusty wire, and the irregular line of the enemy's parapet. Not a living thing to be seen. No movement; desolation like a lunar landscape. Behind the lines there was tramping of feet, blowing of bugles, and all the martial sounds and movements one associates with armies; but in the Line—nothing.

One spot in particular fascinated Rawley: it was where the front line fire trench crossed the *route nationale*. One left the support trench on the crest of the hill and zigzagged down the forward slope by the deep communicating trench that here and there, where a passing head might be visible from Hunland, was roofed with battered sheets of rusty iron. Then two gaunt and bullet-pitted tree trunks that had been visible from various angles off and on for the last few minutes suddenly appeared towering directly above the trench, and a few minutes later one was in the fire trench. One passed two traverses and in the second fire bay the hard thick section of road metal could be traced in the parados behind and below the sandbagged parapet. One peeped through a periscope and saw that one was standing in the middle of a broad road, one's eyes just above the level of its surface. There it ran broad and straight, and grass-grown to the bottom of the slope and up again till it was cut by the brown, tumbled line of the Hun parapet. Tangles of rusty barbed wire and fallen telegraph wire lay across it, and its straight edges were here and there indented by black or grass-grown shell holes; but it was still a road that ran on up the opposite slope to the low, ragged walls and blackened gables of the Hunland village a quarter of a mile away.

In pre-war days the farmers of that village had no doubt walked every day to the fields on this slope and driven their wagons along the road. But for more than two years now no vehicle had passed from one to the other, and no living thing had moved up that dip of the road except at night, when men crawled on their bellies and went in fear of death. It occurred to him that one of the most interesting results of peace would be that a man would be able to walk down that grass-grown bit of road and up into the village beyond. And he wondered whimsically whether no-man's-land would be filled with chattering mobs of Germans and English comparing notes and gaping like tourists.

IV

Rumbald did not like forward observation work. He was quite candid about it. His chassis was not designed, he said, for long tramps through narrow communicating trenches. And anyway, there was never anything to see when one reached the O.Pip. The only bright spot was that good whisky was always to be had in the infantry company headquarter dug-out nearby. And besides, Pete and Piddy liked the job; Pete positively revelled in it and actually killed Huns. Personally, he didn't think that all that watching and scheming and surreptitious registering was worth it, in order to kill a Hun now and then. Life wasn't long enough. No, he preferred the battery in the orchard that was only a quiet stroll from the mess; and since Pete preferred the O.Pip, why not let him do it? That was a fair division of labour, surely.

Rawley, for his part, was quite content to do more than his share as forward observation officer. And Cane, after a mild protest, fell in with the arrangement; for he was equally keen on the offensive spirit, and it irked him to have an officer in the forward O.Pip who never called on the guns except when the S.O.S. rockets demanded retaliation.

Rumbald thus became almost a fixture at the battery, and since two other officers were nearly always there also, he gradually, by reason of other self-created jobs, ceased to do his full share as officer on duty at the guns. He set about improving the men's quarters, and while employed on this job he persuaded Cane to release him from other duties. He was also Mess President, P.R.I., and O.C. Amusements, and in fairness it must be admitted that these useful but unwarlike duties he performed admirably. He was a master of the art of ingratiation, and was always able to raise a car to take him back to buy mess stores or stock for the canteen. He became an institution in the village. Everybody knew him and he knew everybody. The little cottage mess-room became a rendezvous for officers of every branch of the service. Infantry subalterns on their way back from leave dropped in to enthuse over the latest London revue; gunner officers from the neighbouring batteries came in for a chat on the local situation; infantry quartermasters bringing up rations called in to say goodnight and stayed for a drink; and sapper officers waited there for their working parties to arrive. It became a kind of club in which one heard the latest gossip, the latest rumours, and the hottest stories. It was crowded at all hours of the day and night, and Rumbald lounged in his green plush armchair calling everybody by some endearing nickname and dispensing hospitality in the manner of a patriarchal baron, while Rawley, Piddock and even Cane, appearing at intervals for food and sleep, seemed like strangers in their own mess.

The green plush armchair had been the object of much jealousy. Rumbald had annexed it, and it was very irritating to Rawley and Piddock on returning from a long tramp to the O.Pip, or from a tiring spell at the guns, to find the only comfortable chair in the mess occupied by Rumbald or one of his visitors. Piddock's sarcasm was wasted on Rumbald's hearty complacency, and in a fury he searched the whole village for another armchair. He found three or four, but none unclaimed, and in spite of great ingenuity was unable to make off with any of them. Finally, with the help of two handymen of the battery, he set to work to build a settee framework out of lengths of "four-by-two." He stretched wire netting over the seat and back, covered it with new latrine canvas, and stuffed it with straw. The result was a comfortable if rough-looking settee, which was kept in Piddock's room across the passage, and was carried into the mess whenever he or Rawley wanted it.

V

But this leisurely type of warfare was not to continue. Other batteries dug pits in and around the village, and their registering, though done as unobtrusively as possible, did not escape the notice of the enemy. The old mutual agreement to let sleeping dogs lie came to an end. Wagons and limbers no longer were able to roam about the village in daylight in the former carefree manner. The drone of a German plane threading the cotton-wool anti-aircraft bursts became a familar feature of the sky above, and from dawn till dusk the dumpy, livid sickle of a German observation balloon hung motionless and menacing above the slope eastwards.

Tiles and bricks began to litter the streets. Holes like ink-stains appeared in the cottage roofs. Here and there a house-front collapsed and the homely furniture of a cottage bedroom lay in a jumbled heap on the edge of the sagging floor above a tangled garden. And the squat, square church tower was whittled to a ragged tapering finger above a mason's rubble heap. At any time of the night or day and without warning would come that hurtling roar as of an express train, and the terrific crash of the burst, followed by the patter of falling debris and the dense black cloud slowly dissolving above the cottages.

But, although casualties were unavoidable, B Battery fared better than any of the batteries near them. As a sleeping place the cottage was abandoned in favour of the shelters that had been dug in the steep bank at the end of the garden, and Rumbald had his precious green plush armchair carried down to the cellar, although the mess-room upstairs with its window protected from splinters by three tree trunks was still used.

He had nearly finished the improvements he was making in the men's quarters at the guns, and had begun to talk suggestively about new brick horse-standings for the wagon lines. "Doesn't like the look of the weather," remarked Piddock dryly. "Thinks it will be healthier farther back."

Cane, however, while admitting the desirability of new brick horse-standings, and the other schemes for wagon-line improvement which Rumbald enthusiastically sketched, said that they would have to wait, and that for the moment he could exercise his ingenuity on the construction of a new observation post in the support line. "Meanwhile, Rawley and I will be delighted to keep your chair warm for you," observed Piddock maliciously. "And we will post it to your people if you don't come back."

The following morning, therefore, Rumbald in tin hat and gas helmet, looking "all hot and bothered," as Piddock put it, trailed off up the long communication trench in the wake of Cane, to be shown the position of the new O.Pip, and the same evening after dark he was to take up a fatigue party to do the necessary work.

VI

Phillips and Anderson of A Battery were in the mess that night playing bridge with Cane and a sapper captain whom Rawley did not know. Rumbald had already gone out to take up the working party, and Rawley, who was due to relieve Piddock on duty at the guns in a few minutes, lay on the home-made settee watching the game. Occasionally the tree trunks that rested against the wall outside became visible through the dark, uncurtained square of the window as they were silhouetted for a second against the vivid flash of the six-inch howitzer in the next garden. The gun was firing straight over the cottage, and at each blast the roof seemed to lift an inch or two and then drop back, while the flames of the two candles stuck in bottles on the table jumped, and all but went out.

Rawley glanced at his wrist-watch, yawned, and reluctantly put his feet to the floor. He took his steel helmet from a corner of the room and went out. It was very dark in the orchard, but the trees ahead were dimly silhouetted by the greenish glow of Verey lights that now and then soared up from the Line ahead. A little enemy whizz-bang shelling was going on. The lash of a giant whip swept suddenly through the night above his head and a spurt of flame and an ear-ringing crack followed simultaneously in the tangled garden beyond the road. He walked quickly through the orchard towards the guns. Again, out of the night came that vicious lash and earsplitting crack, and in the silence that followed, broken only by the patter of descending earth and stones, he was startled by a cough in the darkness close at hand. He turned towards the sound, and in a few paces reached the low hedge that bordered the orchard. He realized that the cough had come from the road beyond, and he was about to turn back again when he was arrested by a shuffling of feet. He stared intently into the darkness, and was just able to distinguish a row of dark heads on the far side of the road.

"What are you fellows hanging about here for?" he called.

He heard the scrape of a man's feet turning smartly, and Corporal Turner's voice answered, "This is the working party for the O.Pip, sir. We are waiting for Mr. Rumbald."

Again out of the night came that whistling lash, crack. Silence. And then again lash, crack, and a fragment of steel struck a spark from a flint as it smacked into the road.

"It's no good keeping the men hanging about here, corporal," said Rawley. "Get them under cover and parade them when Mr. Rumbald arrives."

"Very good, sir," came the corporal's voice from the darkness, and the soft thud of an invisible hand falling from the salute could be heard.

Rawley strode fiercely between the trees to Rumbald's dug-out. A light shone at the bottom of the steps.

"Rumbald!" he called. "Rumbald!"

"Hullo! Is that you, Pete?" came Rumbald's voice from below.

"Come on out of it. What about that fatigue party?" called Rawley.

"I'm just coming. What's the hurry?" answered Rumbald.

"Just coming be damned. Come on out of it *toute suite*. You've left that party parading on the road and the Bosche is whiz-banging it."

"All right, all right," came Rumbald's voice. "Are you taking up this bloody party or am I?"

"You are, and you should have been off ten minutes ago—and if you are not up by the time I've counted ten I am going back to the mess to tell Cane that you are hiding in your dug-out while the party is waiting on the road. One-two-three-four-five-six—"

The light disappeared and Rumbald came slowly up the steps. "You're always in a hell of a sweat about being a second or two late on parade, aren't you?" he growled. "As a matter of fact I forgot my gas gadget and came back for it."

"Well, you've got it now," answered Rawley grimly.

Rumbald's bulky figure disappeared in the darkness, and Rawley walked over to the guns, but he waited at the top of the control dug-out steps till he heard Corporal Turner's "Fall in!" and the tramp of feet as the party moved off.

CHAPTER IX

I

Piddock opined that things were working up for a lot of unpleasantness. "I recognize the symptoms," he said. "That valley behind Lagnicourt that used to be all truly rural was full of dumps and hutments when I came through it yesterday. There is a labour battalion making up the road out of Heninville and I'm told they've shoved a railway gun back in Mailly wood. And a positive rash of red hats has broken out all over the district. I met three staff wallahs on my way up to the O.Pip today. Brass hats in the trenches are always a sign of incipient offensiveness.

"Yes, I diagnose a push in the offing; though not yet awhile. We haven't stirred up the Bosche quite enough yet. But when he has brought up a lot of new batteries to counter our new ones registering, and when we have another half-dozen observation balloons up and the whole countryside draped with dumps and huts for his airmen to photograph, we shall be ready. In about another fortnight the civilians will be able to give us the date, I expect; and then perhaps in another fortnight after that we shall get our 'secret and confidential' orders for the surprise attack. Oh, it's a great life!"

"Well, I hope you are right," Rawley told him. "I have never seen a push yet, and I would rather like to."

"They are all right at first," agreed Piddock. "But the trouble is that after a few days things get mixed and it becomes a bit difficult to know who is doing the pushing—we or they."

"Well, I will push off to see Anderson and leave you to it," grinned Rawley.

They had been standing outside the battery canteen which had been installed in a cellar, and Rawley went off towards A Battery mess while Piddock went straight on towards the battery position.

Rawley heard the shell coming, and with the speed of instinctive movement went flat. The hurtling, train-like roar leapt upon him out of the distance, engulfing every other sound; but in the half second that he crouched with eyes tightly shut and taut muscles awaiting the impact he was conscious that Piddock, a few yards ahead of him, between the horse pond and the pulverized church, had not dropped quickly enough. Then came the bump of impact and an unfamiliar muffled roar, instead of the expected "cr-r-r-ump" of a five-nine.

He opened his eyes to see a great black plume as high as the ragged church tower poised on the roadside ahead. The fan-shaped crest had a halo of up-flung particles that glittered like countless diamonds in the sun. For a moment it hung motionless and then slowly descended and dissolved; and a brief torrent of rain fell from the clear sky. The dusty white surface of the road around him was pitted with rain-drops, and lumps of wet black mud lay upon it. By the horse pond, which he noticed was now quite empty, the road was obliterated under hummocks of black mud from which trickled countless streams of water.

He could not see Piddock. And then the foul stinking mess stirred and formed itself into the shape of a human figure that rose slowly and stood black and shining and dribbling dollops of mud and water.

"My God!" exclaimed Rawley. "Are you hit, old man?"

The black, featureless head shook emphatically, and the filthy hands rubbed the face so that streaks of grey showed through the damp, black mask. "D-dirty work at the c-cross-roads!" spluttered the voice of Piddock.

II

It was an unofficial regulation of B Battery mess that each officer returning from leave should bring back with him at least one record for the gramophone, and selections from the musical comedies and revues popular in London at the moment were to be heard any evening in the now rather battered cottage in the orchard. Piddock usually selected the programme, wound up the gramophone, and put on the records; and he accompanied each item appropriately with a step dance on the bare boards by the door, by singing American rag-time choruses in a nasally sentimental voice, or by gliding gracefully about the room whilst conversing conventionally with an imaginary dancing partner. Ever since his visit to the Corps concert party with Rawley his favourite air had been "Roses in Picardy." At least once each evening this record, after being flicked with a pocket handkerchief, was put on and the needle and sound-box were carefully adjusted. Then he would refill his pipe whilst listening silently to the verse, but as soon as the plaintive notes of the refrain rang out he would glance across at Rawley and their eyes would meet understandingly.

Rawley had written to Berney Travers, and one memorable evening when the ration limber from the wagon lines brought up the mail came her reply. He remembered vividly standing in the gloaming at the top of the steps of the control dug-out with the unopened letter in his hand. It was one of those rare peaceful evenings when darkness came down upon the front on tip-toe as if afraid of waking some nocturnal monster. The men's gruff voices as they threw out the rations from the limber on the road came to his ears pleasantly subdued by distance. There was a distant rumble of gun fire far to the south, but the immediate front where the first Verey light was glowing halfheartedly against the purple sky was still. Before him the ragged apple trees stood out black and twisted against the dying embers in the western sky.

It was a friendly little letter, written in a round schoolgirlish hand, thanking him for his letter and for the very jolly evening at the Corps concert party. She related one or two amusing incidents that had occurred at her C.C.S.; said that Mary Hamilton wished to be remembered to him; inquired politely after Mr. Piddock; and ended decorously with "Yours sincerely, Berney Travers."

Rawley read the letter three times before putting it into the breast pocket of his tunic, and in the night watches he wrote a reply, sitting on an upturned box at the rough table containing the war map and lighted stump of candle in the control dug-out—a reply interrupted by a call for retaliation from the battalion in front, and completed after a short interval, during which the dark and silent orchard was transformed into a devil's smithy filled with clanging anvils served by intent and swiftly working minions seen kaleidoscopically in the flashes of the guns.

Other letters written in the same cheerful, healthy strain passed between them, and in one of these she mentioned that the Corps was shortly holding a horse show in the neighbourhood of the village and that she hoped to get permission to go to it. Rawley, too, determined to be there if possible, and thus one morning it came about that he and Rumbald were seated together in a car on the road to Hocqmaison. On the previous evening Rumbald had suddenly announced that he was going and had offered Rawley a lift in the car which one of his numerous cronies among the A.S.C., Ordnance, and supply officers was providing, and Rawley, though not at all pleased to know that Rumbald would be there, had accepted the offer in preference to the unsatisfactory alternative of lorry jumping.

III

An open stretch of grass land on the outskirts of Hocqmaison had been converted into the showground, and a very good job Corps Headquarters had made of it. As Rumbald and Rawley walked from the car-park towards the long grandstand that had been erected down one side of the centre arena a number of limbered wagon turn-outs, unfamiliarly resplendent with burnished metal work, snow-white head ropes, and spruce drivers were being judged in a smaller arena enclosed by ropes and whitewashed posts. A band was playing in the larger arena where a number of riders were taking their perfectly groomed horses over the jumps; and here and there were little groups of officers whose long peaked caps, spidery legs and perfect riding breeches would have proclaimed them judges of horseflesh even had they not been wearing the official rosette.

Rawley was very glad when Rumbald was hailed by a rather boisterous group of officers and he was able to wander off by himself. The grandstand was already more than half-filled, but the ladies were so much in the minority that it was an easy matter for him to satisfy himself that Berney was not among the number. He threaded his way between the groups of officers who stood chatting in the open space, between the luncheon marquee and a small arena, and spied her at last watching a fine pair of horses having the finishing touches put to their toilet.

He came up quietly and halted a pace or two away, watching her. For a few seconds she continued to gaze with amused interest at the drivers in grey shirt sleeves and looped hanging braces plying a blacking brush on the horses' hoofs, and then, becoming aware of someone near and gazing at her, she turned her head slowly.

He noted with pleasure the faint wave of colour that spread over her face as their eyes met. But her embarrassment was momentarily only; she turned her face back towards the horses and said, as though continuing a conversation: "Aren't they dears? So proud of their clean bibs and tuckers!"

He came and stood close beside her so that his elbow touched hers as it rested on the rail.

"Are you awfully keen on seeing all this?" he asked suddenly and seriously during a pause in their light-hearted conversation.

She turned her head slowly and looked at him from under the broad brim of her hat. "I am enjoying it; aren't you? But—why?" she asked.

He swung his stick between his two hands without looking at her. "What I mean is, would you hate to miss some of it? Because I have an idea."

"And the idea is?" she asked when he paused.

"About lunch." He made a motion of his head towards the luncheon marquee behind them. "That place will be an awful squash, and I thought we might give it a miss. There is a village tucked away in a valley about a couple of kilometres from here: it's right off the main road. We passed through it on the way here because Rumbald had to see a fellow out Queant way. It looked rather a good spot—no troops—and there was a sort of fair going on—you know, stalls and things in a meadow and those ramshackle old French carts coming in from the outlying farms."

"And the idea is?" repeated Berney.

"To look round and have lunch. There was a rather jolly looking *estaminet* there with tables set out in the orchard. What do you say?"

"I'd love it."

"You would?" he exclaimed eagerly, and flushed with pleasure. She nodded emphatically. "Um-m!"

"But it means walking—two kilometres or thereabouts," he warned her.

"When do we start?" she answered smiling.

He grinned cheerfully and took her by the elbow.

"Now—*toute suite!*"

Half an hour later, as they descended a hillside by a narrow unhedged lane that separated a leafy oak wood from a breast high rampart of growing maize, they saw, within arms length it seemed, the short lead spire and the bleached stone church tower of the village rising foot by foot against the wooded slope beyond. At the bottom of the slope the narrow lane broadened into the village street. It was hung with flags, and several of the doorways had little shrines erected in them. Here and there an ancient long-maned horse, tethered to a ring bolt on a cottage wall, stood patiently with its weight on three legs, with an occasional flick of its long tail on the backboard of the weather-worn cart behind it. The village folk were dressed in their best clothes and were chatting in voluble groups in the roadway; and just beyond the little stone bridge, where the wooded slopes fell back grudgingly to allow a small pasture to nestle between them, a number of gay-coloured booths were occupying the attention of the country folk.

"I would not have missed this for anything," said Berney as they sauntered along the line of stalls. "This is much nicer than the horse show."

The *estaminet*, though a large one, had its resources taxed to the utmost. When Rawley and Berney arrived they found every room filled with the hum of conversation and the clatter of plates, knives and forks; but the alert little proprietress, who somehow managed to remain calm and efficient in the midst of the holiday babel and bustle round her, bade them a smiling '*Bonjour, M'sieu, Madame*,' and led them outside to the orchard. All the tables were already occupied, but in response to the little woman's call a young country boy brought chairs and a small trestle table, which was placed in the shade of an apple tree and promptly covered with a spotless cloth of coarse linen.

"This is rather *bon!*" said Rawley as they sat down. "Now the question is—what are we going to eat?"

"I am in your hands," answered Berney.

"Well," said Rawley, "in France they know a good deal more about these things than we do, and I have always found the best plan is to say, '*Madame, quelque-chose à manger*,' in your best Parisian, and leave the rest to her."

"This is really rather a discovery," said Berney presently. "I'm sure we are the only English people in the whole village."

"That was one of my reasons for wanting to come," answered Rawley. "I wanted to get away from the horse show. I was afraid Rumbald might see us together," he confessed.

She looked up at him and wrinkled her brow in an exaggerated effort to decide what was the exact implication of his confession. "I am not sure whether that is very nice or very nasty of you," she said.

"He is a fellow that always has a lot to say," explained Rawley. "If he had seen us together he would have gone back and made a lot of silly remarks in the mess—and his remarks are not always in good taste."

"You mean that you don't like being ragged?"

"Oh, I can stand chipping as well as most people," he answered seriously. "But if Rumbald had gone back and made some of his so-called jokes I should probably have hit him."

"That's rather nice of you, Peter," she said, becoming serious. "But you must not go fighting every man who makes—silly remarks about girls."

He dabbed his mouth with his napkin viciously and went on quickly and earnestly. "It's not that—it's because it's you. Anyone else—well, I would just tell him to shut up . . . but if he had made one of his cad's remarks about you I should have hit him—hard." He moistened his lips with his tongue: "You see—you're different . . . you . . . I . . ." He floundered helplessly in his embarrassment. "I mean . . ." he tried again, and then giving up the attempt and flushing to the roots of his hair he attacked his food with fierce concentration.

Berney crumbled her bread and stared at her plate. "You mean . . ." she began. "Peter, hadn't we better be frank? You mean—you—rather like me?"

He nodded vigorously with his mouth full. "Um! That's it—awfully. Most awfully."

In the pause that followed, she said softly: "That's very sweet of you, Peter."

"Well, it's out now," he said gruffly, without looking at her. "Though, of course, you knew it all along."

"I did not know for certain," she answered slowly. And then she added: "But I hoped you did."

He looked at her quickly and their eyes met. Hers, in the shadow of her hat, were misty and very tender. She went on very softly, but her words reached him clearly, in spite of the loud buzz of conversation around them. "And, of course, I like you too, Peter—most awfully."

Her eyes were shining like stars, he thought—stars in a mist. He gulped quickly and grinned foolishly. He put out his hand under the little table and found hers, and they ate in silence left-handed and awkwardly for a moment or two.

"Berney," he said presently, "I suppose we are engaged. Isn't it funny!"

"Are we?" she asked, with motherly eyes on his.

He grinned happily. "Well, I mean to say—aren't we?"

She nodded slowly. "Um-m, I suppose we are," she answered softly, and smiled shyly.

"Wouldn't you like to tell everybody? I would," he cried in an eager whisper. "All these dear old farm women."

She nodded with shining eyes. "Dear Peter!"

He squeezed her hand under the table. "Berney," he whispered. "Berney—darling!"

Out again in the village street they bought bulls'-eyes in a little shop with a jangling bell. In another, more pretentious shop window, among such objects as terra-cotta figures, a bundle of Venus pencils, a *croix de guerre* in velvet case, and metal napkin rings embossed with the arms of various towns, Rawley spied a plush rack containing four or five rings. He took Berney by the elbow and led her into the shop.

"You must have one of some sort today," he asserted. "And we will get a proper one as soon as we can."

Two only of the five rings were at all suitable: one a thin gold circle with a moonstone, and the other a red stone surrounded by tiny pearls. The old shop dame watched them with interest as they examined the rings, and her wrinkled old face broke into a smile when Rawley tried one of them on Berney's finger. "*Fiancée, M'sieu?*" she asked, with her dark veined hands clasped on her breast.

"*Oui, Madame,*" answered Rawley proudly. "*Depuis une heure seulement.*" The old dame beamed at them through her thick glasses. The ring set with pearls fitted, and Rawley put his arms round Berney's shoulders as she stood with arm outstretched, shyly admiring it on her finger.

"*La veille guerre ce n'est pas trop mal, Madame*—eh?" asked Rawley gaily. And the dame threw up her hands and cried, "*La guerre! La guerre! Oh, là, là! Mes pauvres enfants.*" From the door of her shop she watched "*les pauvres enfants anglais*" pass up the street.

IV

Dusk found Rawley, a lonely figure, jogging along the pot-holed road between the wagon lines and the battery. Close ahead the leaning wayside crucifix, still guarded by its leafless, shattered trees, stood dark and desolate against the evening sky; and the lonely ragged stump of a church tower jutting darkly across a pearly rift in the purple night clouds proclaimed the village in the gloom beyond. The grumble of distant gun fire came from the south, borne fitfully upon the breeze.

The last grey sunset glow had faded when he entered the mess. There, upon the little mantelpiece lay his spare pipe, just as he had left it before going off that morning; and yet so much had happened since. Cane and Whedbee were busy at the table working out range tables for a shoot which brigade headquarters had just ordered. Piddock, with the aid of the gramophone, was conducting a duet by singing on the long bars between the lines: "Some of the time you think you love a brunette," sang the gramophone voice; and "I know the kind who had a Spanish mother," followed quickly the deep voice of Piddock. "Some of the time you love a blonde, Who came from Eden by way of Sweeden," carolled Piddock. "They may be short, they may be tall: Sometimes they pam-didly um—sometimes they fall, But you love somebody a-ll the time—ter rum ter rum."

At the end he stopped the motor and crossed to where Rawley stood thoughtfully filling his pipe. "Everything go off all right?" he asked.

Rawley looked up and nodded.

"Good show?"

Rawley answered between pulls at his freshly-lighted pipe. "Don't know. I was there only half an hour. We went off and had lunch in a quiet little village nearby." He pressed the charred tobacco into the bowl with the matchbox. "I've been and gone and done it, Piddock."

Piddock cocked an eye at him. "Done what?"

Rawley glanced at Cane and Whedbee whose heads were still close together over the range tables, and he added in a low voice:

"Got engaged."

Piddock gripped and wrung the hand that still held the matchbox. "Put it there, old son. Put it right there."

Rawley grinned. "Thanks—but keep it dark for the moment."

"Sure. But a drink is clearly indicated. Pugh! Pugh! Two gins and its—*beaucoup* gin and *beaucoup* it." They sat down on their home-made settee. "Well, here's the very best!" said Piddock, raising his glass. "The very best to you and—you know."

They set their glasses down, and Piddock rewound the gramophone and put on "Roses in Picardy." They listened to the air in thoughtful silence.

Without warning the frenzied shriek of a shell hurtling through the outer night peremptorily engulfed the sound of the gramophone. The full-bodied ferocious note told that the shell was near the end of its flight, and that the point of impact would be very close. Cane and Whedbee had ceased mumbling figures: their heads went forward in strained attention. During the fraction of a second that elapsed before the inevitable impact the figures in the little candle-lit mess crouched motionless as a panther ready to spring. Only Piddock, with a lightning movement of his hand, whipped his glass from the table and drained it at a gulp.

Then came the rocking bump of impact and a mighty rending roar. The aeroplane fabric that covered the glassless window flew into ribbons before the draught of the titanic blow, and the walls of the mess-room bulged visibly inwards, it seemed, and then swung reluctantly back. Slabs of plaster thudded from the ceiling, and the one picture crashed to the floor.

Cane had relighted the candle before the whine and clatter of flying fragments had ceased. He was grinning at Piddock.

"You're a funny fellow," he cried. "Did you see him, Whedbee? Polishing off his drink! Ruling passion strong in death!"

From the outer darkness came a long-drawn "Oh-e-e-e! Ho-ee-e!" Rawley was first through the door, and stumbling among the debris that littered the road. A fresh hole of unusual size yawned beneath the stars, and a black cavity gaped in the stained lime-washed wall of the cottage beyond. The sound came from there.

Cane, behind him, switched on a torch. The beam shone on the white face of a man in shirt sleeves, sitting upright upon a palliasse. A paper-covered book was in his hand, and from the stump of candle stuck in a cigarette tin on the box beside him a thin spiral of smoke still rose. The beam moved downwards to his legs, and Rawley saw that they were buried beneath the brick and plaster wall which had been blown inwards by the blast of the shell.

It needed half an hour's unremitting effort to release him: the mortar held the bricks together in great slabs, and a pick could not be used.

CHAPTER X

I

IT was now officially admitted by headquarters that a push was imminent. Cane brought the news one evening on his return from brigade. "Zero hour and all that is, of course, still a secret known only to the few brass hats who dwell in and around the holy of holies. But we know this much: there will be no long-drawn-out preliminary bombardment as on the old Somme. Just a short, intense hate, and then our chaps go over."

At night now, every man that could be spared from the guns was employed till dawn in unloading and stacking the great supplies of ammunition that would be necessary for the barrages and the preliminary bombardment. And the many other batteries that had recently taken up positions in and around the village were doing the same. After dark the road was blocked with transport, and two days of ceaseless rain had covered it with several inches of liquid mud. Double teams were necessary, and even then the heavy wagons were frequently stuck.

But at last the necessary amount of ammunition had been brought up and stacked, and everything was ready for the attack on the morrow.

It meant an early start for the gunners, for the barrage was to begin at 3.30 a.m., but Rawley lingered by the gun-pits before turning in. Apart from the tingling sensation of his own expectancy there was nothing to show that an attack would be made within a few hours. The moon, in its third quarter, shone serenely down upon the netting that screened the guns, and threw a chequered pattern upon the floor of the pits. Behind him the ragged edge of the stump of the church was tipped with silver. The noisy howitzer behind the mess was silent. The gunfire was confined to the long-drawn whine and distant crunch of a heavy, and the periodical vicious lash and crack of a whiz-bang. But on the road dark files of men passed every few minutes: they were the attacking infantry moving up to the assembly trenches.

Rawley was called at 3 a.m. Sitting on his bunk, he drank the mug of hot tea his servant brought him. Then he pulled on his boots and went out. The stars glittered coldly overhead, but the moon, now low on the horizon, was a blurred pinkish ball half submerged in the heavy ground mist. The air was damp and chilly.

The barrage opened perfectly in one great rippling roar, and the darkness was dispersed by the myriad flashes of the guns. It was intoxicating and exhilarating this giant's tattoo that filled the vast auditorium of the night with throbbing sound and maintained its pitch tirelessly hour after hour. Dawn came, grey and desolate, and although the dancing flashes of the guns paled before it, the massed drumming of their voices did not cease.

Soon after the sun rose the first walking wounded began to trickle back—men in twos and threes, with supporting arms about each other's shoulders, with bloody bandages about heads or thighs from which the trouser leg had been slit, and each with a white label dangling from a button. They rested on the bank beside the road and drank the water or smoked the cigarettes that were offered them before continuing their journey to the dressing-station. And an adventurous ambulance with its dark-green cover riddled with shrapnel bumped slowly down the pot-holed road with its fragile cargo.

In the gun-pits the men had thrown aside respirators, tunics and shirts, and stripped to the waist sweated at the nearly red-hot guns. Clouds of steam rose from the pools of water on the floor of the pits, water that had been cold before being poured through the bores; and the mounds of empty cases rose higher and higher.

The barrage ran its allotted course and ended, as far as B Battery was concerned, at 10.15, when extreme range had been reached. Everyone was asking "Who has won?" Nobody knew anything of what was happening. The wounded were the only source of information, and their news was very localized and often contradictory. But there had been very little hostile shelling since eight o'clock, and that was a good omen.

B Battery cleaned up and awaited the expected order to move forward. The backs of the gun-pits were broken down in preparation for hauling out the guns. Light kits stood ready packed and the mess functioned on the minimum of kit. Some batteries were already on the move.

The order to move came at last, and almost at the same moment hostile shelling began again on the ridge ahead. Cane rode off in the gathering dusk to choose the new position. The teams arrived shortly afterwards, and the guns, which had already been manhandled out of the pits, were limbered up and driven on to the road.

The whole British Army seemed to be moving forward that night. The road was encumbered with every kind of vehicle—G.S. wagons, eighteen-pounder guns, motor bicycles, 4.5 howitzers, limber wagons, maltese carts, staff cars, caterpillar tractors and eight horse teams of hairies dragging sixty-pounders, besides the usual ration parties, water carrying parties and platoons of relieving infantry. The darkness and the hostile shelling added to the confusion.

Along the ridge beyond the village ran a *route nationale*. Its bordering trees had always been a ranging mark for the enemy's guns. One of the tall poplars lay across its intersection with the narrower road to the front, and the stream of traffic had perforce piled up behind the obstacle. A gang of sweating, swearing men were labouring desperately to remove it. Their figures could be seen hacking and hauling darkly against the glow of a distant burning dump, overhung by an immense black pall of smoke. Shells that approached with a vicious shriek and detonated with a reverberating "cr-rump" ranged at minute intervals up and down the crowded road, and from a copse to the right a heavy howitzer fired periodically, its blast almost unseating the horsemen on the road.

The tree was dragged away and the traffic streamed on, only to halt again a short distance farther on where a ditched six-inch howitzer partly blocked the road. Baulks of timber were taken from a sapper bridging wagon, and dragged to the side of the road; the traffic bumped over them and round the obstacle.

The traffic thinned as it neared the front, and B Battery was able to make better progress. But the hostile shells became more numerous. Close ahead the ruins of a village was lit by their bursts. One landed on the maltese cart ahead of Rawley, and it disappeared.

Rumbald, his steel helmet askew, clattered up beside him. "We can't get through this," he panted. "I will go back and see if I can find a way round."

Rawley jerked out sharply, "We've got to get through." And when Rumbald persisted, he shouted, "Good God, Rumbald, don't you realize this is a battle, and the infantry up there are relying on us for artillery support!"

A shrill, rising scream was cut short by a crash and a spurt of flame on the roadside. His mare reared straight up and came down trembling. In the brief, bright glow Rawley saw Rumbald's big face glistening and streaked with perspiration. "Go back—hell!" he shouted.

He heard the hurtling shriek of a large calibre shell; the darkness lifted about a vivid flash surmounted by a great black canopy of rising earth. He turned in the saddle and yelled through his cupped hands—"Tr-rot!"

The battered gable end of a barn to the left glistened fitfully in the flash of bursting shells. The air sang and hummed with flying fragments of metal. He signalled "gallop" to the gun behind him. The six horses threw their weight upon the traces and stretched their necks. The drivers crouched low in the saddles, the men clutched desperately to the swaying caissons; and the gun behind rocked and bounced and struck sparks beneath its flying wheels.

Again he heard the hurtling shriek of a large calibre shell. The hot blast scorched his face, and the uprearing canopy of earth spread out above him like a pall. With his head bent sideways as to a gale he saw driver Tench slowly bow his head and then slide slowly from the saddle down among the galloping hoofs. By the light of the next flash he saw the huddled body, white face and shock of dark hair strike the road and remain motionless; and then the following gun wheels leapt upon it.

A fire burning in the shattered village spilled a ruddy pool of light upon the shell-pocked road and bordering hummocks of masonry. A driverless limber flashed out from the darkness beyond. Rawley saw the ruddy glow of the fire reflected in the glistening eyes of the terrified horses as they stampeded by with the leaping limber behind. They missed the gun by inches, but thirty yards further on they collided with a hummock of brickwork with a crash that splintered the limber to matchwood, and could be heard above the roar of the barrage.

Beyond the rubble heap of the village in the comparative peace of an occasional whiz-bang Rawley turned his mare and waited. One by one the wagons and guns appeared as long, dark, swiftly moving objects against the red glow of the fire. Piddock, a dark silhouette with tilted shrapnel helmet and bulging respirator, clattered up.

"Dirty night at sea," he growled.

"Any damage?" asked Rawley.

"One wagon scuppered and a team knocked out, and Rumbald is back t'other side of the village with number two gun that's ditched in a shell-hole big enough to sink a battleship."

Major Cane appeared out of the darkness ahead and led them to the new position, a chawed-up depression in the old support line, where rusty wire and shell holes impeded the task of getting in the guns; but an old trench with infantry dug-outs gave accommodation for the men.

II

Soon after dawn Cane and Rawley, accompanied by linesmen, set off to observe and to try to get some idea of the new line held by the enemy. It was Rawley's first view of a battlefield. They came down a gentle slope covered with rank grass and pitted with shell holes, and crossed the old fire trench by one of the wooden bridges prepared by the sappers. In the now deserted trench the rough ladders, made to assist the infantry in going over the top, still leaned against the parapet, and in the bay beneath the bridge one of the early casualties lay on the fire-step, with his muddy boots protruding from the great coat which covered him.

They passed through the rusty wire and knife rests into the low ground which two days previously had been no-man's-land. Here and there a figure sprawled stiffly among the coarse grass and rusty tins, the face already blue-grey and the lips black, between which the teeth glimmered like those of a dead horse. Nearer the old German Line was evidence of the bombardment—countless shell holes, twisted scraps of barbed wire, the iron cases of trench mortar shells, ripped and spread fanwise by the explosion of the charge within, and more gruesome relics: a black German field boot, with an inch or two of shining white shin bone protruding from it.

The German fire trench was too broad to jump. Cut in the hillslope, it was backed by a tortured glacis of chalk. The duckboards were littered with broken revetment and chalk debris. Water bottles, gas masks, rifles, coal-scuttle helmets, and scraps of clothing and equipment littered the fire-step, and its defenders lay in grotesque attitudes among the ruins. One knelt as in prayer, with his head bowed on the fire-step. Another sprawled face downwards on the duckboards. Another sat drunkenly in the angle of a traverse with his cropped head thrown back as though singing a ribald chorus. A thin, red-headed corpse gazed at the sun with one rigid eye; the other side of his face was gone. And the occupants of one dug-out had been literally plastered round the doorway by the explosions of the attackers' bombs. It was all clear and vivid in the bright morning light, and nothing moved.

Farther on, in a saphead, they came upon an overturned machine-gun with a half-fired belt still through the breech. Behind it sat a huge dead German, his black-booted legs spread out on either side in the firing position, his back against an ammunition box. He was tunicless, and his great hands and knotted forearms rested on the faded grey cloth of his breeches, where they had dropped from the firing knob. His grimy open shirt displayed a hairy chest matted with a purple crust from three or four bayonet jabs.

"Stout fellow!" said Cane, as they picked their way past him and up the sap. "But, damn him, he must have done a hell of a lot of damage before they got him."

Through a wood they went by a trench only breast high, where branches, splintered wood, and fallen trunks littered the ground on either side. Above them towered the trees, gaunt and ragged, with limbs hanging lamely or stumps ending in white-splintered manes. And the work of destruction continued. A runaway express train, it seemed, was tearing across the sky, to end in mid-career in a stunning thunder clap; and in the clear sky overhead appeared miraculously a thick woolly black cloud. The sky was soon stained with wispy smears, the drifting ghosts of former heavy shrapnel bursts.

They found themselves at last in the new front Line, which at this point was an old German reserve trench with new fire-steps cut to face the enemy, and were able to shoot the battery from a position in a barricaded communicating trench running out towards the enemy.

III

On their return to the battery they found that it had received some attention from the enemy's gunners. Number two pit had received a direct hit, and the fire which had been started thereby had only just been prevented from exploding the ammunition stacked at the back. Piddock and Sergeant Jameson had spent an anxious ten minutes removing from the danger zone some hundreds of shells that were already almost too hot to touch. And a little later Piddock had been blown down the steps of the mess dugout by a shell which landed on the parados of the trench. His only injury, a glorious black eye, was the subject of much chaff.

"What with one thing and another we've had quite a chatty afternoon," he told them with a grin; but Rawley noticed that the usual clog dance accompaniment to the gramophone was missing that evening.

Day succeeded day and the battle continued. To Rawley they were days of recurring pictures, like figures on a revolving frieze, a kaleidoscope of sound, movement, and colour. The gun-pits with the sunlight streaming through the camouflage netting and mottling the backs and helmets of the sweating gunners; the gun-pits at night, leaping in the vivid flashes of the guns from shadowy mystery to the cardboard detail of theatrical scenery; the gun-pits in the rain, with water sluicing the bleached sandbags and trickling from the drenched netting overhead. The rutted road by day and night, in sunshine and in rain, with wounded in twos and threes trickling down it and little files of steel-hatted men passing up it. The mess dug-out with Cane, pipe in mouth, working out barrage tables by the light of a guttering candle. The tortured lunar-like landscape, hot and reeking beneath a brazen sun, boggy and shining and diluvian beneath a slanting rain, or ghostly and Dantesque in the greenish glow of Verey lights. The skyline familiar in every detail from the clustered bare poles of the wood to the ragged hummocks of the *briqueterie*, smeared by day with the dirty smudges of shell-bursts and illuminated at night by the soaring Verey lights, winking shrapnel bursts, and coloured S.O.S. rockets.

The throbbing roar of the guns was ever present, the crashing concussion of detonating shells, the nauseating stench of foul earth, chloride of lime, wet clothing, and sweating humanity.

No one knew what was happening. The newspapers spoke glibly of victories and substantial gains. B Battery fired countless attack bombardments and put down countless protective barrages in answer to supplicating S.O.S. rockets, but no orders came to move forward.

Typical British battle weather had set in, and after floundering through the water-logged trenches and mud from the O.P. to the battery, one arrived in a state of semi-exhaustion. Rawley, however, was consistently cheerful and even happy. The happiest moment of the day was when, after the exhausting trudge back from the O.P., he stumbled, tired and muddy, down the steps of his dug-out. Presently, as he sipped a mug of hot tea, his servant would pull off his muddy field boots. Afterwards he would strip and towel himself vigorously all over; and the evening ration cart would bring him a letter from Berney. His inward happiness was proof against the outward attacks of cold, fatigue and monotony.

The new wagon lines had become a quagmire, and Rumbald had got his way at last and had gone back to construct new horse-standings. No doubt he was more concerned about the exhausting and dangerous journey to and from the O.P. than with the comfort and health of the horses; but Rawley was glad to be rid of him, for in the confined space of the little mess his presence and personality were rather overpowering.

Rawley himself did not mind the extra duty which one officer the less at the guns entailed, but he was resentful on Piddock's account. Piddock had been shaken by being blown down the dug-out steps, and three days later he had again been blown over by a crump when on his way up to the O.P. Physically he had suffered no injury on either occasion, and he was not the man to talk about his mental reactions. Outwardly he was as cheerful as ever, but on one occasion, during a heavy strafe, his lighting of a cigarette was performed a shade too nonchalantly to deceive the keen eye of a friend like Rawley. If anyone needed and deserved a quiet spell at the wagon lines it was Piddock, not Rumbald.

For days the rain continued, and it became the chief source of discomfort. The old German trench behind the guns was a foot deep in liquid mud. It was impossible to keep the water out of the dug-outs. Clothing became sodden, and clean underclothing freshly put on felt damp and sticky. The guns on their platforms of timber baulks sank deeper and deeper in the ooze, and threatened to disappear altogether as more than one horse and wagon had done.

The ammunition wagons needed two and even three teams to drag them over roads that were like ploughed fields, and the journey from the wagon lines and back occupied from sunset till sunrise. Shells, with delay action fuses, that buried themselves deeply in the earth before detonating, left pits a dozen feet deep into which the unwary fell to be drowned in the foul water that filled them.

The enemy were using a large number of gas shells, particularly at night. When the ghostly Verey lights were rising and falling on the front, they came whimpering and sighing through the darkness like lost souls, the liquid gas within the shell swilling like water in the belly of a trotting horse. The men in rain-washed steel helmets and respirators floundering in the quagmire resembled reptiles emerging from the primeval ooze. The mud itself was impregnated with gas, and few men in the battery escaped scot free in that polluted air. Rawley could speak hardly above a whisper, and for a day Cane lost his voice entirely.

Late one afternoon, after a spell at the guns, Rawley squelched along the trench and down the steep steps to the mess dug-out. A battered acetylene lamp flared on a bracket that had been driven into the glistening damp earth wall of the dug-out. Piddock, who had been on duty at the O.Pip, sat dejectedly on a box. He wore his muddy trench coat, and his dented steel helmet lay on the rough table before him.

Rawley took off his respirator and hung it on a nail. He took out his pouch and began filling his pipe. "Had a good day?" he asked.

Without shifting his position Piddock replied shortly, "Bloody awful!"

Rawley rolled up the pouch and returned it to his pocket. "Dear mother," he quoted conversationally, "this war's a beggar, but don't tell aunty!" He drew at his pipe and threw away the match. "Yes, the fellow who wrote that classic was about right."

To his amazement Piddock thumped the table madly with his fist and shrieked, "Shut up! Shut up! For Christ's sake, shut up!"

In the startled silence that followed, Piddock raised a glass shakily to his lips, and Rawley saw for the first time that it was three parts full of neat whisky. He opened his mouth to speak, but closed it again and remained staring with wrinkled brow at the greasy upturned collar of Piddock's trench coat. Then he took his respirator from the nail and went quietly up the steps.

He went in search of Cane. Piddock was cracking up, and it was a damned shame the way Rumbald was allowed to play the skrim-shanker back at the wagon lines. In the army there was too much of that working the willing horse. A good fellow, just because he did his job and was reliable, was put on dirty job after dirty job, till he either cracked up or got killed, while the shirker, just because he was unreliable, was never put on an important and therefore dirty job. Piddock had never shirked. He ought to have a rest, and Cane ought to give it him.

Near number three pit he met Sergeant Jameson, and in passing asked him if Gunner Davies was back yet.

"Gunner Davies has gone down the Line with a nasty dose of shell-shock, sir," answered the sergeant. "You haven't heard about young Jackson then, sir?"

Rawley had not. Sergeant Jameson had the story from Gunner Davies, told jerkily between violent fits of shivering and teeth-chattering.

On his way back from the O.Pip that afternoon, Piddock, with Davies and Jackson, had been crossing the churned-up area of twisted wire and shell holes that had once been no-man's-land, when the German gunners suddenly opened a heavy strafe with five-nines. Piddock and his two men, progressing by short rushes between the bursts, had nearly reached the edge of the danger zone, when a shell, whose warning scream had been drowned in the crashing detonation of another shell, caught them unawares. Piddock and Davies flung themselves flat just in time, but Jackson was hurled backwards by the black uprearing fountain of earth. A second later, when the fragments were still whining through the air, Piddock rose and ran towards the prone figure. It writhed convulsively as he approached it, but when the tousled head from which the steel helmet had fallen turned towards him he pulled up in horror. Not a vestige of face remained. Where it should have been above the open flap of the box respirator on the chest was now a pulpy, purple mess like trampled bullock's liver, with dark cavities where eyes and mouth should have been.

Davies, who had been Jackson's friend, drew back in terror and began to shout hysterically. Piddock manfully stood his ground till the thing, attracted by the shouts, struggled blindly to its feet and tottered, mopping and mowing, towards him. Then he, too, turned and fled. And the thing followed, mowing and gibbering, till mercifully it stumbled into a brimming shell hole and lay still, half submerged in the slowly reddening water.

Cane was in the control dug-out. He looked up when Rawley pulled aside the gas curtain. "Hullo, Rawley," he said. "News just come from brigade. We go out tomorrow night."

With his thoughts on Piddock, Rawley answered, "And about time too."

Cane grinned and nodded. His own tanned face was as lean as a headhunter's trophy, and there were black caverns beneath his eyes. "Yes, about time. We all look rather like advertisements for patent medicines—before taking."

IV

The relief which took place on the following evening was carried out in record time. There were no guns to be man-handled out of the pits. B Battery was exchanging its guns for those of the relieving battery. A G.S. wagon came up at dusk and started back again as soon as its load of blankets, ground sheets, mess kit, and other kit were stowed into it. Piddock marched off the men as soon as the personnel of the relieving battery arrived, and Cane and Rawley stayed to hand over.

Accompanied by the C.O. of the relieving battery they visited, for the last time, the gun-pits and the telephone and control dug-outs. Then, having handed over maps, S.O.S. lines and other details, they returned to the mess and drank good luck to their successors. Ten minutes later they had picked up their horses and grooms and were on the way back.

The weather, as though repenting of its former treatment of them, was perfect. Stars glittered overhead, and the great yellow disc of the moon hung like a paper lantern above the ragged walls of the village near the wagon lines as they clattered through it. Three hundred yards along the main road beyond, they came up with the rear of the column, Whedbee and Piddock with the old wagons and the guns taken over from the relieving battery. Rumbald had gone on ahead as billeting officer. Tall trees bordered the road across which the moonlight lay in dazzling white bars. Pipes and cigarettes glowed in the mouths of the swaying mounted figures, and the mournful air of a sentimental song could be heard fitfully above the rumbling wheels and jingling accoutrements of the long dark, slowly moving column.

Hour after hour they jogged along through the keen night air. Behind them the Verey lights faded from view and the throbbing roll of the guns sank to a distant grumble. The pulsating drone of a marauding plane, invisible in the silver radiance overhead, and the distant "whu-ump" of a bomb were the only disturbers of the peace. With echoing rumble of wheels and horses' feet the column passed through sleeping villages where the moonlight gave haloes to the whitewashed cottages, where green and red lamps and a silent statuesque sentry, with silver-tipped bayonet, proclaimed a headquarters, or where a line of lorries stood dark and silent in the deep shadow of the houses.

The moon had sunk behind a pine spinney and shone between the black trunks like the eye of a caged tiger, when at last the short-coated figure of Bombardier Wilson, one of the billeting party, rose from the darkness of the roadside and led the way towards the short black church spire that stabbed the sky close ahead. The village street was dark, silent, and deserted till the bombardier tapped on a window. Then an invisible door opened, spilling a flood of light across the road, and the broad figure of Rumbald, pipe in mouth, was silhouetted in the doorway. The bombardier saluted. "Battery just coming in, sir," he said. And a moment later the rumbling of wheels, the clatter of hoofs, and the gruff voices of men, echoed between the houses as the battery came in, halted, and moved off section by section to its billets.

CHAPTER XI

I

PIPE in mouth Rawley sat on the soft grass of an orchard with his back against an apple tree. A map was spread on his knees, and he was engaged in measuring the distance between this village and Hocqmaison, between himself and Berney. On the grass nearby Piddock lay full length with his fingers locked behind his head, gazing upwards at the small white clouds sailing overhead. Down at the stream half a dozen men in shirt sleeves, with boots, socks, and puttees off, were standing in the water and washing clothes. On the bank numbers of shirts, vests, and pairs of pants lay spread out in the sun.

Whedbee, with his hands in his breeches pockets, strolled up and sat down by Rawley and Piddock. He unrolled a tobacco pouch and began filling his curved pipe. "This is one of the best places we have struck," he said appreciatively.

"Touch wood—or we shan't stay," cried Piddock.

"I am," answered Whedbee, holding up his pipe. "I have just sent off a half-limber to get stores," he continued. "We will have the canteen going tonight." He drew appreciatively at his pipe. "And we might arrange a concert tomorrow night. That big barn No. 3 section are in would be just the place for it."

Piddock murmured: "Behold our noble P.R.I. The conscientious exhilarator at work."

"Well, we must keep the men amused," answered Whedbee.

"Then why not organize a crown and anchor tournament," suggested Piddock.

"Too many rival firms," grinned Whedbee. "But we might have a football match tomorrow afternoon. I must see Sergeant Jagger about that. You will play, won't you?"

Piddock groaned. "It's so much like work," he protested.

"And give me a miss," said Rawley. "I rather want to go off for the day tomorrow if I can."

Piddock turned and gave Rawley a significant look.

"You are a pair of slackers," complained Whedbee. "Loafing is a positive disease with you."

Piddock removed the blade of grass from his mouth and regarded the chewed stem. "Rawley's trouble is more organic than that," he said innocently, and he began humming softly, "If you were the only girl in the world."

II

The officers of B Battery gathered in the mess that night were a contented party. They wore slacks and polished brown shoes. Fresh butter was on the table, which was covered with a clean white cloth. The gramophone was playing "Destiny" waltz, and Piddock and Whedbee, clasped amorously in each other's arms, were circling dreamily in a corner. Rawley was playing patience at one end of the table, and Rumbald was showing the mess corporal how to make a new cocktail with some cognac he had got from an old man in the village. Cane was absent. He had gone to Brigade in the neighbouring village, and they were waiting dinner till he returned.

Suddenly a voice was heard outside, and a moment later he came in. He shied his cap on to a chair and unbuckled his belt. "Hullo, Rumbald! What have you got there?" he exclaimed.

"New cocktail: Gunner's Glory! Try one?"

Cane took the glass and tossed off the concoction. "Um! Not bad," he said, pursing up his mouth judicially. He put down the glass. "Well, you fellows, we're not staying long in the country."

"I thought these billets were too good to be true," said Whedbee, breaking off his dance with Piddock.

"How long are we staying?" asked Rumbald.

"We move up and in again tomorrow. Take over new positions tomorrow night."

"Oh, my gawd!" complained Rumbald. "Anyone would think we were the only bloody battery in France."

Rawley glanced at Piddock; but his face was as expressionless as a mask.

"And I've just bought all that canteen stuff," groaned Whedbee. "Where are we going, sir?"

"Somewhere just south of Arras; pretty god-forsaken spot from all accounts. But there is one bright glimmer in the otherwise cloudy firmament: leave is re-opening shortly. You are first on the list, Piddock, you young blighter. Well, come on, let's have some food. I'm going to bed early and make the most of that mattress I've got."

III

All next day the battery marched along the straight, tree-bordered roads, and with the dusk reached the outlying houses of Arras. Here the wheels rattled noisily over the *pavé* of narrow streets where the windows of roofless buildings gaped like sightless eyes. On they went through the *petite place*, where the jagged stump of the once-soaring *hôtel-de-ville* glimmered eerily in the moonlight, and across the huge *grande place*, silent and deserted; through endless streets and little squares where grass flourished between the cobbles and shattered lamp-posts threw crooked shadows on the moonlit walls.

Beyond the city they entered a desert country of rank jungle grass, with here and there an abandoned army hut sagging dejectedly in the moonlight. The soaring Verey lights ahead marked the end of the journey.

Dawn came and revealed the surroundings of their new home. The position lay in a shallow valley; the bottom of which was flat and rather marshy. The stream which flowed through it was enclosed between banks some five feet in height. The guns were dug into the near bank so as to fire across the stream, and were covered with the usual camouflage netting. An old grass-grown communicating trench ran up to the slope behind, and the skyline was broken by weed-grown excavations with here and there a bent screw picket and a tangled strand of wire. The slope in front beyond the stream was also scarred with disused trenches, pitted with shell holes, weed-grown, and littered with rusty tins and wire.

"Quite one of the beauty spots of the western front," commented Cane, as he went round the position in the full light of day. "And we ought to indent for lifebelts; for if Brother Bosche pitches a few heavies into the bank we shall be flooded out in ten minutes."

Cane did not approve of the mess dug-out either. It was dug into the river bank a little distance from the guns. "Wouldn't stop a pop-gun bullet," he growled. "And a five-nine within fifteen yards will probably shake the whole damn thing in on top of us."

CHAPTER XII

I

L EAVE re-opened on the following day, and Piddock went back to the wagon lines in the morning. The adjutant also was going on leave, and he offered to call at the wagon lines and give Piddock a lift back to railhead in a car. And so, after breakfast, Piddock put the yellow leave warrant in his pocket, donned his trench coat and bulging haversack, and set out.

Whedbee turned up for lunch with Phillips of C Battery. C Battery had recently acquired a Minoru cloth, and Phillips was anxious to introduce the game to B Battery. A new sandbag was found and slit up to form a cloth, and the necessary lines were marked on it with a blue and red pencil from Cane's map case. Phillips worked out the odds as nearly as he could remember them, and then, with revolver ammunition for horses and a pack of cards, the game began.

Phillips, to his joy, was banker, but he lost steadily; and he became the butt of a roar of laughter when Whedbee, who had spent his life teaching mathematics, pointed out in his quiet, humorous way, that the odds were so arranged that the bank could not win.

"Never mind, it's a good game," grinned Cane. "And Phillips is the sort of chap I've been looking for for years. Come on, Whedbee, I will show you what I mean about those old oil drums."

Cane and Whedbee disappeared up the dug-out steps, and Rumbald, with pencil and paper, began to work out odds more favourable to the bank. Phillips lighted a cigarette and looked on ruefully.

From outside came suddenly a long drawn whine, followed by a bump and a muffled explosion. The dug-out shook convulsively. Then in rapid succession came again that whine—crash; whine—crash; whine—crash. And at each crash the dug-out flinched, and smoke drifted across the top of the steps.

Phillips made a grimace and looked up. "Much of a roof over?" he asked.

"Wouldn't stop that sort," replied Rawley.

The mess-cook's voice came calling down the steps: "Sir! Mr. Rawley! Mr. Rawley! The C.O. and Captain Whedbee are lying out there—copped it, sir!"

Rawley, followed by Phillips, dashed up the steps. Every three or four seconds a shell, preceded by its hurtling whine, burst with a thunder-clap—"c-r-r-ump!"—and a great uprearing fountain of earth.

"Come on!" cried Rawley. "By short dashes—after the next one." Whine—crash! The three men darted out. Again that swiftly travelling whine hurtled towards them, and they went flat. Crash! They were up again and on. They found Cane lying badly wounded in the thigh and shoulder. Rawley and Phillips took his head and shoulders, and the mess-cook took his legs. They brought him in and laid him on the table, which was still covered with Phillips' improvised Minoru cloth. They left

Rumbald to get busy with field dressings, and went back for Whedbee.

His left knee-cap was shattered, and he screamed when they raised his legs. But with shells still coming in, every five or ten seconds, it was no time for squeamishness. They had brought him nearly to the dug-out when, with a deafening roar, a shell burst within a few yards. They went flat; but when they rose again the mess-cook's fingers were dripping blood from a wound in the arm, and Whedbee uttered no cry when they seized his injured leg and hurried him down the steps. Then as they laid him on the floor they saw that he was dead. A fragment of the last shell had broken his back.

At the end of a few minutes the shelling ceased as suddenly as it had begun, and it was possible to get a stretcher and send Cane back.

II

Rumbald and Rawley returned to the mess dug-out, where the mess-cook was swabbing the table with one hand.

"You get along, Reeves, and have that arm properly dressed," Rawley told him. "And have some antitetanus juice pumped in."

"But there is nobody else here, sir. Corporal Jones has gone to the canteen at Aidecourt."

"It doesn't matter; we don't want anything," said Rawley. "You get along."

He took Cane's compass from the nail on which it hung by its long strap. "This ought to have gone down with his other kit," he muttered. "Well, Rumbald, you are O.C. for the moment."

Rumbald glanced at his wrist-watch. "We shall just be in time to stop Piddock," he remarked.

"But there is no need to do that," protested Rawley. "Brigade will send us another fellow presently, and we can carry on meantime."

Rumbald shook his head. "We are too short-handed," he objected.

"Oh, rot!" retorted Rawley. "Look here, Rumbald, Piddock needs this leave damned badly. He's just about done in. He has been out here longer than any of us, and he has had a pretty thin time lately. This leave may just save him. We can carry on all right till brigade sends us another man."

Rumbald shook his head. "There's too much to do. We want a chap at the O.Pip, and another with the guns, and there's the wagon lines. He can take his leave as soon as a reinforcement comes. Meantime, we'll have him up here. . . ."

"Up here!" echoed Rawley. "Why up here?"

Rumbald rubbed the back of his neck with his hand. "Well, he is more used to O.Pip work than I am, and—"

"Much more used," agreed Rawley, cuttingly. "And what are you going to do, pray?"

"There must be an officer at the wagon lines."

Rawley thumped the table. "Damn you, Rumbald, you can't do that. Piddock is second-in-command now, and if he stays his job is at the wagon lines and yours is up here. Cane always stayed with the guns."

"I'm more used to the battery at the wagon lines," persisted Rumbald.

"More use be blowed! You're not thinking of the battery; you're thinking of yourself. It's just wind up—thinking of your own skin."

Rumbald grinned exasperatingly at Rawley's heat. "Anyway, I'm running the battery now," he retorted. He stood up and looked at his watch. "I must get my servant to pack my kit, and we shall just be in time to stop Piddock before he leaves."

"You can't be such a skunk, Rumbald; you damn well can't."

"You can't stop me," said Rumbald, as he moved towards the steps.

"I can," shouted Rawley. "By God, I can and will. I'll ring up brigade. I'll speak to the colonel." He moved towards the telephone.

Rumbald turned and seized him by the arm. No you don't," he snapped.

Rawley shook him off and stretched again towards the telephone, but Rumbald's big hand gripped the lapels of his coat into a bunch and stayed him. Rawley turned his head slowly and saw the big red face at the end of the arm that held him. The smouldering anger of weeks burst into flame. His fist shot out. "Take your hands off me," he panted.

Rumbald let go his hold and staggered back. His tie and tunic were dribbled with blood. His nose was bleeding like a tap. He rushed forward with fury-contorted face, and Rawley, with no room to retreat, could only duck under the great swinging fists and throw his arms round the thick body.

By sheer weight he was forced back against the dug-out wall, but he locked his hands in the small of Rumbald's back and hugged like a bear. The big body began to pant, and then, step by step, they tottered across the dug-out, Rawley gripping with all his strength and trying to bend his opponent backwards. Rumbald's heel came against a box; Rawley flung all his weight forward, and the pair came down with a crash.

They scrambled to their feet, Rawley panting and furious, Rumbald dishevelled and dangerous looking. He came on again with swinging arms. Rawley, backing before the onslaught, collided with the little table, and the hand he put behind him to steady it closed over an old entrenching-tool handle lying there. He swung it up and struck hard as one of the wild, swinging blows sent him crashing on top of the table.

Rumbald staggered back, one hand to his head; his heel came again against the box, and he went over backwards with a crash.

Rawley sat up on the collapsed table and dabbed the blood from his face with a handkerchief. Rumbald lay where he had fallen like a half-filled sack of corn, his legs apart and his chin tucked deeply into his chest by reason of a pit prop against which he had cracked his head. His forehead was cut and bleeding from the blow of the entrenching-tool handle; and blood from his nose covered his tunic.

Rawley scrambled to his feet and went down on one knee beside Rumbald. The eyes were open and the whites were turned up. Knocked right out by that crack on the head, he thought. And the head was certainly in an uncomfortable position; propped up like that with the chin in the chest.

He linked his arm under Rumbald's shoulder and dragged him a foot or two from the post; and the moment the head was free it dropped back with a thud to the floor and lolled to one side in a horrible manner like a rag doll.

Then it was that Rawley realized that the neck was broken, had been snapped when the head came into contact with the post. Rumbald was dead.

Dead—killed in a brawl! It was true then what was always said about people who took too much care of themselves: that they got themselves killed in an air raid on leave, or were run over in the street. What a great flabby hulk he looked, lying there with his legs wide apart and blood all over his chest.

Rawley rose wearily to his feet, and then plumped down again on the box. His head was whirling. It came upon him in a flash that he would be accused of killing Rumbald. Rumbald lay there with a broken neck and his forehead all cut and bloody from a heavy blow. Striking and killing his superior officer! That meant shooting or hanging.

"My God, what an end! To be hanged for murder in war time, as though killing were a crime. Hanged, when one might be killed any day—and kill, kill hundreds and be called a hero for it."

He stared at the silent figure on the floor. If only the shell that had got poor old Whedbee had got Rumbald instead.

He stood up. What ought he to do? Pick up the telephone and say to the signaller at the other end: "Send the stretcher bearers to the mess; I've just killed Mr. Rumbald." Clear out? There was time. The mess-cook would not be back for another ten minutes or so.

III

He put on his cap and went up the steps. No one was about. The gun-pits and other dug-outs were hidden by the curve of the river bank. A few yards away the weed-grown remains of an old communicating trench began and continued diagonally up the slope. Dark clods of earth from several freshly made shell holes littered the ground. A long-range "heavy" moaned lazily overhead and detonated a few seconds later with a distant crunch.

He crossed the few yards of broken ground and dropped into the disused trench. Broken duckboards and rotting sandbags impeded his steps, and here and there a landslide partly blocked the trench. But once over the crest of the slope and out of sight of the battery he clambered out and turned south-west away from the pot-holed road.

He tramped on like an automaton, avoiding subconsciously the heavy batteries, earth burrows, and derelict huts that dotted this forward area. Occasionally a high-velocity shell lashed through the air and sent the black earth spouting skywards, or a long-range heavy waddled lazily overhead and detonated grumpily in the distance.

Behind him he heard the mournful swish of gas shells—many of them. They sounded very close to B Battery, and he half turned at the thought. But he turned again with a shrug. That was now no concern of his.

He pulled out his pipe and filled it. There was very little tobacco in his pouch; he had left a tin three parts full in the dug-out. He must have tobacco.

He turned towards some huts, on one of which he could distinguish the red triangle of the Y.M.C.A. It was fortunate that he had some money. Whedbee had drawn him a hundred and twenty-five francs from the field-cashier only yesterday. He took a fifty-franc note from his wallet and entered the hut. It seemed very cosy with its tables and benches and shelves with tins of fruits, milk, biscuits, and tobacco. He took his tin of tobacco, stuffed the notes of his change into the ticket pocket in the waistband of his tunic, and went out.

He tramped on away from the huts and the road. A nice mess he had made of things, he thought bitterly. This was the end of everything—of B Battery, of Berney.

He had not a notion what to do. He was driven onward by the instinct of self-preservation. He thought vaguely of stealing some clothes and posing as a civilian till after the war. But of course that was absurd. He spoke French very imperfectly, and how would an English civilian without papers explain his presence in France? He would be arrested and shot as a spy.

He had been a fool to run away. It would have been simpler to have stayed and faced the music. And then he would have been hanged because, instead of blowing Germans to bits with high explosive, he had accidentally broken the neck of a useless skrimshanker like Rumbald. Because Rumbald wore khaki and not field grey, he, Rawley, would be hanged. He had a licence to kill any number of men in grey, no matter how excellent and useful members of humanity they might be, but it was a horrible crime to kill one useless and worthless fellow who wore khaki. What a farce it all was.

He tramped on. The huts, horse-lines, and dumps that lay in rear of the Line were left behind. Around him stretched the devastated area, the old Somme battlefields in which no village, house, or building stood; a belt of desolation thirty miles in breadth, shell-pocked, trench-scarred, weed-grown, and littered with rusty wire, rotting sandbags, mouldering debris of battle and the rubble heaps of flattened villages.

He seated himself on the parados of an old trench and smoked a pipe. He must devise some plan. Various schemes floated through his mind, but none of them was really practicable. In England he might enlist under another name and bury his identity in the ranks; but he was not in England. There was the Foreign Legion, of course. It was said foreigners were enlisted without too many questions being asked, and that once enlisted they were protected from the consequences of anything done before enlistment. He had better make for the zone of the French armies then. In any case, he must get away from the area in which there were units and divisions that knew him.

He rose and tramped on. Darkness fell. Behind him the invisible horizon was lit by the summer-lightning-like flicker of the guns, and their voices were a distant grumble. Overhead an invisible night bomber forged its way through the darkness, but soon the steady pulsating drone of its twin engines dwindled and died away. No cheerful light gleamed in the surrounding darkness. The silence of death and decay brooded over the devastated area.

He tramped on hopelessly, stumbling into weed-grown shell holes, and disentangling his feet from curled strands of rusty wire. He found himself at length on a narrow pot-holed road and followed it.

The sudden scrape of a boot close ahead pulled him up short. A form loomed in the darkness and a voice asked: "Got a match, mate?" He could distinguish the outline of a battered service cap against a starry rift in the clouds. As he fumbled in his pocket, something soft and heavy fell upon the back of his head. He sank drunkenly to his knees. Darkness rushed in.

CHAPTER XIII

I

C ONSCIOUSNESS floated back to him, consciousness of dull pains and aches and particularly of a splitting headache. Rain was falling gently on his upturned face. He opened his eyes without moving. Here and there stars shone from rifts in the clouds, and low down near the invisible horizon a dull red light glowed like an eye. He moved his aching head slowly to avoid the tickling of the long, rank grass which the chill night breeze brushed against his cheek, and at the movement the distant dull red light swayed and kindled to a bright red, revealing itself with startling suddenness as a cigarette in the mouth of a shadowy face.

"So you've woke up, 'ave you!" commented a voice close at hand. The point of light disappeared, and the dark head and shoulders of a man rose against the sky.

Rawley scrambled painfully to his feet and discovered in the process that his belt and tunic were undone. He took a step forward, but the figure backed from him. "Keep your distance," it growled. "If yer don't want a hole in yer shirt."

Rawley plumped down again on the bank. He saw that, although the speaker was short and slight, he held a revolver in his hand.

"All right," he said. "You can put that thing away." He put his hand to his breast pocket, and found that his wallet was gone and that the flaps of his pockets were unbuttoned. His pockets had been ransacked. He held his aching head in his hands. "Well, what's the idea?" he asked.

"Idea! What bleedin' idea?" asked the other.

"I mean you've cleaned me out very nicely. What now?"

"Nothin'. You can clear out."

"Oh—er—thanks!" answered Rawley, with a touch of sarcasm. "But I'm still a bit dicky, and—er—if it's all the same to you, I'll wait a moment."

The other grunted and sat down on the roadside a yard or two away. Rain was falling gently. The distant gun flashes still played like summer lightning along the horizon. Rawley held his aching head in his hands. He wondered why the fellow had stayed. The glow of his cigarette waxed and waned in the darkness and gave glimpses of a sharp, ferrety little face. He was a little dirty weed of a man and a cockney, judging by his voice.

Presently he spoke again. "I'll take my bleedin' oath you saw some stars when Kelly copped you that beauty on the napper!" he chuckled.

His tone was conversational, and without any malice, and it dawned on Rawley that for some reason the fellow was glad of his company. The cigarette glowed in the darkness, and the sharp face behind it was revealed fitfully. The voice continued in a confidential tone: "I saw you was a gunner, that's why I stayed till you come to. You'll be all right in a jiffy."

"Thanks," answered Rawley. He was in truth a little grateful to the fellow for staying. He felt very much alone in the world at that moment, and the devastated area was very desolate and depressing at that hour. An outcast himself, the company even of a guttersnipe was not to be despised. "I suppose you are a gunner, too," he added conversationally.

"Yep," answered the other, and spat. "I was." He threw away the cigarette end and lighted another with a tinder lighter.

Automatically Rawley put his hand in his pocket, but though his pipe remained, his tobacco had been taken. He put the cold stem between his teeth.

"I suppose your hospitality towards a fellow gunner wouldn't rise to giving him a cigarette," he asked. "My tobacco seems to have gone astray."

The fellow hesitated a moment and then fumbled in his pockets. A cigarette fell into Rawley's lap.

"Many thanks," said Rawley. "But my matches seem to have gone the way of my tobacco."

The automatic lighter landed in his lap. He twisted the flint and blew the tinder to a bright glow.

The cigarette was flat and a little bent from long residence in a pocket, but it was a smoke. Rawley straightened it between his fingers and lighted it.

In the silence that followed, the grumble of distant gunfire quickened suddenly to a dull throbbing roll like the muffled beating of side-drums, and the flickerings on the eastern horizon became continuous.

"Kaiser Bill's birfday or something!" commented Rawley's companion. "Nasty 'ate going on."

"Sounds as if somebody is a bit peeved about something," agreed Rawley. "That's mostly eighteen pounders."

"I was eighteen pounders," said the other reminiscently.

Rawley nodded. "Nice little cannon. Though I don't suppose I shall ever fire one again," he added bitterly.

"Why, ain't you going up there any more?" The dark head nodded towards the distant gunflashes.

"No—I suppose not. I cleared out of the battery this afternoon, and—there's no going back now."

"Why . . . you ain't deserted, 'ave you—and you an officer!" The tone was one of shocked righteousness.

Rawley's pent feelings overflowed. "Why, blast you, you thieving little squit, you're a deserter, too, aren't you?"

"Orl right. Orl right. And what if I am?" protested the other.

"Then what the hell do you mean by talking like that? If you think I got cold feet and ran away from my men, you are damn well wrong, and I'll knock your dirty little head off." He checked his vehemence and laughed bitterly. "Well, what's the good of all this anyway? We are both deserters and there's an end of it." He threw his cigarette end on the ground and trod it viciously into the mud with his heel. There was silence for some moments, and then another cigarette landed in his lap. He lifted it between his fingers, and after a moment's hesitation put it in his mouth. "Thanks," he said curtly.

They smoked in silence for some moments. Presently the cockney voice came again, sympathetically: "What are you going to do, mate?"

Rawley blew a cloud of smoke through his nose and laughed shortly. "Lord knows. What do *you* do?"

"Well, that's just it; I was just a-thinkin'."

"Thinking what?"

"Why, that we might be half-sections, you an' me."

Rawley's answering grunt was non-committal.

"You see," went on the other confidentially, "you want a maite in this gaime. It's orl rite scroungin' round on yer own fer a bit, but yer never knows if some of the other crowd won't find where you've hidden your stores and pinch 'em. And it's lonesome out 'ere at night, I give yer my oath." He spat and shivered. "No, I reckon you're ruddy lucky meetin' me. When I fust come out 'ere I lived on arf a biscuit for two days and drank rain water from a shell 'ole. And the fust two nights it rained like only sunny bleedin' France can rain, and I lay in a shell hole under a bit of old elephant iron till I got washed out and nearly froze. And that's what you'd be doing if you hadn't met me. You ain't got no bunk, and you ain't got no grub, and you ain't got no fags. And I've got all of 'em, and what I 'as, my mate 'as too. What do you say?" He came close to Rawley and tapped him on the knee. "Look 'ere," he went on in a confidential whisper, and pulled something from his pocket, "I'll show you the sort of bloke I am. That's 'arf my share, five francs. Kelly, blast 'im, took your fifty-franc note and all the rest, and he give me and Pearson ten francs each. And that's the bleedin' truth, if I never speak another word." He held the tattered note towards Rawley. "There y'are fifty-fifty."

"What's your name?" asked Rawley without taking the proffered note.

"Alf. The other naime don't matter."

"Well, Alf, put that five francs back in your pocket. It's payment for the cigarettes I've smoked, and for the grub I'm relying on you to produce. And as I'm devilish hungry, the sooner you produce it the better it will suit me."

II

They set off together in the darkness along the narrow, muddy, pot-holed road. There was no sound except the distant drumming of the guns and the gentle swish of the rain. The darkness hung like a curtain around them, and once only did Rawley see dimly against the sky the skeleton rafters of some shattered homestead.

Presently they left the road and stumbled among foot-high, weed-grown walls and grassy brick rubble slippery with rain. Beyond the flattened village the ground sloped upwards and was covered with coarse grass and pitted with weed-grown shell holes. Alf led the way, and occasionally gave warning of a tangle of rusty wire or of an old half-filled trench that had to be jumped.

He halted finally and said: "Here we are, mate." But there was nothing to be seen. The flickerings eastwards had either ceased or were hidden by the contour of the ground. The invisible rain rustled mournfully in the darkness. Alf bent down and his dark form was instantly swallowed up. A moment later his voice came muffled from below Rawley's feet. "Come on; it's about a six-foot drop."

Rawley felt forward cautiously with one foot and slithered down through wet grass and weeds into a narrow, muddy trench.

Alf led off again and Rawley followed. Dripping weeds brushed his face and bits of old basket revetment stabbed at his legs. For twenty yards or more they stumbled along, sliding and sticking in the mud, before they halted where the trench was blocked by a fall of earth. A baulk of rotting timber, half-buried in the landslide, bridged low down in the trench a narrow hole, through which Alf crawled. "You stay, mate, till I get a light," he said, as his head disappeared.

A few minutes later a gleam of yellow light appeared, and Rawley squeezed through the hole, feet first. He found himself in a low and narrow tunnel, revetted with rotting timbers and half-blocked with falls of earth. Alf stood with a battered hurricane lantern in his hand, his body bent to avoid the roof timbers. They squeezed under an outward-leaning pit-prop and its burden of loose earth and revetment and scrambled round a mound of loose earth that all but filled the tunnel. Then down several steps to a curtain of dirty sacking which Alf pulled aside. " 'Ere we are, maite, 'ome sweet 'ome."

Rawley followed him past the curtain and found himself in a medium-sized dug-out. A big beam ran across the middle of the roof and was supported in the centre by a great baulk of timber whose base rested on a thick plank half-embedded in the earthen floor. Against the post stood a rough table on which at the moment rested a dirty piece of newspaper, an empty bully-beef tin with jagged meaty edges, and much candle grease. Beyond it stood a crazy wire-netting bed with rumpled brown blankets, and pegged by match stalks to the earth wall above were a number of stained photographs of actresses, torn from illustrated papers. The whole place was indescribably dirty and had a musty, earthy, garlicky smell, like the lair of a wild beast.

Alf put the battered hurricane lamp on the table and looked around him with a grin. " 'Ere we are," he said. " 'Ere we are. The well-known society gent, Mr. Alf Hitchkins, in his boudoir—some-bleedin'-where in France."

The lamplight revealed him to Rawley as a short wiry little man with long unkempt dark hair curling over his ears, bright and rather humorous eyes set in a grimy face, and several days' growth of beard like a strip of black crêpe round his narrow jaw.

"Now for some grub," he said. He went to the other side of the dug-out and pulled down a dirty piece of sacking that was pegged into the earth wall. Behind it was a hole some six feet deep by four feet in height, forming an alcove. From a corner he dragged a battered bucket, with holes punched in it, and set it up on two bricks on the floor of the alcove. Into this he put some scraps of paper and splintered wood.

"You're not going to light that thing in here, are you?" asked Rawley. "We shall be smoked out."

Alf watched the paper blaze up and the wood begin to crackle, and then turning on one knee gave a large wink. "This bug 'ouse might 'ave been built for Hindenburg hisself," he said. "Every modern convenyince. Fireplace and chimbly. The only thing it 'asn't got is a barf room."

He took a fair-sized tin with a wire handle from under some rubbish, filled it with water from a petrol tin, and hung it over the blaze by means of a rusty bayonet. Then he cleared the table by tipping the rubbish on to the floor. He set out a tin of bully beef, four rather mouldy army biscuits, a battered enamel mug, and an old mustard tin.

"It's the cook's night out, and the kippers 'avent come cos it's early closin' dye, but I'm stunnin' the fat 'eaded Fray Bentos." And he set to work with a jack-knife to open the tin. A small handful of tea thrown into the boiling water completed the preparations.

They sat on upturned boxes on either side of the rickety table and ate the beef from the tin with the aid of pocket knives.

"Where do you draw your rations?" asked Rawley, as he sipped his nearly black tea from the mustard tin.

Alf transferred a lump of bully-beef from the point of his jack-knife to his mouth.

"Scrounge it," he answered, masticating vigorously. "There aint 'arf a lot of stuff lying around these old trenches. I've got a nice little stock of bully, and I had some jam too, but that's all gone. Oh, it aint 'arf bad out 'ere. We live like perishin' fightin' cocks sometimes, I give you my word. Why, a few weeks ago the boys 'ad a raid on a canteen at

Morpas. It was one of Kelly's stunts, and I come back 'ere with a perishin' bread sack bulgin' with tins of crab, and pork and beans, and Maconochie, and fags by the 'undred. Proper Christmas day in the workus, it was."

Rawley broke one of the board-like biscuits by hammering it on the post beside him and dropped a piece into his tea to soften. "Who is Kelly?" he asked.

"Kelly! Why, he's the perishin' Fairy Queen. A bloke what's a sight too free with his dukes—so it don't do to argue with 'im."

"I see," said Rawley. "Sort of unofficial O.C. devastated area. A deserter, I suppose?"

Alf nodded and went on between spasms of mastication. "He's an Aussie. They say he shot a perishin' red-cap down at Etapps. I ain't never seen his billet 'cause he don't encourage visitors, but they say he lives like a bloomin' duke, down there in the old Jaeger Redoubt—armchairs, brass beds, and a pianner—proper Buckin'am Palace it is, from all accounts."

Rawley refilled his teacup by dipping the mustard tin into the can of tea on the fire. "Stuff he's looted from round about, I suppose," he remarked.

Alf nodded. "And then he's got 'is lidy friends in Armeens. They brings 'ome some passionate Percy, and while he's gettin' on with the love-making, Kelly socks 'im one and takes the dibs."

"What! Do you mean he goes into Amiens and lives with women there!"

"Lord, yes! And brings two or three tarts out 'ere when the red-caps get busy in Armeens. He's a proper coughdrop, he is—he and his perishin' bodyguard."

"Bodyguard!"

"Yars. That's what we calls 'em. They're his mates he brought with him from Etapps. About half a dozen of 'em, and they ain't arf a 'ot lot neither. They all mess together in the Jaeger Redoubt, and they've got Lewis guns, Vickers, and bombs, and thousands of rounds of ammo. It would take a bleedin' brigade to clean them out."

From force of habit Rawley took his pipe from his pocket, and then remembering that he had no tobacco, he put it back. But Alf jumped up from his box and thrust his arm into a hole in the revetting boards. He returned to the table with one hand held behind his back, and then, in the manner of a conjurer, made some elaborate passes with the other hand, and finally produced a dusty half-packet of ration tobacco from behind his back.

"No, I say," said Rawley. "I can't take that. Is that all you've got?"

"Go on," persisted Alf magnanimously. "I smoke fags." And he took a half-smoked cigarette from behind his ear and lighted it at the candle.

Rawley filled his pipe with the dry dusty mixture in the packet and drew at it appreciatively. "How do you—that is we—stand with regard to Kelly and his push?" he asked.

"We keep out of their perishin' way," answered Alf. "But when he has one of his field days—cleanin' out a canteen or something—after he and his lot have taken their fancy he lets us other chaps muck in."

"Who are the other chaps?"

"Why the chaps that don't belong to Kelly's bodyguard There's several of us livin' round 'ere in these old trenches mostly working in pairs. But I never took to any of 'em, and kept on me own."

"And you and the other chaps have nothing to do with Kelly?"

"Not more than we can help."

"But you were with him tonight. You said it was Kelly who took my money."

"Yars. He copped me and Pearson for a fatigue."

"Fatigue! He makes you do fatigues for him?"

"Yars. Carrying water this was, only he heard your perishin' footmarks on the *pavé* and he shoves me into a hole and tells Pearson to arsk you for a light; and then ups and socks you with a bit of sandbag."

Rawley nodded thoughtfully. "We must get our own back on Mr. Kelly one of these days," he said.

"I'm with you there, mate," agreed Alf. "Only he carries a gun and I ain't forgot about that perishin' red-cap at Etapps."

Rawley yawned and pulled back his cuff, only to remember that his wrist watch had been taken. "How the deuce do you ever know the time!" he said. "Though I suppose it doesn't matter out here."

"No, nor the date neither," agreed Alf. "But I know both," he added with an air of pride. From his breeches' pocket he fished a battered Ingersoll tethered by a greasy lanyard to his braces. "Brigade time is eleven fifty-three pip emma," he announced. "And the dite is"—he peered at a small calendar that hung among the pictures of actresses above his frowsy bed—"is the thirteenth."

"I might have known it," remarked Rawley cynically.

"Now don't get down'earted, mate! 'Ere you are, spending a holiday in Sunny France for nothin'. Why, you'd pay quids to come to a plice like this in peace time!" And he began to whistle cheerfully "Roses in Picardy!"

To his amazement Rawley leapt from his box and, with a face white with passion, shouted: "For God's sake stop that row."

"Orl right, orl right," answered Alf in an injured tone. "I thought a little music might cheer you up."

Rawley plumped down again on the box. "Never whistle that tune again," he said vehemently. "Never let me hear it again."

Alf produced a pile of sandbags from his dump of salvage, and with these and a mud-caked spare blanket Rawley made his bed. He pulled off his field boots and put a sandbag on each foot. As he took off his tunic his thumb slid into the little waist-band pocket and encountered crisp paper, and it was then that he remembered that he had absent-mindedly put the change from a fifty-franc note there. He transferred the notes quietly to his breeches pocket. He was glad they had escaped the fingers of Kelly; they might be very useful later on. He regretted the loss of the other money, but still more he regretted the loss of the wallet that contained it; for behind a mica shield in one flap was a photograph of Berney. He took off his collar and tie, and was ready for bed.

Alf blew out the candle, rolled himself up in his frowzy blankets, and cried " 'Appy dreams"; but for a long time Rawley lay awake watching the dying embers glowing in the darkness and listening to Alf's heavy breathing and the scurryings of rats.

CHAPTER XIV

I

RAWLEY awoke cold and stiff the next morning. The warm light of flames flickered on the dark-brown earth-wall of the dug-out, and the dancing shadow of Alf as he knelt before the brazier was bent grotesquely where the head and shoulders overlapped on to the ceiling.

Rawley put on his tunic and pulled on his boots. He thrust his hands into his breeches' pocket and with tousled hair stamped up and down the narrow space. Another tin of bully-beef and two of the hard, unappetising biscuits constituted breakfast, but the strong, hot tea was very welcome. He felt his stubbly chin and eyed his grimy hands as he warmed them on the tin of hot liquid, but there was no water to spare for washing. The source of supply was a well in the flattened village they had stumbled through the night before, and in the dug-out Alf had enough for drinking purposes only.

After breakfast, however, they set out carrying the three petrol tins possessed by Alf and an old and bleached canvas bucket of which he was very proud. Rawley followed him through the hole under the landslide into the grey daylight of a rainy autumn morning. They clambered out of the muddy, weed-grown trench and set off for the village. A cold, blustering wind drove the rain in their faces. Alf had a tattered ground-sheet tied with string about his shoulders, but Rawley could only turn up the collar of his tunic about his collarless neck.

In daylight the place was even more depressing than at night. They were descending a gentle slope into a wide depression, bisected by a narrow and half-obliterated road. The low weed-grown banks of old trenches straggled in all directions. Here and there wooden stakes or bent screw pickets grew forlornly from the barren soil, and tangles of barbed wire lay like black cobwebs on the tortured earth. To the right, in the lowest part of the depression, the narrow road petered out, and the brimming shell holes lay in such profusion as to produce the illusion of a vast net—countless circles of stagnant, scum-covered water strung together by narrow strips of barren soil. A few ragged walls and blackened tileless rafters marked the site of a village, and half way up the slope beyond, the bleached and ragged trunks of a leafless wood stood gaunt and dead, like hop-poles beneath the low, grey clouds. The only distant view showed the same desolate country undulating in a dreary tundra to the rain-swept horizon.

The two men, trudging through the mud, seemed to be the only living things in the landscape, and when a solitary bird rose ahead of them and shot away on the wind, Rawley exclaimed, "By jove, there's a pigeon!"

Alf pulled his dripping ground-sheet closer about his shoulders. "Going back to the perishin' Ark," he growled.

They reached the village through which they had stumbled in the darkness of the previous night. By daylight it was but a few parallelograms of ragged, foot-high walls, though here and there a blackened rafter or a bent and rusty iron bedstead protruded from the weed-grown rubble of brick and plaster. Alf led the way to the well, and they filled the three cans with water. Then Rawley stripped to the waist and washed as well as one can in a leaky canvas bucket without soap or towels. He put on his damp shirt and sodden tunic, and they plodded back up the slope.

II

These first few days in the devastated area were active ones for Rawley. He had no desire either to meditate upon his position or to speculate about the future. The time that elapsed before sleep came to him each night in the tomb-like darkness of the dug-out was all too long for that purpose, and he realized that the hours of daylight must be fully occupied if the fruitless thought cycle of bitterness, desperation, and despair was not to daze his reason.

He threw himself feverishly into task after task. Many journeys were made to the lifeless wood on the hillside, and the splintered branches were dragged to the dug-out and stacked for firewood. The accumulated filth of months was swept from the dug-out floor, stuffed into a sack, and emptied into a shell hole. Some measure of comfort was introduced into the cheerless den. Among Alf's gleanings from that once populous trench system were a pair of wire-cutters, some rusty nails, and an old German saw-bayonet; and with these simple tools Rawley constructed shelves on which to stow their belongings, a wire-netting bed for himself and—his greatest triumph—an easy chair with wire-netting seat and back.

But all this was not done in a day nor all at once. Many hours were spent in exploring the neighbouring and more remote trenches in search of the salvage on which they depended for their supplies.

It was the pioneer-like atmosphere of these expeditions that appealed to Rawley. Tramping through those deserted trenches that stretched with all their ramifications mile after mile across that wilderness of grass-grown shell holes, rubble heaps, and dead, shivered trees, he could well imagine himself to be an explorer who had stumbled upon the mouldering dwellings of some dead and long-forgotten race. And down in those burrows underground where they had lived were the evidences of that race—evidences that sometimes told a story of comedy or tragedy more eloquently than any of the excavations in ancient Pompeii. For sometimes he would enter a dug-out to find it just as its former occupants, German or British, had left it; mouldy blankets on the beds, a half-burned candle stuck to the table, illustrations torn from magazines pinned to the walls and bearing dates in 1915 and 1916, half packets of mildewy cigarettes, and once a gramophone with a warped record on the turntable.

Alf, however, was interested only in the practical side of these explorations. He inspected an abandoned dug-out with the speed and thoroughness with which a tramp will go through a dustbin, often taking objects which Rawley would have considered not worth salving, but unerringly rejecting the really worthless. On the good days they would return to their dug-out with their sacks stuffed with an odd variety of lumber: a tin or two of bully beef maybe, half a dozen candle ends, a few periodicals and tattered books, a mud-encrusted puttee and a grimy sock, a chipped enamel mug and a rusty fork, and perhaps a frowzy blanket or an old gum boot. One day they found an unopened drum of paraffin and were heartened during the long and difficult journey back to the dug-out by the knowledge that it was many future hours of cheerful light that weighed so painfully on their shoulders.

On these expeditions they seldom saw a soul. Occasionally in the distance Rawley saw one of the other outcasts moving furtively across country to disappear presently into some burrow. They were like rats that appear for a few moments in search of scraps and then go to earth again. Occasionally among the rubble heaps of a flattened village the figure of an old peasant woman would be seen wandering forlornly in search of some relic that would identify a particular heap as her home. Only on the few main roads that switchbacked across that desolate country, straight and white like the wake of a ship on the ocean wastes, was there any constant movement. Sometimes on his salvage expeditions Rawley came within sight of one of these, and from the shelter of the wilderness would watch a company of infantry trudging towards the Line, or a convoy of supply lorries roll by on the distant road. Once he saw a battery of eighteen pounders on the march and crept closer. Water ran from the shining steel helmets of the men and their heads were sunk low in the upturned collars of their British warms as they jogged along slowly through the rain. No doubt they were cursing the mud, the weather, and the Line that lay ahead, but Rawley envied them with all his heart.

III

One morning, when the December sun had broken through the clouds, and the wet weeds and grass that straggled over the trench side glittered in the cheerful light, Rawley was returning to the dug-out with a petrol tin of water. He rounded a crumbling traverse, and in the old fire-bay beyond came suddenly face to face with a stranger. The man had evidently heard him coming, for he was waiting there in the middle of the old fire-bay with one hand thrust into his breeches' pocket, and his eyes, as they met Rawley's startled look, wore an expression of amused and contemptuous hostility.

He was a very big man, standing well over six feet, and the service rifle that was slung by a strap over one broad shoulder looked little bigger than a boy's air-gun. He was hatless and collarless and wore a civilian tweed jacket, undone so as to display a dirty pink flannel shirt. Beneath the jacket a bulging revolver holster was attached to the leather belt which supported his khaki cord riding breeches. Mud-spattered field boots completed the equipment.

Rawley had recovered from his surprise and was about to pass on, but the big man turned slowly and put one of his feet on the crumbling fire-step, thus blocking the way. He did not speak, but he continued to regard Rawley with the same baleful and disconcerting smirk.

Rawley put down the petrol tin and broke the silence: "Well!" he said.

The other continued to regard him for a few moments longer in silence. "Well!" he repeated at last, in a deep, gruff voice. "And what the hell do you think you're doing here?"

Rawley was feeling uncomfortable under the man's intense and hostile gaze, but he shrugged his shoulder and answered, "Much about the same as you, I suppose."

The other grunted and spat. "And who the hell asked you to come?"

"No one," answered Rawley. "But I should have thought there was enough room for both of us in this God-forsaken place."

The other raised his eyebrows and nodded his head. "Oh, you would, would you! Well, that depends." He rested his elbow on his upraised knee. "And so you're a deserter, Mr. Officer! I've heard of you." And his eyes travelled slowly and insolently over the stained braid on the cuff of Rawley's unbuttoned tunic, the tarnished buttons, the collarless shirt, unshaven chin and tousled hair. "And you got the wind up when the guns went bang, and ran away, eh!" he continued slowly, with curling lip.

Rawley controlled his temper with great difficulty. "It's true I'm a deserter," he retorted, "but not through cold feet. And what the hell has it got to do with you, anyway!"

The other withdrew his foot from the fire-step and grinned unpleasantly. "What it's got to do with me is that I don't want white-livered little bastards crawling round here. Do you understand that, little Mr. Officer?" And very deliberately he dealt Rawley a stinging blow across the face with his open palm.

Rawley staggered sideways with flaming cheek, and then leapt forward in fury. His left cracked home on the big man's jaw; his right thudded into the big body. The man stepped back out of reach, slipped the rifle from his shoulder, and put up his fists. Rawley went at him again. He got one more blow in under the long arms, and then one of the huge fists shot out and knocked him off his feet on to the floor of the trench.

He struggled up again painfully. The big man stood waiting for him with an anticipatory grin on his face. Rawley went for him again, but he had no chance. The big man was not only vastly superior to him in weight, height and reach, but was also more than his match in skill. Rawley feinted and dodged and hit desperately, but the big man blocked all his punches, and, waiting for a favourable moment, very deliberately and scientifically dealt Rawley a blow on the jaw that rattled every tooth in his head and stretched him almost senseless on the floor of the trench.

He lay motionless for a few moments. Then slowly and painfully, by digging his fingers into the wall of the trench, rose shakily to his feet. He was covered in mud from head to foot and the blood from a cut lip furrowed the grime on his chin. He tottered a pace towards his opponent who stood watching him with arms akimbo, but his shaking legs gave way and he collapsed.

The big man sat down leisurely on the fire-step. He gripped the back of Rawley's tunic with one huge hand, and yanked him on to the fire-step beside him. Then he took a cigarette case from his pocket, stuck a cigarette in the corner of his mouth, and pushed the case under Rawley's nose. Rawley, sick and giddy, leaning back against the trench wall, shook his head; but the big fellow shoved the case against his chest and growled menacingly, "Go on, take one."

Rawley raised a shaking hand and fumbled at the case, whereupon the fellow plucked out a cigarette, unceremoniously jerked up Rawley's chin with his hand, and poked the cigarette between his lips. Then he struck a match and lighted both cigarettes.

"Um. You've got more guts than I thought," he said presently, in a voice that was almost friendly. "What did you desert for if it wasn't cold feet?"

Rawley did not reply.

"Come on now," growled the other, in his old menacing tone. "And the truth, mind, or I'll knock your flaming head off."

Rawley turned his aching head slowly and looked at the weather-beaten face thrust close to his own. "I don't see what the hell it's got to do with you," he said. "But if you must know, I quarrelled with a senior officer and hit him."

The other blew a cloud of smoke from his nose and looked at Rawley sideways. "What did you hit him for?" he demanded, after a pause during which he seemed to have been considering whether he could believe this.

"He was one of those swine who always wangle out of unhealthy jobs," answered Rawley. "And when during a little shelling he wanted to stop a fellow's leave so that he himself could go back out of it, I saw red."

"Saw red!" echoed the big man contemptuously. "Why didn't you shoot him? That sort's best dead."

"He is," said Rawley. "That's why I'm here. He went over backwards and broke his neck."

The other chuckled. "Well, that's not so bad after all," he conceded. He stood up and slung the rifle over one shoulder. "Well, Mr. Neckbreaker, understand that I'm boss here, and you'll have to hit damned hard to break my neck. Get in my way and—phut!" He made a significant movement with his fingers. "Jump to it when I give the word, and you can take your pickings with the rest." And with that he turned and sauntered off round the traverse.

IV

The degrading discomforts of the life worried Rawley. He had borne discomforts with the battery patiently and cheerfully, for they were part of the necessary business of getting on with the war; but filth and squalor were hard to bear when the sense of mortification for the common good was lacking. In the gun-pits some degree of personal cleanliness was always attainable. In times of stress one might have to wait two or three days for a shave; and even if one became lousy, always sooner or later came the luxury of a hot bath and clean underclothes. But living here, in an abandoned dug-out of the devastated area, he had to go unshaven. He had no razor. He had no soap, except when he was lucky enough to find a hard, gritty morsel in one of the old trenches. He had only the clothes he stood up in, and they were filthy. One night he heated a can of water on their fire and washed his undergarment as well as he could without soap. He stood wrapt in a blanket during the task, and when he put on his clothes on the following morning they seemed little cleaner for all his efforts.

The matter did not worry Alf; but Rawley found it insupportable. What he needed was a change of undergarments. It was impossible to go frequently through that ordeal of going naked, but for a blanket, while one washed the garments and waited for them to dry.

He found a way out of the difficulty one evening at dusk when he found himself in the neighbourhood of a shattered village. This village lay on the outskirts of the devastated area, and though badly battered was more than a mere heap of brick and rubble. Tiles were gone from the roofs; walls stood ragged against the sky, and many of them were but tumbled piles of bricks, but the shell of many of the cottages remained.

The whole front wall of one cottage had been removed by shell or bomb as neatly as though sliced by a knife, and the interior gaped open to the street like a doll's house with the front removed. Bricks and smashed furniture littered the floors and faded paper hung in strips from the walls. A staircase with a shattered banister-rail led upstairs to a room where overturned bedroom furniture hung precariously on a sagging floor and threatened an avalanche into the street. Odds and ends of garments were mixed up with the litter, and against the back wall of that upper room was a chest with half-open drawers spilling clothes.

It was these that Rawley coveted. One or two of the less damaged cottages on the outskirts of the village were occupied by an A.S.C. unit, and two Nissen huts stood in a weed-grown field nearby. Otherwise the village and the surrounding country were deserted.

Rawley lay down to wait for darkness.

Lights appeared in the occupied cottages and in the Nissen huts. The strident screech of a gramophone was wafted fitfully on the breeze. Outside one of the huts a man was singing, and the silhouette of his head and shoulders came and went against the light square window. Then he opened the door, releasing for a moment a flood of light and a strident burst of gramophone, and closed it behind him.

Rawley entered the tiny village from the other end and flitted along the road to the cottage. He picked his way cautiously over the bricks and fallen furniture on the ground floor. He groped his way step by step up the cranky staircase, praying that it would not collapse beneath him. Fortunately that chest of drawers was against the wall where the sagging bedroom floor would be at its strongest. He sidled along with his back to the wall and reached the chest.

The top drawer was half open. He put in his hand and pulled a bundle of damp clothing on to the top of the chest. He held up the garments one by one in front of him so that their outlines showed against the night sky, framed in the shattered cottage front. They were all women's clothes. He tried to get at the next drawer, but the top drawer was warped with the damp and would neither close nor come out. The next drawer itself was slightly open, but would not move further. He was afraid to pull hard lest he should send the whole chest toppling down the sloping floor into the road. He tried the bottom drawer. It did not move. He pulled again harder, and to his joy the front came out in his hand. He pulled out the pile of garments inside, and tested them against the night sky. They were men's garments.

He took trousers, shirts, pants, vests and socks and rolled them into a bundle under his arm; but before he could move away the lights of a car or lorry flooded the road below him, and he crouched motionless and helpless beside the chest till the dark shape of a lorry rumbled past and the road was dark again. Then he sidled back along the wall to the little landing. As he groped his way round to the head of the staircase his head became enveloped in something hanging on the wall. It was a damp-smelling jacket. He took it and went cautiously down the cranky stairs and out across the road to the open country.

CHAPTER XV

I

T HE question of supplies became acute. They discussed ways and means. "Kelly copped a lorry full of canteen stores the other day," said Alf.

"How did he manage it?" asked Rawley.

"Well, he knew all about the lorry, you see—where it was going and what time. He and another chap stopped it on the road and got a lift. There was two chaps on the lorry. One chap driving and another bloke on the back. Kelly and his mate sat in front beside the driver. Then when they got to a bit of road with nothing in sight, Kelly loses his cap, and the driver stops for him to pick it up. Kelly and his mate jumps down, picks up the cap, and then Kelly goes to the front of the lorry and says to the driver: 'Struth, look 'ere!' 'What is it?' says the driver. 'You come and have a look,' says Kelly, staring hard at the ground. So out jumps the driver and comes round to have a look. 'Where?' he says. 'Under there,' says Kelly. And when the bloke bent down to look, Kelly lays him out with his little sandbag. Then he calls the chap at the back: 'Here, something's wrong with your mate.' So out jumps the other chap, and while he is bending over his mate, Kelly slogs him too. Then they drove off, cached all the stuff and burnt the lorry. He's a one, is Kelly. All canteen stuff, too—tinned crab, Ideal milk; proper stuff, I tell you."

"Yes, but we aren't going to do any sandbagging," objected Rawley. "I don't mind relieving the E.F.C. of some stuff, but I draw the line at that."

"We might pinch some stuff from a ration dump," suggested Alf.

"That's more like it," said Rawley. "The Q.M.G. owes me some rations."

Alf grinned. "I know the very place," he went on eagerly. "They bring the stuff up by lorry at about ten at night, and the horse transport collects it at about six in the morning."

"How far away?" asked Rawley.

"Goodish way. Ten kilos about."

"That's all right. So long as it's not too near home."

"They take about an hour to unload. Then we shall have to wait for the blokes at the dump to go to sleep. I know, 'cause I won a sack of bread from there before."

"What about sentries?"

"Only one. We can dodge him or pull a sack over his head."

"We'll dodge him. If the G.S. wagons come at six, the dump men won't turn out before five. That gives us five hours or thereabouts. We ought to be able to take a lot of stuff in that time without being seen."

They set out soon after dark carrying empty sacks. A drizzling rain was falling, and they trudged along over the rough ground with old waterproof sheets round their shoulders. The usual pale flickerings of gun flashes rippled to and fro on the eastern horizon. Rawley trudged along in gloomy silence. Darkness and the mechanical exercise of walking always stimulated his thoughts. And they always followed the same cycle. They began with a nagging sense of impotence and resentment, passed on to bitter comparisons between his present predicament and his previous happiness, took refuge in re-living and idealizing that happiness, came back to reality and groped desperately for some hole in the net which entangled him, and finding none, refused to think of the future and took refuge in the present.

His thoughts followed that course tonight. This expedition that sent him a dirty, unshaven, bedrabbled outcast tramping through the wilderness with a guttersnipe to steal from a dump disgusted him. Only necessity had made him consent to it. But having consented he found excuses for it. The primitive law of self-preservation overrode all others. Even in civilized English law it was held on occasion to abrogate that paramount one, thou shalt not kill. There was a distinction between taking Government stores and ordinary theft. Men in no such predicament as himself "won" or "scrounged" things and boasted of it. But it was the pettiness and meanness of it that disgusted him. It was a skulking mean business for one who had been an officer. Open brigandage would be less repugnant.

He alternated between two states of mind. On the one hand he clung desperately to some shreds of self-respect, arguing that Lieutenant Peter Rawley, R.F.A., and the unshaven outcast of the devastated area were the same person, and should be governed by the same rules of conduct. There was an outward transformation due to force of circumstances. The inner man was the same. Other circumstances might reverse the transformation. He must keep his self-respect. Were that once lost it would need more than a bath, a shave, and new clothes to restore it.

On the other hand his common sense told him that there should be no connection between these two Peter Rawleys. They lived in different worlds amid different environments. And man was the product of his environment. Morality was a question of geography. There was no fixed universal code. And to all intents and purposes the two Peter Rawleys lived in different continents. The rules of conduct which applied to the one should not apply to the other. The rules of European society were evolved for that society and applied to him no more than to the natives of Central Africa. He was now a deserter and an outlaw; common sense demanded that he should live as a deserter and an outlaw.

The native of Central Africa, living according to the rules of conduct of his society, is content. But the European living in their midst must forget Europe if he conforms to those rules. Rawley could not forget. As he trudged on through the darkness his eyes saw the cheery cottage mess-room, Piddock clog dancing to the gramophone, and poor old Whedbee, spectacles on nose, reading his paper. He saw the gun-pits and the gunners dappled with the shadows of the camouflaged netting. He heard Piddock's cheerful laugh, Whedbee's slow, deliberate voice, and Cane's crisp word of command. He felt again that unexpressed cheerful spirit of comradeship that seemed to say "we are all in this rotten show together; let's make the best of it—a short life and a gay one." And now he was out of it all and alone. And he saw the little table beneath an apple tree outside a French village *estaminet*. He heard Berney's voice say, "Peter, hadn't we better be frank." He saw her eyes in the shadow of her hat, misty, and very tender. "And, of course, I like you, too, Peter—most awfully."

Alf's high-pitched voice and atrocious accent dissolved the picture. "Along this 'ere track, maite."

Rawley dragged his thoughts back to the present and jumped the ditch to a muddy track. The throbbing drone of a night bomber passed over their heads and died away.

"What made you take to a country life?" asked Rawley.

"What cher mean? Bunk from the perishin' battery?"

"Yes. But don't tell me if you don't want to."

Alf trudged along for a moment in silence. "Oh, I don't mind tellin' yer," he said presently. "You see, it was like this. We was up at Arras on the Ridge. The Canuks had been pushin' Jerry off the top, and he was crumpin' everything something awful. Talk about mud! Struth! Ten horse teams got stuck with a half-limber and wouldn't budge. So we started sending up ammo on pack horses. We had a lot of canvas bags with pockets in 'em. You slung the bag across the horse's back and put three or four rounds of eighteen-pounder in the pockets on each side. Me and some more blokes was taking up about a dozen pack horses when Jerry opened out. The first two landed on the side of the track and set the horses kicking. The next landed under the bombardier and blew him and a horse into a shell hole twenty yards away. Then things started properly. There was a sausage balloon up that must have been spotting for them. Proper merry hell it was. I was hanging on to a head rope and the bitch was pullin' my perishin' arms out. Then Nobby Clarke let go, and his horse came backwards into mine and sent it arse over tip. I rolled out of the way into a shell hole, and when I looked out, there was my bastard streakin' away like a Derby winner.

"I didn't worry about that. I stayed where I was till it got a bit quieter. Then I crawled out and had a look round. There weren't nothing there except two or three dead horses and a lot of crump holes. So I started back. Then I met a battery sergeant-major with some blokes. 'Where are you off to?' says he. So I told him what happened. 'Where are the rest, then?' says he. 'Gone on, I expect, sergeant-major,' I says. 'Then find your perishing beast and go after 'em,' says he. 'What the hell do you mean by coming back before you've handed over your ammo to the battery.'

"Back I went. But there weren't no horse in sight and Jerry was crumping the track ahead; so I cut away off to the right and started back again. I done about half a mile when up pops that bleedin' sergeant-major again. 'Hullo,' says he. 'You've been quick.' I started to explain, but he would'n hear nothing. 'I know what's wrong with you, my lad,' says he. 'You're under arrest.' And he tells another bloke and a bombardier to take me back.

"'What are they going to do with me, bombardier?' I says. 'They'll shove you in the stragglers' cage, I expect,' says he. 'And then you'll be for a court-martial.'

"Well, when we came over a hill and I see a lot of huts and a lot of Jerrys in a prisoners' cage and a couple of our blokes in a little cage beside it, I says to myself, 'Alf, once you're in that cage your number's up.'

"Just before we reached the cage we crossed a road and the bombardier stopped on the other side to arsk a bloke something. While we was standing there a long convoy of lorries come along and so I says to the bloke beside me, 'Lord, look at Jerry up there!' He looks up, and I dodges across the road between a couple of lorries. There were a lot of huts on the other side, and the first thing I see is a box with a knife on it and a dixie and a lot of spuds beside it. I whipped off my coat, and cap, sat down on the box and started peelin' spuds. I kep' my head down, but I heard a lorry put on its brakes quick and a bloke cursing and blinding, and then out of the corner of my eye I saw the bombardier and the other chap dodge out from between two lorries. They stopped a moment and looked each way, and the bombardier sings out to me, 'Hey, chum, did you see a chap run across the road just now? Which way did he go?' I pointed with the knife over my shoulder, and they set off running up the hill behind me. Then I went off quick the other way."

"And here you are," said Rawley.

Alf grunted. "Here I bleedin' well am."

II

They trudged on through the darkness and the drizzling rain. Far away to the left an occasional moving light showed where one of the straight main roads switchbacked uncompromisingly across the desert. Alf waved a hand in its direction. "There 'yare," he said. "That's it. And when we get there we've got about another two kilos to the ration dump."

The track converged upon the road, but they did not follow it to the junction. The road itself, they felt, was unsafe for such as they. Lorries or cars passed intermittently and parties of men might be met too suddenly to allow of concealment. They turned off the track and moved parallel with the road. The going was rough and boggy, but it was safe. More than once, however, they lost direction in the darkness and blundered nearly on to the road or found themselves wandering out into the desert again. Then the lights of a passing lorry would enable them to recover direction.

They halted at length opposite three or four lights, one of which, in the shape of a square, came unmistakably from a window covered with aeroplane fabric. "That's it," said Alf.

They crept forward cautiously to reconnoitre. The dark outline of two Nissen huts took shape against the sky. Bordering the road was a low wooden structure like a railway platform. They settled down to wait. Two tiny lights appeared in the distance, disappeared and reappeared some seconds later nearer and larger. The hum of a car reached their ears, and then it flashed past, its headlights mottling the uneven surface of the road with shadows. Then darkness closed in behind it. A dimly lighted lorry rumbled slowly by, and the slap, slap, slap of a piece of loose rubber on one of the wheels was audible long after it had passed. In one of the Nissen huts men were singing. The words rose and fell with the rhythm: "We were sailing alo-ong on moonlight ba-a-ay. . . ." The rain still drizzled down; a loose bit of latrine canvas flapped mournfully in the gusty breeze.

Rawley pillowed his head on his arm and dozed. He was brought back to full consciousness by the sound of voices and Alf's elbow in his ribs. A number of men had come out of one of the huts, and the dark shapes of two lorries stood throbbing beside the platform-like structure on the roadside. There was an exchange of banter between the lorry drivers and the men from the huts and then the throb of the engines wavered and subsided. Dark figures moved in the rear of the lorries, chains clinked, and the backboards clattered down. The work of unloading began. Sacks, boxes, metal drums, cases, and a few stone jars were dumped on to the platform whereon an N.C.O. stood holding a lantern, and a sheaf of papers. At last the work of unloading, checking, and signing was done. The backboards were pushed up and secured; the drivers started their engines and climbed into their seats. A few cries of "Goodnight, George—Goodnight, Charley," and the lorries rumbled on their way.

The light from the open door of a hut fell upon four men staggering under the weight of a folded tarpaulin. They heaved it on to the wooden platform and pulled open the stiff folds. The sergeant held a lantern whilst they dragged it over the pile of rations and tied it down. Then the men clumped back towards the hut.

The watchers saw the corporal of the guard and heard the mutter of his voice as he read the guard orders to the sentry by the light of the open door. Then the door closed, and only the dull light from the windows shone through the darkness. Later these too were extinguished, and the sound of voices tailed off and ceased. Only the scrape of the sentry's boot on the road or the bump of his rifle butt as he ordered arms broke the silence.

Alf nudged Rawley. "What about it?"

"Yes. I think so," whispered Rawley.

They discarded their tattered ground sheets and crept towards the wooden platform. They moved cautiously, inch by inch, for the night was very quiet, and they had to feel their way over the rough ground in the dark. They reached the shelter of the platform and halted. Peering under it they could distinguish the dark bars of the sentry's legs on the road beyond as he shuffled his feet and hummed a tune. The platform itself was some three feet above them as they lay prone in the mud and opposite them the tarpaulin was secured by a lashing through an eyelet and round one of the platform supports.

Rawley rose on one knee and untied the lashing. "I'll go under and pass out the stuff," he whispered. He raised the tarpaulin over his head and cautiously rose to his feet. Inch by inch he wriggled himself over the edge on to the platform.

It was very dark under the tarpaulin, and he had to trust to his sense of touch. He knew that as long as he remained on that side of the platform and kept reasonably flat, the bulge of the tarpaulin, caused by the pile of rations, would mask from the sentry on the road any undulations caused by his passage. He was as it were in dead ground. But the shifting of box or case, quite apart from the danger of noise, might cause a movement of the tarpaulin or an alteration of its shape that might attract the sentry's notice. He must move only such boxes as did not actually support the tarpaulin.

His hands, feeling forward in the darkness, encountered the rough, hairy wood of a box. It was a small box, about three feet long and unopened. He had no means of knowing what it contained. He tried to lift it, but lying on his chest with his elbows to the ground he could use only a fraction of his strength. He dragged it an inch towards him, but the noise of its scraping on the planks, magnified in the confined space under the tarpaulin, made him hurriedly desist and lie motionless with straining ears.

But the sentry had not heard. Rawley heard the crash of his rifle butt as he ordered arms and stood at ease; then, after a few moments, he paced off again, humming. Rawley resumed his blind exploration. A bulky sack was the next object his hands encountered, and they told him that it contained bread. He took from his pocket the jack-knife he had salved and slit the coarse fabric. But even with bread he had to be careful. He found that when one or two loaves were removed the others tended to roll into the vacated places with quite audible bumps.

He started back with four loaves, but he found that with each arm stretched out encircling two loaves he could not get his elbows to the ground to support the weight of his body as he crawled. He had to leave two behind. He realized that the whole job would be a far slower one than he had anticipated.

Alf raised the tarpaulin as soon as he felt Rawley's body moving under it. He nodded approval of the bread and placed each loaf noiselessly in one of the sacks they had brought. Then Rawley went back and returned with two more loaves. It took him nearly half an hour to fill their sack with loaves.

Alf twisted up the top of the sack and put his mouth close to Rawley's ear. "That's enough bread," he whispered. "I'll take this back a bit and hide it in case we have to make a run for it later. See if you can find some tins of butter and Maconochie, mate. And don't forgit one of them jars of rum."

Rawley nodded and disappeared again under the tarpaulin. He dared not tackle the unopened cases; he wanted to find an open one from which he could take the tins one by one. He found a large square tin, no doubt containing tea, but remembering that thin tins of that nature are liable to produce sudden noises, he left it alone. Then his fingers touched the cool smooth side of a rum jar. He must take that, but the problem was how to move it. He crawled up beside it, and turned on his back. Cautiously he tipped the heavy jar over until it rested on his stomach; then with his knees slightly bent to form a cradle for it, he crawled backwards by means of his elbows and heels.

Alf's approval of this find was unstinted. He nodded his head emphatically several times, and in elaborate dumb show drank the health of the sentry on the road.

Rawley disappeared again under the tarpaulin. He crawled up beside one of the rough wooden cases, and guided by his sense of touch, inserted the blade of his jack-knife under the lid. He increased the pressure gradually, but the board did not move. A sharp jerk might do it, but that would almost certainly splinter the wood with an audible crack or produce a loud squeak as the nails were prised up. There was nothing for it but to explore farther in the hope of finding an opened box.

He began to burrow in among the cases and sacks and tins and crates. It was very slow work. The old civilian jacket he was wearing caught frequently on the corners of cases and held him, and he had to be particularly careful in moving his feet lest his boots should strike against a box or tin. But his perseverance was rewarded. Somewhere he judged near the middle of the dump he found several open cases partly full of tins. In the darkness he examined the contents by his sense of touch. In one case there was no mistaking the peculiar shape of bully beef; another held round flat tins that might contain either butter, salmon, crab or dubbing. In another the tins were round and long; that might mean jam or pork and beans. He took a sample of each and started back.

In the dim light they examined the booty, Alf kneeling in the rank grass and Rawley lying flat on the platform, with his head protruding from the tarpaulin. They classified it as one tin of butter, one tin of jam, one of pork and beans and one of rabbit. Alf nodded approval, and Rawley went back for more.

Inch by inch he wriggled in again among the sacks and cases, and reached the place where his outstretched hand should have touched one of the open boxes. Crates, sacks and cases hemmed him in, but none of them were open. In the dark, with only his sense of touch to guide him, he had gone astray. Somewhere within a yard or two of him must be those open boxes, but they were as completely lost as if they had been dropped into the sea, and he was seeking them on the ocean bed.

He lay still for a moment and tried to think out to which side he had strayed—to right or left. The planks of the platform on which he lay did not fit closely together; there were gaps between them through which blew chilly draughts, and now as he lay over one such crack he saw the coarse grey grass and earth below slowly dawn in the headlights of a car approaching along the road. The long shadows of the grass shortened and lengthened and moved this way and that as the car bumped over the pot-holed road, and the light increased rapidly like a stage dawn, till he could see worms twisting and glistening in the powerful flood.

He took his eye from the crack and tried to distinguish the dim shape of sacks and cases about him, hoping that enough light would filter through to allow him to find those open cases before the car passed. Then he realized that the car had stopped. The light had ceased to grow stronger; nor did it wane. The grass shadows were motionless and clear-cut like stage scenery. The low hum of the engine flared up and ceased. He heard the clatter of the sentry's rifle and the smack of his hand on the butt. Then followed the unmistakable clash of a car door being closed and the scrape of feet on the road.

It was time for him to go, he felt, but with those strong headlights flooding the tarpaulin the slightest movement would be noticeable. The footsteps were passing to the right, towards the huts, but he could still hear the scrape of the sentry's feet near him. He wondered what Alf was doing. Judging from the direction of the shadows of the grass and platform supports the car stood a few feet from the end of the platform, and its headlights would therefore light up all the ground beneath the platform and part of the back as well.

Voices sounded from the direction of the huts, and then came the tramp of several pairs of feet. The voices grew clearer. "Well, we'll just have this off and check up that chit and then I will get on," said one.

He heard men stumbling and moving on both sides of the platform, and he realized with chill that they were untying the lashings of the tarpaulin. Heavy boots clumped on the platform and made the boards vibrate beneath him. Then a strong beam of light revealed the upper part of the crate beside him, and he lay like a watcher in a dark valley when the sun is on the mountain tops. They stripped off the heavy tarpaulin; a sergeant swung a lantern, and he lay there uncovered like a wood louse when a brick is removed.

III

"Hullo! What the devil!" exclaimed the sergeant. And he reached out a hand and dragged the apparently sleeping figure to its knees. "What the hell are you up to?" he demanded, holding up the lantern, so that its light fell upon the disreputable figure.

"What's that, sergeant?" said a voice from the road. The sergeant jerked Rawley to his feet. "A Frenchy, sir, after rations. I found him here under the tarpaulin—shamming sleep."

Rawley was dragged down to the road where the lights of the car fell full upon him. An A.S.C. captain and subaltern eyed the miserable-looking object from head to foot. What they saw was an old man with bent shoulders and knees, long, tousled hair, grimy face and unkempt scrubby beard. He wore a dirty shirt of nondescript colour, no collar or tie, a tattered mud-stained jacket and baggy, muddy-kneed corduroy trousers, tied with string around his waist. His hands were filthy, and the nails long and black.

"Looks like the boy whom France forgot!" commented the subaltern.

The A.S.C. captain spoke in halting French. "*Qui êtes-vous? Que faites vous sous le—le drap là?*" He waved a hand towards the tarpaulin. "*Vous volez les choses Anglais*, eh?"

Rawley shook his head vigorously, and waved his hands in the manner of the French peasant, and then broke into a torrent of incoherence punctuated here and there with a word of French.

The officer rubbed his chin. "What the hell does he say. They all talk so damned fast. Look here, Mosu. *Parlez lentement, très lentement. Et prenez garde. Il est très serieuse pour vous.* Come on now. What—er—*que faites vous ici?*"

Rawley went off again into a torrent of incoherence, and then stood twisting his hands and wobbling his head in the manner of an old Frenchman he had seen suffering from shell-shock.

"He's dippy," said the subaltern.

"Or shamming," said the captain. "Search him, sergeant."

Rawley's pockets were turned out, but they revealed nothing more illuminating than an old jack-knife and some bits of string.

"Anything gone from the dump?" asked the captain.

"There's a bread sack slit open here," called one of the men presently. "And there's several loaves gone by the look of it."

"What has he done with them, I wonder," said the captain. "Can't have eaten several loaves." He turned again to Rawley. "*Vous avez prenez les pains, n'est-ce pas?*"

Rawley took refuge again in voluble incoherence.

"Oh, damn the fellow!" exclaimed the captain impatiently. "He's probably only some old daftie trying to steal a mouthful, but we had better hand him over to the French Mission or the A.P.M. Put him in the guard-room, sergeant. I will take him in to Peronne when I come back."

The corporal of the guard was called, and the prisoner was handed over. The corporal jerked his head towards the guard-hut and took his prisoner by the sleeve. "Come on, Charley," he said. And Rawley shuffled off between his captors.

The guard-hut was small, but its occupants consisted only of the corporal, the two men not on sentry-go, and their prisoner. A short form ran along the wall facing the door, and here Rawley sat, staring vacantly at the floor and twisting his hands and wobbling his head whenever he felt that eyes were upon him. He felt that his only chance was to sustain this role of a harmless half-wit in the hope that the guard would become careless and allow him an opportunity of making a sudden dash for it. He could not hope to deceive the A.P.M. with his incoherent pseudo-French.

The guard took little notice of him. The corporal read a tattered, paper-covered novelette by the light of a candle-end stuck in a tin, and the two men played some obscure card game on the floor. Once he heard a faint tapping on the wall of the hut behind him, and wondered whether Alf were trying to signal to him. He waited till the two men on the floor made some remark to each other, and then, under cover of the sound, he cautiously tapped back. An answering tap followed. It was cheering to know that he had not been abandoned, although it did not seem possible that Alf could be of any help at the moment.

The time passed slowly, and Rawley's hopes rose when the corporal glanced at the watch hanging on a nail above his head and said, "Just time for you to go on, Baker." For a few moments during which the relief took place there would be only one man in the hut. Then it ought to be possible to make a dash for it. But his hopes fell again when he heard the sentry's voice outside the door. "What's the time, corp? Ain't George ever coming on?"

The corporal tightened his belt and rose to his feet. "Come on," he said. One of the men also rose grumbling to his feet and took up his rifle. They went outside, and as Rawley had feared, the relief took place within a yard of the door. In a few moments the corporal was back again, and the relieved sentry was drinking tea from a canteen.

The men dozed, but always one of them was sufficiently awake to make any attempt at escape hopeless. Rawley sat on, sick at heart, fighting against his desire to sleep, hoping against hope that at the last moment some chance of escape, however desperate, would present itself. But none did. Dawn came and when the sound of voices and of men moving about outside told him that his vigil had been useless he allowed his eyes to close.

He was awakened by someone shaking his arm. One of the guard stood beside him with a mug of hot tea and a chipped enamel plate of greasy pork. "Here y'are, Charley. Muck in. Make your miserable life happy." He 'mucked in,' and the hot strong tea and the pork and bread, which was a banquet in comparison with his previous breakfasts of broken biscuit and bully, put new life into him.

IV

Towards the middle of the morning the captain of the previous night returned, and Rawley was taken from the guard-hut and put into the back of a car. "Here, Ellworthey, you come along with him," said the captain. "And see that he doesn't jump out." An A.S.C. private climbed in beside him, and the car moved off.

They went south through country new to Rawley, but the same dreary landscape stretched around him—weed-grown, shell-pitted earth, villages that were mere heaps of rubble, derelict huts, and woods that were clumps of bare, white splintered poles. Occasionally the truncated chimney of a *sucrerie* stood ragged against the sky or a rusty perforated water tank hung drunkenly on its twisted supports. The road switchbacked through the wilderness between the white splintered corpses of its bordering tree stumps.

The car stopped before a house in one of the shattered streets of Peronne. A sentry stood on guard beside the two splinter-pocked brick pillars that led to the little rubble-littered garden beyond. The heavy iron gates were open; one of them lay among the weeds and tumbled bricks in the garden, and the other, rusty and ripped and perforated like a colander, hung crazily from one twisted hinge. Rawley was taken from the car and led over the broken pavement of the garden path towards the house. Many of the tiles had gone from the mansard roof and the rafters showed skeleton-like beneath. The ornate brickwork and stone facing of the windows was pitted by splinters, and the window spaces themselves were filled with yellow aeroplane fabric. He was led up three chipped stone steps to the hall and into a small room on the left.

He was relieved to find that it was a guard-room and not the office of the A.P.M., for desperately though he still clung to the hope of escape he could not disguise from himself how small his chances would be once he were examined by that officer. Outside in the hall the A.S.C. captain who had brought him to Peronne was talking to another officer, and he gathered from the conversation that he was to be lodged in the guard-room pending the return of the A.P.M., who was away at the moment.

The men of the guard were just about to have their dinner. They were taking mess-tins and knives and forks from packs which hung from nails on the wall. One of them in shirt sleeves and with tousled hair came in drying his face on a grubby towel, and a moment later there came a cry of "Dinner's up!" and a man entered carrying an iron dixie of hot stew. Rawley was given a share and a battered lead spoon to eat it with.

The men paid no attention to him; they sat on their kits on the floor and jabbered noisily as they ate. Rawley sat on the floor at one end of the room facing the door. The room was bare of furniture, and the plaster of the wall behind him was furrowed fan-wise by splinters that had evidently passed through a window in the wall on his left from a shell-burst outside. This was the only window in the room, and like those in the front of the house was covered with aeroplane fabric which imparted a warm, rich orange light, like summer evening sunshine. A black, twisted bit of wire, like a dirty bootlace, hanging from a broken ornamental medallion on the ceiling was all that remained of the electrolier, and the laths showed through in many places from which the plaster had fallen. The door was open, but Rawley's view of the narrow hall beyond was limited to a portion of the staircase with its banisters as it cut diagonally across the upper part of the doorway. Below the staircase was a small cupboard door standing ajar.

Occasionally men passed along the passage, men in shirt sleeves and often with greasy caps, and Rawley concluded that the old kitchens at the end of the passage were occupied by cooks and fatigue men. Feet also passed up and down the staircase, but they were visible only from the knee downwards. Some of them belonged to officers and some of them to men, and he guessed that the offices of this headquarter were upstairs, and that the ground floor was occupied only by the guard, cooks, and orderlies.

The time passed with torturing slowness to Rawley, who maintained his vacant stare at the floor, the restless twisting of his hands and nervous movement of his head. Nobody paid any attention to him. The men played their games, wrote letters, and argued as though he were not there. He could think of no plan of escape; he could only wait on events and seize the first chance that offered itself. At any moment the A.P.M. might return and his examination begin; but he was helpless. He could only wait and hope.

From outside a voice came faintly, "Turn out the guard." And then a powerful voice bellowed, "Guard! Turn out!" Immediately the guard-room was in a ferment. Men dropped the letters they were writing and the novelettes they were reading, leapt to their feet, seized their rifles, and ran out straightening their caps and equipment as they went. In a moment, with the exception of Rawley, the room was empty.

Rawley too leapt to his feet. Another such chance could not be expected, and in a moment or two the prisoner would be remembered, and one of the guard would return. He snatched up a fork that lay on top of a mess-tin and slit from top to bottom the aeroplane fabric covering the window. He parted the tattered remnants and prepared to vault through, but paused with his hand on the sill. Beyond it lay a brick and rubbish-littered yard, bounded by a high wall and the kitchens of the house. The cooks and fatigue men would probably see him, and even if he got away over the wall, he could hardly hope in daylight to escape the hue and cry which would be raised.

He left the window and tip-toed to the door. The hall passage was empty. From one end of it came the sound of the cooks' voices in the kitchens; from the other came the rattle of the rifles as the guard presented arms outside in the road. Upstairs a door banged and heavy footsteps sounded overhead. He whipped open the little cupboard door under the staircase and crept inside.

Heavy footsteps came down the stairs over his head, and he lay still till they had passed. Then he crept forward, feeling cautiously ahead with his hands. Dirt and old sacks was all that his fingers encountered and he crept on till the descending stairs which formed the roof barred further progress. He covered himself with a sack, wedged himself under the bottom stair, and lay still.

A moment later steps passed along the passage beside him, and then followed a sharp exclamation and a shout: "Corp! Corporal! Here! That old Frenchy, he's bunked." The corporal's voice was heard cursing outside, and several pairs of feet ran along the passage. Then the distant shouting told Rawley that the corporal and his men had gone through the window into the yard outside.

He could only trust to his ears to tell him how his chances varied from moment to moment. Men passed to and fro along the passage; footsteps went up and down the stairs over his head; three voices, one dominating one, raised in argument, sounded from the direction of the kitchens; in the guard-room across the passage a man was cursing to himself as he moved about, only the word "bloody" which occurred very frequently being distinguishable; and occasionally voices sounded distantly from the road or from the yard at the back. But no one opened the little door and looked under the stairs, and gradually the hurried movement ceased. The men were back in the guard-room; he could hear a low growl of voices, doubtless discussing his disappearance, and occasionally a voice was raised so that a string of oaths was distinguishable.

His hopes began to rise and he began to plan the next step. It was obvious that nothing could be done before night. Then, however, with darkness outside, the wandering orderlies and cooks in bed and asleep, and only the guard to elude, it ought to be possible to creep away. His present sense of some security produced relaxation, and he became acutely aware that he had not slept for many hours. He pillowed his head on his arm and dozed.

He was aware vaguely from time to time of footsteps passing over his head and of voices in the passage, and then came a long blank period from which he was aroused by a crash close beside his ear. He started up and struck his head with violence on the stair above. The bump restored him to consciousness of his surroundings, and with pounding heart he lay breathless in the dark, listening. Heavy footsteps were passing along the passage, and then came a second crash that he recognized as the thud of a rifle-butt on the floor. The footsteps died away and he breathed freely again.

He had been asleep for some time, he thought. The house was strangely quiet. No sounds reached him from the guard-room across the passage. Faint footsteps could be heard crunching the rubble of the wrecked garden outside; they rang out more clearly as they mounted the stone steps to the door, and then thudded loudly along the passage beside him, two pairs of them. They halted, moved on a pace or two, and then ceased. The corporal changing sentries, he thought. Faint sounds of movement reached him from the guard-room, and a muttered word or two, and then silence.

He waited what he judged to be ten minutes or a quarter of an hour, and then, disentangling himself from the sack, he crept towards the cupboard door. A faint strip of light that was just distinguishable from the surrounding darkness showed that it was ajar. He halted and held his breath while listening. The stair cupboard faced the guard-room door, and if that door were open any of the guard awake inside might see the cupboard door move. He would have to take that risk.

He waited another five minutes, and when still no sound reached him from across the passage he opened the door an inch.

He could see down the passage towards the rear of the house, but the passage was dark except for a faint glow close at hand which must come from the guard-room. Either the guard-room door was nearly closed or, if it were open, the light inside must be very faint. He opened the cupboard door another inch. Still no sound. He pushed it a further three inches and cautiously put his head through the opening.

The guard-room door was nearly closed, and the passage was illuminated only by the narrow bar of light which escaped from the candle inside. Rawley pulled in his head and considered the situation.

Should he crawl down the passage to the rear of the house, or up the passage to the front door? Down the passage to the rear seemed the obvious way to take, but somewhere in the rear of the house the cooks and orderlies were sleeping, there would be a door to open, and he did not know the geography of the house. In the front of the house a sentry was posted, but that grave disadvantage was somewhat counterbalanced by the fact that the breeze blowing down the passage had told him that the front door was open, and that he knew the lie of the land. He decided to try the front.

He opened the door a few inches more and crawled silently into the passage. Round the door he went, closing it behind him, and inch by inch past the partly open guard-room door. The sound of a slight movement came from within, and he crouched motionless and listening while debating what to do should someone come out into the passage. He would not be able to get back under the staircase. That door was closed. He would have to leap to his feet and bolt through the open front door.

But no further sounds came from the guard-room, and after a moment's pause he crawled on. It was a laborious progress, for he went on his knees, keeping the toes of his heavy boots up lest they should scrape on the floor. He rounded the angle of the foot of the staircase and reached the open door. The night breeze fanned his face. Cautiously he rose to his feet. There was not sufficient light behind him to betray him to the sentry on the road. He reached the edge of the top step, shifted his weight to one foot and leaned one hand heavily on the door post. Cautiously he lowered his foot to the next step and shifted his weight to it. He could not distinguish the sentry's form, but he could hear his feet scrape occasionally on the road.

He reached the bottom of the steps and stood on the narrow paved path that was gritty and liable to scrape underfoot. Under cover of a movement of the sentry he stepped off on to the rubble-littered garden. He went bent double and with great care to avoid displacing the fallen bricks, and reached the dividing wall. It was some seven feet high and ragged in places where the coping had been shattered. He chose a spot where the bricks seemed firm and moved a hummock of bricks and mortar to the foot. He was thankful that there was no moon. He could judge of the sentry's movements only by sound, and when he heard the familiar clash of sloping arms he mounted his stepping stone and drew himself up. The scrape of his toes against the bricks was drowned by the sentry's movement. He lay flat on the top of the wall for a few moments and peered into the darkness below him. Another wrecked and rubble-littered front garden lay there. He waited for the sentry to move off on his short beat, and then he lowered himself to the full extent of his arms and let go.

He landed on a pile of fallen bricks and rolled over. The noise made him lie still and listen, but when no sudden pause in the scrape of the sentry's boots on the road occurred he rose, reassured, and picked his way across the little court to the far wall. The gate to his right, leading on to the road, would be too close to the sentry for safety. He climbed the next wall into the next little garden and crept towards the gate, but the gate, a large iron one, hung crankily upon its hinges. There was not room enough to squeeze through, and if he attempted to open it farther it would creak abominably. He climbed the far wall and found the little forecourt beyond filled with a great mound of bricks and timber from a house which had fallen in. The wooden framework of the roof lay tilted across it.

His only course was to crawl over the rubble under the shattered roof; he dared not climb over the crazy beams. The going was slow and precarious. The fallen slates snapped under his weight and tended to slither over the bricks and rubble. Above him the gable timbers and fragments of slates still clinging to the laths showed like leafy branches against the night sky. He slithered gently down the far side of the heap of rubble and crept through the broken gate to the road.

He was now nearly fifty yards from the sentry, and the night was dark. He turned to his left along the street; another fifty yards should bring him to the open country. But he went slowly and cautiously. There might be other sentries in the street, and a sentry at night standing motionless against a wall is invisible from a distance of a few yards. He moved slowly and stopped often to listen. Once the lights of a lorry drove him from the road, and he crouched behind a broken wall till it had rumbled past, but though a light shone dimly here and there among the shattered buildings, he encountered no more sentries and passed the last few houses of the town in safety.

He was in a part of the country that was unfamiliar to him, and he could only follow the road along which he had come that morning in a car. It was a good fourteen miles, he estimated, to the ration dump where he had been captured, and he had to make a detour around huts and take cover when any vehicle approached; for it was probable that his escape had been made known to the troops in the immediate neighbourhood. The night seemed interminable as he tramped along, hour after hour, through the darkness, lit only by the faint flicker of gunfire on the eastern horizon, while the chill night breeze wafted to his nostrils the pungent scents of death and decay from the shattered country around him. The drizzling rain had turned to sleet and was silently covering the road with a thin carpet of white.

Dawn found him cold and wet, still trudging along the straight switchback road. The snow and sleet had ceased to fall, and his boots left wet black imprints on the road. Slowly the grey light strengthened over the snow-powdered landscape and revealed two low black Nissen huts crouching on the slope ahead. They looked forsaken and forlorn in that featureless desert, but he recognized in them the ration dump that had been the scene of his capture. Away to the right, converging on the road, was the track that he and Alf had followed. He cut across country to it and was soon out of sight of the dump; but it was well after midday when he stumbled through the flattened village by the well and ploughed through the melting snow and mud up the slope to the old trench and Alf's boudoir.

CHAPTER XVI

I

A LF sat on his frowzy wire-netting bed with his bare arms clasped about his shins. His scraggy bearded chin rested on his knees, and a half-smoked cigarette drooped from the corner of his mouth. A lock of dark tousled hair hung down over his contracted brows. His bright bird-like eyes were fixed on Rawley. Rawley, also in shirt sleeves, lay stretched full length upon his bunk, his eyes fixed broodingly upon the damp clay wall of the dug-out, his long-stemmed pipe clenched between his teeth.

For a week and more he had not been outside the dug-out except now and then to draw water from the well, or to bring in firewood, and even these necessary duties he performed only after blasphemous protest. His former restless energy had gone and was replaced by slothful moodiness. The oil lamp hanging from the great roof timber threw a yellow beam across the greasy, food-stained table and litter-strewn floor. The dug-out was filthier than on the night he had first entered it. He gave neither help nor encouragement to Alf's half-hearted and sporadic efforts to tidy it.

For the moment they had food in plenty. Alf had brought back the stores which Rawley had taken from the ration dump, and some days later Kelly had organized a raid on an E.F. canteen. After he and his immediate followers had taken what they wanted, the other outcasts had been allowed to help themselves. Rawley and Alf had filled two large bread sacks, and Rawley had seen to it that several tins of tobacco were among the booty. Ever since he had sprawled on his bunk, smoking and brooding. Sometimes he picked up a tattered magazine, only to fling it away after reading a page or two, and then he would refill his foul pipe while his eyes glowered sombrely at the damp clay wall before him.

Without unclasping his hands Alf worked the cigarette into the other corner of his mouth by moving his lips. "What's the use of gettin' chovey about it, chum? It ain't 'olesome," he said. "I always says it's a pore bleedin' heart what never rejoices." He removed the cigarette and spat on the floor. "Come on," he went on in a wheedling voice, " 'ave a bit o' life. 'Ave a bit o' guts." He hopped off his bunk and relighted his cigarette-end in the flame of the lamp. Then he perched again on the bed and began to sing: "She was po-ere but she was honest; the victim of a rich man's whi-im." He broke off to screw up his face and waggle one finger in his ear. He withdrew the finger, examined it critically, and went on again with gusto: "It's the saime the 'ole world over: it's the poor what taikes the blaime; it's the rich what take their pleasure. Ain't it all a bleedin' shai-ime."

Rawley took the tattered book from his knees and hurled it across the dug-out. "Shut up," he cried viciously. "Blast you!"

Alf took a cigarette from behind one ear and lighted it with the stump of the old one. Then he drew up his knees and began again. "Did I ever tell you about that little French bit I picked up at Lillers? Coo, she wasn't 'arf a hot little bitch . . ."

Rawley put his feet to the floor and got up menacingly. "Will you or will you not shut that foul mouth of yours?" he shouted.

"Orl right, orl right," grumbled Alf, and then added, when Rawley turned away, "I didn't know this was a flamin' Salvation Army!"

Rawley paced up and down the narrow dug-out, sucking fiercely at his pipe. "My God!" he complained. "Haven't I got enough to put up with without having to listen to your foul talk. Isn't it enough to have to endure your filthy habits? My God! Here I sit day after day in this damned pig-sty with a dirty little guttersnipe, who can talk about nothing except women and his belly." He turned fiercely and shouted, although Alf had not spoken: "Stop it, I say! Stop it! I'll wring that filthy unwashed neck of yours if you open your mouth again."

Alf assumed an expression of injured virtue and turned reproachful dark eyes on Rawley; but Rawley had turned away and now sat on his bunk with his head clasped in his hands. "I'm sick of this lousy hole," he groaned, and all the fire had gone from his voice. "My God! I'm sick of it."

Alf regarded him with hostility. "Oh, put a sock in it," he cried. "Do you think I like this perishin' bug-'ouse any more than you do? But what's the use of chewing the rag?" He spat with disgust. "You fairly give me the belly-ache, you do. Grouse, grouse, grouse!" He turned away and began to sing: "Grousin', grousin', grousin', always bloody well grousin', early in the morning from Reveille till Lights Out." The song had restored his natural cheerfulness, and he broke off to say in sympathetic tones: "Now looke here, chum, what we want is a bit o' cheerin' up. A bit of a sing-song. That's the stuff to put a 'eart into the troops." He scratched the back of his tousled head thoughtfully, and then his furrowed brow cleared. " 'Ere! I'll tell yer what we'll do." He smacked his thigh. "We'll go to the perishin' Pip Squeaks. Struth we will!" He fished his huge watch from an inner pocket and glanced at it. "They're over at Evigny, an' the hut's fifty yards from the 'ouses." He jumped off his bunk enthusiastically. "Come on. We can git right up close an' hear the 'ole bloomin' show buckshee."

Alf's enthusiasm had conveyed some shadow of interest to Rawley. He raised his head and said doubtfully, "Well, I suppose it can't be worse than staying here."

"Course not," said Alf. "Come on. 'An put a jerk in it, or we shall be laite for the orchiestra's openin' bars!"

Thus it came about that two dirty and dishevelled outcasts trudged several miles through the mud and ruin of the old battlefields to lie in a ditch beside an army recreation hut. But listening to the familiar choruses that swelled from within, they forgot that they were wet and muddy, they forgot the chill wind and the dreary desert around them, and they cursed when the rumble of a convoy of lorries drowned the voice of a singer.

"She'll tell you what you're ter do, dear, if you look in 'er eyes," sang Alf softly. "That's a fav'rite o' mine—that an' 'Thora.' Coo, I wish 'eed sing 'Thora'—lovely thing!"

Those familiar airs, drifting plaintively through the night, were a torture to Rawley. They were an insistent reminder of happier days and of all that he had lost, but he deliberately went down into the depths of despair, and found a melancholy joy in contrasting his present plight with that last occasion on which he had listened to a concert party. He recalled every incident of that evening—the comic bicycle ride with Piddock, the meal at the officers' club, Berney sitting close beside him in the crowded hut and the exact expression of her eyes in the shade of her hat and the intonation of her voice as she had turned to him and asked why he was staring at her. And then that walk to the village in the moonlight beneath the trees and the wonderful moment in the lane beside her billet. He recalled every look, every inflexion of her voice, and took a morbid delight in the pain he was causing himself.

Alf enjoyed himself thoroughly and chuckled with delight at the obvious humour of the comic songs; but Rawley, sunk in his abyss of self-pity, was silent, and when the plaintive air of "Roses in Picardy" came from the hut he dug his hands in the mud and groaned.

The singing of "God save the King" roused them, and they crept from the ditch and stole away. Alf chattered light-heartedly as they plodded through the darkness, but

Rawley, with his eyes fixed on the flickering gunflashes on the horizon, answered not a word.

II

Alf brought news one day of a projected raid by Kelly. "All I know is that it's tomorrow," he said. "They say it's on a canteen in a village, but they don't know really. Anyway, Kelly wants the whole issue tomorrow morning, so it's going to be a proper go. He ain't had the 'ole lot out for months. We'll take four of them sacks, and if we don't come back with a nice little lot of stuff it won't be my fault."

Rawley had not seen this band of outlaws at close quarters before, and when a little before midday they assembled in the neighbourhood of the old Jaeger Redoubt, he eyed them with interest. There were about thirty of them all told, and although they had all been soldiers and most of them wore some article of military clothing or equipment, a casual glance would not have revealed that fact. Thick plasterings of dried mud covered them from head to foot, and it was only on looking closer that one perceived such incongruities as a stained and tattered tunic above a muddy pair of civilian trousers or an old corduroy peasant jacket above an almost unrecognizable pair of military riding breeches. All were dirty and unshaven, and there were beards varying from short, black wiry stubble to dirty tangled growths several inches in length. Two or three wore civilian greatcoats that had once been black, and with the torn, mudstained skirts flapping about their legs and their untidy beards hanging down over the ravelled upturned collars they looked like outcasts from a ghetto. Some wore sandbags tied with string about their legs; others had made a hole for their heads in brown army blankets and fastened them round their waists with wire or rope. One man wore a coat of stained ground sheets laced together.

Hats were in keeping with other strange garments. There were two or three steel helmets, but torn and shapeless service caps, battered homburgs and greasy civilian caps predominated. There was also a battered straw, a bowler, and even a woman's bonnet. Several men carried rifles, and one or two had dirty web equipment buckled over civilian jackets and overcoats. And two men wore muddy field grey with faded red numbers on the shoulder-straps. These, Rawley learnt, were Germans who had been hiding in the devastated area with their former enemies ever since they had found themselves on the wrong side of the Line during one of the Somme battles of 1916.

The men stood about in groups of two or three, and what little conversation there was, was carried on in subdued tones. Each group kept to itself and displayed no desire for the companionship of another group. They eyed one another suspiciously and even hostilely. Evidently there was no camaraderie of common distress among this collection of outcasts. It was each man for himself.

When Kelly appeared at the head of his six intimates a hush came over the motley assembly. His appearance, though strange enough, was in striking contrast to that of the collection of dirty, ragged tramps before him. He wore a pair of polished field-boots, a mackintosh, and a German officer's cap with a shiny black peak. A leather belt supporting a revolver holster was buckled outside the mackintosh, and a rifle hung by a web sling from one shoulder. Behind him his six companions were dressed in varying combinations of military and civilian clothing, but all were shaven and clean. And their clothing, though incongruous, was unstained and apparently comparatively new.

He stood for a moment like a general at the head of his staff eyeing the scarecrows before him with a contemptuous little smile, and then he turned on his heel without a word and strode off. The tattered outcasts trailed after him.

On the long march which followed, the little groups preserved the aloofness which they had already shown during the assembly at Jaeger Redoubt, and when from time to time the roughness of the country necessitated a convergence upon a track, they waited sullenly for their turn and followed one another at intervals. And they debouched once more into scattered groups as soon as the nature of the country permitted. And yet as it seemed by tacit agreement, some sort of march discipline was observed; for when nearing a main road the groups made use of the contours of the ground to approach unseen, and crossed it one by one when absence of traffic made it safe to do so.

Three hours of marching brought them to the edge of the true devastated area. Before them lay a country in which woods, though damaged, were more than clusters of bare poles, and villages, though not free from the marks of war, were yet habitable. They halted in a wood while Kelly gave the final directions to his companions. The spot had been well chosen. Behind stretched the waste of the devastated area; before lay a village and cultivated fields. One narrow road meandered from the village over the bare downland beyond. Three or four miles away on a hill-top the spire of a church rose above a cluster of trees. Except for the near village and the distant church spire no habitation showed in all that sweep of country.

Kelly gave his instructions tersely. The only troops in the village were a small A.S.C. unit. His six intimates would deal with that. No telegraph wires ran through the village; the one military telephone cable would be cut. No traffic might be expected upon the road, but nothing must be allowed to pass out of the village or through it. They were to help themselves and get back as soon as possible. Finally they were to stay where they were until he gave the signal to advance.

Followed by his six companions he left the wood and strode down the hillside, but halted in a little hollow about halfway between the wood and the village. One of his companions went on alone. He was dressed in ordinary clean fatigue with a web belt. There was nothing in his appearance to arouse suspicion, and his mission was evidently to reconnoitre and to cut the telephone cable connecting the A.S.C. orderly-room with other units. He reached the village and disappeared from view down a narrow lane between cottages.

The outcasts sat beneath the trees on the edge of the wood and waited. The pale wintry sun was already low on the horizon, and the slight mist gave promise of a frost to come. The smoke rose almost vertically from three or four chimneys in the unconscious village below, and hung in little hazy grey palls a few feet above the pots as though too lazy to rise farther. A woman was pegging washing on a line between two fruit trees in a cottage garden, and on the big stretch of brown plough that separated the wood from the village an old peasant was working, moving between the furrows with slow, angular movements. Kelly and his companions were invisible in their little hollow.

A quarter of an hour passed. The hornet hum of a flight of aeroplanes flying high passed overhead and died away. A little girl and two cows ambled down a track to the right. And then Kelly's scout reappeared. He emerged from one end of the village, left the narrow road and came striding across the plough towards the hollow. A little rustle of sound rippled on the edge of the wood as the outcasts stirred expectantly.

The scout had disappeared in the hollow, but he reappeared a few moments later with Kelly and the others. The group began to move towards the village, but Kelly who was the last to go, before he turned away, swung his hand underarm in the signal to advance.

The outcasts among the trees scrambled to their feet and streamed down across the plough towards the village. The old peasant straightened his bent back as they passed, and stood looking after them with his knotted old hands hanging awkwardly at his sides.

Kelly and his intimates reached the village fifty yards ahead of the others and disappeared from view. Rawley and Alf, side by side, were a little in front of the other outcasts, but Alf twitched Rawley's sleeve. "Step short," he cried. "If there's any trouble let someone else get it first." Each carried a long bread-sack over one shoulder, like a bandoleer, with the two ends tied together with string under the other arm. Alf carried his revolver in a pocket, but Rawley was unarmed except for an entrenching-tool handle.

Presently they found themselves in a narrow rutted lane between two cottages and an orchard. It was that down which the scout had first disappeared. It led them to the main, and indeed only, street of the village. Several of the outcasts were already there prowling along with rifles at the ready like bandits in a film drama. A woman carrying a bucket opened a cottage door as three of them were passing, and at the sight of them she screamed, dropped the bucket, and slammed the door. A few yards down the street a lorry was drawn up on the cobbles close to a house. The wooden notice-board hanging outside the door proclaimed it to be the A.S.C. unit's office. The half-dozen men inside had already been held up by Kelly's bodyguard, and were now herded together in a small back room. Two of the outcasts had been pressed into service to guard them under the command of one of the bodyguard.

Outside the A.S.C. unit's little canteen a sorry-looking horse was being harnessed to a dilapidated spring-cart, and Kelly's companions were busily engaged in transferring the contents of the canteen to the cart. Doors and shutters had closed as by magic, but the outcasts set to work with rifle butts, crowbars, and any farm implements that came to hand to batter them open. Kelly, watchful and alert, strode up and down and urged them on. Many of the villagers fled through their back gardens and reached the open country, but the screams which rose now and then above the shouts, thunderous blows, splinter of wood and tinkle of broken glass proclaimed that some had been less wise.

The throb of a motor-cycle was drowned in the uproar, but it did not escape the attentive ear of Kelly. He whipped round in time to see at the end of the street a despatch rider turn his machine and shoot back the way he had come. Kelly slipped the rifle from his shoulder and rested it against a pump that stood on the cobbles by the roadside. Five full seconds passed before the crack of the rifle echoed in the narrow street. The despatch rider sped on his way for another twenty yards; and then his machine swerved and crashed head on into the wall of a barn. Kelly re-shot the bolt of his rifle and lowered the weapon with a satisfied grin.

Dusk was descending upon the stricken village. The street was littered with broken glass and the splintered wood of doors and shutters. The raiders in their search for loot had spared nothing. The contents of presses and chests had been wantonly flung through the windows, and bed linen and articles of female attire now hung forlornly on bushes and garden shrubs, and lay trampled into the mire. Two chests of drawers that had been pushed bodily from an upper window lay smashed in the street below, vomiting their contents over the muddy *pavé*. The cottages had been stripped of everything that was valuable and movable. Even chairs and mattresses that had been dragged out and then abandoned as too cumbersome lay here and there upon the road.

The raiders moved from house to house, cursing and quarrelling over the spoils. Figures passed bearing strange burdens. One man had three chickens slung over his shoulder, and the blood from their recently cut throats dribbled down the back of his coat and left a trail on the road behind him. Another had a feather bed rolled up and roped to his shoulders. A man in a stained black overcoat had two hams dangling from his web belt. One man had a half side of bacon lashed on his chest like a breastplate. Nearly all carried bundles of blankets and clothing.

The scene nauseated Rawley. He had half filled his sack in the wrecked canteen with articles left by Kelly's companions, but he refused to plunder the cottages. "I've sunk low enough, my God!" he cried savagely to Alf's importunities. "But not to this." Alf's philosophy was more accommodating. "If I don't take the stuff, some other bloke will," was his point of view. He was laden with a ham, two long French loaves, three bottles of wine, and a locked leather suit-case he had unearthed in an upper room.

Darkness had come, but lights showed here and there through the broken windows and revealed the raiders in twos and threes eating and drinking in the wrecked little cottage rooms. Some had already drunk much and were shouting and singing uproariously. From one cottage where a lamp had been overturned a pillar of smoke was rolling up into the night. Suddenly a tongue of flame leapt from the thatched roof and shed a ruddy glow over the shattered street.

Rawley grabbed Alf by the arm as he emerged from a cottage. "I've had enough of this," he cried. "And so have you, you ruddy little ruffian."

Alf agreed. "There ain't much left," he said philosophically. "And that perishin' fire'll bring visitors. We'll clear before the trouble starts."

Glass crunched underfoot as they went down the street where the broken fragments glittered in the light of the dancing flames. The roof was now blazing furiously, and in the cottage garden, dangerously near the falling sparks, half a dozen drunken raiders with linked hands were howling and dancing like madmen. Rawley's last view of the flame-lit village street before he turned uphill towards the dark line of the wood showed him the tall dark figure of Kelly dragging a struggling girl from a cottage door. He half turned back, but Alf seized his arm and dragged him on.

CHAPTER XVII

I

I T was a long and dreary tramp back to the dug-out, and they arrived almost dead beat. Rawley flung himself full length upon his bunk, too tired and sick at heart even to smoke. Alf crept under his frowzy blankets and dozed. Hunger, however, roused them. Unlike the majority of the raiders, they had eaten little since morning, and as soon as the more immediate aches of fatigue had subsided, they began to think of food and the luxuries they had brought from the village. The ham was set out on the rickety table, one of the bottles of wine, a long French loaf, some real fresh farm butter and a tin of peaches. It was a feast, and they did full justice to it. The wine and the food dispelled what remained of their fatigue, and Rawley, with his pipe drawing well, and his bootless feet wrapped in soft, comfortable sandbags, was no longer in despair.

"Damn that swine Kelly," he cried. "I've had enough of him, the murdering hound. I've done some pretty bloody things since I took to this God-forsaken devastated area, but I draw the line at murder and rape and robbing and burning old women's cottages. If I can't live without that, I'll starve. But I can live without that. My brains are as good as Kelly's—and a damn sight better. And I'm going to use 'em. I'm going to scrounge my own rations, and there will be no murdering and burning about it. It's the E.F.C. and the War Office that's going to lose; not old peasants and their wives."

Alf paused in his job of trying to pick the lock of the suit-case with a bit of wire. He was worried about it. It was a beautiful leather suit-case, and he was sure there was something valuable inside. He did not want to have to smash the lock. He was only half listening to what Rawley was saying. He re-bent the wire and again inserted it into the lock. "But Kelly won't stand for that," he said conversationally. "We'll have to join in his stunts. An' if he twigs you're gettin' stuff on your own, he'll make you share out."

"He damn well won't," cried Rawley decisively. "Because he won't know anything about it in the first place, and he won't get the chance in the second. I'm going to clear out of this. There's plenty of room in this God-forsaken desert, and I'm going to find a place that's a good many miles from Mr. Kelly and his gang of hooligans. You can stay if you like."

Alf forgot his suit-case. He regarded Rawley with dismay. "What, you going to leave 'ere!" he cried. He glanced round the dug-out which had never before seemed so cosy. "You going to leave all this—what we've taken weeks to make all cushy!"

Rawley nodded. "I expect there are other palaces in the devastated area nearly as luxurious as this," he said, with a grim smile. "But you are not bound to go unless you want to."

Alf took a cigarette from one of the new tins they had brought from the village. He lighted it with care at the lamp and sat down again on his bunk. He surveyed the dug-out in silence, the cigarette held between the first finger and thumb of one of the dirty hands that rested on his knees. He flicked away the ash and took another puff, and by projecting his lower lip sent the smoke spurting upwards past his face. He watched it a moment with upturned eyes. Then he said, shortly, "I'm with yer, mate."

"Good for you!" said Rawley. "Then we'll stick together, and we'll make a damn sight better and cleaner living than Kelly does."

"Yes, I'm with you," went on Alf solemnly. His hands still rested on his knees, and a spiral of smoke rose from the cigarette between his finger and thumb. "I didn't never go to no Sunday school, but I reckon Kelly's a bit too hot for me. I didn't 'arf get the wind up when that fire started. Arskin' for trouble, that was." He flicked the ash from his cigarette and took another puff. "This district's going to be bleedin' unhealthy afore long, mark my words. I can see it acomin'. Yes, mate, you're right. We'll move afore someone calls for the rent."

Rawley knocked out his pipe and opened a fresh tin of tobacco. "The question is, where to go," he said, as he pushed the strands into the warm bowl. "Of course, the farther the better." He got up and took from a shelf some old maps he had found in various dug-outs. "The scheme would be to take a little stuff with us and go exploring. Then when we have found a suitable place, we can dump the stuff and come back for the rest." He opened the maps and scanned them thoughtfully. "Do you know, I believe it would be safer and in many ways more convenient to find a place on the edge of the devastated area near a main road." He studied the maps again. "Somewhere in the neighbourhood of Albert for instance. That's far enough away from Kelly to be quite comfortable and near enough to places like Bapaume where there ought to be canteens and dumps worth looting. Unfortunately I don't know that part of the world."

"I do," said Alf. "Too bleedin' well. I was there all '16, ever since we come down from Bethune for the Somme." Suddenly he smote his thigh with such vigour that the cigarette between his fingers dropped to the floor. He picked it up and stuck it into the corner of his mouth. "Boy, I know the very place! We was there in August '16. We 'ad the guns on the edge of a little wood, though there weren't much of a wood about it, if you know what I mean. We rigged up bivvys in an old Jerry trench what ran through it. And the orficers had a cushy little place in a cellar. Yer see there was an 'ouse in the middle of the wood, what 'ad been knocked flat, 'an they had the mess in the cellar underneath. It was one of them arched places—you know, like them places under a church. Keep out the biggest stuff and dry as a bone. I went down there once with a message for the captain, and coo, it looked orl right! They had a lot of them saucy French coloured pitchers round the walls, and a proper white tablecloth on the table. Looked just like home, it did."

"Whereabouts was it?" asked Rawley.

"Nigh to Contalmaison; betwixt there and La Boiselle. But it warn't too healthy then, 'cause Jerry was in Ovillers and shootin' pretty nearly into our backs. But we pushed him out of that on September 13th."

Rawley was studying the map. "You must have been somewhere here," he said, dabbing a finger.

Alf peered over his shoulder. "What's that place there?"

"Poizières."

"That's right. We was facin' Poizières, only you couldn't see it from the battery 'cause the guns was in a holler. Contalmaison, or what was left of it, was on our right, on the other side of the holler."

"I've got you now," said Rawley. "There is a little valley west of the village. You must have had this road running diagonally across your flank. It runs through Poizières—to Bapaume."

"That's right," said Alf excitedly. "The Bapaume road. It was about 'arf a mile away. You could see it when you went up to the top of the slope."

Rawley made a mark on the map. "This one-over-a-hundred-thousand map only shows the big woods, but I've fixed the spot within a hundred yards or so. It sounds as though it were just the place we're after. Anyway, we will go and have a look at it." He folded up the map. "We'll turn in for a spot of sleep and then off we go."

Alf lighted a fresh cigarette from the stump of an old one and swung his legs on the bunk. "Coo, why didn't I think of that before!" he exclaimed. "Why, we shall be a 'eap better off there than we are 'ere."

Rawley was taking off his coat. "What about water?" he asked suddenly.

"There's a well belongin' to the 'ouse, but we never used it," said Alf.

"Well, there is bound to be one in Contalmaison, anyway."

Alf rose with a yawn, and began to take off his coat, but he stopped with his arms outstretched as a sudden thud sounded from the shaft leading to the trench. "Did you hear that?" he whispered.

They both stood motionless looking towards the shaft. A moment later the noise was repeated. "Someone knocking at the door," said Rawley. They always blocked the narrow entrance of the shaft with a baulk of timber, wedged into place with a small pit-prop.

Alf's face had grown pale under its covering of dirt. "The bleedin' red caps," he whispered.

"Not likely—so soon," said Rawley.

Alf recovered himself and took his big revolver from the shelf over his bunk. "I'll go and have a listen," he whispered, and tip-toed off up the steps.

Rawley heard the sound of muffled voices, and then of footsteps approaching. Alf came back into the dug-out, followed by a man whom Rawley recognized as one of Kelly's bodyguard.

253

"It's a message from Kelly," said Alf. "He says we've got to clear out."

The man looked round the dug-out and then at Rawley. "Yes," he said. "There's going to be trouble over that little dust up this afternoon. Some of the A.P.M.'s push came into the village soon after we left, and they'll be nosing around here before long, I shouldn't wonder. You're all to come right along to the redoubt. That's Kelly's orders." He nodded towards the two rifles that Alf kept in a corner. "Bring those along and all the ammo you've got. We'll give that bloody A.P.M. the surprise of his life if he comes nosing round here."

Rawley had been regarding the speaker with silent hostility, and something of this must have showed in his face, for the man added sharply: "Now then, jump to it. Pack up and clear."

"Don't worry, we're going to clear out all right," said Rawley. "But you can tell Kelly to go to hell. We're not going to his redoubt to shoot down honest men just to help to save his dirty skin." The man had turned towards the shaft, but he spun round at Rawley's words, and there was an ugly look on his face. "Oh, you're not, aren't you!" he growled. "Too bloody proud to fight, eh!" He spat contemptuously on the floor. "Feet too bloody cold, you mean. You think you're going to clear out and save your own flaming skin. P'raps you think you'll put yourself all right with the red caps by showing them where your pals are cached. I should ruddy well smile! Too bloomin' soft-hearted to shoot honest men!"

Rawley whipped up Alf's revolver from the table. "Honest men, yes, but not you and your sort. Clear out, quick!"

The fellow backed slowly with contracted brows. "All right," he growled. "But don't you think you'll get away with this." Then he turned suddenly and dived up the steps.

Rawley followed slowly and re-blocked the entrance with the baulk of timber. He wedged it firmly with the pit-prop and returned to the dug-out.

II

Alf was sitting dejectedly upon his bunk. "You didn't ought to have done that," he said. "Kelly's a fair devil when he's riled."

Rawley flung the revolver noisily on the table. "Kelly can go to hell," he cried.

"But why didn't you tell that bloke we was coming to the redoubt, then when he'd gone we could've nipped off on the quiet," persisted Alf, in an aggrieved tone.

Rawley thumped the table with his hand. "Because I'm not going to bother to lie to a swine like that," he yelled.

Alf shrugged his shoulders and got off his bunk. "Well, we've done it now, anyway," he said, with a resigned sigh. "And the sooner we *partit* from this neighbourhood the better." He picked up a sack and began filling it.

Rawley watched him moodily for a few moments, and then picked up another sack. "I suppose you're right," he admitted. "No good meeting trouble when you can avoid it."

Alf did not pause in his task of stuffing tins into the sack. "Too true," he agreed. "Once I get on top there, you won't see me for dust."

Rawley threw down his sack. "Look here," he said. "It's no good just stuffing things in. We can't take everything, that's obvious. And it's very doubtful if we shall be able to come back for more later. So let's decide what we are going to take. It's no good loading ourselves up so that we can't move."

They spread their possessions out on the floor—their store of food, tools, candle ends, blankets and clothing. Rawley surveyed them with his hands in his pockets. "Well, it's pretty clear that we can't take a quarter of that," he said.

Alf nodded dolefully. "It do seem 'ard lines to 'ave to leave all that good stuff," he complained.

"Well, let's eliminate," said Rawley. He indicated the battered gramophone, and its one warped record with his toe. "That's out, anyway. And we can't take the lamp or the oil; therefore the candles must come. The ham comes, of course, and the bulk of the tinned stuff. There's those two remaining bottles of wine. Can't possibly take them. Must drink 'em before we go, that's all. Then blankets; must have those. And we'll roll up some underclothes inside 'em." He pulled his blankets from his bunk. "We will roll up the blankets first and strap them on, and then we will see how much more we can carry comfortably."

Rawley spread his blankets on the floor, placed his spare underclothes and one or two treasures on top, and began to roll them up. A dull thud from the direction of the steps stopped him. He paused with his head raised, listening. A scraping noise came faintly from the top of the shaft. Neither spoke. The scratching and bumping noise continued. Rawley rose from his knees and silently took one of the rifles from the corner. He pulled back the bolt. The magazine was full. He re-shot the bolt, sending a round into the breach. Alf too rose to his feet, and his hand went out to his revolver.

Rawley walked to the foot of the shaft and stood with one foot on the bottom step. He held the rifle lightly in his two hands. He shouted up the shaft, "Keep out of here. You haven't got an earthly. We can shoot you down one by one as you come—and we will if you try it."

There was no reply. The noises had ceased, and an uncanny silence reigned. Rawley moved from the foot of the shaft and glanced round the dug-out. His glance rested on the lamp that hung from the centre beam. His eye travelled from it to the shaft; then he moved the lamp to a nail nearer the wall. "They might try to shoot out the light," he said, in a low voice.

They waited side by side for the attack, their eyes fixed on the foot of the shaft, their ears strained to catch the slightest sound. But none came.

Rawley lowered the butt of his rifle to the floor. "They've thought better of it," he said. "They would not have stood an earthly, and they know it." He lifted his foot to step over his roll of blankets on the floor, but he never completed the pace. A great gust of hot air leapt from the foot of the shaft, caught him up, and hurled him to the floor. The light was extinguished; the dug-out vibrated as though rocked by an earthquake; and a mighty roar smote his ear drums.

He lay where he had fallen, half stunned by concussion, but his experiences under bombardment in the gun-pits had taught him to think quickly in moments such as this. One hand still retained its grasp of the rifle, and before the earth, splintered timber and stones had ceased to hurtle through the darkness, he dragged himself to a sitting position and pushed forward the safety-catch. "Alf!" he cried. "Alf! Look out; they'll try to rush us now."

Alf's voice grunted from the darkness beside him. No other sound, except the trickle of a few pebbles down the steps, broke the silence. "You all right?" whispered Rawley.

"Yes."

"Got your revolver?"

"Yes."

A gallery of a deserted coal mine could not have been darker or more silent. The air was heavy with the acrid smell of high explosive.

They had looted a packet of matches from the village canteen. Rawley had a box in his pocket. "Look out," he whispered. "Keep your eye on the shaft. I'm going to strike a light. If anyone appears—shoot."

A match scraped on the box, and a little flame spluttered up, disclosing smoky fumes wreathed like a fog around them, and Alf propped on one elbow, his revolver pointing somewhat shakily towards the shaft foot. The floor of the dug-out was littered with earth and stones. No sound came from the shaft.

The lamp lay smashed beside the overturned table, but among the stores that were spread out on the floor lay their collection of candle ends. Rawley slipped his left arm through the sling of his rifle and crawled forward, holding the half-burned match in his right hand. He propped up a candle end and lighted it. Then without removing his eyes from the foot of the shaft, he righted the table with one hand, placed the candle on it, and rose to his feet.

Alf too rose cautiously.

Rawley, with a finger on the trigger guard, tip-toed to the shaft, paused a moment listening, and disappeared up the steps.

He was back in a moment, and leaned his rifle carelessly against the wall. "Well?" whispered Alf, who stood holding his revolver ready.

"It's all right," said Rawley in natural tones. "You can put that down. They're not coming."

Alf slowly lowered his revolver. "'Ow do you know they ain't comin'?" he demanded.

Rawley pulled his pipe from his pocket, shook some earth from the bowl, and began filling it deliberately. "'Ow do you know?" repeated Alf.

Rawley did not look up. "They can't," he said. "They've blown in the shaft."

Alf's jaw dropped. "Watcher mean?" he said.

Rawley jerked his head towards the shaft. "Go and see for yourself."

Alf gazed at Rawley for a moment, and then he stumbled quickly across to the foot of the shaft and disappeared. He re-appeared slowly, dropped his revolver on the table, and sat down on his earth-sprinkled bunk. He rubbed the back of his neck with a grimy hand. "Yars they've got us all right," he said dejectedly.

Rawley threw away the match with which he had extravagantly been lighting his pipe. "What do you mean—'got us'?" he demanded.

"Got us!" repeated Alf, with vehemence. "Bloody well got us. We're buried alive, ain't we? An' all through your ruddy yappin' with that chap."

"Not a bit of it," said Rawley. "We can dig ourselves out."

"What, with a trenchin' tool!" exclaimed Alf, with caustic sarcasm. "We ain't got nothin' else, you know that. An' there's thirty foot o' muck there, if there's an inch."

"It will be a long job, I know," said Rawley. "But we've plenty of time. We've any amount of grub and water—how about the water, though!" He strode across and inspected the tins. "One full and one half full, including several handfuls of earth. That's enough, if we go easy." He came back and sat down on the edge of his bunk. "What they have forgotten is"—he nodded towards the little alcove where the bucket fire was kept—"is that. They've forgotten the pipe. If they'd blocked that up, we would have been suffocated."

Alf took a brighter view of the situation. "Oh, well," he said, "I s'pose you're right. We might 'ave been foot-sloggin' it outside an' 'ere we are still in 'ome sweet 'ome.

It's a perishin' ill wind what blows nobody no good! But they've made a bleedin' mess," he added, as he surveyed the rubble-littered floor.

"Oh, well, let's clear it up," said Rawley. He put the ham on the table and flicked off the dirt with a bit of rag.

"'Ow do you reckon they did it?" asked Alf.

"Shoved a six-inch or a toffee apple outside the plank and touched it off with a plunger. Easy enough."

Alf went down on his knees and shook his blankets to rid them of the soil which covered them; but the thud of some heavy object falling in the alcove made him pause and turn his head in that direction. And at the same moment Rawley, it seemed, went mad; he leapt upon Alf like an avalanche and knocked him flat.

A stunning, ripping crack smote the ear-drums like a blow; the candle went out; and a number of deep-toned buzzing noises, like a flight of bumble bees, droned noisily across the darkness and ended in a series of sharp smacks and dull thuds.

Rawley released his hold. "All right?" he asked.

"What the hell was that?" panted Alf.

"Mills' bomb. I saw it just as it landed. The swine must have dropped it down the chimney." He began to crawl across the floor. "Don't get up," he said. "There may be more to follow." His outstretched arm touched the table leg, and he raised himself, and felt along the top for the candle. He found it, and felt in his pocket for the matches. But he did not strike one; instead he put the candle in his pocket. "If they look down the chimney they will see the light," he muttered. "We shall hear it drop, anyway." He tilted the table on to its side and dragged it back to where Alf lay. They crouched behind it listening.

Rawley could hear the beating of his own heart and Alf's laboured breathing; there was no other sound except the intermittent scuffling of a rat behind the revetment. He held his breath and strained his ears. He thought he could detect a faint sound in the direction of the chimney. Yes, he was sure now: a scraping noise, but very faint.

A second explosion shook the dug-out, but the sound was muffled and seemed to come from above. Stones pattered on the earth floor and clattered as they hit the invisible bucket. Then silence settled down once more.

Rawley took the candle end from his pocket and lighted it. He scrambled to his feet and righted the table. Alf too rose gingerly. "Is it all right?" he asked.

Rawley did not reply. He stood looking down at the stones and earth that was mingled with the wood ash in the fire bucket and lay on the floor round about. Then he put his head down and looked up the chimney.

"Look out!" cried Alf. "If they drops another . . ."

Rawley turned from the alcove and looked round the dug-out without speaking. Then he strode across to Alf's bunk and took a cigarette from the tin on the shelf above. He lighted it at the candle and puffed at it for a moment. Then he strode to the alcove and puffed smoke across the bottom of the chimney. The blue wreaths curled lazily along the low roof of the recess; a little disappeared slowly up the chimney.

Rawley dropped the cigarette into the fire-bucket, and went and sat on the edge of his bunk. Mechanically he pulled out his pipe and filled it. Alf watched him in silence. "What 'ave they done?" he asked at last.

Rawley pulled the table to him and lighted his pipe at the candle. "They've blocked up the chimney," he said.

"Are ye sure?" demanded Alf.

"'Fraid so; there's no draught."

Alf dropped rather wearily on to the edge of his bunk. His face was a little pale. He rubbed the back of his neck with his hand. "Well, that's torn it, right up the leg. Can't we do nothin'?" he asked in a strangled voice.

"I don't know. I'm trying to think. Of course, we ought to put that out." He nodded towards the candle. "And I ought not to smoke. Burning up air. But what's the odds, anyway."

"Couldn't we dig ourselves out?"

Rawley shook his head. "Not in time. The devil of it is, that chimney is a good thirty feet long, and we've got nothing that would go up—not that it would be likely to be any good if we had." He looked round the dug-out, estimating the latent possibilities of each article it contained. Suddenly he jumped to his feet. "By jove, of course—the rifles!" He took his rifle from the floor where it had fallen, and pushed forward the safety-catch. Alf, too, had dived for his rifle and was ramming a round in the breech. Rawley suddenly dropped his butt on the floor. "Wait a minute," he cried. "Go easy. They may still be up there, and if we clear the chimney, they'll only block it up again. We must let them think they have done it all right, and give them time to go away." He sat down again on the edge of his bunk.

Alf stood with his rifle balanced in his hands. "I don't like waitin'," he said. "Fair gives me the creeps, it do. Supposin' the air give out. . . ."

"It won't yet awhile," said Rawley. "We will wait ten minutes by your watch. Hang it up where we can see it."

Alf put down his rifle and hung up the watch. "Seem to be gettin' pretty phuggy already," he said nervously.

Rawley had thought the same himself, but had not liked to put his thoughts into words. "It's the fumes from the H.E.," he said carelessly. "If we put out the candle it will help."

But Alf shook his head vehemently. "No, mate; if I'm going west, let's 'ave a light. It'll be more cheerful-like than in the dark." He rubbed the back of his neck and glanced at the watch. "Supposin' the rifle won't clear it."

"It must," said Rawley. "Let's see—how much earth will a bullet penetrate? It's in *Musketry Regs*. What is it now? . . . three feet, I believe. That's if it's loose earth. If you ram it tight the resisting power is less. The earth up there is probably pretty tight, so we'll go through three feet all right. There can't be more than six or seven feet of earth wedged in the pipe, if that. So we have only to keep shooting away, and we must get through. By the by, how much ammunition have we got?"

"There's pretty nearly a full box," said Alf.

"No trouble on that score then. You see, we must get through—unless—"

"Unless what?"

"Unless—well, unless they've wedged a dud in the chimney. But no, they cannot have done that. There would have been no need of that explosion then. They've either blown in the top of the chimney or exploded a grenade a little way down. It sounded to me like a grenade." He glanced at the watch. "Another five minutes."

Alf groaned.

"Look here, how about a drink to put some buck into us?" suggested Rawley. "We can't take those two bottles with us, anyway. Come on." He took up one of the bottles wrapped it in a sandbag, and neatly knocked off the neck. He filled their two mugs and pushed one towards Alf. He raised his mug and glanced round the dug-out. Then he stood up and bowed towards his rifle that leaned against the wall. "Here's to Mr. Lee-Enfield," he said. "Short Mr. Lee-Enfield—coupled with the name of that pushing little fellow Mr. Mark Six, or whatever it is, Three-O-Three."

"'Ear, 'ear!" said Alf with a grin. "Bleedin' well 'ear, 'ear—an' more perishin' power to his push." They drained the mugs.

"How's that?" said Rawley.

Alf smacked his lips, and pushed his mug forward. "Fill up, chum. It ain't no good keepin' that broken bottle. Another pint of this tack an' I'll push kebs over."

Rawley glanced at the watch. "Right'o. Just time for another."

Alf lighted a cigarette and they drank again. Rawley put down his empty mug and rose. "Time, gentlemen, please," he said. He took his rifle and moved towards the recess. Alf followed. Rawley pushed forward the safety catch and thrust the barrel up the chimney. Then he pulled it down again and turned to Alf. "Is the chimney straight?" he asked.

Alf nodded.

"Sure? I mean, we don't want to shoot into the ground."

"There's a bit of a slant," said Alf. "But you can see daylight when you look up."

Rawley examined the chimney. "I see," he said. "It slopes this way a bit." He went down on one knee, rested the butt of the rifle on the other, and held the barrel in the centre of the pipe. "Here goes," he said. "Stand clear."

The report was deafening in the confined space, and was followed by a little avalanche of earth down the chimney. Rawley shook the earth from the bolt and sent another round into the breech. "Bring that cigarette here," he said. He held the cigarette under the chimney, but the smoke displayed no great tendency to rush up it. "Ah, well, can't expect to do the trick first go off. We shall have to peg away at it. I'll empty the magazine and then try it."

He fired the other nine rounds and stood up. Alf held the cigarette underneath, but with no result.

"We've brought down some earth anyway," said Rawley. "You have a go now, while I reload."

He dragged out the box of S.A.A. and took out a handful of clips. The already vitiated air was now heavy with the reek of burnt cordite. There was no longer any need to hold a cigarette beneath the chimney. The fumes hung in wreathes that made breathing difficult. Alf was firing round after round up the chimney.

"Steady!" warned Rawley. "Make sure you're not plugging into the side of the pipe higher up, or you will do more harm than good."

Alf ejected the last case from the breech and drew his hand across his damp forehead. "It ain't 'arf gettin' stuffy in 'ere," he said. "Do you think we'll do it, chum?"

"Rather! You load up again while I have a go." Rawley fired each round deliberately, pausing before each pressure of the trigger to ensure accuracy of aim. And he turned his eyes frequently to the fumes that clung lazily to the low roof of the recess. He thought he detected a slight tendency to float up the chimney. Alf stood ready with his rifle reloaded. Rawley put out his hand for it. "Let me carry on for a bit," he said. He fired three more rounds deliberately, pausing after each to watch the behaviour of the fumes. After the third round the fumes slid round the edge of the chimney in a small continuous stream like an inverted water-fall. He fired several more rounds before his rifle and hands were deluged with a small avalanche of earth. Then he stood up. The fumes in the neighbourhood of the chimney were gravitating towards it, moving faster and with more decision as they neared it, till finally they whisked round the edge and up out of sight.

Rawley leaned his rifle against the wall and sat down rather wearily on his bunk. "All clear!" he said, and felt for his pipe.

Alf mopped his face with a dirty rag. "I don't mind sayin'," he confessed, "that put the wind up me proper."

"Me, too," agreed Rawley. "Anyway, it's all right now."

"Now we got to dig ourselves out."

"Not now. Personally, I'm pretty nearly all in. The best thing we can do is to turn in for a bit; and then we'll go at it like navvies when we wake up."

Alf demurred. He did not like the feeling of being buried like a corpse even though there was now plenty of air. Why not start digging at once.

"What, for half an hour—and then be too tired to move for hours after?" objected Rawley. "No. Turn in and have a good sleep. We shall get through twice the amount of work in half the time when we are fresh. After all, that blessed landslide won't run away." And so they crawled into their bunks and were soon asleep.

CHAPTER XVIII

I

R AWLEY was first awake, and he lay for some minutes in the intense darkness going over in his mind the events of the previous hours. He was reassured to find that the air was comparatively fresh, for he had been unable to rid himself entirely of the fear that Kelly's gang might have heard the noise of the firing and returned to re-block the chimney. At last he put out his hand and felt for the matches on the shelf above the bunk. He struck one cautiously and lighted the candle stump on the table. He propped up a tattered magazine to shield the light from Alf who lay snoring in the other bunk.

Their stores, with the exception of the ham, still lay on the floor. He surveyed them thoughtfully. Where was the ham? Why, yes, he had put it on the table to flick the dirt from it just before that first bomb came down the chimney. And then the candle had gone out, and—oh yes—he had upset the table so as to form some sort of protection against further bombs. The ham must be on the floor somewhere then.

He found it almost buried under loose earth, and he replaced it on the table after removing as much of the dirt as possible. The long French loaf was more easily freed from its covering of earth, and the butter was cleanly wrapped in paper. Tea was the difficulty. They needed something hot to warm them for the long task that lay ahead, but he dared not light a fire. One of Kelly's gang might see the smoke. There was one bottle of wine left, but wine at breakfast was not very enticing. He looked through the articles which Alf had looted from the canteen and found what he needed, two slabs of solidified alcohol, refills for a Tommy's cooker. With one of these he boiled enough water for a mug of tea each, and then he awakened Alf.

They ate an excellent breakfast. Rawley insisted upon it; and Alf needed little encouragement. They had ample supplies. More, perhaps, than they would be able to carry away, and they would work the better for a full meal.

After breakfast they piled their stores in the corner farthest from the shaft, and set to work. Their only implement was an entrenching-tool, and they arranged that one should dig in the shaft whilst the other, armed with a board, shovelled the loose earth from the step and piled it in a corner of the dug-out. With such a small implement progress was necessarily slow, and other difficulties soon presented themselves.

Rawley had taken first turn with the entrenching-tool, and after twenty minutes hard digging, when he had made a tunnel some two feet in diameter and three feet in length, the roof came in and not only covered the two steps he had cleared but the third as well. Alf then took a turn at digging, but no sooner had he made a tunnel a few feet in length than a like catastrophe occurred.

Rawley suspended operations and lighted his pipe. "If we go on like this," he said, "the roof will keep coming in and we shall have to go on digging till we've dug out all the earth on top—and that's a good thirty feet. The only other thing to do is to revet the tunnel with timber. And the question is, where is the timber coming from?" He looked round the dug-out. "We can break up those boxes, and those few floor boards will have to come up. And we may be able to take a plank here and there from the walls. We'll make the tunnel as small as possible—just big enough to crawl through and if we put the planks like an inverted V, that will save one bit of wood each time on the roof. Come on, let's get to work. Where is that saw?"

By experiment they found that when two planks about two and a half feet in length were propped against each other with their bases some two feet apart, it was just possible to crawl under them. Alf set to work with the saw, and Rawley resumed digging, but he found, as soon as the first two revetments were in position, that although it was not difficult to crawl under them it was no easy matter to dig. The confined space made it impossible to swing the entrenchment tool, and he had to remove the handle and use the blade as a scoop. Also it was very tiring to dig while lying flat on the chest; and the only way of getting rid of the loose earth was to push it down one's side with one hand, and then by bending the knee as far as possible, scrape it out behind to Alf with one foot. However they persevered, and when the tunnel was nearly seven feet in length, knocked off and ate another meal.

But the work became harder and more difficult as they progressed. The confined space made breathing so difficult that ten minutes or a quarter of an hour was as long as one could dig without a rest, and there was the ever present fear that a pair of the planks would slip and block the tunnel behind one. It took several minutes to crawl up the tunnel to the point of working, and more than double that time to worm one's way out backwards.

Rawley indeed did have an accident. While scraping the earth back behind him his foot displaced a board and brought down a small avalanche of earth that blocked the tunnel behind him. Fortunately Alf was in the tunnel at the moment and was able to scrape away enough earth with his hands to allow him to replace the revetment.

When the tunnel reached the top of the steps Rawley wormed his way out backwards into the dug-out and announced his intention of knocking off for the night. They were both utterly worn out, and it was obviously unwise to continue. They ate a meal in a depressed silence which the last bottle of wine was unable to relieve. Though tired out, Rawley found it impossible to sleep. He tossed from side to side on his narrow wire-netting bunk, and when at times he did doze, it was only to dream that he was still working on the tunnel, or to awaken with the horror of entombment upon him. The prospect of the morrow appalled him. The thought of again entering the tunnel terrified him. His thoughts revolved in an endless circle; sleep would not come.

At last he abandoned the pretence. He cautiously lighted the candle and shielded the light from Alf, whose regular breathing came from the opposite bunk. He filled his pipe, that one soothing companion of all his troubles, and with the first few fragrant puffs his mind ceased to revolve futilely in a circle: it began to work constructively.

He rummaged in his box of odds and ends for a pencil. He opened the half-used field message book and began to draw a sectional plan of the dug-out, the shaft, and the gallery that led up to the trench. He drew it roughly to scale, using one side of the little squares into which the paper was divided to represent one foot. There were ten steps in the shaft that led immediately from the dug-out, then followed a gallery some sixteen feet in length, sloping upwards and ending in three steps up into the trench. They had dug the tunnel to the top of the shaft; there remained the gallery and the three steps to be traversed. Looking at the diagram, he saw clearly now what he had realized subconsciously for some time; they would never be able to complete the tunnel. Apart from the doubtful possibility of their being able to endure the strain of working in and digging so long and small a tunnel, there was not enough timber left to revet it. They had already taken from the walls of the dug-out nearly all the timber that could be removed with safety.

The realization of this, however, did not depress him. His feeling was rather of relief at the knowledge that he would not have to work again in that detestable tunnel. But some other way out must be found, and he set to work to tackle the problem.

He started, as it were, from first causes. The passage to the upper air was blocked by a fall of earth caused by the explosion, presumably of a shell. This had no doubt caused the roof to collapse in the neighbourhood of the explosion, but surely not the whole length of that gallery and shaft. For at least half the distance that separated the dug-out from the trench the timber roof must still be in position, although the passage itself was blocked with earth. Therefore, theoretically, that cramped and terrifying tunnel should be necessary only to traverse the actual place where the roof timbers had collapsed. But where was that place?

He turned again to his diagram. About half way down the sloping gallery there had been a fall of earth, round which he and Alf had always had to squeeze when entering or leaving the dug-out, and it was at this bottle-neck that they had erected the baulk of timber wedged with a pit-prop that they called their door. Kelly's men had not forced this; therefore the explosion had taken place on the far side of it. Almost certainly they had placed the shell on the other side of the "door," and exploded it there. If that were so, it was probable that only a section of the roof timbers in the middle of the gallery were shattered, and those in the shaft were almost certainly intact. The earth that blocked the steps was due merely to the steepness of the shaft. If they could clear this out, the actual tunnel would be needed only in that collapsed section in the middle of the gallery. The plan would be not to dig along the floor as they had done up to now, but to dig along the top just under the roof timbers, and to start the tunnel only when they ceased.

Having worked this out to his satisfaction, he climbed again into his bunk, blew out the candle, and in a few minutes was asleep.

II

When Rawley awoke it was to find that Alf had already been up some time and that breakfast was ready. During the eating of it he told Alf the result of his nocturnal meditations and submitted the diagram for verification. Alf thought that the gallery was longer than Rawley had drawn it, but expressed his unqualified delight at the news that he would not have to start work again immediately in the tunnel.

They began digging at the top as Rawley had suggested, and found that, with the increased room and air, the work proceeded much faster than formerly. The few remaining planks were used to stop the earth from sliding farther down the shaft, and then a tunnel was dug about two feet in diameter just under the roof beams, the digger crawling over the earth that covered the steps. They found as Rawley had anticipated that the roof beams were intact, and they reached the entrance to the gallery after a little over two hours digging. They had not progressed more than about four feet along the gallery, however, before the entrenching-tool struck a hard substance. Rawley, who was digging at the time, called for a candle, and by its light found that the obstacle was a thick baulk of timber buried in the soil. This was evidently one of the roof timbers. The

275

baulk lay diagonally across their tunnel, the upper end resting on one of the side timbers of the gallery, the lower end disappearing into the surrounding soil.

They had now reached the collapsed sector where tunnelling would be necessary, but Rawley foresaw a new difficulty. Ahead of him these shattered roof timbers lay, no doubt, embedded in the soil at all angles, and the difficulty of digging the tunnel that was now necessary would be greatly increased by having to go over or under these timbers whenever they were encountered. The problem required thinking out. They had already wasted much time and labour by hasty action, and he had no intention of making a second mistake. They had been at work for over three hours. He decided to take their midday meal and think over the problem.

"It's quite simple really," he said to Alf as he lighted his pipe at the end of the meal. "The explosion would shatter the timbers and probably raise them a little, and then the earth on top would come in and fill the gallery. Therefore, the timbers must be—most of them at any rate—below their normal position. If we dig our tunnel upwards a bit then, just above the old level of the roof, we ought not to strike any timbers. And now we must crawl up that damned tunnel of ours and bring out the planks; for we shall want them for the new tunnel."

They tossed to decide who should go first, and Alf won. So Rawley wormed his way up the narrow tunnel and very gingerly removed the last two supporting planks. He managed to slide them over his back and push them away with his feet. Then he moved back a bit and removed the next two planks. He removed three before the unsupported part of the tunnel fell in, and then the rush of earth flowed into his face and nearly suffocated him. It was a terrifying experience, lying as he was in complete darkness; but when he had wormed back a foot or two the rush of earth ceased. It made it very difficult, however, to remove the end pair of planks which were now completely embedded in soil. He managed it at last without any further fall of earth, and then he wormed his way back to the dug-out for a rest.

Alf then took his turn and brought out several more pairs of planks, and finally all were removed without accident. But the operation had taken them nearly as long as the whole digging of the larger tunnel under the roof. Alf wiped the sweat from his face with a grimy hand. He made no attempt to disguise his dislike of narrow tunnels. He was obviously not looking forward to the digging of the new one. He said that they had done enough for one day, and suggested that they should turn in and leave the beginning of the new one for the morrow.

Rawley disagreed. He disliked the tunnel, he said, as much as Alf did—perhaps more—but that was all the more reason for splitting up the work into short stretches. If they dug only four feet tonight that would be four feet less to dig tomorrow, and they would be very glad of those four feet before tomorrow was out.

And so they set to work. One point Rawley found he had forgotten: the fact that by digging along the top instead of along the floor of the gallery they had deprived themselves of a firm base on which to rest the inverted Vs. At the first attempt the edges of the planks gradually drove into the soil by reason of the pressure above, but they overcame the difficulty by resting the inverted V upon a third plank which formed the floor of the tunnel. And although the amount of timber they would need was thus increased by one third, Rawley was confident that they would have enough.

He produced his diagram to prove his contention. The gallery, they were agreed, was roughly sixteen feet in length. The explosion had taken place nearly in the middle—that was to say, some eight feet from the top of the shaft. Four feet from the top of the shaft they had reached the limit of the roof's collapse. That was presumably four feet from the centre of the explosion; and presuming that the damage on the far side was of equal extent, a further four feet should bring them to the undamaged roof again. The tunnel then would be only eight feet in length, and they had ample timber for that. They drove their tunnel three feet and then turned in for the night.

III

The next morning they continued the work in good spirits. Alf went in first and extended the tunnel to seven feet; and then Rawley took his turn whilst Alf in the larger tunnel under the sound roof passed up the revetting planks and shovelled out the loose earth. Rawley added a foot, put up the V-shaped revetting planks, and wormed forward again. He added a further two feet and discovered, whilst making a firm bed for a floor plank to rest on, that there were timbers beneath him. He cleared away some of the earth that covered them and satisfied himself by feeling over them that they were the roof timbers of the gallery undamaged and in position. They had bridged the gap, but by digging their tunnel a little high, were now on top instead of under the roof timbers beyond.

Rawley wormed his way back a foot and cleared the soil from the top of the roof timbers. He went back a further foot before he found the edge of the gap where the roof timbers had collapsed. Then he dug down and under. And very glad he was to feel a substantial roof over his head again.

It was time for Alf to relieve him at digging, but he was too near success now to stop. With a firm roof overhead, and plenty of room to swing the entrenching-tool, the work progressed rapidly. Barely four feet of the new broad tunnel had been dug before the earth seemed to melt from his entrenching-tool and light flowed over him like cool water. It was a very subdued light, but the blessed light of day nevertheless. The roof was close above him, and he lay on his side looking down a slope of loose earth. At the foot of the slope were the steps leading up into the trench by the entrance that was partially blocked by the old landslide. Through the small gap under the fallen beam subdued daylight now streamed.

Rawley shouted the good news to Alf and scrambled down the slope. A few moments later they stood side by side in the trench drinking in the clean air and revelling in the clear light of day, and at that moment the dreary landscape that stretched about them seemed the most beautiful they had ever gazed upon.

At last Rawley turned. "Well," he said, "now we must go back, pack up, have a meal, and clear."

Alf grimaced. "I never thought we'd get up here no more," he said. "But now we are up 'ere, I don't like goin' back again. Do you? S'posin' that perishin' little tunnel come in!"

"It won't," said Rawley. He spoke shortly, for he was very much of Alf's way of thinking. "And besides, what about our stores! Are we going to leave all those?"

"I s'pose not," said Alf gloomily.

"Come on, I'll go first," said Rawley.

They reached the dug-out in safety, and recommenced the task of packing that had been interrupted so dramatically. Then they ate their last meal at the little table and prepared to leave. Alf went first with a rope in his hand. He crawled through the eight odd feet of narrow tunnel and then, by means of the rope, dragged his rolled-up blankets after him. The rope was passed back and Rawley's blankets were drawn through. Then the other stores were dragged through in like manner. Rawley was about to follow when a shout from Alf stopped him. "My suit-case, chum!" he called. "Struth, I nearly forgot all about it. It's un'erneath my bunk."

Rawley went back, found the suit-case, and returned; but they had the greatest difficulty in passing it through the narrow stretch of tunnel, and when it stuck half way, refusing to budge either forward or back, Rawley lost his temper. "Hell take your rotten suit-case," he cried. "It has got nothing in it except junk, I expect, and now it has blocked the tunnel with me on the wrong side." They dared not use any force for fear of displacing their revetment, but by long and patient coaxing, during which Rawley's head and shoulders were in the low tunnel, and he momentarily expected the roof to descend upon him, they slid it along inch by inch. Finally Alf pulled it out with an exclamation of triumph, but the incident caused a tension between them that lasted for an hour or more.

Up in the trench they divided the stores, slung the rolled blankets over their shoulders, and shouldered their sacks. In addition they each carried a rifle and twenty rounds of ammunition. Alf carried his precious suit-case across his chest to balance the weight of the sack to which it was tied. Rawley had the tattered maps.

They followed the trench down to the ruined village from which they had so often drawn water; then, after assuring themselves that no one was in sight, crossed the grass-grown road and struck across country up the slope by the shattered wood. The ground was rough and, heavily loaded as they were, they made slow progress. Rawley had decided to cut straight across country towards the cellar which they had chosen for their future home. He had set his map as nearly as possible before leaving the trench, but he had no compass to guide him, and was marching by the glow of the sun that was occasionally visible behind the clouds.

Prudently they kept a sharp look out around them. And it was fortunate they did so, for as they were descending a gentle slope they came suddenly upon a little party of horsemen in a sunken road below. The horsemen, five in number, were sitting motionless on their animals, with their backs towards Rawley and Alf. Two of them, side by side, were apparently studying a map. It was a tense moment for the two vagabonds. By silent agreement they had dropped flat. To retreat back over the slope seemed too dangerous, and yet it was dangerous to remain where they were. One of the two horsemen studying the map had stretched out his arm and was pointing to his flank; at any moment he might turn in the saddle.

Rawley glanced despairingly about him. Fifteen yards to his right were the remains of a building of some kind—a low jumble of broken bricks, and an upsticking beam or two. Rawley whispered to Alf and began to crawl. The sack on his back seemed clamorously conspicuous and impeded his movement. He lowered it gently into a shell hole beside him and left it. Alf had stopped. Burdened as he was with the suit-case in front, the sack behind, and the blankets over his shoulder, crawling was impossible. Rawley pulled out his knife and went back. He cut the cord that held the suit-case and sack together. The old sacks might escape notice, but the suit-case would be startlingly visible: that would have to go. They crawled on, Rawley cursing the suit-case which Alf held awkwardly under one arm. They kept their eyes on the little group of horsemen not thirty yards distant, and at every impatient tapping of a hoof upon the road they dropped flat and lay still.

They reached the shelter of the mound of bricks at last and paused. They breathed more freely, but they did not feel safe. One or more of the horsemen might mount the slope and discover them crouching there. Rawley raised himself cautiously and examined the pile of debris in front of him. It consisted of a low bank of broken bricks, the remains evidently of an outer wall; beyond that, in what had been a room, was a hollow littered with plaster rubble; and beyond that again lay the fallen roof, a broken, blackened lattice-work of rafters, still covered in one place with broken slates. Under that their chances of escaping detection would be greatly improved.

They crawled with difficulty over the low barrier of bricks and crossed the filthy reeking hollow beyond. The fallen roof lay almost flat on the rubble, but they found a small space near the flattened peak of the gable and crawled under. There was room enough to lie comfortably under the slated portion, and the slates, though sufficiently damaged to allow them to see what was going on outside, were not so broken as to make their hiding-place dangerous. Furthermore they could now see the heads and shoulders of the horsemen on the sunken road. "If only we 'adn't left our perishin' sacks out there we might have 'ad a bite of somethin' while waitin' for the procession to pass," complained Alf.

"You have got your suit-case," retorted Rawley. "Have a bite at that."

He watched the horsemen with some anxiety. The sword scabbards and rifle buckets proclaimed them to be cavalry troopers. Four of them had dismounted, and while one walked the four horses slowly up the road, the remaining three climbed the far bank and settled down in full view of the hiding-place. The remaining man put his horse at the near bank and rode up the slope, passing between the shattered building and the sacks but without giving a glance to either. He disappeared from view over the crest.

The scrape of a match caused Rawley to turn sharply. Alf, his knees up and his back against a hummock of masonry, was in the act of applying a lighted match to the cigarette that dangled from one corner of his mouth; but before the flame could burn the tobacco, a hand knocked both cigarette and match on to the rubble. "You blasted fool," whispered Rawley. "Those fellows over there are facing this way and they would spot the smoke in a moment."

Alf recovered the bent cigarette from between two bricks at his feet. "Awkward beggar!" he growled as he straightened it between his fingers. "They wouldn't 'ave noticed nothin'. It ain't as though they was looking for us."

"I'm not so sure of that," answered Rawley. "We can't afford to play the fool, anyway."

Alf relapsed into grumpy silence; Rawley kept watch. The only sounds that reached him were the murmur of voices from the men below, and the klop of hoofs on the road as the horses were walked slowly up and down.

The light was gradually failing, and the mist that was so common over all the devastated area was shrouding distant objects one by one. Alf was dozing, and Rawley himself found the cold and silence were slowly wearing down his wakefulness.

He was aroused by the thud of hoofs behind him. Three horsemen rode out of the dusk and beside them plodded a man on foot. And as they rode slowly down the slope, passing within a few yards of his hiding-place, Rawley had confirmation of the suspicion that had troubled him for the past hour. In the slouching figure beside them he recognized one of the outcasts of the devastated area.

The men sitting on the bank rose at their approach, and the usual gruff interchange of chaff took place between them. The fast-gathering darkness made it difficult to see what was going on, and Rawley had to be guided by his ears. He heard the sound of rough English voices mingled with the jingle of bits. Then boots scraped on the road, and he heard the restless movement that a horse makes when a man climbs into the saddle. Feet pawed the road intermittently like instruments tuning up, and then, following a gruff "Walk March!" the whole orchestra of hoofs broke suddenly into sound. He watched the road where it was visible for fifty yards as a pale strip in the gloom and a few moments later saw the cavalcade pass as a dark slowly-moving shadow. It disappeared and the echo of the hoof beats died away.

" 'Ave they gone?' asked Alf in a hoarse whisper. "Well, I ain't sorry. What wiv draughts in me ear'ole and 'arf bricks in the back of me neck I ain't slep a wink. Roll on duration! What about movin'?"

"Presently," said Rawley. "We will give them a few more minutes to get right away. We've got to go dashed carefully. Kelly did us a good turn when he blew in our shaft."

"What'yer mean?"

"I mean that while we were digging our way out Kelly and his crowd were being rounded up. Didn't you see that chap those three fellows brought in just before they went off? He was one of the mob that raided the village. I expect they have cleaned up Kelly and now they have got the cavalry out rounding up the stragglers. We've got to go mighty carefully. No more daylight trekking, that's certain. One pipe and then we will start. Hold your coat open while I strike a match. We are taking no chances now."

IV

It was quite dark when they left their hiding-place. They recovered their sacks from the shell holes and set out. Rawley insisted that the rolled blankets should no longer be carried round the chest like a bandoleer. If they were hung loosely over one shoulder the whole of the impedimenta could then be dropped in a moment. He said it was absurd to take the suit-case, but Alf was adamant on this point. He declared that it balanced the sack on his back, and he had to carry it, so it was his funeral anyway.

They descended the slope and crossed the sunken road. There was no moon, but there were rifts in the clouds through which the stars shone, and Rawley set his course by the occasional glimpses he had of Altair and the Great Bear. It was a very unsatisfactory method, but no other was available.

They plodded on side by side at a steady pace and in silence. The exertion and the load they carried kept them warm in spite of the chill night air. They had eaten nothing since midday, but Rawley refused to stop. He said they could not afford the time that would be lost in stopping to open sacks and tins. When they had gone to earth in their new home it would be time enough to think of eating. They had brought two battered water-bottles with them and had quenched their thirst before leaving their hiding-place under the shattered roof.

Hour after hour went by, and the ceaseless plodding through the formless night produced in Rawley a kind of numbness of the brain. His limbs moved without his volition. It seemed that he was doomed to march to the end of time through a formless, endless and darkened world. He had no notion of his whereabouts. In that desert from which all landmarks had been obliterated the map was useless. He had set out from the dug-out on a course which, if accurately adhered to, would bring him straight to his destination, but he knew how difficult it was to march across country at night even with the aid of a compass. The rough-and-ready methods he was forced to use left all too much latitude in which to go astray. And in addition they had to make several detours to avoid hutments; and after these it was almost certain that they had not always got back even to the rough line they were following. The only course was to go ahead and trust that Alf would recognize some locality. One thing, however, Rawley had decided upon, and that was not to continue the march longer than two hours before dawn, unless Alf could say for certain that they were close to their destination. The best part of two hours might be required to find a suitable hiding-place, and they must be below ground before the darkness lifted.

They trudged on wearily like automatons, and the only variation in the movement was when some fracture of the ground caused them to lengthen or shorten their pace and the occasional hitch given to sack or blankets. Rawley estimated that barely three hours of darkness remained.

A huge truncated pyramid loomed up darkly to their left, its outlines ragged and undefined in the murk. Rawley broke the long silence. "What on earth's that?" he whispered. They turned towards it by silent consent. The ground was much broken by ancient shell holes and shallow trench remains. The huge shape bulked broader and higher as they approached. It was mottled with pale grey streaks and patches, and quite suddenly they found themselves at its foot. It towered above them, a gigantic pimple of earth on a high plateau. Its surface was furrowed and pitted; rank grass grew upon it, but the underlying chalk showed in streaks and patches. "My God, it might be Silbury Hill!" muttered Rawley.

Alf made a sudden exclamation. "I know where we are, mate," he cried excitedly. "This 'ere's the old Butte de

Warlincourt. Don't I know it! Proper 'ealth resort it was in '16—I don't think."

"I've heard of it," answered Rawley in a low voice. "Don't shout. But whereabouts is it?"

"Bapaume way."

"Yes, but north, south, east or west?"

"It's before you come to Bapaume."

"What, west of it? Wait a minute—how does it lie with regard to that road, the Albert-Bapaume Road?"

"You can see it from the road easy."

"But which side of it—north or south? Coming from Albert, say, is it right or left?"

"Right—an' it ain't more'an about fifteen kilos from Albert."

"Good—we're getting near. Now let me think." Rawley did not think it prudent to strike a match so near a road, but he had studied the map so carefully that he carried a plan of its main features in his mind. The Albert-Bapaume road, he remembered, ran diagonally across the map— roughly S.W. and N.E. If they marched between those two points, N.W. that was, they must strike the road. Then they must follow the road in the direction of Albert and turn off it southwards at Poizières—that was if Alf could recognise a pile of bricks as that village. He turned his attention to the sky. Gaps in the clouds were rare and the clouds moved sluggishly. He had to wait several minutes before a glimpse of the Great Bear gave him the direction of the Pole Star. Then he faced it, turned half left and set off.

They came upon the road in a few minutes, one of those straight French roads that switchback uncompromisingly across the country as though drawn with a ruler; but they did not venture to follow it. They went back a few yards and moved parallel with the pale glimmer on their right.

"We haven't much time," whispered Rawley. "It will be dawn in something under three hours. It's fifteen kilometres to Albert, you say; how far to Poizières, do you think?"

Alf thought for a moment. "Not more'an eight or nine, I reckon."

"Well, it will take us the best part of an hour and a half to do that—and then this cellar of yours I made out to be about two kilometres south of that. And we have got to find it, too. By jove, we shall not have much time if we're not to be caught by the dawn."

"Don't you worry, old cock," answered Alf confidently. "There are thousands of perishin' dug-outs round this ruddy place."

They plodded steadily along. Once they dropped flat while a lorry rumbled along the road with rattling chains and flapping cover. That was the only sound that broke the silence.

Once to their right they saw the framework of a raised water-tank dark against the sky, and they went warily till it had disappeared in the gloom behind them. Then a few low mounds of brick rubble announced that they were passing over a village. Beyond it to their right the wedge-shaped nose of a tank pointing upwards showed dimly against the night sky. Rawley halted. "Is that a derelict or not?" he whispered.

"A derelick," said Alf. "I remember him. This 'ere's Poizières."

They turned south. Crumbling trenches lay everywhere about them. To their left the ground sloped down to a shallow valley. "Keep just below the crest on this side and follow the slope," said Rawley. Some minutes later some stark, ragged tree trunks stabbed the night sky ahead. "There's your wood," said Rawley. "Or I'm a Dutchman."

Alf was dubious till they came upon a grass-grown rutted track fronting the stark trees; then he said, "You're right, mate. That's where we 'ad the guns—why, you can see some of the pits now. Come on, we'll soon be 'ome." And he led the way confidently in among the shattered tree stumps. Presently they were stumbling over the brick rubble remains of a building. " 'Ere we are," whispered Alf. "I'll go an' hinspect the billet." He slipped off the sack, suitcase, roll of blankets, and rifle, and revolver in hand moved cautiously around the pile of rubbish.

He was back again in a few minutes. "It's all right, mate. There ain't nobody there. There's a bit of water on the floor, but one of the old bunks is there and a bit of a table. We'll be as snug as a bug in a rug in a couple of shakes." He shouldered his load again, and Rawley followed him round the heap of rubble, through a tangle of brambles, and down a number of brick steps. Ten minutes later they were both asleep.

CHAPTER XIX

I

THEY awoke rested, but ravenously hungry. They therefore ate a substantial meal, washed down with the water that remained in their water-bottles. They thought it unwise to light a fire until they had satisfied themselves that there were no troops in the neighbourhood. At the end of the meal Rawley lighted his pipe and inspected his new home by the light of the candle that was perched on two bricks. It was a small cellar some fifteen feet square, with a vaulted roof. The brick floor was dry except where a small pool of water had collected in a hollow at the foot of the steps. An old wire-netting bunk stood against one wall, and an overturned table with a broken leg completed the furniture. A rusty oil drum, punched with holes to serve as a brazier, stood on three bricks in a corner.

There was plenty of work to be done. There was the table to mend and a second bunk to be constructed. Timber was to be had for the gathering in the wood above, and they had brought a dozen or more nails with them. But they needed some wire netting.

Rawley went up the steps to prospect. It was just after three o'clock in the afternoon, and he went cautiously. The steps reached the ground level among a heap of rubble overgrown with brambles, and were thus most satisfactorily screened from the view of anyone who might chance that way. He walked to the edge of the wood and surveyed the prospect. Some five hundred yards away beyond a slight depression were the remains of a village, a few heaps of mouldering bricks; one white ragged wall a few feet high, the remains of the church, and two or three shivered tree trunks standing stark against the grey sky. He made the complete circuit of the little wood. On the second side a crumbling trench protected by a tangle of rusty wire ran along its margin; on the third, the bare slope was patterned with a network of old trenches, the old German Line of '15, he surmised; and along the fourth ran a weed-grown rutted track and a shallow zigzagging communicating-trench.

On his way back he noticed the rusty iron cylinder of a pump lying by a small mound of brick rubble. Where there is a pump, there is a well, he told himself, and he set about looking for it. The mound of brick rubble was probably the remains of an outhouse in which the pump had been, but though he probed all over the area with the broken handle of the pump he could find no trace of the well. The narrow pump shaft had evidently been effectively blocked by rubbish and fallen bricks. He was just giving up the task as hopeless when a memory of a boyish holiday spent on a Norfolk farm occurred to him. He remembered there just such a pump in the long brick-floored kitchen, and a yard or two outside the kitchen door there had been a circular stone flag with an iron ring in it. He had tugged at that ring with boyish curiosity, and he remembered how the farmwife had come out and scolded him, telling him that underneath was a well so deep that one waited half a minute to hear a stone splash in the water below.

He left the little mound of rubbish and walked slowly in a circle round it, stamping the ground and foraging among the grass and rubbish with his toes. He completed the circle and began a wider one. Half way round, his stamping feet struck a firm surface that rang hollow. He cleared away the grass and dirt and disclosed a circular flagstone with an iron ring, the double of the one he had tugged at as a boy. The flagstone was heavy and sealed with dirt, but, using the pump handle as a lever, he managed to move it far enough to allow a stone to pass through the gap. He listened and heard a slight splash far below. He returned to the cellar well pleased with the results of his exploration.

II

Alf was standing by his bunk with his back to it as Rawley came down the steps; something half-guilty in his attitude suggested that he was trying to hide something. Rawley glanced at him curiously, and then, with a smile and a nod towards the suit-case that was too long to be completely hidden, he said, "Got it open at last?"

Alf nodded rather shamefacedly. Rawley made no comment. "You was right," said Alf at last. "It's full of clothes."

Rawley allowed himself a little smile. "Well, what did you expect it to be full of—gold and jewels? But never mind that. I've found the well. And it seems O.K. as far as I can see. It will save us a hell of a lot of trouble—and danger. It's only a few yards off." Alf brightened up. "That's good work, mate," he said.

Rawley nodded. "Yes, I'm rather pleased with that effort. All we want is a bucket and a rope."

Alf rubbed the back of his neck. "The bucket's easy," he said. "Ought to be plenty of cans lying round 'ere. But the rope—is it a long one?"

"Um—I dropped a stone down, and it sounded pretty deep."

Alf looked gloomy. "We won't find a rope, mate. An' if we do it'll be rotten after being out 'ere all this time."

"Shut up, grouser," retorted Rawley. "How about telephone cable! There ought to be plenty of that in some of these old trenches."

"I s'pose so," agreed Alf reluctantly.

"Of course there will. And we'll go out and find some presently. You've got that wretched suit-case on your chest. Cheer up. After all, you know, clothes will be useful." Then he began to laugh as a thought struck him. "I say, they weren't women's clothes, were they?"

Alf indignantly denied the suggestion. "They're orficers' clo'es," he said. "Proper square pushin' togs. You 'ave a look." And he lifted the lid.

Rawley took out the garments one by one. There was a service tunic with the black maltese cross of the Army Chaplain's Corps on the lapels, a pair of breeches, puttees, a soft cap, and shirt —everything in fact except boots and Sam Browne. There was a waterproof sponge-bag, containing a sponge, shaving soap, a small housewife, containing buttons, needles, thread, and a small pair of scissors; a safety razor in a leather case, a small mirror, and a brush and comb. A note-book, half filled with a pencilled scrawl that was almost illegible, a field cheque-book for drawing from the Field Cashier, and a book of Common Prayer completed the list.

Rawley lighted his pipe and regarded the pile of garments thoughtfully. Alf was trying on the tunic. Suddenly Rawley looked up. "Don't mess up that tunic," he said. "I've got an idea."

"Why, you 'ad one only last week!" said Alf.

Rawley ignored the sarcasm. "I've got some money," he went on.

"An' so 'ave I," retorted Alf proudly. "Five francs I've 'ad for the last couple o' months and a ten-franc note Kelly's bright lads overlooked in that canteen."

"Well, I have some, too," said Rawley. "When Kelly and you so neatly knocked me on the head that night and took my wallet I had just changed fifty francs, and I stuck the change in my waistband pocket. Kelly didn't find it."

Alf grinned. "Good egg! That's one up agin Kelly. But it ain't no use 'cause we can't spend it."

"But that's just it, we can," retorted Rawley. "If I put on that uniform—"

"An' a fine sight you'd look," retorted Alf contemptuously. "'Ave a look at your dial in that lookin' glars."

"Oh, I dare say. But there's scissors and shaving-tackle there, and I'd soon have this off." He fingered his beard.

"Bit risky, ain't it?" asked Alf dubiously.

"Of course, but then I'm not likely to meet anyone I know. And besides, I've changed a lot since I've lived out here. I always had a moustache; I'll take that off. Damn it all, clean shaven and dressed up in a padre's kit, I don't believe I'd be recognized if I did meet someone I knew. And think how useful it would be. I could buy any stuff we wanted and find out what is going on."

Alf nodded. "Ay, it'd be useful—that it would. Still, a bit risky."

"I don't believe it would be a bit more risky than just sitting here," asserted Rawley. "After all, odd officers are always blowing in and out of the mess, and no one ever thinks of asking a lot of questions about them. And padre's kit is just the thing for the job. Nobody ever bothers what a padre does or where he comes from. He's just the padre. By jove, it's a great scheme! You'll see."

III

Just before dusk they explored some of the old German trenches in the neighbourhood and collected several hundred feet of old telephone cable. From a number of battered petrol tins, buckets, and old cans of all descriptions, they selected two petrol tins and a small oil drum. Using the oil drum as a bucket, they filled the petrol cans from the well and returned to the cellar.

297

While Alf busied himself with making a fire, Rawley took the nail-scissors and mirror from the suit-case. He hung the mirror on a rusty nail, but, at the first glimpse of himself in the glass, he paused, scissors in hand, and regarded his reflection with horror. He had been disgusted by the appearance of Alf and the other outcasts, and though he had known that he himself must look much the same, he was shocked, nevertheless, now that for the first time he was confronted with his own image. He saw the face of a stranger—an unsavoury, dangerous-looking character, with dirty, lined face and bright furtive eyes, whose furrowed brow and ears were draped by tangled, uncut locks, whose chin and collarless throat were hidden by a ragged, unkempt beard. He peered curiously at the revolting spectacle, nodding his head slowly as one by one he recognized latent points of resemblance with the reflection he had known. Then, as though rousing himself from an evil dream, he raised the scissors purposefully and clipped off the unkempt beard close to the skin. He nodded with satisfaction at the improvement he had made in his appearance, and attacked the ragged moustache. "Alf, my lad," he cried boyishly, "heat some water; I'm going to have a shave presently."

Shaving was a painful process, but he completed it at last, and surveyed the result with satisfaction. "That's not so bad for the first go off," he said. "If I have another tomorrow morning, I ought to get it pretty smooth. And now for a hair-cut. Come on, you must be barber. Fetch the comb. I'll sit on the bunk."

Alf snipped away with the nail-scissors while Rawley held the mirror, and gave directions from time to time. At the end of it he stood up and turned his head that way and this in the glass. "Well, you will never make your fortune as a barber, Alf," he commented. "But it's certainly an improvement."

Alf, with arms akimbo, was critically surveying the result of his handiwork. Suddenly he strode to the corner in which their stores were piled, rummaged there for a moment, and then, with an air of triumph, banged a small tin down on the table.

"What's that?" demanded Rawley.

"Dubbin," announced Alf proudly. "I brought one tin along 'cause I knew it'd come in handy."

"What's the idea?"

Alf did not reply at first. He opened the tin, pushed back his frayed and threadbare cuffs, smeared his fingers with dubbing, and approached Rawley with hands raised. "'Air oil," he explained, with a grin.

Rawley backed. "Here, wait a minute!"

"Make you look a proper toff!" said Alf ingratiatingly.

"That really isn't a bad idea," agreed Rawley, after a moment's consideration. "But I tell you what I will do; I will put it on tomorrow after I've had a bath."

They had their evening meal, and after it Rawley spent the time before turning in for the night in making ready for his adventure on the morrow. He still had his Sam Browne, which he wore as a belt under his French peasant jacket, and the cross-strap he had used as a rifle sling; but the difficulty was to make them presentable since he had no polish or brass cleaner. Pipe in mouth he set to work with a rag, and after laborious rubbing restored some semblance of polish to the belt. The brass parts he cleaned with brick dust, and polished with a rag. "Well, anyway, no one expects a padre to glitter like a brass hat," he sighed as he inspected the result of his labour, and he made a mental note that his first purchases at a canteen must include cleaning kit and a tin of brilliantine.

IV

Alf was facetious the following morning as Rawley made his toilet. "Sorry I ain't got no fice powder, Gertie," he grinned, as he watched Rawley vigorously towelling himself with the padre's towel. "But I can hoffer you a pinch o' brick-dust to put a rosy blush in them cheeks o' yours." Rawley's reply caused Alf to hide his face coquettishly, and cry, "'Ush, 'Ush, Gertie. Wot languidge!"

"Well," said Rawley, when he was dressed, "what's the verdict?"

Alf inspected him carefully from head to foot. "You'll do, mate," he said solemnly. "You'll do. But you oughter stoop a bit; most parsons 'ave a 'ump. An' you wanter stick yer chin out as though you'd been usedter shovin' it over the top o' one of them dorg collars. You've got it in too much like a bloomin' soldier."

"Have I?" said Rawley, with a pleased laugh. "God, it's good to feel like a soldier again! But I won't forget." He put on the cap. "Well, I'm off. When I come back, I will whistle 'Old soldiers never die,' and you will know it's me. Cheer'o!"

"Good luck, mate. 'Ere, an' I say, you'd better take this." Alf produced his revolver.

Rawley turned on the steps. "No—I shan't want that. You lie low here till I come back. Cheer'o."

CHAPTER XX

THE night had been clear and frosty, and rime still furred the debris and dead branches that carpeted the little wood. But the sun shone from a cloudless sky, giving shadows to the shivered trees and colouring pale orange their dead, barkless trunks. Rawley interpreted the sunlight as a good omen. He paused for a moment by the grass-grown track that bordered the wood, and then, taking his courage in both hands, crossed it boldly and followed a half-obliterated footpath that would bring him to the Bapaume Road.

He experienced a pleasurable feeling of excitement and exhilaration that was fostered by the keen air and bright sunlight, and he strode rapidly up the gentle slope. At the top he came in sight of the road. It was less than three hundred yards from him, running straight in either direction till it topped a slope and disappeared. Half-right on the rising ground lay the ragged brick heaps of a shattered village and, glowing redly in the sunlight, the rusty upturned nose of the tank they had passed on their night march. Half-left, in a hollow, lay another ruined village, beyond which the road rose over a trench-scarred slope and disappeared.

He reached the road and turned left down it towards the village in the hollow. A G.S. wagon was ambling towards him, and as it passed, the driver dropped his hand and jerked his head like a mechanical doll. Rawley

returned the salute and strode jauntily on. The incident
had given him confidence. It was good to move above
ground again in daylight, and he revelled in this new-
found sense of freedom. He reached the village in the
hollow, which his map told him must be La Boiselle, and
looked about him with interest. Huge mine craters lay on
both sides of the road, mighty pits in the chalk, forty, fifty,
and sixty feet deep. This must be the old no-man's-land
of 1915 and pre-July '16, he thought; and those crumbling
trenches on the slope he was ascending were the old
British Line. He trudged on up the slope, and on the crest
paused as a new world came into view.

Below him lay a town, a battered little town, but
beautiful in the clear air and sunlight. The red-brick walls
and chimneys glowed warmly in the morning light, and
the surrounding country was green with that green of grass
and leaves that was so restful after the ash-grey growth,
pounded chalk, and bare clay of the devastated area. A
tree-bordered road ran like a taut white tape up the green
slope beyond, and the trees at the top stood out clear-cut
and toy-like against the clear pale sky. A tall, brick church
tower, rosy in the morning light, rose proudly from the
clustering roofs and chimneys, and the bent and gilded
figure at the top glittered like a heliograph above the
countryside. He had no need to consult the map; this could
only be the famous Hanging Virgin of Albert.

He walked on and reached the first houses. Most of
them were shuttered and deserted, and many were tileless.
He turned up a narrow street and found himself in the

shell-pocked square at the foot of the gashed church tower, with the flashing figure with outstretched arms poised like a diver above him. A green staff car and a flying corps tender stood on the broken *pavé*. He stopped a Tommy and asked him if there were a canteen thereabouts, and the man directed him up a street to the right.

A young A.S.C officer came in as he was making his few purchases. He nodded and said, "'Morning, padre. Glad to see you are patronising our canteen." Rawley offered a cigarette, and they left the canteen together. "You are not teetotal, I hope, padre," said the young officer, as they stood in the street. "Come along to the mess and have a drink." They went a few yards up the street and entered a café that had been abandoned by its owners. "Well, what is it to be, padre—whisky, vermouth, or mother's ruin?"

Rawley chose whisky. A Tommy brought in a bottle and a tantalus. "Well, happy days!" said the A.S.C. officer, raising his glass. "You in the town?" he added conversationally, a few moments later.

"I just came to buy a few things," answered Rawley, guardedly.

"Better stay then, and have a spot of lunch with us."

"Well, that's awfully good of you," agreed Rawley.

The other officers came in for lunch, and Rawley was very guarded during the meal. He kept carefully to the role of a conscientious chaplain, ignorant of military matters, and rather worried and anxious about the keeping of army regulations. He learned among other things that this was a Mechanical Transport mess, that they were Army troops, and that there were several Labour Corps units in the neighbourhood engaged in clearing up the old battlefield.

"Well, it's not often we have a padre in the mess," said the A.S.C. captain. "It must be months since we had one here. I'm afraid you will find us rather a Godless lot, padre. But if you want to arrange a church parade, go ahead by all means."

Rawley was glad to learn that there were no real chaplains in the neighbourhood. "Thank you," he said. "But I haven't called professionally, so to speak—and besides, as you are not in my parish, I'm afraid I'm cadging a lunch under false pretences. I—I feel rather guilty, eating up others' rations."

The captain laughed. "That's all right, padre. Don't you worry about that. We always have several rations in hand. We feed all the odds and ends in the neighbourhood. Our ration strength bobs up and down like a temperature chart, and when in doubt, we bung on a couple."

Rawley suddenly determined on a bold stroke. He sighed. "Rations always worry me," he said. "I cannot cope with all these forms. When I was first on my own I was attached to one unit after another, and every time they changed I went without rations. The new lot said I could not draw them for two days, and I ought to have let them know earlier, or drawn from the other lot." He sighed again, rather pathetically. "Of course, you people always know when troops are moving and all that, but nobody ever tells a padre anything, and I never knew they were moving till they were actually gone."

"Bad luck, padre," said the captain. "Have some more beer; it's French, but wet. So you went without rations?"

Rawley nodded. "But I got tired of that," he continued, with an air of gentle pride in his own astuteness. "And so I went to the senior chaplain about it, and he arranged for me to draw rations from Bapaume."

"Bapaume! That's a goodish step!"

"Yes, that's it," said Rawley. "But I had to get them from there; it was something to do with Corps and Division and Army. I didn't understand it, but there it is."

"Good old red tape!" commented the captain.

"Of course, it would be much more convenient to draw them from someone in Albert."

"Why not?" said the captain. "I should, if it's nearer. No good tramping miles for nothing."

"I might ask," said Rawley, doubtfully. "But I expect I should not be allowed to—Army instead of Corps, or something."

"Why ask?" said the captain. "I should just attach myself to somebody, and leave it at that."

"But wouldn't there be some regulations or something?"

"You're too conscientious, padre," grinned the captain. "Take my advice and never ask anybody in the army for anything that you can get yourself. When you've tried and can't, then it's time enough to chase the brass hats. What the deuce does it matter to anyone where you draw rations from! You are entitled to rations, and common sense says draw them from the most convenient place—whether it's Army, G.H.Q., or the bloomin' War Office itself. I would just fix it up on your own and say nothing to nobody."

Rawley assumed an expression of worried indecision.

"How many rations do you want?" asked the captain.

"Two—only two. Myself and my man."

"Can your man come in here for them?"

"Oh, yes!"

The captain lit a cigarette. "Well, send him along. I'll draw them for you."

"That is very good of you," said Rawley. "But, well—really. Supposing when they go through these indents, or whatever you call them, they found my name and—well, wouldn't there be a dreadful fuss?"

The captain laughed. "We don't put your name down, you know, padre. But don't you worry. They can't check my indent. It's never the same two days together. We get so many odds and ends passing through—and between ourselves we don't go short. Of course, it ought to go in forty-eight hours in advance, but you send your fellow along tomorrow, and it will be all right."

"That's awfully good of you," said Rawley with real gratitude.

"Not a bit. But, let me see, two rations are pretty small. Your chap had better draw for three days at a time, and come every third day. If you come with me presently, I will show you where our quarter-bloke hangs out, and I will tell him your fellow will be coming along tomorrow."

II

It was a very elated young padre who, later that afternoon, swung out of Albert up the Bapaume Road. He marched along confidently and whistled as he walked, but the tunes were not hymn tunes, and some half-hour later, as he approached a pile of debris in a little wood, it was not by accident that the tune was "Old Soldiers Never Die."

Alf's face, in the light of one candle end, wore a relieved look. "Got back all right then, chum!" he said. "I've been as nervous as a blinkin' cat the 'ole time you been away."

Rawley put his few purchases on the rickety table. "Yes, here I am again—all present and correct."

Alf was turning over the tin of polish, soldier's friend, brilliantine and toothpaste. "Is this all you got?" he asked gloomily. "Didn't yer git no grub?"

"We don't want any," answered Rawley, as he took off his belt.

"P'raps not now, but we bloomin' well shall afore long."

Rawley shook his head. "No. We are going to draw rations," he said, with a mysterious smile.

"Rations! Here—get out! What d'yer mean rations?"

"What I say. The padre has arranged to draw rations for himself and servant from an M.T. unit in Albert. We draw three days' rations every third day."

"Garn!" exclaimed Alf derisively. "What, an' rum ration as well, I reckon," he added sarcastically.

"And rum ration as well," repeated Rawley. "When there is one." And he told Alf what had happened.

Alf sat on his bunk and rubbed the back of his neck in a characteristic manner. "Well, that's a proper knock-out. Drorin' rations!" Suddenly he looked up with a serious face. "Who's going to drore 'em?" he demanded.

"You are," said Rawley. "And you start tomorrow."

Alf shook his head. "No, I ain't. Not me. I'd never get away with it. An orficer might, but not a ruddy gunner. No, chum, you'll 'ave to draw 'em."

Rawley pointed out that it would excite comment for an officer to draw rations, even though he were a padre, that the risk was small, and that since he himself had taken the greater risk in asking for them, Alf might do his bit, and take the lesser.

Alf was only half convinced. "And besides, I can't go like this," he added triumphantly.

"No—you aren't fit for C.O.'s parade at the moment," Rawley conceded. "But we will soon alter that. Hair cut, shave—by the by, did you have a moustache or were you clean shaven? Before you took French leave, I mean."

"I 'adn't no moustache," said Alf sulkily.

"Well, we will give you one now, then. A good, walrusy, Old Bill moustache. You can wear my old breeches; your cap will just pass muster—for a padre's servant, that is. The difficulty is your tunic; I'm afraid that's beyond repair. I suppose the only thing to do is to try to steal one."

Alf rubbed the back of his neck. "Look 'ere, chum, do you really mean I've got to go?"

Rawley nodded. "I am afraid so, Alf. We can't afford to chuck away a chance like this."

Alf nodded gloomily. "You don't think they'll cop me?"

"When we've rigged you up with that moustache I honestly think that the chances of anyone recognizing you are about one in a million. I tell you, I found it as easy as pie—and so will you. Don't talk more than is necessary, that's all."

"All right, chum, I'll go." And then he suddenly brightened and smacked his thigh delightedly. "Blimey! Drorin' rations—ain't that a scream!"

"And now we have to think out about that tunic," said Rawley.

"You leave that to me, mate. As soon as it's dark we'll go out. You show me where there's some troops, an' if I don't come back wiv a tunic or somethin', I'll eat my hat."

Alf kept his word, and later that night he returned to the cellar, wearing a soldier's greatcoat that effectively concealed his disreputable tunic. Then Rawley set to work with scissors and comb, and before they turned in for the night their preparations were complete for drawing rations on the morrow.

They walked into Albert together. Rawley had decided that this was best. It would enable him to point out the position of the M.T. unit and thus avoid the necessity of Alf asking questions of other troops; and it would give Alf confidence. And Alf gained confidence rapidly. No one gave them a second glance as they crossed the square beneath the shattered tower of the cathedral. Rawley with his slightly hunched shoulders, rather ill-fitting tunic, and clean-shaven face looked a typical padre, and Alf with his shaggy moustache, shabby cap and greatcoat with a sandbag rolled up under one arm looked the typical old soldier who, by reason of bad feet or wounds, has been given a light job as batman to a town major or padre.

Rawley walked back and waited for Alf on the Bapaume Road. Half an hour later Alf reappeared with a broad grin and a well-filled sandbag. "Everything in the garden's luvely," he said as he came up. "I jes said I've come for Capting Parker's rations and the quarter dished 'em out like a bleedin' lamb."

"Good," said Rawley. "But don't you forget to salute me in public. We have got to be careful about details."

III

Fresh meat and vegetables were such luxuries that for the two days following that first drawing of rations food filled the entire horizon. They vied with each other in thinking out new methods of cooking, and the hours between meals were devoted to the preparation of the next. It was the one topic of conversation and of thought. But soon the novelty wore off, and Rawley found the time hang heavy on his hands. In the old dug-out in the centre of the devastated area he had had to get his supplies by craft or by stealth, and although he had bitterly cursed the necessity it had provided an object in an otherwise objectless life. The necessities of living had occupied the mind and the body. But now there was nothing to occupy either. The bare means of living were provided, and apart from the duties of cooking, eating, and drawing water from the well, body and mind lay fallow.

After his long sojourn as an outcast in the deserted battlefields, that first walk into Albert, decently clean and clothed, had seemed a heaven of delight; but after three or four visits, on those alternate days that he was not cook, the delight faded. It was dull walking about aimlessly, with nothing to do and with nothing constructive to occupy one's thoughts. He envied the men he saw about him. No doubt they were cursing the war and wishing themselves back in civilian life, but they were doing something; they had some object to which they were striving—if it were only to get the job done and go home. He realized bitterly that it is better to have an unpleasant job than no job at all. And at first the risk he ran of arrest as a spy or deserter had given a zest to his walks abroad, but now he was so familiar with his surroundings and moved about so freely and without question that the danger seemed almost negligible, the more so since he had learned that his old division had moved northwards from the area.

He had borrowed a magazine from the M.T. Mess and had read it from cover to cover. He had no books. Quite suddenly it occurred to him that there was nothing to prevent him from going into Amiens to buy some, and he asked himself why he had not thought of it before. It was a splendid idea; and he grew as excited as a schoolboy at the prospect of being in an undamaged, civilized town, and of looking at the windows of real civilian shops. And Alf's suggestion that it might be a bit risky only added zest to the adventure.

IV

He set out on the following morning, leaving Alf shaking his head dolefully in the cellar. His intention was to walk to Albert and try to pick up a lorry or car, but he had barely set foot upon the Albert road before a lorry rumbled up behind him coming from the direction of Bapaume. He asked the driver if he were going anywhere near Amiens. The driver was: he was going through Amiens to Flixecourt. Rawley climbed up into the broad front seat, and the lorry rumbled on its way.

It was one of those bright, mild days that come sometimes early in the year and give a foretaste of spring. Even the rubble heaps of the old battlefield looked almost friendly in the cheerful light, and as the lorry topped the rise by the old British front line, Rawley saw again as he had seen on that first morning walk the Hanging Virgin of Albert flashing golden in the sunlight.

The lorry rumbled on through the narrow *pavé* streets of the town, across the square that, by reason of the levelled buildings surrounding it, was twice as large as its pre-war self; swung left-handed into the narrow street where the tangle of twisted metal in the shattered Schneider factory resembled a gigantic bramble bush, crossed the bridge over the grass-grown railway and climbed the hill beyond. The shattered roofs and splinter-pocked walls of the houses had been left behind. Trees bordered the road. Real trees: not splintered stumps of dead barkless wood, but trees with branches overhead already budding with the promise of spring. The road switchbacked undeviatingly across the low hills, and occasionally to his left, when the hedgeless plough-land dipped in widening curves to a transverse valley, he saw across the countless furrows some peaceful tree-embowered village in the Ancre valley below. Rawley, on the front seat of the moving lorry, enjoyed it all as a schoolboy enjoys his first homecoming.

The country became more wooded, villages more frequent. Woods, red with young shoots, nestled in the folds of the ground, and at times bordered the road. One fleeting glimpse he had of Amiens cathedral, grey and sunlit in the distance.

The driver slowed at last, where a broad road diverged to the left. "I'll have to drop you here, sir. I go straight on, and lorries aren't allowed in the streets of the town anyway."

Rawley climbed down and took the left-hand road. Presently it became a broad boulevard with trees and a cycle track on either side and houses. He reached the iron bridge over the Somme and saw the city before him, tree-shaded quays by the river, and the old houses rising to the great grey bulk of the cathedral.

He walked down the Rue des Trois Cailloux feeling rather like one treading the streets of fairyland. The civilians, particularly the women and girls in pretty frocks, and the shops containing groceries, high-heeled shoes, fish and game, feminine hats, toys, silk stockings, gramophones and pianos, chocolates, and carpenters' tools, seemed as though they must have been transported from some happy land of fancy, so remote were they from the splintered wood and bricks, mud, filth, and desolation of his recent surroundings.

He wandered slowly through the streets like a spirit revisiting the scenes of its earthly life, watching, as it were from a distance, the busy passers-by, lingering at the shop windows, and automatically returning occasional salutes. He remembered much of the city from his one previous visit, and he found that unconsciously he had begun to retrace his steps of that day not so very long ago that now seemed to belong to another life and another age. He went under the archway and stared across the cobbles at the glass door of the baths; he peered through the glass between the mounds of pastries into Odette's tea-shop. He found the little restaurant where Rumbald, Piddock, Penhurst and he had had that riotous and rather scandalous dinner. In broad daylight in the narrow side street it looked shabby and depressing. And he went down to the canal and sat on the bench under the trees, where he had sat that night in the darkness, listening to the hum of hostile aircraft.

Here he ate the sandwiches he had brought with him. He had been sorely tempted to enter an hotel and order a good lunch. But prudence had prevailed. It would have been a shameful waste of his diminishing funds, and he had compromised with the temptation by promising himself tea in a tea-shop, which would be equally enjoyable but less expensive. He found a paper shop in a corner of the Place Gambetta, and bought an English newspaper and two paper-covered novels.

He turned into a tea-shop shortly before four o'clock. Several British officers were already having tea, but he found a little table in a corner. A French girl in a diminutive fancy apron came to take his order, and he was dismayed to find himself stuttering with embarrassment; but she was a self-possessed little lady and seemed neither flattered nor disturbed by the effect she had produced upon the shy young English padre. She brought his tea, and it was only some minutes later that he remembered the procedure, and rose, plate and fork in hand, to choose his cakes. The incident turned his thought to the tea-shop in Doullens, where he and Berney on their first meeting had chosen cakes together and had chaffed each other upon their choice. He returned to his lonely table with all his animation gone.

One or two other British officers came into the shop, and lastly a young chaplain. There were no vacant tables, and the man, after a brief glance round, came and sat down at Rawley's little table. "I hope you don't mind," he said. Rawley did mind, but he murmured politely, "Not at all." Conversation with a real chaplain would have pitfalls, and he eyed the man covertly as the waitress came to take the order.

Evidently he had not been in France long, for he wore the black tie which had been discarded by most chaplains in the field. Not long ago, Rawley thought, he had worn the roman collar and black stock. He was probably rather green, and that was a point to the good. His own role, he decided, must be that of the old hand who discouraged the talking of shop.

The conversation opened in the English fashion with the weather. The man obviously wanted to talk, and Rawley let him talk. It would give Rawley a chance to finish his tea. When he tired of talking about himself, and began to display some curiosity about his fellow padre, then it would be time for Rawley to excuse himself and leave.

Meanwhile he sat and listened, putting in a word here and there to stimulate the flow. He might learn some useful points that would help him to sustain his role of a padre.

He learnt that his diagnosis was correct. The young clergyman had been in France only three weeks. He had reported to a Headquarters that he did not know the name of and had hung about for several days doing nothing. Then he had been billeted in Amiens, where he had met an older padre who was running a canteen and ministering to the needs of various details of troops in the neighbourhood. The older padre had then been ordered to report to a division in the Line and the younger man, not knowing what else to do, had taken over the canteen, which he was still running. He was enthusiastic and desperately anxious to be of use, but he had received no orders, and so he remained in the billet originally allotted to him, ran the canteen, and held a service whenever he could scrape together a congregation, which was seldom. He spoke to Rawley as an older and more experienced man. What should he do?

"One of the first principles out here," said Rawley, "is not to go looking for trouble. It comes without any looking for. Just sit tight and do what you can. They have forgotten you, I expect. One fine day some brass hat will take his feet off the mantelpiece and have a look at the papers they have been resting on. Then he'll discover you, and they will send you chits and things and bundle you off to some godforsaken spot. My advice is to sit tight and see what happens.

The young chaplain sighed. "It's all rather different from what one expected," he said. "Very different from a country parish. I am from Yorkshire. What part of the country do you come from?"

"The Channel Islands," answered Rawley at a venture.

"Oh yes. Beautiful place, I've heard. Let me see, you are in the Winchester diocese, aren't you?"

Rawley nodded and rose. "I must be getting back," he said, and took his leave.

CHAPTER XXI

I

Rawley paid other visits to Amiens. He had discovered a cinema, and when he grew tired of walking the streets, there he could sit and pass in pleasant forgetfulness some of the hours that hung so heavily on his hands. His improved conditions of life had only increased his desire for further comfort. He enjoyed the mere act of sitting on the little tip-up seats in the cinema, and he thought it worth the price of a beer or coffee to sit on the padded red plush seat of a café. Once he was strongly assailed by a temptation to spend the night in an hotel in a real bed in a comfortable room, and he was only restrained from yielding to it by the realization that it would be tempting Providence in the form of the A.P.M. to sign a false name in the register.

On one of his visits he encountered the young chaplain he had met in the tea-shop. They had a drink together in a café and smoked a pipe. The young chaplain was obviously attracted to Rawley. He was lonely, feeling himself something of an outsider among the officers who came and went on leave, or to and from the Line. And Rawley was glad of somebody to talk to now that he found that it was easy to keep the conversation to safe topics.

One evening as Rawley was walking down the Boulevarde d'Alsace, intending to lorry-jump back to Albert, he met the young chaplain hurrying in the opposite direction. He seized Rawley by the arm. "Come back and have some dinner with me," he said. Rawley demurred. "Come on," the other insisted. "It's my last night in Amiens. I got orders about half an hour ago. You are the very man I wanted to see; I haven't the faintest idea what I have to do, and you can tell me everything. In return I'll stand you a jolly good dinner at the Godbert."

"Well, if you put it that way," said Rawley, and he turned back.

They went into the palm-decorated foyer of the Godbert and ordered the meal. "It must be a real good one," said the chaplain. "We will start with oysters and brown bread and butter."

"I have no quarrel with that," agreed Rawley. They worked through the menu together and decided on each course.

"About drinks," said the chaplain. "I'm afraid that's rather my weak suit. Port and champagne is about the limit of my wine knowledge. I leave it to you."

Rawley suggested Chambertin, and the chaplain agreed. They were shown to a table in the long-mirrored room where the lights, white napery and glittering glass made Rawley feel that this was the summit of those steps of respectability and civilization that he had begun to climb with the cutting of his ragged beard in the cellar near Albert. At a table close by there was a girl actually in evening dress.

They began with a Martini and then broached the Chambertin. The chaplain grew voluble. "I'm awfully glad I ran into you," he said. "You see, I'm in an awful hole.

I have got to go off early tomorrow morning. I got orders not more than an hour ago, and when I met you I had just been to the station to see the R.T.O. My train leaves at six-thirty."

"Where are you going?" asked Rawley.

"Somewhere near Arras, the R.T.O. said. I have to report to the fifty-sixth division."

"Oh yes, I know them," said Rawley. "London Territorial division."

"Are they a nice lot?" asked the chaplain. "You see, I'm rather nervous about going up for the first time."

"I just happen to know they are London Territorials and that they have quite a good fighting reputation, but beyond that I don't know anything about them. I've never met them. But tell me, what is the trouble? What are you getting all hot and bothered about?"

The chaplain took a gulp at his glass. "I haven't packed up yet."

Rawley laughed. "Well, that's easy. If you have a pile of stuff you just dump what you can't take, that's all."

"But I don't know what I ought to take, so I am relying on you to come along and show me."

"What, after we have finished this meal!" exclaimed Rawley. "What sort of time do you think I shall get back to Albert, pray?"

"Must you go back tonight?" asked the other coaxingly. "I can put you up if you like. There are two beds in my billet. You must come. There are dozens of other things I want to ask you about."

Rawley laughed. "I don't see why you cannot ask them now, but if you really want me to I will go along to your billet for a little time. I'd be a swab to refuse that after this excellent meal you have given me."

They left the Godbert and walked along the quiet Rue des Jacobin. It was a clear cold night, and the stars glittered metallically above the darkened streets. "What a hardy chap you must be!" exclaimed the chaplain, who was muffled in a thick British warm. "Aren't you perishing without a coat?"

"Not a bit," answered Rawley. "I hardly ever wear a coat these days," he added more truthfully.

They turned into a dark and narrow street between tall, cliff-like houses. Their footfalls rang out noisily on the ornamental pavement. The street was deserted at that hour, and no ray of light escaped from the rows of long-shuttered windows. The chaplain halted before a brick-arched doorway. "Here we are," he said.

The door opened a few inches in response to his knock, and then at the sound of his voice was opened more widely. Rawley mounted two steps and stood in complete darkness. The door closed behind him, a switch clicked, and he found himself in a large ponderously-furnished hall, somewhat dimly lighted by a shaded electrolier. The chaplain led the way up a carpeted stair. He turned down a long corridor dimly lighted by a little oil lamp on a table, and threw open a door. "This is my billet," he said. "Not too bad—considering."

Rawley found himself in a large and lofty room. Facing him were two long French windows, curtained with lace, through which could be seen the white blistered paint of the closed shutters beyond. Heavy plush curtains undrawn hung on either side of each window, and there was a frill of the same thick material along the top. Two beds, with heavy maple panels at head and foot, stood against one wall, with a thick tapestry bell-pull between them. A huge maple press, a marble-topped chest of drawers, and a dark green plush armchair, and a table covered with a plush cloth, completed the furniture.

Rawley moved slowly across the threshold. "No—not too bad," he echoed with a smile. "Better than you are likely to get with your new division, anyway."

The chaplain dragged a new-looking valise from the bottom of the press and set to work to pack. He would not allow Rawley to help him. He was to direct operations, he said. And so Rawley sat in the armchair, smoking his pipe and giving advice.

"What do I do about paying for this billet?" asked the chaplain, looking up suddenly.

"You don't pay," answered Rawley. "You fill in a billeting return which goes to some French authority, who pay the money and claim from the British Government. It goes in every week, I believe."

"But I haven't got a billeting return and I've never had one?" answered the chaplain.

"Somebody has been doing it for you, then—Town Major, or whatever they have here, I suppose. Whom do you draw your rations from?"

"I really don't know. My man always brings them."

"Then I expect he tells the ration people about the billet also. By the by, where is your servant? Are you taking him with you?"

"Oh, no. I don't think so. He belongs here. He's a permanent base, or whatever they call it. But I don't know where he sleeps. He comes in every morning and gets my breakfast, and again for lunch at midday."

Rawley filled his pipe. "Don't you mess with anyone then?"

"No. Bull brings my rations and cooks them for breakfast and lunch, and I usually get an evening meal somewhere in the town. He looks after the canteen for me, too. And I want to talk to you about that. You see, I haven't seen Bull since midday and he doesn't know I'm going. And I shall be gone tomorrow when he comes again. You see, I give him the money and he borrows a limber from somewhere and buys the stuff for the canteen, and he bought a new lot yesterday. And that was what was bothering me when I met you. I can't take all that stuff with me, and I thought I should just have to leave it and not be able to tell Bull about it either. That's why I wanted you to come back here. I thought that if you stayed here for the night you could see Bull tomorrow morning after I have gone, and you could tell him about the rations and the billet and all that. And I thought perhaps you would do something about the canteen stuff for me—either take it up to your people or get Bull to sell it out and then collect the money. In either case, you're welcome to it. I have made a good few hundred francs out of it which I am taking up to this division to start something there. But I can't take the stock, and you would be doing me a good turn if you would take it off my hands."

Rawley blew a cloud of smoke towards the ceiling. "That's jolly good of you. All right then, I will see your bloke, Bull, tomorrow and fix it up." He eyed the comfortable looking box-mattresses on the beds. It was months since he had slept in a real bed, and these had clean sheets and pillows. "And if you insist on my staying the night," he added with a smile, "I suppose I must. Lying in that bed will certainly be more comfortable than bumping back to Albert on a lorry."

The chaplain produced a clean pair of mauve pyjamas. "I brought out four pairs," he said rather shamefacedly. "So I was going to leave these behind, anyway. My kit is bulging as it is. And now I think we ought to turn in. I have got to be up jolly early tomorrow."

II

It was some time before Rawley got to sleep. He had been used to lying closely rolled in two or three blankets with the ends tucked tightly under his shoulders and neck to keep out the draught, and now the very comfort of being able to stretch his legs in loose clean pyjamas in a broad, soft bed kept him awake. He lay with widespread legs, relaxed in the darkness, and though he could see nothing except two faint glimmers of light from the heart-shaped holes in the window-shutters, he was acutely aware of the peace and comfort of the room. Gradually, however, his thoughts became confused and disconnected, and he dropped into a deep sleep.

He was awakened by someone moving near him, and as he turned over and drowsily opened his eyes the two faint bars of light from the shutters recalled to him his whereabouts. A dim form was bending by the other bed. "Hullo, are you awake?" came the voice of the chaplain. "Don't you get out, but I have got to look slippy; it's nearly a quarter-to-six."

Rawley jumped out of bed, and the chaplain switched on the electric light. "Now what can I do?" asked Rawley. "What about breakfast?"

"I shall not have time for that," answered the chaplain, who was pulling on his clothes. "I'll pick up something at the station."

"That's absurd," protested Rawley. "You won't get much at the station at this hour, and if I know anything of army trains it will probably take you all day to crawl up to Arras. Haven't you got anything here?"

"A few biscuits. I don't know where Bull keeps my rations. He will bring them along later and cook my breakfast. You will eat that, of course. I will pick up something on the way all right."

"You don't know these French trains as I do," said Rawley doubtfully. "You ought to have brought something back from the Godbert last night. Eat the biscuits, anyway. How are you getting your kit down to the station?"

"I'll have to carry it, I suppose."

Rawley laughed. "You are a hopeless fellow. Look here, as soon as I'm dressed I will run out and see if I can find somebody or something to take your valise along." He put on his collar and tunic. "You get along quietly. I'm off, and in any case I will be back in time to give you a hand down to the station."

Rawley opened the door and felt his way along the corridor and down the dark stairs. He fumbled with the heavy front door and opened it. Dawn was breaking, but the light was not yet strong, and the street wore the cold, deserted air peculiar to towns at that hour. He set off briskly through the chill air, his feet echoing loudly on the pavement. He turned into a broad tree-lined road that was deserted except for a workman in a blue blouse at the far end. But the rumble of wheels on cobbles came from a street to his left. He doubled along the pavement and to his joy saw an army limbered wagon rattling towards him. Within five minutes he was back at the house with the limber.

The chaplain was buckling the last strap of his valise as Rawley burst into the room. "Are you ready?" cried Rawley. "I have got a limber for you outside."

The chaplain buckled on his belt and looked round the room. "Yes, I think I have got everything. I'm leaving several odds and ends. Do what you like with them."

He put on his British warm. Rawley shouldered the valise and went down the stairs. The driver put the valise in the limber, and the chaplain climbed in after it. He wrung Rawley's hand. "Thanks awfully," he said. "Oh, and look here; give this to Bull, will you? It's his wages. And see that he gives you a good breakfast. Goodbye, and again—thanks awfully."

When the limber had rattled out of sight round the corner, Rawley turned back into the house. He went into the lighted room and looked about him with fresh interest. It was his now for the moment. Two or three books and an old pair of slippers lay on the floor. There was a little pile of torn-up letters on the plush tablecloth, and on the marble-topped chest of drawers was a basin half full of water, a bit of soap in a soap dish, and a crumpled towel.

He took off his coat and collar and washed. Then he switched off the electric light, opened the long French windows and pushed back the shutters. An ornamental railing ran across the lower part of the windows which looked on to the narrow street. Some of the shutters in the houses opposite had already been opened. The air was fresh, but the sun was now up, and he picked up a book and pulled the armchair to the window.

III

About an hour later a tap sounded on the door, and a short, thick-set man came in carrying an enamel jug of steaming water. He paused at the sight of Rawley sitting by the window, and looked inquiringly round the room. Rawley put down his book. "Captain Chivers has gone," he said. "He got orders last night too late to let you know, and he went off early this morning. He asked me to tell you, and he sent you this."

The man put down the jug and took the money Rawley held out to him. "Thank you, sir."

"Oh, and Bull, I'm eating his breakfast."

"Very good, sir. It's a bit o' bacon this morning."

"Good!" said Rawley. "And I'm ready when you are."

"I'll 'ave to cook it first, sir. But I'll get on with it right away." He turned back on his way to the door. "And 'ow do you like the tea, sir? Captain Chivers liked it 'ot and strong."

"Hot, Bull, but not too strong," said Rawley.

"Right you are, sir. Oh, an' there ain't only condensed this morning."

"That's all right," said Rawley.

The man paused in the doorway. "I've got a tin o' jam, sir—plum an' apple."

"That's splendid! Bring that, too," said Rawley.

Private Bull returned later with the breakfast. He spread a moderately clean white cloth over the plush tablecloth, and put upon it a knife and fork, a plate containing two rashers of rather fat bacon, half a loaf of bread, a teacup and saucer, a small tea-pot and a cardboard carton of jam. He dusted his hands lightly together as he looked over the table. "There you are, sir," he said. "I don't think I've forgotten nothin'. Shall I give your belt and buttons a rub while you are eatin' it?"

"Yes, please," said Rawley. "And then I want you to show me the stuff in the canteen. Captain Chivers has turned it over to me."

"I see, sir." He fumbled in his breast pocket and produced a dog-eared note-book. He opened it where it was bulged by a pile of small notes and placed it on the table beside Rawley. "That's yesterday's takings, sir, an' the list. I 'ave added it up, but it come out 'alf a franc short somehow. Captain Chivers always used to give a look at it while he was a-having his breakfast."

"Righto," said Rawley.

Bull picked up the belt and tunic, but paused in the doorway. "Since you're taking over from the other captain, I s'pose I'll drore rations as usual, sir."

Rawley arrested the teacup that was half-way to his mouth, and held it poised in mid air. Then he set it slowly back in the saucer. "Er, yes—yes, for as long as I'm here," he said.

"Well, you never know, sir, you may stay here for duration. Captain Chivers thought he'd be here for a couple o' days an' he was 'ere over a month. He reckoned they'd forgot all about him, but as I used to tell 'im, there are a lot o' worse places than this in France he might a' been forgot in."

"That's very true," agreed Rawley.

"Yes, that's what I tell him. Well, I'll give these 'ere buttons a rub, sir, and then I'll tidy up a bit."

Left alone in the room, Rawley ate his bacon and drank the hot tea with a thoughtful air. His intention had been to sell out the canteen stock and to come into Amiens in a few days' time to collect the money from Bull. Now, however, he toyed with other ideas. Bull had evidently interpreted his words to mean that he was taking over from Chivers, not only the canteen stock, but the canteen itself as a going concern and the billet and rations also. He looked round the furnished, civilized room and particularly at the comfortable bed, and asked himself why he should not stay here at least until the stock was sold. The risk was not very great. Once a thing was started it was easy, except in exceptional circumstances, to carry on without suspicion. He knew the way these things were done. Some officer permanently in the town would sign the billeting return as a matter of course, and Bull would draw rations from some quartermaster-sergeant who would probably never know that Chivers had gone, and if he did know he would take it as a matter of course that another padre had taken over. No one had ever bothered about Chivers; why should anyone ever bother about him? The prospect was dazzling: a comfortable billet in Amiens, rations, a servant to cook one's meals, and the profits of the canteen to play with. He glanced once more round the comfortable room that could be his, and decided to risk it.

IV

After breakfast he lighted his pipe, and sat in the comfortable armchair by the window to think matters out. It would be impossible to bring Alf into Amiens. He would have to stay in the cellar and draw rations as usual from Albert. He, Rawley, could go to see him occasionally and take him little comforts. Then there was the question of kit.

He would have to have some kit. Bull would think it peculiar for an officer to arrive with no change of underclothes even, and only the few articles from Alf's looted suit-case. He turned over the money Bull had given him. Together with what remained of his money it amounted to just over a hundred and fifty francs. It was hardly enough for the purpose and he needed a reserve for re-stocking the canteen. At Ordnance, of course, one could get stuff without paying for it. One produced one's field-cashier's book and signed a form. He had the field-cashier's book of Captain Parker, whose uniform he wore. Since the book was lost, Parker might have cancelled it. The field-cashier would know that, but it was hardly likely that Ordnance would, since with them the book was not used as a cheque-book, but only as proof that the holder was an officer. But then, again, if he signed as Captain Parker, A.C.D., Parker would have to pay for his things, which was rather mean, and also when Parker saw the items deducted from his pay he might repudiate them, tell the story of his suit-case lost in that raid in the village, and set the military police on tracing the impostor. That would be highly dangerous.

He pondered the problem till he had solved it to his satisfaction. Then he went out into the town.

He bought a set of A.S.C. badges in the Rue des Trois Cailloux, cap badge and collar badges; these with an indelible pencil completed his purchases. He walked down the Boulevard by the station, jumped a lorry going in the right direction, and an hour and a half later walked down the steps of the cellar.

Alf greeted him with joy. "Coo! I thought they'd got you this time, mate," he said. "Watcher been on the tiles all night!"

Rawley told him what had happened and what he intended doing. "But the devil of it is," he concluded, "I can't take you with me, there is nowhere where you would fit in, and if you came it would spoil the whole show and they would probably nab us both. My idea is for you to stay here—you will be drawing double rations, by the by—and I will come out to see you now and then and bring anything you want."

Alf was awed by the audacity of the plan. "Coo, if that don't take the perishin' kitty!" he exclaimed smacking his thigh. "Livin' in a proper billet! But you're right about me, mate. O' course, I'd rather 'ave you with me, but I'll be all right if you come out an' see me now and agin. An' then if things get awkward for yer in Armeens, you can come back 'ere."

"And now I must go and draw my kit from Ordnance," said Rawley, with a grin. He opened the suit-case and took from it the field-cashier's book. It was a long cheque-shaped book, containing perforated forms and counterfoils. On the cover was written in indelible pencil, Captain W. F. Parker, A.C.D. The letters standing for Army Chaplain's Department were fairly far apart. Rawley dipped a finger in some grease on the table and smeared the cover so as to obliterate the final D. Then with an indelible pencil he wrote an S between the A and C. The cover now read, Captain W. F. Parker, A.S.C. He put the book in his pocket and stood up. "Well, cheerio, Alf. I will come and see you tomorrow or the day after and tell you how I'm getting on. Meanwhile, take this, but don't for heaven's sake get tight on it, or you may talk and find yourself in a guard-room." He put a twenty-franc note into Alf's hand and went up the steps.

In Albert he made his way to the Doullens road. No doubt there was an Ordnance depôt in Amiens, but it would be safer, he decided, to get his kit in Doullens. He waited ten minutes or more for a lorry going in the right direction, and had just begun to despair of finding one, when a fast travelling Vauxhall car shot out from Albert. The driver slowed in response to Rawley's frantic arm wavings, and when the car gathered speed again Rawley was seated beside the Supply Officer in the back seat. In a little over half an hour they reached the junction with the Amiens road just outside Doullens.

Rawley got out and, when the car had disappeared from view, went behind a hedge and changed his black chaplain's badges for those of the A.S.C. which he had bought in Amiens. Then he marched boldly into the little town.

So intent had he been upon his plan that it was not till he saw an ambulance standing among a number of cars in the little square that he realized that this was the Doullens he had visited in happier circumstances, and that Berney might actually be in the town at that moment. The thought filled him with momentary panic, and he asked himself whether she would recognize him, changed and clean-shaven as he was. He was torn between a desire to avoid her and a great longing to see her, and yet not be seen; and as he strode briskly along the street he scanned the faces of the passers-by with eager dread.

But he reached the Ordnance depôt without any misadventure, and here, as he told himself, it was as easy as taking milk from a baby. He produced the field-cashier's book, signed the form as Captain Parker, A.S.C., and selected his kit. He took a brown Wolseley valise, a trench coat, underclothes and other articles of small kit. He rolled them up in the valise, and gave a passing Tommy five francs to carry it to the Amiens road. A lorry dropped him on the outskirts of Amiens in something over an hour and a half, and he left the valise with an old woman in a chandler's shop. He walked back to his billet and, when Bull came in, sent him to fetch the valise. That night he dined at the Hôtel de la Poste and afterwards enjoyed the luxury of reading in bed in a comfortable room with an electric light switch over his bed.

CHAPTER XXII

I

IN the course of the following days Rawley settled down to his new life. The canteen was flourishing, and he went one morning with Bull in a borrowed limber to the Expeditionary Force Canteen to buy a fresh stock. Every morning at breakfast he went through the accounts of the previous day. Every evening he dined at one or other of the hotels or cafés of the town. And laden with delicacies of food, drink or tobacco, he paid flying visits to Alf in the cellar near Albert.

He was no longer ignorant of the course that events were taking. He bought an English paper every day, and from the officers he met in cafés or hotels he learned both what the men in the Line and the people at home were discussing. Among the troops the topic of the moment was the expected German attack. It was generally agreed that it was coming, that it was coming soon, and that when it did come, it would be the father and mother of all the pushes that ever were. Some went so far as to prophesy the date and exact frontage of the attack. Most were optimistic, but there were others who professed distrust of the new defence system of isolated redoubts with a battle zone in rear.

One afternoon he was sitting on the red plush seat of a café in the Rue des Trois Cailloux with an engineer officer he had met casually a few minutes before. "Good spot, old

Armeens!" eulogized the sapper, sipping his drink and eyeing the passers-by. "Take my advice, padre, and make the most of it while you can; it won't be for long."

"You mean this Bosche push is going to upset things," said Rawley.

"Well yes, I suppose it will when it comes," said the sapper, fishing a cigarette case from his breast pocket. "But I wasn't thinking of that." He glanced suspiciously to right and left and added in a low voice. "Amiens is going to be closed to the troops!"

"Why, what is the idea?" asked Rawley, as casually as he could.

The other took a gulp at his glass, and continued in a low voice, "Another spy scare. I was up at Army this morning, and I heard them discussing it. I remember they did it once before, just before the Somme show. No one allowed in or out without a pass. I was going on leave at the time, and the M.P.s wouldn't even let me off the station to get breakfast. They collared some fellow and shot him. He was running one of the hotels, the Du Rhin, I believe."

Rawley began slowly to fill his pipe. "How long is this going to last?" he asked.

"Oh, I don't know, a week, a fortnight or a month—till they get whoever they're after. Meantime, I shall have to do without my oysters at Josephine's—blast them! But I'm coming in tomorrow night to have a final bust if I have to desert for it."

"Is tomorrow the last day then?" asked Rawley.

The sapper nodded. "According to what I heard at Army. Come in tomorrow, padre, and do yourself well. After that you won't get in without a special pass."

Rawley went straight back to his billet as soon as he had parted from the engineer officer, and sucked thoughtfully at his pipe as he strode along. Obviously he would have to leave Amiens tomorrow if what had been told him were true. He would have to leave his comfortable bed and billet to go back to the cellar. It was a great nuisance, and the necessity of moving could not have come at a more awkward time. He had restocked the canteen only yesterday. He was therefore rather low in funds and burdened with stock that he could neither sell nor take with him. Perhaps the best thing would be to get Bull to pack up the stock in two or three old wooden cases, trusting that in the course of a few days he might be able to borrow a limber and get the cases sent up to the M.T. people at Albert, where he, Rawley could call for them.

He hunted up Bull in his billet and gave him instructions. He said he had been ordered to join a division on the Cambrai front and was leaving tomorrow. The train left at such an unearthly hour in the morning that he had decided to lorry-jump to Albert and Bapaume. He would therefore want Bull to carry his valise to the Albert road.

He went back into the town and had tea. He might as well make the most of his last day in Amiens, and the shops and lights and people seemed to have grown brighter and more attractive now that he was leaving them. He had not very much money, but he would make the most of it; he would pay a final visit to all the haunts which he had frequented during the course of his enforced role of a man-about-town.

II

Early in the evening he went into the l'Univers and ordered a drink. Two or three officers were sitting in the cane chairs in the little lounge. He looked down at the rose coloured carpet and wondered if ever again he would have a carpet beneath his feet. He finished his drink and prepared to go. A girl was coming round the bend of the stairs, and as he crossed towards the door, they met. She glanced at him casually, but her look of frank self-possession changed swiftly to one of startled interest. His heart pounded against his ribs.

This was the meeting he had dreaded—and longed for.

Her eyes widened slowly; her face was paper white. "PE-TER!" The word came in an intense vibrant whisper, and she clutched his sleeve for support. "They told me you were—DEAD."

To him it seemed that the lounge was revolving rapidly, forming a coloured shining frame encircling her pale face and eyes, but he kept his head, and with one hand under her elbow, piloted her to the door. She went unresisting. The cool air outside cleared his brain a little. She was speaking; whispering; "I know it's you, Peter. I know it's you—really you, but tell me it is. Tell me."

"Yes—it's me," he answered in a strangled voice.

"Thank God!" she whispered. "Thank God."

Her hand still clutched his arm. He stole a look at her. Her face was flushed and her eyes were bright. His brain was clearing. He led her down a side street where there was little light and no traffic. "If you know . . ." he began. "But I can see you don't. Aren't you—aren't you wondering . . . don't you want to know. . . ."

She hugged his arm. "No. Not now. I know that you are alive. Nothing else matters."

They walked on in silence. Ahead the moonlight glinted on water. They sat down beneath a plane-tree on that bench whereon he had rested that night of his first visit to Amiens. He took her hands and held them close against his face. "Berney," he began. "Berney, it's such a long and dismal story. . . ."

She laid her cheek against the hand that held hers. "Let us leave it till tomorrow. Tonight I am content to know that you are alive and still love me."

He kissed the palms of her hands. "But tomorrow I must leave Amiens," he said.

"I can bear even that now I know that you are safe," she murmured.

"But we must be practical," he insisted, "though God knows I wish we could sit here for ever, you and I. But our time is so short. Tell me—tell me what you know. What did you think—what did you do when I—I. . . ."

"I had no reply to my letters, and I was terribly afraid," she said in a voice that quivered with the remembrance of that fear. "I wrote to Mr. Piddock to ask if anything terrible had happened to you."

"Ah!"

She covered her face with her hands. "Oh, Peter, it was dreadful. I tried so hard to carry on and be—be worthy of you, but I was all dead inside. Mr. Piddock's letter was so kind and sympathetic, but he said you had been killed."

"Ah!" Rawley nodded his head slowly. "Dear old Piddock. That was the kindest thing he could say."

"He said that you had been buried in a dug-out with another man—killed instantaneously when a shell went through it. Why did he say it, Peter? Why did he say it? And why, oh why, did you leave me all this time in agony without a word, without one tiny little word just to say that you were alive! It was cruel—cruel of you, darling. When I saw you in the hotel there I thought I was suffocating; and then I saw that it was really you, and all sorts of things went rushing through my head. I thought that perhaps you had grown tired of me and had kept away on that account, but then your eyes told me that wasn't true, and I didn't care about anything alse—you were alive and had the same dear look in your eyes. I'm so happy—so happy."

He held her shoulder closely and mumbled incoherently.

"But why, Peter, why did you let me suffer so long?" she murmured.

"I—I thought it best that you should forget me," he mumbled. He felt her body stiffen slightly in his arms and he went on quickly. "I had to leave the battery—I ran away—deserted. You see, there was a fellow there—Rumbald, you've heard me speak of him before—a shirker—we were always quarrelling. In the Line you get on each other's nerves—hate each other. It went on working up and up. One day it came to a head. He was going to give another fellow a job that he ought to have done himself and funked doing. We'd had two officers killed that day already. We were both mad with rage. We were alone in the dug-out and we started fighting and I killed him. And so I cleared out."

He had released his grip in anticipation of her shrinking, but her body did not move. "But why—why," she asked in a low puzzled voice, "didn't you write to me or see me?"

He laughed hoarsely. "Well—I mean—a fellow who's a deserter and killed another man. . . .!"

"But isn't that what everybody is trying to do, and didn't he deserve to be killed?"

He laughed mirthlessly. "Oh, I dare say. He deserved it a good deal more than most of the Germans we have been doing our best to kill—but the authorities wouldn't take that view."

She sat up suddenly. "Peter! You—you are in danger then!"

"I expect they would shoot me if they caught me," he said easily.

She clung to him, fearfully. "Oh, Peter!" She shook his arm insistently. "You must hide. Where can you go."

He soothed her. "I'm safe enough here for the moment," he assured her. "So long as I'm out of Amiens before tomorrow night. And I have a safe enough place to go to. Too safe! My risk would have been much greater had things been different and I had been—been with the battery. Don't let that worry you, sweetheart. What worries me is you—and what will be the end of it all." He took her hands and held them tightly. "You, see," he went on quickly and doggedly, "I had to live somehow after that—that business in the dug-out, and that's why I'm dressed up as a Padre and living like a mountebank—by my wits. And before that I lived out there." He swung an arm. "In the devastated area . . . in old dug-outs and trenches . . . like a savage . . . with other miserable wretches . . . bandits. And . . . Oh, Berney, dear, don't you see, I'm an outcast . . . a deserter . . . there's no hope . . . no future. . . ."

She clung to his arm. "My poor, poor Peter." She went on earnestly. "But Peter, darling, there must be hope. I can't believe that finding you alive after all this terrible time of sickening fear . . . I can't, can't believe it's just a cruel joke. There must be a future. There must. There shall be."

He shook his head sadly. And then, with a swift change of thought, she cried in alarm, "Where are you going tomorrow . . . not, not back to that terrible life?"

He reassured her and told her about Alf and the cellar, painting the account in bright colours to comfort her. "It's really quite snug," he concluded. "You need not worry on that score. Why, we draw rations, and it's far more comfortable and safe than being with a battery on the Line."

She was silent for a few moments, and then she said in a low voice, "It's terrible for you, Peter, terrible, I know, but I can't, I simply can't be depressed about it now; I'm too thankful and glad to find you alive. I can face anything now that I know that. Something will turn up. Something must happen. I feel it will. Anyway we have had this time together. No one can take that away from us. Whatever happens we shall have this memory and the knowledge that we—that we love one another."

"I have lived on memories," he said huskily. "I never thought to see that dear look in your eyes again. I dreaded meeting you . . . dreaded seeing another look . . . after what has happened I thought . . . a fellow . . . an outcast. . . ."

She laughed happily. "You old goose," she murmured and snuggled against his shoulder.

The March night air was chilly and he felt her shiver. "Selfish brute, I am," he said. "You are getting cold and you've had no food. We will go and have a meal, a real bust. Do you remember the last we had together? That lunch in the orchard?"

She squeezed his arm. "But, Peter, is it safe?"

He laughed at her fears. "Why, I've fed in some place or other here every night for a fortnight or more. But I don't think we will go to the Godbert tonight. Somewhere quieter, where we can talk."

He took her to one of the less-known hotel restaurants that was patronized more by the native French themselves than by British officers. It was quiet, and their table in the corner was situated far enough from the other diners to give them privacy of conversation. And the food was excellent, but their eyes sought each other so persistently across the table that they had little time to notice what was on their plates.

Berney sipped her wine thoughtfully, and then she slowly put down her glass, and looked up. "Peter, I've got a simply wonderful idea!"

He nodded, gazing hungrily at her glowing cheeks and eyes sparkling in the shade of her hat. "Which is?"

"I'm supposed to be going to England tomorrow. I'm leaving the C.C.S. I have been posted to an ambulance column with the Royal Berks Hospital at Reading, but they have given me a fortnight's leave before I have to report."

He nodded his head slowly.

She fingered the stem of her glass and then looked at him with starry eyes. "Peter, can't we get married and have a fortnight's honeymoon!"

He reached for her hand across the table and laughed unsteadily at the dazzling prospect she opened up. "But, Berney darling, where could we go?"

She had laid her other hand on his and went on eagerly. "To your cellar. It would be such dear, delicious fun. Alf could find another place for the time being. You said there were lots of dug-outs and things near, and. . . ."

"Berney, Berney dear, I couldn't let you do that even if it were possible—which it isn't."

"But why?" she protested.

"How could we get married, dear?" he said gently. "I'm what I am. No padre would do it."

She nodded her head slowly. "Um—I had not thought of that. But you do want to marry me, Peter?" she asked after a moment's silence.

"Berney!" he exclaimed with an eloquent look.

She fiddled with the stem of her glass and went on without looking up. "It isn't our fault we can't get married, is it? We would if we could. Peter—Peter, couldn't we—couldn't we have the honeymoon, anyway?"

He made some inarticulate sound, and she went on quickly and earnestly. "Life is so—so uncertain, Peter. I know a man who wanted to marry a girl at home on his last leave. Her people said it was too short—ten days. And so they didn't and he went back and he was killed. Now she is heartbroken. Why shouldn't we take happiness while we can? There is no certainty for anybody of anything—except the moment, and I am so greedy of life and joy and happiness. And we couldn't love each other any more even if we were married." Her eyes fell. "Peter, am I very wicked?"

"Wicked!" he exclaimed with an unsteady little laugh that was strangled by a gulp. "Berney, you're . . . you're an angel." He knit his brows and rested his head on his hand like one crazed. "But I should be wicked," he faltered like one repeating a lesson, "I . . . should be . . . wicked if . . . I let you . . . do it." He raised his head suddenly and defiantly. "No, no, no, you must not do it. I'd be a cad to let you."

She was silent, but her eyes were fixed on his, appealingly. "And besides," he went on lamely, "it would not be any easier at the end."

"But we should have had our fortnight," she said, in a low voice.

He looked at her with imploring eyes. "Berney, Berney darling," he cried miserably, like a drowning man. "I cannot argue about it. You would beat me in two minutes. God knows I'm holding out against myself only by a hair. I can't hold out against you, too. But I *know* I ought not to consent, and I'm clinging to that blindly—clinging to my last shred of decency. If I loved you a little less I should have given in already. Berney—Berney, help me."

She squeezed the hand that held hers. Her eyes were misty. They turned again abruptly to their food and ate fiercely and in silence.

IV

It was getting late when they left the restaurant, but they did not take the shortest way back to the l'Univers They moved slowly through the dark, narrow streets, and found themselves again on the quay by the canal. Both were silent with the thought of the parting that was so near. They sat down on the bench beneath the plane-tree.

"Peter," she whispered. "You will see me off tomorrow?"

He nodded miserably.

"My train leaves a little after ten. You—you want me to go by it?"

He nodded without speaking.

347

"Two weeks," she said softly, as though speaking to herself. "Two little weeks of happiness out of—perhaps a whole lifetime. It seems such a little to ask of life."

He felt his strength of will slipping from him. He struggled blindly to resist, but with her arms around his neck, her body in his arms, and her cheek against his, it was a losing battle he fought, and he knew it. His denials became less vehement and ceased. He consented.

Now that the cloud of separation was lifted from their minds they were eager and radiant. They talked of practicalities. It was settled that he was to go to the l'Univers in the morning and have breakfast with her; then he would go out to the cellar and make ready for her. Meantime she would do some shopping and would jump a lorry so as to arrive in Albert in the neighbourhood of five o'clock. He would meet her there, and together they would walk back through the dusk to the cellar.

At the top of the deserted Rue Lammartine they parted. For a few wonderful moments he held her again in his arms, and then, with a whispered "Till tomorrow, Peter darling," she crossed the Rue de Noyon and disappeared into the Hôtel de l'Univers opposite.

V

Back in his billet, he undressed and got into bed, but sleep did not come to him. He lay staring into the darkness, while his active brain rehearsed the events of the evening, and made plans for the morrow. Already with Berney he had superficially discussed practicalities and, in their joyous enthusiasm, they had joked and made light of difficulties; but now, as he lay alone in the darkness, without the intoxicating pressure of her hand on his arm, going soberly over the mundane essentials of bare existence in the devastated area, subconsciously the conviction grew that he was acting selfishly and like a cad. And as he lay tossing in the darkness, while the fight went on with the nagging voice that would not let him enjoy that which he so ardently desired, a new thought came to disturb his peace. It came as a suspicion and grew to be a certainty: she did not intend to go at the end of the fortnight. She intended to sacrifice herself for him and share his outlawry and hunted existence to the end.

Filled with a new strength and resolution he switched on the light and climbed out of bed. He filled four or five sheets of a ruled block with writing. Read them through, tore them up, and began again. The final draft covered less than a sheet. It read:

"Berney darling,—If we lived together for a thousand years we could not be happier than we have been tonight, or love each other more. It was only here, alone in my billet, that I realized what you intend, and what your sacrifice means. But even now I know that, were your dear eyes on mine and your lips pleading, I should give in. And so, like a coward I am running away. For your own sake I dare not see you before I go. When your dear eyes are reading this I shall have left

Amiens, and it will be useless and only dangerous for us both to try to find me.

"Berney, you are angry with me, perhaps, but if ever you doubt my love, read again this letter. Darling, I am very, very sad, but very, very happy, and you must be very happy, too.

"In my thoughts I shall be with you always, always, darling, whatever happens.

"Peter."

He went back to bed, but slept only fitfully. He had left a shutter open, and was up with the first streaks of dawn. He dressed hurriedly and without shaving. He packed his immediate necessities in a haversack, and his other kit in the valise. Then he put on his trench coat and went out. He found Bull shaving in his billet, and he gave him orders to get the valise out to the Albert road as soon as possible. Then he set off briskly through the town.

A sleepy old waiter in a baize apron was sweeping the doorway of the Hôtel de l'Univers. Rawley handed him the letter with instructions to give it to Miss Travers as soon as she came down. He walked on round the corner into the Place de la Gare and entered a café. The café was not yet officially open for the day, but the matronly proprietress took compassion on him and brought hot coffee and rolls. Opposite him was the great glass front of the station, and the slope that led down to it, and he wondered which pavement Berney would choose when she passed that way a few hours later. He envied the walls that would see her pass though he could not. But he wasted little time on vain sentimentalizing. He finished his breakfast and walked down the Boulevard Alsace towards the Albert road.

As he crossed the bridge over the river a lorry overtook him. It was going to Bapaume, the driver said, and Rawley climbed up beside him. At the T roads at the end of the Boulevard, Private Bull, a cigarette in his mouth, was sitting on the valise. The lorry stopped and the valise was taken on board. Rawley said goodbye to Bull, and the lorry rumbled on its way. An hour and a half later it rumbled through Albert and out along the Bapaume Road. He left it in a deserted spot in the neighbourhood of Poizières, and shouldering the valise, tramped towards the cellar. He was in no mood for Alf's primitive conversation, and was relieved to find the cellar empty; but fearing that its owner would return shortly, he dumped the valise in a corner and went back up the steps.

CHAPTER XXIII

I

IT was late afternoon when he returned from a long tramp across country. Alf had returned and was glad to see him. "I saw your posh kit, chum, so I knew you was back, and that it wasn't just an afternoon tea call."

"I'm back for keeps," said Rawley. "There's a spy hunt starting in Amiens tomorrow, and I thought it healthier to clear out before it began."

"Too ruddy true," agreed Alf. "But look 'ere, mate, you've turned up at an awkward moment." He ran his fingers through his tousled hair. "You see, it's like this, I turned up as large as life at the M.T. Quarter's stores to draw three days' rations this morning—and the shysters 'ad gorn. A bloke what I saw peelin' pertiters said they went yesterday. Anyway, they're gorn and," he spread out his hands in exaggerated French gesture. "No more ruddy rations—compree?"

Rawley rubbed his stubbly chin. "Um! That's awkward. I've brought nothing with me either—though there's a whole canteen of stuff back in Amiens. I hope to get it out here in a few days, but I dare not go back for it now." He sat down on the edge of Alf's wire bed. "What other units are there in Albert now?"

"Only odds and ends. I tried to cadge a dixie of stew from the bloke what was peelin' pertiters, but he wasn't

352

'aving any. Yer see we ain't got nothing in the 'ouse 'cept a couple o' biscuits—mark IV bomb proof."

"And I've got two francs left in the wide," said Rawley, jingling the coins together.

"Well, we'll 'ave to go on the scrounge again, I reckon," said Alf. "And I know a place where we can scrounge all right. I've been lookin' round all day trying to win a bite o' something. I went right into Bapaume on a lorry, but there weren't nothin' there; but jes' the other side I come across a camp. There weren't no one in the camp 'cept a couple o' P.B. blokes, and it looked to me as though the troops had jes' gone out of it. Anyway, I come across a canteen. It was shut up, but I looked in the winders, and there was the stuff all piled in boxes ready to take away. I reckon them blokes got orders to move in a hurry, an' they're sendin' a limber for that stuff tomorrow, so if we go up tonight, we'll get there fust."

Rawley grimaced. "My luxurious life in Amiens has spoiled me for this sort of thing," he said with a wry smile. "Still, I suppose it has got to be done. A couple of P.B. men, you say?"

"There may be more, but I only saw a couple."

"Can we get up to the place under cover?"

"Sure. There's a deep ditch run right alongside the hut."

"Full of mud, too, I expect," commented Rawley.

"It ain't too clean," admitted Alf.

Rawley glanced down at his clean tunic. "If I spoil this, bang goes our chance of drawing rations again."

Alf nodded. "We'd better take our posh togs off and put on our old civvies for this job," he suggested.

II

They set out soon after dark, dressed in their disreputable peasant clothes. Each carried a sack slung across his shoulders, and Alf carried a rifle. A slight mist was rising, and as their clothes made it unsafe for them to use the road, the going across that uneven, shell-torn country was necessarily slow. They trudged along silently side by side. The mist thickened as time passed, and they had difficulty in distinguishing objects at five yards distance. The occasional muffled report of a gun gave them the direction of the Line, but they were uncertain of their exact whereabouts. They turned half-left, hoping to strike the road, but another hour went by and the same impenetrable grey vapour surrounded them, and there was the same uneven ground underfoot.

They had hoped to reach their objective a little before midnight, but midnight was now past and they had not yet located Bapaume. They rested on a hummock of chalk. "We are lost," said Rawley. "We have been walking in circles probably. Our only chance is to find the main road; and when we do find it we had better go straight back, or we shall have daylight upon us. Then if the mist suddenly rises and we find ourselves in the middle of a camp, we shall be in the soup."

They set off again at right angles to their former line of march. Another hour went by, but no road or identifiable landmark appeared. The fog seemed to have grown more dense. They came upon a narrow weed-grown track and halted. "Tracks lead to roads," said Rawley. "But which way?" They listened for the rumble of gunfire eastwards, but the guns were silent or their voices were muffled by the fog. The mist drifted about them in clammy wreaths, and they seemed to be alone in a dead world. Now that the crunch of their boots was hushed, the silence was uncanny. "Fair give yer the creeps," shivered Alf.

Rawley had no notion of direction, but he set off at a venture along the track. It led them down a steep slope, across a marshy flat, through some bricky hummocks, and ceased. The situation was becoming desperate. Both were dog-tired and hungry. Long since they had abandoned their object of finding the derelict canteen; they had but one desire: to find their way back to the safety of the cellar and sleep.

They trudged on, hoping against hope. They moved through a silent, invisible world, penned as it were in a tiny grey chamber that moved when they moved, and halted when they halted. They moved slowly and stumbled as they walked; it was agony to drag one leaden foot after another. They no longer kept a sharp look out into the mist ahead, although they knew that at any moment they might stumble upon a sentry. They were past caring; the longing to rest and sleep had numbed all other feelings.

A wire entanglement loomed dimly to their right, but in their exhausted condition they but glanced at it and did not notice that the pickets seemed to be unbent and the wire taut. A trench yawned at their feet, and they halted on its brink. The hope of finding a place where they could rest was uppermost in the minds of both. A yard to the left, the dark rectangle of a dug-out entrance shadowed the mist. They dropped clumsily into the trench and stumbled down the steps. Rawley swung his flash-lamp. The place was bare and the chalk walls leapt up dazzlingly white in the sudden glare. In a dazed way he was aware that the place seemed new. They dropped upon the floor, and in a few minutes were asleep.

III

Rawley was dragged back to consciousness by a feeling of being violently jolted. He had dreamt that he was sliding swiftly down a snowy slope in a large box, and just at the steepest part when the box was travelling at its swiftest an elephant had loomed suddenly in the fog right ahead. The resulting thud and jolt had awakened him. He sat up with a start. A noise like a few pebbles bouncing down steps came from the darkness, but the sounds ceased almost before he was aware of them. He rubbed his sleep-laden eyes and turned over. And then in the darkness and silence he became aware of another sound. It was a gentle throbbing, almost inaudible, undercurrent of sound like that of a smooth-running engine in a stationary motor car.

He scrambled to his feet and switched on his torch. Alf lay inert on the floor like a half-filled sack of corn, his head pillowed on one arm. Rawley switched off the light and tip-toed to the dug-out steps. That undercurrent of sound was louder now, and it came from above. He went slowly up the steps. Pebbles and loose earth crunched beneath his boots. The mist hung thickly in the trench above, but it was of a pale luminous colour that told that dawn had come. Up there above ground there was no mistaking the meaning of that continuous rumble of sound. It was the drumming of a heavy barrage. And were confirmation needed, a second later the scream of a shell tore the mist above his head, to be followed by the familiar bump and crashing roar of the explosion. He turned and clattered down the steps with the whine of flying fragments in his ears.

He roused Alf and spoke with suppressed excitement. "There's a hell of a barrage going on up there."

"What's that got to do with us?" complained Alf sleepily.

"A lot," retorted Rawley. "In the first place it means that it has come—the great Bosche attack, I mean. And in the second, there's heavy stuff landing pretty close. That means we must have wandered a long way east; we're among the troops, and the sooner we get out the better."

He swung his torch round the dug-out and for the first time really noticed that it seemed to have been dug recently. But he said nothing, and they went up the steps. The rumble of the barrage went on ceaselessly. Alf was impressed by it. "Struth! Someone's 'aving a 'appy birfday," he exclaimed.

They moved along the trench through the mist. Alf stumbled over something, and they pulled up precipitately. The obstacle proved to consist of two boxes. One was an open box of S.A.A.—small arms ammunition—the other a small case of iron rations. A waterproof sheet and a half-filled bread sack lay beside them.

"Out of the trench," whispered Rawley. "It's occupied." He stuffed two or three tins of beef into his pockets and climbed out. Alf took a loaf and three or four of the linen bandoleers of ammunition and followed. "If there's goin' to be dirty work, we might as well 'ave some ammo," he whispered as they went cautiously forward. They heard voices behind them and passed a belt of wire, but they knew their direction was right by the steady drum fire behind them.

Once they stopped and lay flat while a party of men went by. The column was invisible in the mist, but the rattle of equipment and the dull thud of feet sounded quite close. Shells detonated noisily at intervals. To their right they heard the crunch of wheels on a road. The light was increasing, and it was possible to distinguish objects fifteen or twenty yards distant. Sounds of movement came fitfully from all sides, and they halted with beating hearts at every tree stump or battered wall that loomed indistinctly in the mist.

"This is too dangerous," said Rawley at last. "We may walk into a party at any moment, and if the mist rises we're done. We must find somewhere to lie up. We have had a narrow escape as it is. That is the rear battle position we have just left. That dug-out was brand new. They are manning them now. Another ten minutes and we should have been caught."

Weary though they were they went on quickly but with infinite caution. They stumbled suddenly among the brick rubble of an isolated cottage. Alf lay down on guard while Rawley prowled about. There seemed to be no cellar or hiding-place, but at last under one corner of the pile of splintered wood and plaster he discovered a small brick cubby-hole, half underground. It was half full of plaster and broken bricks, but empty would just be big enough for two men to crawl into. They cleared out the debris and crawled in.

They ate ravenously of the tinned beef and the loaf of bread. The sounds of battle went on, and they discussed in whispers the meaning of each distant fusillade of musketry or stutter of machine-gun fire. Occasionally the deafening roar of an aeroplane engine passed over their heads. But they had slept no more than an hour or two in the dug-out, and now that the immediate pangs of hunger were satisfied, fatigue exacted its due. They dropped again into a deep sleep.

IV

When Rawley awoke he was astonished to find that night had come, but his first movement was checked by a whispered warning from Alf. "Shush, chum! There's some ruddy gunners not mor'n five yards away. When I woke up bout an 'our ago there was a bloke standing an' talking just outside. Gave me the fright of my life, it did."

Rawley lay silent in the darkness. From the sounds that reached him he knew that a battery was bivouacked all round him, and that for the moment, at any rate, it was impossible to get through them unseen. All sounds of gunning had ceased, and the night was very quiet. He argued from this that the German attack had failed, but the occasional Verey lights that soared into his view through a chink in the debris seemed very close.

Hour after hour they lay cramped and aching in the darkness, but no chance of successful escape offered.

As dawn approached the quietness of the night gave place to intermittent gunfire, and with the first filter of grey light into their cramped hiding-place the throbbing rumble of a heavy barrage broke afresh. Several heavy shells burst quite close, shaking their little cubby-hole violently and sounding a tattoo of fragments on the debris above them. The sound of rifle and machine-gun fire came in gusts of fierce intensity that told of infantry attacks pressed home. Low-flying aeroplanes tore overhead with sudden brief tornadoes of sound, and the earsplitting pom, pom, pom, of the field battery nearby added to the din.

"Proper dorg fight!" said Alf. "Somebody'll get 'urt if this goes on."

"I'm dying to have a look at those guns out there," said Rawley. "There they go again—battery fire. They must have got a hell of a good target. Aren't you just itching to fire one of the little beggars again?"

"Not 'arf! But I ain't too 'appy about our billet, chum. I reckon that machine-gun's getting closer."

Later they heard the jingle of harness and the thud of hoofs. "By gad, they're getting the teams up," whispered Rawley. "They're going back."

They heard the thunder of hoofs and the creak of wheels as the guns and wagons drove by. Alf thrust his head out cautiously. "They've gone, mate," he announced.

They crept out and started back. The mist was still thick enough to shroud objects at a distance of more than thirty yards. The shelling was fairly heavy. Great dark uprearing fountains spouted now and then in the mist, and overhead heavy shrapnel burst with a stunning thunder-clap though the accompanying thick woolly cloud was but dimly visible behind the grey pall. They descended a grassy slope to a broad, flat depression where a dead Tommy lay huddled by a deep black shell crater. Rawley picked up the rifle and hurried on.

The ground rose again gently to a low crest outlined against the sky. Rawley pulled up suddenly near the top. "The mist is lifting," he exclaimed. "We had better wait a bit and have a look at the lie of the land." To their right was a short length of disused trench from which they could observe unseen. They dropped into it.

Ahead the mist seemed to be as thick as ever, but behind them visibility had improved greatly. Below them in the depression they had recently crossed they could see the dead Tommy quite plainly, though he must have been nearly two hundred yards away, and the slope beyond was clear, a low grassy hill, bare except for two or three shivered tree stumps. To their left, seemingly behind them, a machine-gun was stuttering in short bursts.

Movement caught the eye on the slope opposite. Two or three little figures were coming over the crest. " 'Bout time we walk marched," remarked Alf. Rawley, watching the distant figures, saw for an instant against the sky the silhouette of a long-necked helmet and high square pack. "My God, they're Bosches!" he cried.

They regarded each other with consternation. "Jerry's broke through," grunted Alf. Moved by a common impulse they picked up the rifles. Rawley adjusted the sights. "About five hundred, I should think," he said. He rested his elbow on the parapet of the shallow trench, cuddled the butt against his cheek and took aim. At his second shot a figure fell. But the others came on. They were trickling over the skyline all the way along the crest, and the slope was dotted with moving figures. But there was not a vestige of cover, and Rawley, firing deliberately, picked off man after man. Alf was blazing away light-heartedly. "Like a ruddy shooting gallery," he cried as he rammed another clip into the magazine. "Walk up, walk up! All you ring you 'ave."

Rawley cast anxious eyes towards his flanks. "We shall have to get back. They will be round behind us if we stay too long."

They fired ten rounds rapid, rammed in a fresh clip, and climbed out of the trench. Bullets were cracking and whispering overhead, but twenty yards covered at top speed brought them to dead ground. They dropped into a walk and went down the reverse slope. The hollow below them was still bathed in mist, and shells that from their sound seemed to be British, were bursting somewhere ahead. Half-way down the slope they found themselves again enveloped in mist. At the bottom they jumped a ditch and ran suddenly into six or seven figures standing on a narrow road. They recognized the coal-scuttle steel helmets and high square packs of German infantrymen, but retreat was impossible. Bayonets were at their throats. Their rifles clattered on the road; their hands shot up.

V

In the very first-half second that he stood there with his arms raised above his head, Rawley realized with grim clarity the full significance of their position. They were caught, caught in civilian clothes with arms in their hands. It would be useless to claim treatment as prisoners of war. By the rules of international law they were liable to be shot. He felt strangely calm and detached as though he were a spectator of this drama rather than one of the principal actors in it, and he scanned the faces of his captors without emotion though he knew that he would find his fate written there.

There was no comfort to be found in the hard eyes that met his and that travelled ominously over his tattered civilian clothes. Barely two seconds had gone by since the first encounter. It needed only one impetuous word to set in motion the common impulse to plunge bayonets into these treacherous civilians.

A Feld-Webel pushed his way through the little group of men and confronted the two. He shouted at them angrily in German. Rawley answered calmly and clearly, "We are British soldiers," and repeated in French, "*Soldats anglais.*" A torrent of exclamations, unintelligible but clearly hostile, broke from the German infantrymen. They pointed to the ragged civilian clothes, the dropped rifles, the linen bandoleers. The Feld-Webel silenced them and spoke again threateningly and accusingly to the prisoners. Rawley shook his head and repeated his assertion that they were British soldiers.

The Feld-Webel gave an order and the two prisoners were marched up the road. Thirty yards brought them to a place where the banks on either side rose to a height of six or seven feet. Half a dozen German wounded sat on the grass; one of them was being bandaged by a stretcher-bearer. Ten yards farther on was a chalk quarry cut in the side of the sunken road. An officer was coming towards them. The party halted while the Feld-Webel spoke to the officer. Rawley's ignorance of German prevented him from following the conversation, but the drift of it was clear. The officer spoke to him in German. Rawley shook his head and replied in English. The officer spoke in halting French. Rawley repeated his parrot phrase, "*Soldats anglais.*" The officer shrugged his shoulders and walked slowly away. He seemed to be bored with the whole proceeding. A runner brought him a message, and the party stood waiting while he sat on the bank and read it.

The Feld-Webel, standing stiffly to attention, put in a word as the officer signed the receipt form. Without glancing up the officer said something and made a motion of his head. The Feld-Webel saluted quiveringly, about-turned, and bawled an order.

Two men marched the prisoners the ten odd yards up the road to the quarry and halted them against the chalky cliff. The remaining men back by the Feld-Webel were falling in in single rank. That curious feeling of being a spectator still clung to Rawley. He heard a shell whine overhead and detonate on the hillside above him; and he noted with detached interest that it sounded like a British sixty-pounder. He also noticed with the same dream-like detachment that a party of three British prisoners, including an officer, were being escorted up the road.

Alf's face was pale under its covering of dirt, and every few seconds he moistened his lips with his tongue. "I 'ope them blokes 'ave got safety catches," he whispered hoarsely. "Playin' about with firearms like that."

Another shell came whining through the mist; its snoring hum increased rapidly to a savage resonant roar and it burst on the side of the road with a majestic pillar of spouting earth and vibrant hum of flying metal. The two men, half-way back to the firing party, had dropped flat with the speed of long practice. One of the firing party lay limply on the ground, the others cowered under the bank. Another savage whirlwind of sound swooped down through the mist and sent chalky boulders hurtling through the air.

Rawley, crouching at the foot of the chalk cliff, heard an explosive grunt. He lowered his hunched shoulders, and saw Alf lying face upwards beside him. He had the pathetic, uncomplaining look of a bludgeoned mouse. There was a large hole in his chest, and his face had that grey transparent look that Rawley had come to know so well. "Just what I was . . ." he began, but the words ended in a dry gurgle and his jaw dropped.

Another shell detonated lower down the road, and the splinters came droning through the air like giant bees. Rawley saw that the opposite bank was sloping, and not more than ten feet in height. He leapt to his feet, dashed across the road and scrambled up. In the thin mist on the bare slope beyond he was an easy mark, but no bullets followed him. He ran hard for fifty yards, and then dropped into a jog-trot. Intermittent machine-gun fire came from his left, and an occasional shell snored overhead and detonated behind him. Once, half-left, he saw two or three figures in coal-scuttle helmets passing through a broken farm gate, and to his right a few minutes later he saw a little party of British troops trudging along a track westwards.

He reached a half-demolished barn, and lay down panting in the lee of a ragged hedge. A yard or two away the body of a Tommy lay half in, half out, of the ditch. It hung head downwards, and the bayonet scabbard and blue enamel water-bottle were flung upwards across the sagging back. Rawley's throat was parched with thirst. He had drunk nothing for many hours. He crawled over to the body and took the water-bottle.

He had already had proof how dangerous were his peasant clothes. He dragged the body clear of the ditch and turned it over. Rather gingerly he unbuckled the web belt and pulled off the equipment. The greatcoat was more difficult to remove. The heavy arms gave no assistance. But he managed it at last, and unbuttoned the tunic. That also was not removed without a struggle in which the dead seemed doggedly to combat the efforts of the living.

He pulled off his mud-stained peasant coat, and buttoned on the tunic. The greatcoat would only hamper his movements; that he flung over the half-undressed corpse. His civilian trousers were faded green corduroy, muddy and torn. He unwound one mud-caked puttee from the corpse, but then, overcome with disgust, he cut it in two with the dead man's jack-knife, and bound a half round each shin. He buckled on the equipment, retrieved the steel helmet and rifle from the ditch, and went on. Now at least, if captured, he could claim treatment as a prisoner of war, and among the retreating British troops he would pass unnoticed as a straggler.

The mist was clearing. Splintered trees and the ragged hummock of flattened villages were the only landmarks, and he recognized none of them. The country seemed deserted. Once he saw a cavalry patrol moving along the margin of a splintered wood, and he saw a line of men digging on a distant hill slope. He crossed a broad main road, running almost at right angles to his line of march. It was deserted, and its bordering trees were shivered stumps.

An hour later he passed round the ragged stump of a *sucrerie* chimney, and ascended a long slope. From the top he had a wide view. The splintered wood and plaster heaps of several villages dotted the hollows and slopes, and to his right, northwards, a grey pimple of chalk stood out prominently on a scarred, flat-topped hill. He knew his whereabouts at last.

At dusk he stumbled down the steps of the cellar. Alf's wire-netting bunk stood against one wall; his own valise rested in a corner. The smart brown suit-case lay under the bunk. He put his shrapnel helmet on the rickety table, and gazed at the familiar place with dazed eyes. It seemed weeks since he and Alf had left it. It was odd that nothing had changed. He dropped wearily upon the bunk and slept.

CHAPTER XXIV

I

S UBDUED daylight filtered down the cellar steps. Rawley was at breakfast. It consisted of the dead Tommy's iron ration—a tin of bully beef, three biscuits, and tea. After it he filled the petrol cans at the well, stripped off his filthy clothes, and washed. Shaven and dressed again in officer's uniform, he went up the steps. He thought he would walk into Albert and find out what was going on. Gunfire sounded very close, and east and south the sky was smeared with shrapnel bursts. Already he had seen enough to know that things were going very badly for the British Army.

On the Bapaume Road he met a party of about sixty men led by a second lieutenant. Their badges and shoulder-titles displayed a variety of units—British line regiments, highlanders, labour corps, and A.S.C. The young officer said that they were returned leave men who had been formed into platoons on the quay and rushed off to the danger zone. "They are collecting Town-Majors' batmen, cooks, and sanitary men, I'm told, padre," he said. "I've got some labour corps fellows myself, and I don't believe they've ever handled a rifle before. Thank God we've got a navy. Well, I suppose we shall meet Jerry up this way somewhere. Cheerio, padre." And the little party trudged on.

Rawley watched them disappear over a rise and followed slowly. He had half a mind to go back and attach

369

himself to the party. But after all, he knew little about infantry work. If they had been gunners now.

Half-right, to the south-east, the gunfire sounded loudest, and without any definite purpose, he turned off the road and walked in that direction. An hour's walk brought him to the rear of the forward zone. He passed some gun-wagons halted in a hollow, the wagon lines of some battery. Red telephone cable crossed his path and was looped over a rutted track on two tall poles striped black and white. Another hollow was full of cavalry horses, and from behind a bluff to his right two sixty-pounder guns barked every few seconds.

He crossed a narrow, sunken road, up which a four-wheeled-drive lorry was slowly towing a howitzer, and ascended a long, bare slope. From the top he looked across a slight hollow to the debris of a village on the slope beyond. By the powdered rubble heaps a battery of field-guns was in action, and he stood watching the little vivid flashes of light followed by the stabbing "pom, pom-pom-pom-pom" of the salvoes.

As he stood there a solitary figure came along the ridge towards him. It proved to be a young artillery subaltern who saluted punctiliously as he came up. "Can you tell me where I can find the 254th South Midland Battery?" he asked.

"I don't know at all," answered Rawley; "unless it's that one over there. What is the latest news?" he added.

"I don't know, but things seem to be rather bad." He laughed a little self-consciously. "You see, padre, I've only just come out, and it's all rather strange at first."

Rawley nodded. "You haven't chosen too good a time either."

The young officer went on as though he were glad of somebody to talk to; "Yes, it's awfully strange at first. People told me to go to Division and to go to Brigade and I rode about on wagons and lorries and tramped miles. And I lost my kit too. But I found brigade in the end. They were in a funny little farm-house with a big hole in the roof. They told me to report to this battery. Do you think it's that one over there?"

"I don't know," answered Rawley. "But I would walk across and ask, if I were you."

Just as he moved off a shell roared overhead and burst a hundred yards to the rear. The young officer turned and regarded the plume of earth and smoke with a comic raising of the eyebrows. Rawley laughed. "That's a five-nine," he said. "You want to keep clear of those chaps."

"I will," called back the young officer, and strode on.

He had gone barely a hundred yards when Rawley saw him suddenly break into a run. Simultaneously came the hurtling roar of another shell. The luckless flying figure flung itself flat as the ground rocked to the bump and the column of flying clods spouted not a yard from him. The black inverted pyramid subsided, but the figure did not rise. Rawley went across the bare hill slope at the double.

The artillery subaltern was dead when Rawley reached him. His steel helmet had fallen off, and there was a piece of metal as big as a pocket knife embedded in his temple. Poor devil, he had had little enough run for his money.

Rawley walked slowly away, his eyes fixed wistfully upon the battery among the rubble heaps across the dip. They had but five guns in action; they had probably been fighting continuously since that murderous barrage broke more than two days ago. But they were giving as good as they got—good luck to them. How futile and impotent one felt, being a spectator in times like these!

He turned suddenly back towards that shell crater and its huddled victim. Why not? he asked himself. Every man must be of value at such a crisis; and he was an experienced workman. His own division, he knew, was up North; it was unlikely that anyone would know him. But what did it matter, anyway, as long as they would let him take a hand with the guns.

He went down on one knee beside the body and exchanged the chaplain's Maltese crosses on his lapels for the bronze grenades of the artillery. He gently raised the battered head and slipped from over it the sling of the box respirator; then he detached the leather-bottomed haversack and clipped it to his own Sam Browne. He remembered that he did not know the man's name. It would be necessary to know it, for the poor fellow had been to brigade and they had probably informed the battery that he was coming. He felt between the collar and neck for the string and pulled out the identity disc. Lt. Kemp, it had on it, R.F.A., C. of E. He put on the steel helmet and was ready.

He met the battery sergeant-major as he came up the slope with the jagged brick heaps of the ruined village above him. "254th South Midland, sergeant-major?"

"Yes, sir."

"The C.O. here?"

He pointed to an officer seated on a heap of rubble. "Over there, sir."

Rawley went across and reported. The major looked tired and gaunt. He eyed Rawley up and down. "Right section," he said. "You've got a sergeant who knows his job." Rawley saluted and went with a new feeling of happiness to the section. Presently the major himself came along and stood watching for some minutes. "You been out before, Kemp?" he asked suddenly. "Yes, sir," answered Rawley. The major nodded in a satisfied way and walked off.

II

About three o'clock in the afternoon the Bosche attacked. Rawley, who was acting as forward observation officer on the forward slope in front of the guns, saw them streaming over a ridge less than a thousand yards away. The battery awoke to frantic vigour, and the white fleecy puffs of low, bursting shrapnel soon built up a long-wreathed cloud in the still air. It was not easy to see what was happening. The ears were the only guide, and the very extravagance of the sounds made discrimination difficult. The hard rattle of machine-guns rose and fell amid the crackle of musketry. High explosive detonated with its reverberating "c-r-ump" and spouting columns of earth; heavy shrapnel burst overhead with stunning thunderclaps and thick woolly clouds of smoke; and low-flying aeroplanes roared over the battery and machine-gunned the crews.

Infantry began to trickle back, bearded, hollow-eyed men in the last stages of exhaustion. They trudged past the battery singly and in twos and threes, without a glance to right or left. Heavy machine-gun fire came from the right flank where the enemy had penetrated up a broad, shallow valley. The major had the guns slewed round forty-five degrees and fired over open sights. A depleted squadron of dismounted cavalry came up the slope and passed forward by the guns. The men looked tired but determined. "For God's sake sit tight and stop those fellows coming back," roared the major to the captain in command as he went by.

The guns were nearly red hot, and mounds of brass cases lay beside the trails; the shields were dented and silvered with bullet and shell fragments; and the personnel had been reduced by one third. But the machine-gun fire grew no louder. It grew spasmodic and became silent for long intervals. The hostile shelling died down. By dusk an unnatural calm reigned over the battlefield.

The men lay down almost where they stood and slept beside the guns. Rawley passed the night among the rubble heaps in a shack made of a groundsheet spread over a broken wall, and he too was asleep almost as soon as he had closed his eyes.

Dawn came cold and misty, and the weary gunners stretched their cramped limbs and warmed their hands on the canteens of hot tea. Heavy rifle fire punctuated by the staccato bursts of machine-gun fire broke suddenly from behind the thin grey curtain that hung over the ground. Conway, a Canadian subaltern who had spent the night as F.O.O. among the infantry, called for battery fire on S.O.S. lines, and immediately the covers were off and the guns were vomiting frenziedly into the mist. Time passed and the sound of rifle fire dwindled. Odd stragglers came through the mist. Conway said he was coming in. He could see very little, and the Bosches were round behind him on his right. Little parties of infantry passed slowly and sullenly. The major ordered up the teams and halted them in a little dip a hundred yards to his left rear.

Conway came in with his signallers and cable. Close behind him came a few of the dismounted cavalry and the captain to whom the major had spoken. "God in Heaven," stormed the major, "are you going back! What about my guns!"

"What about my squadron!" echoed the captain with a wry smile. "That's all that's left of 'em." He indicated the half-dozen men halted behind him. "It's no good, major. They scuppered our posts and got up quite close in the mist before we could see them—hundreds of 'em. We worked our bolts till they jammed with the heat. And there's nobody left." The major ordered up the teams, and one by one the guns went back.

The mist cleared as they went along. To the southward there was heavy hostile shelling. Little groups of men could be seen lining a railway embankment. They were very few and seemed to be unsupported by artillery. In the distance beyond the embankment the country was dotted with black slowly-moving blobs which field glasses revealed as small columns of German infantry. The major had the guns unlimbered, and they came into action at four thousand yards.

Hostile shelling increased as time went on. A five-nine burst under number two gun, overturning it, killing the crew and smashing the recoil buffer. The major was hit in the leg and the arm by shrapnel, but he refused to go back. He sat in a shallow hole behind the guns and carried on. Half an hour later he was again wounded in the groin by a splinter of H.E. and had to go. Rawley heard Nisbett, the other subaltern, call across to Conway, "I'm sending the major back. He wants me to go to the teams and wagons and the skipper is to come up and take over the guns."

A little time later Rawley's sergeant said, "I see the Captain has come, sir."

Then during a lull he heard Conway's voice cry cheerily: "Hullo, Piddock! You've come up to a nice little dog fight."

Piddock! Rawley's heart quickened its beat, but he did not look round. Conway's voice went on, "We've only four guns left now, so we've amalgamated two sections. I'm taking this one, and the new chap, Kemp, is taking the other. That's him over there—quite a stout feller."

Rawley heard no footsteps, but he knew that the captain was walking towards him. He did not turn; he went on stolidly with his self-imposed task of laying the gun. He wanted to prolong the doubt that something inside told him was a certainty.

The sergeant at his elbow said, "The captain, sir."

Rawley turned slowly. It was Piddock; a little leaner perhaps and with three stars on his cuff, but otherwise the same old Piddock. Their eyes met. Piddock's were filled with amazement; and then his face lighted up. "By God, it's old Rawley!" he cried. He seized Rawley's hand and wrung it. "I thought you were dead, old son!"

Rawley was a little touched by the warmth of his greeting. "It was good of you to think that," he muttered hoarsely.

Piddock linked his arm in Rawley's and walked him a yard or two from the guns. "Good of me!" he echoed. "I don't know what the deuce you mean—or how on earth you turned up here; but I know I'm damned glad to see you, you old devil!"

"Piddock," said Rawley earnestly, "I don't care what you do with me after—all this, but let me carry on now. It's the one thing I ask—for old time's sake."

Piddock rubbed the back of his head under the brim of his steel helmet. "I don't know what the hell you're talking about," he exclaimed. "But as for carrying on—good Lord, yes. What else? I'm mighty glad to have you, old son."

"Thanks," mumbled Rawley gratefully. "And, I say, you won't let the others know yet, will you? Remember, I'm Kemp for the moment."

Piddock stopped. "Look here, old bird, either I'm tight or you are. Are you fit to carry on?"

"Don't play the fool with me, Piddock," cried Rawley. "I'm deadly serious. Damn it, you know you can trust me."

Piddock nodded and squeezed Rawley's arm. "I know, but you seem so damned queer. And this Kemp business...."

"Can't I be Kemp, just for the moment—till its over?" pleaded Rawley.

"Call yourself Hindenburg if it amuses you, old son," cried Piddock. "We'll have a crack about this later; meantime—let's get on with the purple war." And he walked off with a puzzled expression on his face.

III

Nightfall brought respite to the weary men. The barrages died down to the perfunctory shelling of the old quiet sector trench warfare, and the familiar Verey lights soared majestically in the darkness. Even the machine-guns were silent or awoke only at long intervals to stutter a few rounds and be quiet again like men turning over in their rest. It seemed as though the sated god of war dozed and muttered uneasily in his sleep.

Rawley and Piddock sat beneath two battered sheets of galvanized iron laid across an old weed-grown trench. Piddock enveloped in an open British warm with high up-turned collar sucked at a foul old pipe and regarded Rawley whimsically. "Of course I'm all agog to know what you've been up to," he said. "Dying and then turning up again here and calling yourself Kemp and all that!"

Rawley regarded the glowing brazier they had made out of an old bucket. "Supposing," he said after a moment's silence, "supposing first of all you tell me what happened that afternoon after—after I disappeared."

Piddock extended his soiled field boots towards the the brazier and moved his pipe to the other side of his mouth. "Well, I was down at the wagon lines, you know, waiting to go off on leave. The adjutant rolled up and we were just going to start when Crookshaw came along and said he'd been ringing the battery and couldn't get any reply. I told him the line had probably gone and he had better send somebody out to mend it. Then Cane's servant turned up with his kit and said Cane had gone back with a bad Blighty one and that poor old Whedbee had been knocked out. I thought I ought to find out from you how things were going; so I rang up brigade, and brigade said they couldn't get any reply from you either. The adjutant and I then thought it was time we went up and had a look round. So up we went.

"Before we got to the battery we met Sergeant Jameson and another fellow coming back. He had a long and doleful story to tell. He said that soon after that bit of hate that knocked out Cane and poor old Whedbee the Bosche suddenly fairly plastered the position with gas—but of course you know all about this."

"No—go on," said Rawley.

"Well, anyway, Jameson said the stuff came in all of a sudden and so thick that a good number of the men were half gassed before they got their respirators on; and even then they found it beginning to leak through. It was some new potent stuff of the mustard variety.

"Well, Jameson went along to find you, he said you and Rumbald were in the mess—the mess, of course, being out of sight round that curve of the river bank. Well, when he came round the curve he saw that a big one had landed on the mess and brought the whole damned issue in as Cane always said it would one day. He collected a party at the double and they set to work to try to lift up the roof. It was a pretty unpleasant job apparently. You know what it's like working in respirators and with the Bosche shelling hard all the time. They got the roof up a couple of inches or so, far enough to prove that it was flat on the floor and that if anyone were underneath he couldn't be alive. Then they chucked it and cleared out. Half the fellows were on their backs and the other half were blundering about like drunks. So we posted you and Rumbald as missing, believed killed.

"And didn't you dig out the mess dug-out later?" asked Rawley.

Piddock knocked out his pipe on the heel of his boot. "No. You see the place was reeking with gas and we had to leave it for a bit, and meanwhile Jerry slogged it heavily. When we went back we found he'd knocked in the river bank in a couple of places and the whole position was a marsh. We had a hell of a job getting the guns out. More than half the battery had been evacuated from that damned gas, and so division sent us back. And incidentally I had a fortnight in the most topping little village you ever saw, miles away from the nearest bang and then I went on leave. So we never went back to that rotten position."

"Then you never found Rumbald's body?"

"No—nor yours," he added with a grin.

Rawley burst into a peal of laughter, but there was no merriment in it. "Well, that's good," he said. "Damn good, that! A pretty rotten mess I've made of things!" He nodded his head slowly. "And you thought Rumbald was killed by that roof coming in!"

"Naturally; and you too. Wasn't he then?"

Rawley shook his head. "He was dead before that roof came in. That's why I cleared out—deserted." He looked up with a wry smile. "You see, I killed him."

Piddock took his pipe from his mouth and regarded the glowing bowl with raised eyebrows. "Look here, Rawley, old son, all this may seem quite ordinary to you, but personally I'm a bit out of my depth. You've been chucking the most amazing remarks at me ever since you did the bally resurrection trick at the guns this afternoon. Suppose you tell me all about it. Remember I'm a thickheaded cove with Mark 1 brains."

Rawley took the pouch held out to him and slowly filled his pipe. "The moral of the story is 'Look before you leap,'" he said, with a wry smile. And he began, while Piddock listened without comment. "So you see, I've made a pretty box up of things all round," he ended.

Piddock thrust a bit of paper into the brazier and relighted his pipe. "Um," he agreed. "But the question is, what can we do about it."

"There is nothing we can do about it," Rawley told him. "I'm a deserter—and that's all there is to it."

Piddock grimaced. "Not a deserter, old son—at least not in the ordinary unpleasant sense; and anyway, except you and me, no one knows it. So we can wash that out. Officially, you are missing, believed killed; but the problem is to revive you and account satisfactorily for the interval. You see, although this chap Kemp is dead, you couldn't keep that up, because when things have settled down again—if they ever do—his people will be writing and there will be all sorts of complications. If it had been old Conway now, it would have been easy. He hasn't a relation in the world. Went to Canada as a kid and lived in a shack in the wild and woolly North West ever since. He doesn't know a soul in Europe. But damn it all there must be some way out, if only we could think of it. Anyway it's up to me. After all it was through me you got into this mess. I must put on my thinking cap." He knocked out his pipe. "Well, old son, what about it? I'm losing my beauty sleep. I think 'kip' is indicated, as the troops say."

CHAPTER XXV

I

T HE next two days were strenuous ones for man and beast; endurance was stretched to limit and beyond. The battery marched and fought and fought and marched without respite and without rest. But Rawley was content; he was even happy. Once more there was an object in life, something that demanded all one's strength of body and of will. For the moment he was no longer a pariah; he was back again with the pack, inspired by the contagion of human effort concentrated to a single purpose. One might suffer hunger, thirst, fatigue, pain, death, and fear, but one suffered neither futilely nor alone. Consciousness of a noble purpose spurred one's flagging efforts; hardships borne in common fed the warming fire of comradeship.

The battery marched and fought and fought and marched, bending before the flood that day after day rolled farther westwards—sweeping before its angry crest the fast submerging wreckage of the human dam it had already broken. Somewhere behind them, they hoped and prayed, another dam was being built, against which the fierce grey flood would beat in vain. So they fought on without respite or relief, helpless to stem the advancing tide, but fighting stubbornly to delay it.

One more gun had been crippled and abandoned, but the little unit of half a hundred men, worn out by ceaseless labour, lack of sleep, and constant shelling, moved doggedly across that smashed and pounded desert, halting while the gun numbers worked like fiends to hurl a hurricane of shrapnel from the two remaining battered and nearly red-hot guns, then retreating to avoid extinction. In front of them was but a straggling line of hollow-eyed and bearded infantry, the remnants of a score of units mixed with the gleanings of the back areas, farriers, labour corps, town majors' batmen. Ranges that began at five thousand yards dropped steadily to as many hundreds; fuses were set almost at zero; and the gun shields rang like bells under the hammer blows of direct rifle fire; then up thundered the racing teams and the leaping guns were snatched again from the threshold of destruction.

Those desperate days sucked all volition from that devoted remnant; they responded only to one unconquerable idea that galvanized their exhausted bodies long after their numbed minds had ceased to function. At the call to action men lying log-like in the depths of fatigue sprang up and worked with frenzied vigour at the guns; and when the cease-fire sounded dropped where they stood and slept beside the trails. Like mechanical dolls when a penny is dropped into the slot, they functioned vigorously and efficiently, to lapse into death-like inertia the moment the need of action had passed. Thus did Piddock, hollow-eyed and gaunt, lead his devoted little remnant through the wreck of an army.

II

The end came one bright spring day. They had reached the limit of the old Somme battlefields. Behind them lay green country undefiled by war, where woods were bursting into bud and the white, tree-bordered roads ran back towards the distant spires of Amiens. Since morning the battery—if battery it could be called—had been in action in a shallow S-shaped valley. Heavy shrapnel rumbled across the sky and burst overhead with stunning thunderclaps. Machine-gun fire waxed and waned. The warm spring sun beat down upon the weary sweating men.

Morning wore on to afternoon, and bullets began to whisper down the valley from the north. It was a situation which they had learned to expect. The enemy had found another gap and were trickling through it round the flank. Soon the position would be untenable: the haggard infantry would come trudging back, and the grey tide would lap westward again.

The guns were manhandled round and fired up the valley at the threatened flank. But the whip and crack of bullets overhead increased in volume; a machine-gun began its bedlam chatter; and the exhausted infantry began to stagger back.

Piddock ordered up the teams. They came at the gallop, but that machine-gun, traversing like a scythe above the grass, brought them down as they circled by the guns. Piddock, at the head of a little band of helpers, cut four unharmed beasts free from the kicking, struggling mass, and hooked them to a limber, while Rawley's gun-crew planted shell after shell in the neighbourhood of that damnable machine-gun. Ready hands swung the trail to the limber and the gun went off at a mad gallop.

A fresh team started for Rawley's gun, but never reached it. Men and horses came down in a kicking, struggling heap. It was evident that the gun could not be got away, and Piddock sent word to Rawley and his crew, firing and crouching in the shelter of the gun-shield, to abandon it and retire.

Shrapnel pursued the one retiring gun as it crossed the high ground. Conway was hit in the neck and slid from the saddle, but they put him across the crupper of Piddock's mare and rode on. A mile and a half back they unlimbered and came again into action. Infantry in artillery formation were moving up across the fields behind them—fresh troops at last. "And about bloody well time!" growled a haggard gunner, as he watched them move by.

Piddock's orderly rode in leading a couple of horses. "Where's Mr. Kemp? Did he get away all right?" demanded Piddock.

"I delivered your message, sir," replied the man; "and Mr. Kemp said he would just fire a few parting rounds at the machine-gun; but I have an idea, sir, that—"

"That what?"

"That he intended to stay, sir. He sent the remainder of the section back with me, except three men with him, serving the gun."

"But he may have come away after you left."

"I don't think they could have got away, sir. We found it pretty warm when we came. Jerry was just working over the crest. There weren't any troops in front of us. And just as we dropped into dead ground by that old water-tank, I had a look back, and the gun was still firing, sir, searching for that machine-gun."

A fresh battery unlimbered on the ridge near Piddock's solitary gun, and came into action. The afternoon wore on to evening, and evening to night, and every hour the voices of fresh guns joined the roaring chorus on the ridge. Gradually an indefinable feeling of mastery crept over them; they felt in their bones that this time no infiltration of the enemy to a flank would render retirement inevitable. The great attack in the West had been brought to a halt.

In the fast failing light Piddock surveyed his little remnant of haggard scarecrows. "One gun we've brought through," he said musingly to Nisbett, "one gun, two officers and a round score other ranks. Poor old Conway gone today—and Kemp. And one gun. But Jerry hasn't got it anyway. He's still on the slope above that last position they tell me; he never got down to the gun itself, though I expect it's chiefly scrap iron now. Anyway, as soon as it's dark enough I'm going to take out a couple of fellows to see if there is anyone left."

III

After dark Piddock and two volunteers passed out through the line of shallow rifle-pits down to that S-shaped depression that had now become no-man's-land. The rising roar of gunfire of the past few hours had dwindled with the coming of darkness, and only an occasional round lashed through the night and burst with a gong-like crash.

Here and there a rifle cracked sharply, and a round went whimpering down the valley like a lost soul. Eastwards from the German slope an occasional Verey light soared up and shed its ghostly blue-green glare above the ground. Then they crouched motionless till it sank and expired.

They passed the dim shape of one of their limbers, tilted sideways on one wheel, and the dark heap of the slain team beyond. Then, quite suddenly, Piddock saw the gun. A Verey light soared up and as it sank slowly he saw the grotesque elongated shadow of the twisted shield, barrel, and broken wheel-spokes glide across the grass. "There it is," he said, as they went forward again.

A voice from the ground to his left answered his. "Is that the captain? This way, sir. It's Gunner Higgins."

Piddock knelt down beside the dark form. "Got it badly, Higgins?"

"No, sir. I'm all right. One of them damned typewriter ones in my leg; that's all. But poor old Baker and Jones have gone. Jones went about an hour ago. I told him to try and stick it. I said I knew you'd come out after us as soon as it got dark."

"And Mr. Kemp? He gone, too?"

"He's over there by the gun, sir. I tried to drag him away from it because Jerry's got a machine-gun trained on it— thinking we might try to get it away, I s'pose—but his leg's all smashed up and he couldn't stand it. But I heard him groaning a short time ago."

They found Rawley a yard or two from the battered gun. He was unconscious, but when they lifted him to the stretcher the pain of the movement revived him for a moment, and he seemed to recognize Piddock's voice. The two men lifted the stretcher; Piddock slung Gunner Higgins across his shoulder by the fireman's lift; and the little party turned its back upon the soaring German lights and made its way towards the British lines.

IV

A long green and white train was running slowly down the line between Amiens and Boulogne. Prominently upon the white woodwork of each coach was painted the red cross of the Geneva Convention. Inside were long tiers of wire bunks that folded flat against the white walls when not in use; but at the moment they were all in use. Each was furnished with sheets and blankets, and on each white pillow lay a head, though some were hidden in swathes of bandages.

Rawley lay on the top tier of bunks with a cradle over his shattered leg to raise the blankets. Ahead of him lay long weeks in hospital and inevitable arrest. He felt weak and broken. Through the partly-open window he could see a level stretch of marshland bounded by dark, pine-covered dunes with here and there patches of dazzling white sand.

A sister came down the alley between the bunks and paused beside him. "I have a letter for you," she said kindly. "It's marked private and confidential. Do you think you could manage to read it yet?"

He nodded and murmured weakly, "Yes."

His fingers, answering sluggishly and like strangers to the commands of his brain, fumbled as they tore open the envelope and unfolded the letter. It was from Piddock.

"Well, old son, you are off to Blighty, and here am I still in beau-ti-ful France! But things are looking up. Comic Cuts says that the old Bosche has been brought to a standstill all the way down the line. Anyway, on our particular bit he is still sitting on the slope overlooking our poor old gun, and our fellows are sitting opposite and giving him a good plastering. We came out of it with one gun, one officer—myself—and twenty-two other ranks. Poor old Conway—a stout fellow, if ever there was one—was wounded coming back and died that night; and Nisbett stopped one a bit later and has gone down the line. So they pulled us out of it, and here we are in the most peaceful little burg you ever saw, waiting for new guns, officers and men. It is quite close to your C.C.S. and I hoped to come in and have many a crack with you. But they told me today that they were sending you to Blighty tomorrow, and that's why I'm writing this letter.

"I have fixed it all up for you, old son, so don't you be a B.F. and go and spoil it all! You just sit tight and obey orders—damn you! After we brought you in that night I had a brain-wave. Poor old Conway was lying there, too, and it occurred to me to swop your identity discs. There won't be any complications because, as I told you, he hasn't a relation in the world—and no money either, but you won't mind that. If I get cashiered for making false returns, and come down to playing a tin whistle outside your billet, I know you'll spare me a penny. Anyway, on my casualty return I have sent in Conway as Kemp, and you as Conway.

"A nice little sister at your C.C.S.—by the by, I think I shall have to visit that C.C.S. again, even though you aren't there!—a sister at your C.C.S. told me that officers could usually choose which hospital in England they wanted to go to, provided it wasn't full; and I told her to have you sent to the Royal Berks at Reading. And, furthermore, I have written to Miss Berney Travers to say that a Lieutenant Conway will shortly be arriving at her hospital, and will she go and see him. Also, she is not to be surprised if she finds that this aforesaid Conway cove bears a remarkable resemblance to a certain Peter Rawley she once knew. So that's that.

"Well, old son, give my love to Blighty and all the pretty girls—including Miss Berney. God bless you, my children! May you grow in wisdom and wealth, and may your offspring be as the sands of the seashore for multitude; and when your Uncle Piddock comes to see you, may you greet him with a bottle of the best in either hand.

"Cheerio,

"Yours ever,

"CHARLES PIDDOCK."

Rawley turned his head away to the window. He felt very weak and emotional. Through the narrow open slit the twin lighthouses of Paris-Plage were coming into view, and beyond them, in the shining offing, a lean grey destroyer was slipping through the white-flecked water with a vapoury smudge above each funnel.

The sister came back down the alley-way and paused as her glance fell upon his face. She followed the direction of his eyes and nodded understandingly. "You will be in England tonight," she said softly. And then she bent swiftly and flicked away the tear that had welled on to his cheek.

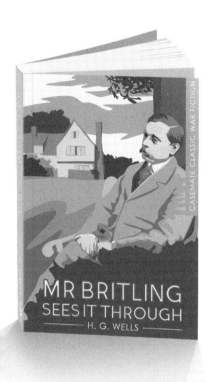

Mr Britling lives in the quintessentially English town of Matching's Easy in Essex. He is a great thinker, an essayist, but most of all an optimist. When war arrives he is forced to reassess many of the things he had been so sure of. The war brings great change – Belgian refugees come with dreadful stories and everywhere it seems there are young men dressed in khaki. The family's young German tutor is forced to head back to Germany, and Mr Britling's seventeen-year-old son enlists in the Territorials. Day by day and month by month, Wells chronicles the unfolding events and public reaction as witnessed by the inhabitants of one house in rural England.

Written in 1916 when the outcome of the war was still uncertain, the semi-autobiographical *Mr Britling Sees it Through* is a fascinating portrait of Britain at war and an insight into Wells' own ideals.

August 2016 | ISBN 9781612004150

MR BRITLING
SEES IT THROUGH

H. G. Wells

Set deep in the mountains of southern France, this charming short novel tells the story of Roux, a man from the Cèvennes Mountains who refuses to join the army at the outbreak of World War I. Instead, he flees and hides in the hills, returning only occasionally to the farm where he left his mother and sisters. The people of the valley condemn his desertion and hope the police will find his hideout. But as the months and the years go by, and the horrors of the trenches become known, the local population starts to understand Roux's actions. In *Roux the Bandit* Chamson explores questions of perception, morality and conscience with a lightness of touch coupled with an atmospheric picture of life in World War I-era rural France.

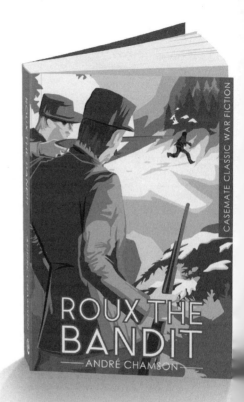

August 2016 | ISBN 9781612004174

ROUX THE BANDIT

André Chamson

PASS GUARD
AT YPRES

Ronald Gurner

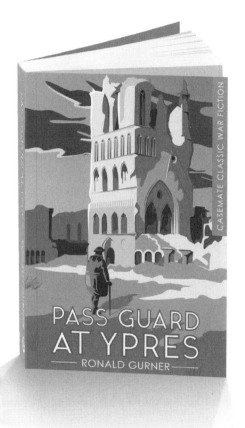

A platoon of inexperienced British soldiers crosses to France in excited and nervous anticipation of what is to come. They find themselves at Ypres, where the battle-weary Allied troops are dug in, surrounded by slaughter. With their young, upright officer Freddy Mann, they are soon in the thick of it, burying the dead, suffering the terror of bombardment, and being picked off by snipers. The action unfolds through the soldiers' eyes, focusing on Freddy Mann's journey from idealistic officer fresh from school to battle-hardened cynic. Barely hanging on as those around him are killed, maimed and traumatised, Freddy suffers a crisis of faith, losing his belief in both the war and in everything he once stood for.

August 2016 | ISBN 9781612004112

In *The Somme* and its companion *The Coward*, first published in 1927, the heroics of war and noble self-sacrifice are completely absent; replaced by the gritty realism of life in WWI for the ordinary soldier, and the unflinching portrayal of the horrors of war.

Written under the guidance of the master storyteller H. G. Wells, they are classics of the genre. *The Somme* revolves around a futile attack in 1916 during the Somme campaign. Everitt, the central protagonist is wounded and moved back through a series of dressing stations to the General Hospital at Rouen. Both in and out of the line he behaves selfishly and unheroically, but despite this his circumstances and the conditions around him make his actions easy to understand. Based on A. D. Gristwood's own wartime experiences, critics have said that few other accounts of the war give such an accurate picture of trench life. *The Coward* concerns a man who shoots himself in the hand to escape the war, during the March 1918 retreat – an offence punishable by death. He gets away with it, but is haunted by fear of discovery and self-loathing.

April 2016 | ISBN 9781612003801

THE SOMME

ALSO INCLUDING THE COWARD
A. D. Gristwood

In the Mesopotamian desert during World War I, the leader of a British patrol is shot and killed, by an unseen enemy. The officer is the only one who knows their orders and has not told anyone else where they are located. From then on the sergeant has to try to lead the men through a hostile desert landscape which is full of invisible Arab snipers. One by one they are picked off, and the group of diverse characters from different backgrounds has to try to come together in order to survive. The decision making process proves far from easy as tensions and prejudices from their former lives come to the fore.

This thrilling tale of suspense goes right to the last page and was a best seller in the 1920s. The novel was filmed twice, by Walter Summers (as *Lost Patrol* in 1929) and by John Ford (as *The Lost Patrol* in 1934).

April 2016 | ISBN 9781612003788

PATROL

Phillip MacDonald

Towards the end of the war as the Germans are in their final retreat in November 1918, a British raiding party stumbles across a strange and eerie scene in a ruined chateau, under fire. Following the strains of a familiar tune, and understandably perplexed as to who would be playing the piano in the midst of shellfire, they discover a German officer lying dead at the keys, next to a beautiful woman in full evening dress, also deceased. But the officer is the spitting image of G. B. Bretherton, a British officer missing in action. So follows a tale of mystery and identity which is an authentic account of conditions at the Front.

First published in 1930 this remarkable thriller, with a highly unusual plot, won *Bretherton* comparisons to John Buchan and the best of the espionage writers. John Squire, the influential editor of the *London Mercury* said 'of the English war-books, undoubtedly the best is *Bretherton*.' The *Morning Post* thought it 'one of the best of the English war novels. I do not expect anything much better.' *The Sunday Times* pinpointed its dual attraction: it was both 'a mystery as exciting as a good detective story and an extraordinarily vivid account of trench-warfare'.

April 2016 | ISBN 9781612003764

BRETHERTON
KHAKI OR FIELD-GREY?
W. F. Morris

UNDER FIRE

Henri Barbusse

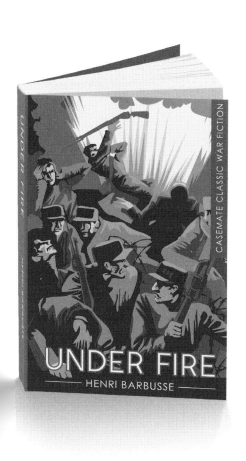

Set in early 1916, *Under Fire* follows a squad of French volunteer soldiers through the eyes of an unnamed foot soldier, who participates in and also observes the action. It combines soaring, poetic descriptions with the mundane, messy, human reality of soldiers living in their own excrement. Then slowly names and features are given to the men who emerge from the mud, from the dignified leader Corporal Bertrand, to the ebullient Volpatte and the obsessive Cocon. Intermingled with details of how they navigate daily life in the putrified atmosphere of the trenches are both harrowing descriptions and a political, pacifist argument about this war and war more generally.

Caught up in events they cannot control, the soldiers go through their daily routines: foraging for food, reading letters from wives and mothers, drinking, fighting in battle, and in heavily realistic scenes which the novel is noted for, discovering dead bodies in advanced stages of decomposition; the human detritus of a brutal conflict. Through it all, they talk about the war, attempting to make sense of the altered world in which they find themselves. *Under Fire* drew criticism at the time of its publication for its harsh realism, but won the Prix Goncourt. The original translation by Fitzwater Wray which first appeared in 1917 is published here. It captures the essence of the era; a glossary is also provided to help with unfamiliar vocabulary.

April 2016 | ISBN 9781612003825